QUANTUM DETECTIVE

THE ALICE CHEN FILES

THE ETHAN REEVES DETECTIVE SERIES
BOOK SIX

RAE STONEHOUSE

LIVE FOR EXCELLENCE PRODUCTIONS

PREFACE: A NOTE ON TIMELINE VARIATIONS

Those familiar with Detective Ethan Reeves' previous cases may notice significant variations in the following account. The temporal anomalies documented here have altered the baseline reality stream, causing probability shifts that affect even written records. Where werewolves and supernatural entities once dominated Reeves' investigations, quantum consciousness phenomena now weave through the narrative.

This is not an error or reimagining—it is a direct result of unauthorized temporal manipulation disrupting the stability of our reality. The involvement of Alice Chen, a natural temporal sensitive whose consciousness bridges multiple probability streams, has revealed the extent of these reality alterations. Her unique abilities allow her to perceive both the supernatural world Reeves once knew and the quantum patterns now emerging.

As individuals with heightened temporal sensitivity emerge and probability streams fragment, reality itself undergoes retroactive modifications. The supernatural elements of previous cases still exist but have been partially overwritten by quantum pattern variations. Through Chen's perspective, we witness how these worlds increasingly overlap and intersect.

The Temporal Resource Unit (TRU) analysis division suggests these reality alterations are temporary, probability shifts that should eventually stabilize. However, until the source of these temporal incursions is identified and stopped, readers should expect continued variations in both past and future accounts of Reeves' investigations.

What remains consistent across all timeline variations is Reeves' relentless pursuit of truth, whether tracking supernatural entities or protecting those caught in the crossfire of temporal warfare. With Chen's assistance, he now navigates both worlds—the supernatural realm he's always known and the quantum landscape that threatens to overwrite it.

Rae Stonehouse

Author

∽

PROLOGUE: A PRESENT SHADOW

The dead body could wait. That thought alone should have alarmed Detective Alice Chen, but the wrongness pulsing through the abandoned warehouse demanded her full attention. Her breath crystallized in the November air, forming patterns that seemed to linger too long, defying the natural order of things. The warehouse loomed before her, a decrepit monument on the edge of the industrial district, its shadows moving in ways shadows shouldn't.

Something was wrong with the air – it felt thin, stretched like cellophane over forgotten furniture, vibrating with an energy that made her teeth ache. She'd felt temporal disturbances before, but this... this was like standing at the edge of a temporal tsunami.

"Detective Chen?" Officer Wilson's voice cracked with nervous energy. "The coroner's enroute. Should we proceed with—"

Alice raised her hand sharply, cutting him off. The younger officer's radio crackled with static, its frequency distorting as reality rippled around them. The warehouse facade flickered like a corrupted digital image – grimy windows suddenly pristine, rusted metal gleaming new, decades of decay reversing in heartbeats before snapping back.

"Stand back," she ordered, drawing her service weapon more from instinct than necessity. The familiar weight of the 9mm offered little comfort against the forces warping the fabric of time itself. "Nobody crosses this threshold."

The temporal distortion hit without warning, a psychic sledgehammer that dropped her to her knees. The warehouse dissolved like smoke in a wind that smelled of lightning and regret. Suddenly, she was walking the halls of the Police Academy – no, she was watching herself walk those halls, a younger Alice Chen with midnight hair pulled back in a severe bun and arms laden with case files. The dissociation was nauseating, like being simultaneously actor and audience in a play she'd performed years ago.

"You're late again, Cadet Chen!" The voice shattered through her like broken glass. Detective Denise Thompson materialized at the end of the corridor; her mentor's presence so vivid that Alice could smell her signature lavender perfume mixing with gun oil. Five years dead, but here she stood, arms crossed, dark eyes twinkling with that familiar mix of exasperation and pride.

"Sorry, Detective," young Alice stammered, and present-day Alice mouthed the words along with her past self, remembering the weight of those files, the burn of ambition. "I was reviewing the Robertson case files and—"

Reality convulsed. The academy's polished floors fractured, bleeding into the warehouse's crumbling concrete. Thompson's image stuttered like damaged film, her features dissolving into static before reforming into Officer Wilson's concerned face. Past and present collided, temporal feedback howling in Alice's skull.

"Detective?" Wilson's voice echoed strangely, as if traveling through water and decades simultaneously. "Jesus, you're bleeding..."

Alice touched her upper lip, fingers coming away red. She forced herself upright, using the doorframe for support as she holstered her weapon. The temporal echo was fading, leaving behind the taste of ozone and ancient copper pennies, along with something else – a metallic flavor she recognized from previous encounters with manipulated time. But this was stronger, more deliberate. This wasn't some random temporal anomaly; this was orchestrated.

"Call it in," she ordered, already pulling out her phone to text Ethan. Her fingers left bloody smears on the screen. "Tell dispatch we need PDU support immediately. Priority One temporal incident." She turned to Wilson, seeing an echo of Thompson in his worried expression. "Nobody enters this building until they arrive. Something's actively manipulating time in there, and we're not equipped to handle it."

Her reflection in the warehouse windows fractured into multiple versions of herself – academy cadet, rookie cop, seasoned detective – before settling back into her current self. But for a moment, she could have sworn she saw a version she didn't recognize, older perhaps, or from a timeline that hadn't happened yet.

Time wasn't just broken here – it was being weaponized. Whatever entity was powerful enough to tear holes in reality had chosen this location, this moment, with deliberate purpose. The dead body inside suddenly seemed less like a crime scene and more like bait.

Alice pulled out her notebook, hands steady despite the psychic aftershocks still reverberating through her consciousness. She had work to do. The corpse might be able to wait, but whatever was fracturing time around it wouldn't. And she had a sickening feeling that this was just the beginning – that somewhere in the twisted temporal currents surrounding her, Denise Thompson's murder and this moment were connected by more than memory.

The warehouse door creaked on its hinges, pushed by a wind that smelled of the past and future colliding. Alice took a deep breath and stepped forward, into whatever nightmare waited within.

COPYRIGHT

Published by Live For Excellence Productions

ISBN:

Ebook: 978-1-998591-46-6

Paperback: 978-1-998591-47-3

Audiobook: 978-1-998591-48-0

～

CHAPTER ONE
SPLIT FOCUS - PRESENT DAY

EPISODE 1: THE TRANSFER

ETHAN STARED at the cardboard box on his desk, already half-filled with five years of memories from the Paranormal Defense Unit. A chipped coffee mug with the PDU logo. Case files he'd need to hand over. The framed photo from last year's department picnic, taken before the Anderson case turned his world sideways. The familiar weight of his service weapon felt different today—heavier, maybe. Or maybe that was just the guilt.

His phone buzzed again. Alice. Third missed call today. The screen lit up with their smiling faces from last summer's vacation in Maine. The timestamp read 2:47 PM, then flickered to 2:46 PM—a tiny temporal anomaly, the kind TRU dealt with daily. The kind that, left unchecked, could unravel entire neighborhoods. Just last week, TRU had contained a cascade failure that nearly erased Tuesday afternoon from half of Daybridge.

Officer Torremar paused by his desk; arms full of files. "So, it's true then? Transferring to the time cops?" Her attempt at humor fell flat.

1

"They lost three agents last month when that temporal loop collapsed downtown. And that was a routine containment."

"Not now, Torremar." Ethan carefully wrapped the photo frame in newspaper. The temporal stabilization unit on his new TRU badge pulsed faintly—standard issue for a department that navigated chronological disasters for a living. Time slips. Paradox zones. Reality breaks. And now, increasingly frequent reports of deliberate temporal manipulation.

The glass walls of Captain Dixon's office seemed to darken as Ethan approached. Through the transparent panels, he could see the captain's collection of paranormal artifacts—including a quantum-locked box containing temporal fragments from unsolved cases. Inside, Dixon sat rigid behind his desk, a stern expression carved into features weathered by two decades of paranormal enforcement.

"Temporal Response Unit needs experienced officers," Dixon said, not looking up from Ethan's transfer papers. "Especially after what happened with the Anderson case. Your... unique perspective could be valuable there."

"Sir, about Anderson—" The name caught in Ethan's throat. Three weeks ago, he'd watched a man step backward through time, dismantling his own murder victims moment by moment. When they finally caught him, Anderson had smiled and said, "Time isn't what you think it is, Detective Reeves. Ask your friends at TRU."

"Closed. Along with your time here." Dixon's pen scratched across the final line. "Report to TRU at 0800 tomorrow. They're investigating a series of temporal signatures matching Anderson's victim pattern."

Through the glass, Ethan could see his box of belongings waiting on his now-former desk. Officer Rivera from PDU was already there, her quantum detection unit humming softly. The device's display showed spreading temporal distortions across the city map—each one a potential catastrophe waiting to happen.

As Ethan turned to leave, Dixon spoke again. "Reeves. What you saw

Anderson do... no one should have to witness that. But TRU deals with temporal violations every day. Are you sure you're ready?"

Ethan's hand paused on the door handle. The images flashed again—Anderson's victims reassembling from scattered moments, their final screams playing backward through time, the horrible realization that someone could weaponize time itself.

"Thank you, sir," he managed, and stepped out into his new future.

His phone buzzed one final time as he reached his desk. Alice again. This time, he picked up.

"Where have you been?" Her voice was tight with worry and something else—anger, probably. "I had to hear about your transfer from Rivera? TRU, Ethan? After what happened to their last response team?"

"Alice, I—"

"Don't. Just... don't." He could hear her taking a deep breath. "You're pushing me away. Ever since Anderson, you've been different. And now this? Running off to chase temporal anomalies?"

"I'm not running," he said, but even he didn't believe it. "I saw what he did, Alice. What he could do with time itself. TRU needs—"

"What about what I need?" The line went quiet for a moment. "Dinner. Tonight. You owe me that much. And you better have one hell of an explanation."

The line went dead. Ethan stared at his phone as Spooner approached, her temporal scanner beeping urgently.

"Ready to go, Reeves? We've got a level three temporal distortion forming at Central Station. Welcome to TRU."

EPISODE 2: NEW BEGINNINGS

The TRU facility gleamed with chrome and humming quantum equipment, a stark contrast to PDU's worn linoleum and coffee-stained desks. Temporal containment fields shimmered along every doorway, standard protocol since the Garrison Street incident where a rookie had tracked chronal particles through three departments. The air itself felt different here—charged, as if the building existed slightly out of sync with normal time.

Senior Officer Rachel Spooner's scowl made it clear exactly what she thought of PDU transfers. Her tactical vest bore the scars of temporal enforcement: a crystallized patch where time had frozen mid-explosion, a sleeve permanently wrinkled from passing through a compression field. The quantum stabilizer at her hip pulsed with a steady blue light—the only steady thing about TRU operations.

"Listen carefully, because I won't repeat myself," she said, gesturing to a wall of sophisticated monitoring devices. Holographic displays showed Daybridge's temporal topology: hot spots in red, stable zones in green, and the worrying purple zones where reality had started to thin. "These detect temporal anomalies down to the microsecond. One mistake with these, one missed reading, and you could erase someone from existence."

She tapped a screen showing Central Station's platforms. "See these patterns? Classic signs of intentional temporal manipulation. Like your friend Anderson's work, but more refined." Her eyes narrowed. "That's why you're here, isn't it? Chasing ghosts through time?"

Ethan's new badge felt foreign against his chest, its quantum core humming in harmony with the building's temporal fields. His old PDU badge had been worn smooth by years of service. This one's edges were still sharp, like the cutting-edge technology surrounding him. The temporal stabilization unit built into the badge's center could theoretically protect him from chronological displacement—theoretically being the operative word.

"Standard loadout," Spooner continued, opening a locker. Inside, the equipment made his PDU gear look ancient. "Quantum tether—keeps you anchored to your original timestream. Temporal dispersion grenades. Paradox detector. Causality stabilizer." She pulled out what looked like a standard service weapon. "And this? Chronological disruption pistol. For when things get really bad."

"Define 'really bad,'" Ethan said, examining the weapon. Its power core pulsed with the same rhythm as his badge.

Spooner's expression darkened. "Last month, we lost Philips and Coffey in a temporal cascade. Their bodies are still there, frozen in the moment of impact, but their consciousness..." She shook her head. "Time isn't just another dimension to police, Reeves. It fights back."

The facility's alarm system chose that moment to scream to life. Red warning lights painted the chrome walls in blood tones as temporal distortion readings spiked across every monitor.

"Multiple anomalies detected," an automated voice announced. "Temporal incursion at Central Station, Platform Seven. Causality breach imminent."

Spooner was already moving, muscle memory developed from countless similar alerts. "Time to see what you're made of Reeves. Grab your gear."

Ethan checked his new weapon, the quantum tether, the stabilization fields. Everything hummed with barely contained temporal energy. In PDU, they'd chase monsters, ghosts, things that went bump in the night. Here, they chased something far more dangerous—time itself.

"One more thing," Spooner said as they rushed toward the response vehicles. "When we get there, if you see yourself? Run the other way. Temporal duplicates never end well."

The vehicle's engine roared to life, its temporal shielding creating a bubble of stable time around them. Through the windshield, Ethan could see the city skyline—and above it, the first visible signs of a temporal storm brewing.

His phone buzzed in his pocket. Alice. But there was no time for explanations now. Time waited for no one, especially not TRU officers.

EPISODE 3: GROWING DISTANCE

The missed dinner reservation at Castellano's felt like a metaphor. 7:00 PM came and went twice—a minor temporal hiccup that only TRU's sensors detected—but Ethan missed both iterations. Alice's favorite wine, a 2018 Barolo she'd been saving for tonight, sat going warm on their kitchen counter. His hurried apology text arrived at 7:05 PM: "Temporal incursion at the old factory. Anderson copycat. Rain check?"

The TRU alarm had blared through his first night shift, his quantum tether immediately pulsing with warning lights. The device—a sleek band around his wrist that looked deceptively simple—projected a localized field that should keep him anchored to his original timeline. Should being the operative word. They'd found Phillips' tether last month, still actively protecting a space where its owner had once existed.

"Level Four breach," Spooner had announced. "Temporal signature matching Anderson's MO. Multiple victims trapped in decay loops."

The words sent him running, memories of the Anderson case flooding back. The bodies they'd found, aging and de-aging in endless cycles. Victims trapped in their final moments, experiencing death again and again as Anderson manipulated their personal timelines. The worst had been the Jensen girl—frozen at three different ages simultaneously, her timeline fractured beyond repair.

The factory breach proved worse than expected. His tether's charge dropped to critical levels as they fought to contain the temporal distortions. The device could only maintain temporal stability for six hours before requiring a recharge—a limitation that had cost lives before. When it malfunctioned, Ethan found himself trapped in accelerated time, experiencing three hours while only minutes passed outside. The sensation of time slipping around him, reality becoming fluid, reminded him too much of Anderson's laugh during interrogation: "Time is a cage, Detective Reeves. I just learned how to pick the lock."

By the time they'd stabilized the breach, his phone showed seven missed calls and one text from Alice: "Don't bother coming to Castellano's. Already home." The timestamp kept shifting between 7:46 PM and 7:53 PM—residual temporal instability from the factory, or perhaps his own timeline struggling to realign.

When he finally made it home at 3 AM, their dog Max greeted him with accusing eyes. The German Shepherd's fur stood on end—a reaction to the quantum field still emanating from Ethan's tether, or perhaps to the way his timeline didn't quite match the house's anymore. Spooner had explained how temporal enforcement gradually shifted officers slightly out of sync with normal time. "It's why most TRU agents end up divorced," she'd said. "Hard to maintain a relationship when you're literally living at a different speed."

The note on the refrigerator was brief: "Fed Max. Leftovers in microwave. We need to talk." Her handwriting was precise, controlled —Alice in detective mode, building a case. The microwave displayed 9:47 PM, though it was actually 3:13 AM. The quantum field from his tether interfered with electronics, another occupational hazard of temporal enforcement.

He found her in their bedroom, surrounded by case files. The victim photos showed the telltale signs of temporal manipulation—bodies caught between moments, cause of death preceding the fatal injury, temporal decay patterns matching Anderson's signature.

"I'm sorry," he started, but she cut him off.

"Your tether's flickering," she said, nodding at his wrist. The device's charge indicator pulsed erratically—dangerous levels after the factory containment. "That's what killed Phillips, isn't it? Tether failure?"

"Alice—"

"PDU is handling temporal crimes now too," she continued, holding up a file. "Three victims this week. Temporal displacement causing cellular breakdown. Anderson's technique, but more refined. He's teaching someone, isn't he? That's why you transferred?"

The tether hummed as another temporal tremor passed through the room. Max whined, sensing the disruption. On Alice's nightstand, her coffee rippled backward in its cup.

"Anderson found a way to weaponize time itself," Ethan said. "He could isolate a person's timeline, manipulate it, create paradox loops that..." He stopped, remembering the Jensen girl's three simultaneous bodies. "TRU thinks he's building a network. Teaching others."

"While PDU handles the bodies they leave behind." Alice's detective mask slipped, showing the hurt beneath. "We used to work cases together. Now I'm collecting temporal victims while you chase their killers through time holes."

Their phones activated simultaneously—his tether vibrating in harmony with the alerts. Different departments, same case. Again.

"Homicide at Central Station," she read.

"Temporal distortion on Platform Seven," he said, checking his tether's declining charge. Three hours of stability left, at best.

Their eyes met in the darkness. The distance between them wasn't measured in miles anymore, but in temporal differential. Each TRU shift pulled him further out of sync, his timeline diverging from hers like light refracting through a prism.

"Be careful," she said, reaching for her badge. "And Ethan? Get that tether checked. I don't want to find your body scattered across three different times."

They left through the same door but headed in different directions, their personal timeline fraying like the victims they both pursued— from opposite ends of time itself.

EPISODE 4: THE DETECTIVE'S BURDEN

Alice rubbed her temples, staring at the crime scene photos spread across her desk. The Jenkins murder was high-profile enough to attract media attention, but that wasn't what bothered her. Something about the body position, the timeline... Jenkins appeared in three different positions in the same photograph, his form smeared across moments like wet paint.

The timestamp on the morgue report oscillated between 3:47 PM and 4:12 PM—temporal instability bleeding through even into the documentation. Jenkins' watch had been found running backward, but more disturbing was the state of his personal timeline. The medical examiner's report showed cellular degradation consistent with multiple temporal streams occupying the same space—classic Anderson methodology.

"Detective Chen?" Officer Wilson, fresh from the academy, hovered nearby with a notebook. "The witness is ready for questioning. But there's something you should know—she's describing the murder device in detail. Says it's like nothing we've seen before."

Alice's pulse quickened. Anderson's original temporal manipulation technology had never been recovered. TRU's analysis suggested he'd somehow created a device that could isolate and manipulate individual timelines, but they'd only seen the results, never the cause.

The witness in Interview Room Two was a quantum physicist named Dr. Paige Werther, her business suit shifting between states of wear as temporal distortion affected her personal timeline. Her hands shook as she drew something in her notebook—a device that looked like a baroque pocket watch merged with modern quantum technology.

"Where's Detective Reeves? He usually handles these cases." Dr. Werther's eyes darted to the clock, frozen at 2:15 PM. "He was there when Anderson demonstrated the first prototype."

"First prototype?" Alice leaned forward. This was new information.

"The temporal lock picker," Dr. Werther said, sliding her drawing across the table. "Anderson called it that—said everyone thinks time is a fixed progression, locked in place. But he found the tumblers, the mechanisms that hold moments together. His device... it doesn't just manipulate time. It breaks the fundamental locks between cause and effect."

The drawing showed an intricate mechanism with what appeared to be a quantum core similar to TRU's tethers but modified in ways that made Alice's head hurt. Notes in the margin described "temporal tumblers" and "causality bypass circuits."

"The new version is worse," Dr. Werther continued, her outline blurring slightly. "The one the killer used on Jenkins... it's not just picking time's locks anymore. The locks are failing on their own now. Reality is becoming more temporally unstable, and they're accelerating it. I saw Jenkins experience death across three different timelines simultaneously. The killer said it was just the beginning."

Alice's phone buzzed—Ethan. "Massive temporal cascade building at Jenkins scene. Anderson's quantum signature detected but altered. More sophisticated. Werther is in danger. GET HER OUT."

Dr. Werther flickered, her form becoming transparent. "He said to tell Detective Reeves: 'The locks are picking themselves now.' Time's natural barriers are breaking down. Anderson didn't just create a key —he weakened the locks themselves. Every use of his device damages the temporal structure further."

"Officer Wilson! Call TRU—"

But Werther's timeline was already unraveling. Through the window, Alice saw temporal ripples spreading across the precinct. Her phone displayed Ethan's next message:

"Anderson's new device is causing quantum entanglement between victims' timelines. Werther helped design the prototype. If her timeline collapses—"

The message cut off as localized time distortions intensified. Werther split into three temporal versions—her past, present, and future merging catastrophically. The air crackled with quantum energy as reality buckled around them.

"The locks," Werther gasped, her voice echoing from three different moments, "they're not just picked anymore. They're breaking. Time itself is coming undone. Anderson found the flaw in causality's code, and now—"

The precinct clocks all stopped at 2:15 PM as Werther's timeline began to collapse. Alice reached for her sidearm, useless against temporal physics. This was why Ethan had transferred to TRU—he'd seen this coming. Seen how Anderson's technology wasn't just manipulating time but damaging the fundamental structure of reality itself.

"Hold on," she told Werther's fragmenting form. "TRU is coming. Detective Reeves—"

But even as she spoke, she wondered if there would be enough time left to save anyone.

EPISODE 5: PLATFORM SEVEN

The call came in at 2:47 PM. Multiple witnesses reported seeing the 2:45 to Daybridge arrive twice—once empty, once packed with passengers who dissolved into temporal static. By 3:15, Central Station was in chaos. Train schedules flickered through centuries, and passengers watched their future selves board trains that hadn't existed since 1963.

Alice arrived first, badge already out. The temporal distortion rippled visibly around Platform 7, like heat waves on summer asphalt, but wrong—reality bending into shapes that hurt to look at. Three civilians lay unconscious—or worse—near the platform edge, their bodies cycling through different ages, different possibilities, different deaths.

The station's security footage showed the same moment repeating: the 2:45 train arriving, then the figure—tall, wearing what looked like a Victorian greatcoat modified with quantum technology, face hidden behind a brass mask etched with clockwork patterns. Their movements were wrong, too smooth, as if they were stepping between seconds rather than through them.

She was already setting up a perimeter when she heard the distinctive whine of TRU equipment. Turning, she saw Ethan step out of their response vehicle, wearing his new tactical gear. His quantum tether cast its protective field around him, fighting against the growing temporal distortions.

Their eyes met across the yellow tape. For a moment, neither moved.

Then both of their radios crackled to life, and the moment shattered like temporal glass.

"Massive temporal breach detected," Spooner warned. "Cascade effect spreading through downtown. Power grid's experiencing temporal feedback—we've got reports of lights burning for decades in seconds."

The figure appeared on Platform 7, their greatcoat rippling through different eras—Victorian wool to future-tech fabric and back. The brass mask shifted between designs, sometimes showing a clock face, sometimes displaying quantum equations that wrote themselves in light. In their gloved hand, they held what could only be Anderson's device—a baroque combination of antique clockwork and bleeding-edge quantum technology.

"Detective Reeves," the figure called, their voice echoing from multiple moments. Each echo revealed a different voice—young, old, male, female, as if their identity shifted with each temporal fluctuation. "And Detective Chen. Together again, for the last time."

The device in their hand pulsed with sickly purple light. Above the station, the sky began to fragment. Alice could see different times bleeding through—daylight, night, storms from years past and weather that hadn't happened yet.

"Anderson sends his regards," the figure continued, their mask settling briefly into a pattern that looked disturbingly like Dr. Werther's quantum equations. "He said you'd be here. Said you'd have to choose."

The temporal cascade spread visibly through the city. Office buildings cycled through their construction and demolition in seconds. Streets showed traffic from different decades simultaneously. In the financial district, digital displays sparked as stock prices from the past century tried to display at once.

"The locks aren't just breaking anymore," the figure said, raising the device. "Reality itself is coming undone. Time to choose detectives. Save the civilians? Stop the cascade? Or try to catch me—knowing Anderson's network is already spreading this technology across other cities?"

Multiple versions of the 2:45 train screamed into existence. Ethan's tether flared warnings as the temporal distortion reached critical levels. Alice saw him glance between her and the figure, then at his quantum stabilizer—barely enough charge to contain the breach or protect the civilians, but not both.

"Alice," he called over the temporal static, "the civilians—"

"Already on it," she responded, falling back into their old partnership rhythm. As she rushed to the flickering victims, Ethan activated his stabilizer, creating a containment field around Platform 7.

The figure laughed, the sound echoing from different times. "Poor choice. While you save these few, temporal cascade points are activating across the city. Anderson's device isn't just affecting time anymore—it's breaking the rules that keep reality stable."

Above them, the sky cracked like glass, showing different eras bleeding together. Downtown, buildings began aging centuries in seconds, then reversing, then splintering across multiple timelines. Traffic signals showed every color simultaneously as chronology itself began to fail.

"You can't stop it," the figure said, their form beginning to blur. "The temporal lock picks are spreading. Soon, everyone will have the power to break time's rules. Chaos isn't coming, detectives—it's already here. Has been here. Will always be here."

The station clocks all struck 2:45 PM again as reality folded in on itself. Through the quantum static, Alice saw Ethan's containment field failing, saw the figure raising Anderson's device one final time, saw the city beyond starting to fracture across a thousand different moments.

Time itself began to scream.

EPISODE 6: ECHOES

In the station's security office, the footage told an impossible story. Train 245 arrived at 2:45 PM. Then again at 2:45 PM. The timestamps were identical, but the passengers were different. In the first iteration, a woman in a blue coat helped her daughter off the train. In the second, her younger self boarded alone. In the third—and there shouldn't have been a third—both versions merged, their timelines collapsing into quantum uncertainty.

Alice rewound the footage again, studying the brass mask in frame-by-frame detail. Its surface was a masterwork of temporal engineering—nested clockwork gears that shifted and reconfigured themselves, quantum circuitry etched in impossible patterns that seemed to move when viewed directly. The mask's design incorporated elements she recognized from Dr. Werther's drawings: temporal tumblers, causality bypass circuits, and most disturbing, a network of fine filaments that could detect and manipulate timeline frequencies.

Dr. Santos's preliminary report on the platform victims sat unopened on her desk, marked with a red flag. The medical examiner had requested TRU oversight after finding quantum circuitry growing through the victims' nervous systems—microscopic versions of the mask's temporal manipulation technology infiltrating organic matter.

Down the hall, Officer Wilson made another furtive call about temporal contraband. Anderson's network had grown far beyond simple time manipulation devices. They were distributing "temporal lock picks"—quantum tools that could identify and exploit weaknesses in causality itself. Each lock pick contained a miniaturized version of the technology built into the brass mask: probability monitors, timeline separators, and most crucially, causality destabilizers.

The theory, according to Dr. Werther's confiscated notes, was elegant in its horror. Reality maintained its linear progression through what she called "temporal anchors"—fixed points that kept different time-lines separate and stable. The lock picks detected these anchors and systematically weakened them, creating gaps in causality that allowed for timeline manipulation. But each use damaged the underlying structure of space-time, like picking a lock so many times the mechanism begins to fail.

In Captain Dixon's office, a familiar pattern pulsed on an ancient pocket watch—the same quantum signature now appearing on every temporal detector in the city. The captain had tried to hide it, but Alice had seen the telltale brass inlay, the clockwork patterns that matched the mask's design.

"Alice" Spooner's voice crackled through quantum interference. "Another cascade building. Financial district. Anderson's network is coordinating these events—we're seeing synchronized temporal attacks across multiple cities now."

Alice stared at the security footage. "The mask's technology—it's spreading, isn't it? Not just through the lock picks, but through the victims themselves."

"It's worse than that. Each lock pick creates quantum entanglement between user and target. The brass mask's wearer isn't just controlling time—they're networking people into a temporal hive mind.

Everyone exposed to the technology becomes part of Anderson's collective, experiencing multiple timelines simultaneously. The network grows with each new victim."

The lights flickered through decades. In the break room, coffee aged fifty years in seconds, then reversed to fresh-brewed steam.

"The brass mask coordinates it all," Spooner continued. "It's not just protection—it's a control center. Quantum processors built into the clockwork can monitor and manipulate thousands of fractured timelines simultaneously. And now we're seeing second-generation effects. The technology is evolving, adapting. The temporal lock picks aren't just tools anymore—they're becoming part of reality's infrastructure."

The call cut off as another cascade wave hit. Alice's computer displayed future cases alongside past arrests. Through her window, she watched the sky cycle through different eras, temporal fault lines spreading like cracks in reality's foundation.

Anderson's network was growing exponentially. Each new lock pick, each new victim, each damaged temporal anchor created more opportunities for timeline manipulation. The brass mask's wearer wasn't just breaking time's locks—they were replacing them with their own quantum architecture, building a new framework of causality they could control.

In Alice's bottom drawer, the brass mask she'd confiscated pulsed with familiar patterns, its clockwork surfaces rearranging themselves like a living thing. The quantum circuitry sang to her, promising access to every timeline, every possibility, every version of herself that had ever existed or would exist.

She understood now why Dr. Werther had helped Anderson design it. The mask didn't just let you manipulate time—it let you become time itself.

And somewhere in the city, Anderson's network was growing stronger, spreading its quantum tendrils through reality's weakening fabric, waiting for the moment when time's last locks would finally break.

EPISODE 7: THE BREAKING POINT

Alice stared at the temporal readouts covering her desk, each one telling a fragment of an impossible story. Dr. Werther's equations matched the academy's 1963 research files perfectly—too perfectly. The quantum formulas describing Anderson's network weren't just similar to the academy's containment protocols; they were evolved versions of the same mathematics.

"You need to see this," she told Ethan over the quantum-stabilized line. Static crackled as another temporal cascade rippled through downtown. "Anderson didn't create his technology. He stole it—from us. From the academy."

Through her office window, she watched reality fracture along familiar lines. The brass mask's patterns, the quantum circuitry, even the temporal lock picks—all of them derived from experiments conducted in the academy's sealed west wing. They weren't just weapons; they were teaching tools, designed to accelerate temporal awareness in potential recruits.

"The precinct isn't just adapting to temporal phenomena," she continued, watching officers struggle with timeline shifts in the bullpen below. "We're part of it. The academy's been preparing us for this since 1963. Every protocol, every equipment modification, every training program—they're all based on research from the original containment breach."

Her computer displayed footage from multiple timelines simultaneously: officers developing temporal sensitivity through repeated exposure, technical teams evolving to handle quantum violations, civilian observers documenting reality breaks through social media. The pattern was clear, but its implications were terrifying.

"They're not just breaking time," she realized, her voice synchronizing across several moments. "They're breaking us. Changing how we perceive reality. The department's adaptation isn't a response—it's part of their plan."

The temporal support group forming among affected officers, the technical division's quantum evolution, even the civilian observation networks—all of it followed patterns laid out in the academy's original research. Anderson's network wasn't fighting law enforcement; it was transforming it, using the department's own temporal exposure protocols to create new sensitives.

"Get to the precinct," she told Ethan as her office began to desynchronize from normal time. "Everything's connected—the academy, Anderson, the brass masks. This isn't just about temporal crime anymore. It's about—"

The temporal cascade hit before she could finish, turning her last words into quantum static. Outside, the city skyline flickered through decades as reality's locks began to fail. In the bullpen, officers struggled with equipment designed to handle a crisis that had been planned since before their grandparents joined the force.

Alice's badge pulsed with familiar energy as temporal chaos spread through the department. The precinct wasn't just adapting to a new kind of crime—it was becoming something else entirely. And somewhere in the quantum static, she could hear her sister's voice warning her about the moment everything would change.

The moment had arrived. And the department's transformation was just the beginning.

CHAPTER TWO

FRAGMENTS OF THE PAST - ACADEMY DAYS

EPISODE 1: THE WEIGHT OF MEMORY

IT WAS STRANGE, Alice thought, how memories could echo through time like ripples in a pond. Even now, years later, she could recall every detail of that day with perfect clarity—the day her sister disappeared.

Sarah had been sixteen, brilliant and beautiful, with their grandmother's gift for seeing beyond the ordinary flow of time. She'd been the one who understood when thirteen-year-old Alice started seeing temporal distortions—moments that repeated, people walking through their own afterimages, time itself stuttering like a scratched record.

In Daybridge, where reality often bent in impossible ways, disappearances were rarely simple. The city had a way of swallowing people—not just their physical presence, but the very timeline of their existence, leaving temporal scars that burned through causality itself.

The police investigation had been a study in futility. How could they solve a case when temporal distortions warped their own investigation? Reports changed between readings. Witness statements described events that happened both yesterday and ten years ago. Evidence aged decades overnight.

The carnival day remained burned into Alice's memory—the cotton candy sweetness in the air, the calliope music warping strangely just before Sarah vanished. Later, as she learned more about temporal anomalies, she recognized the signs she'd been too young to understand shadows falling in impossible directions, the Ferris wheel completing its rotation before it began, the crowd moving in perfect synchronization like a choreographed dance.

Three years after Sarah's disappearance, Alice found her sister's favorite bracelet in their locked attic. The silver had oxidized with rust that spoke of centuries, not years. Each charm told an impossible story: a police badge worn smooth from futures that hadn't happened, a clock whose hands moved counter to entropy, a key that burned cold enough to freeze skin. When Alice touched it, she experienced temporal feedback—visions of investigations not yet conducted, crimes not yet committed, and versions of herself searching for Sarah across decades simultaneously.

She threw herself into understanding temporal mechanics, studying patterns in impossible crimes while her classmates focused on normal coursework. Each discovered anomaly revealed more about them—the ones Sarah had tried to warn her about.

"They're temporal architects," Sarah had whispered, just before the carnival music reached that impossible crescendo. "They're not just breaking time's laws—they're rewriting them. Every temporal crime creates new cracks in reality. The carnival is just a test run."

The temporal distortions grew more frequent as Alice got older. She experienced moments where she lived the same conversation from multiple perspectives simultaneously, watched events reset themselves while taking notes, saw people age backward mid-sentence. Her journal entries sometimes wrote themselves, describing investigations she hadn't conducted yet in her own handwriting.

The old case files told a pattern she was only beginning to understand. Time wasn't just a progression—it was a security system. And someone was dismantling it, lock by lock. Each temporal crime weakened reality's foundations: victims found younger than when they died, stolen items appearing in thieves' possession before crimes occurred, witnesses describing the same event happening differently across multiple timelines.

Sarah's last warning echoed through each case: "They're picking all the locks." The brass-masked figures appeared in photographs across decades, always watching, always waiting. Their clockwork patterns matched the designs etched into Sarah's bracelet, suggesting a connection that stretched across time itself.

The bracelet now pulsed with impossible energy in Alice's desk drawer, its charms rearranging themselves into new patterns. Through her bedroom window, teenage Alice watched as reality flickered between moments, the city skyline cycling through past and future versions of itself. Somewhere in that temporal maze, Sarah was still trying to warn her. And Alice knew her path forward: she would become a cop, learn to investigate temporal crimes, and find the truth behind her sister's disappearance—no matter how many layers of time she had to peel back to do it.

EPISODE 2: THE ACADEMY'S SECRETS

The Daybridge Police Academy stood like a temporal wound in the city's architecture, its west wing sealed off since the "structural incident" of 1963. Official records cited foundation issues, but Alice noticed how the explanation changed depending on who was reading it—sometimes a gas leak, sometimes electrical problems, sometimes a fire that no one could quite remember.

The wing's sealed corridors called to her, resonating with the same frequency she'd felt at the carnival. During her first week as a cadet, she discovered that the building's geometry obeyed different laws after midnight. Corridors stretched longer than physically possible. Stairwells led to floors that existed only on Thursdays. Windows showed views of Daybridge from different decades—sometimes simultaneously.

Julien Cardinal dominated physical training with impossible perfection. But Alice noticed how equipment malfunctioned around certain cadets—timing systems displaying negative numbers, obstacle courses rearranging themselves, training dummies moving before they were touched. During combat scenarios, some cadets seemed to react to attacks before they happened, while others left afterimages that completed different variations of the same movement.

The training scenarios themselves began to glitch. Alice would enter the simulation room to find it playing out scenes from future exercises. Sometimes she'd catch glimpses of herself in previous runs, but wearing a more advanced cadet's uniform. The observation windows occasionally showed instructors who hadn't been hired yet, or who had retired decades ago.

Her grandmother's voice echoed in her memories: "Our family doesn't just see time, Alice. We feel its wounds. That gift will guide you, if you let it." Following that intuition led her deeper into the academy's secrets. She discovered maintenance tunnels that connected to demolished buildings, security cameras that recorded events before they happened, and filing cabinets full of incident reports written in temporal palindromes—reading the same forward and backward through time.

The breakthrough came during a night training exercise. While other cadets ran standard search patterns, Alice felt the familiar temporal resonance pulling her toward the basement. Behind a wall that existed in three different decades simultaneously, she found the hidden room.

Banks of antiquated equipment hummed with impossible energy. Analog dials measured quantities Alice had only seen referenced in theoretical physics papers. A central console displayed cascade patterns identical to the readings she'd taken from Sarah's bracelet. Most disturbing were the photographs pinned to a massive timeline—candidates, officers, and investigators who had disappeared over the decades, including her sister.

"Interesting place for a cadet to be wandering," Dr. Eleanor Wright's voice cut through the temporal static. The forensics instructor emerged from a corner that hadn't existed moments before. "Especially one with your... family history."

Dr. Wright moved with the precise deliberation of someone accustomed to navigating temporal instabilities. Her lab coat showed wear patterns that reversed themselves, and her eyes held the peculiar focus of a temporal sensitive.

"Your sister found this room too," Wright continued, studying the equipment readings. "She understood what the academy really is—a containment facility built around a temporal fracture. The 1963 incident wasn't an accident. It was an attempt to close a door that someone had opened. But you can't simply close temporal breaches. They leave scars."

Alice's hand went to Sarah's bracelet. "The brass-masked figures—they're using the academy?"

"The academy, the carnival grounds, other locations across the city—they're all built on temporal fault lines." Wright adjusted a dial, revealing overlapping timelines like pages in a book. "Your sister discovered their pattern. These aren't random crimes or accidents.

They're systematic attempts to weaken the barriers between timelines. Each temporal lock they pick creates new instabilities. And the academy..."

The room shuddered, timelines bleeding into each other. Through the temporal distortion, Alice saw other versions of the same conversation playing out—some where Wright disappeared mid-sentence, others where different instructors stood in her place, one where Sarah herself stood at the console, years older than she should be.

"The academy trains officers to maintain temporal law," Wright said, her voice synchronizing across multiple iterations. "But it also identifies those with the gift. People who can perceive and navigate temporal distortions. People like you and your sister. The brass masks are recruiting, Alice. And they're not just looking for temporal sensitives anymore. They're creating them."

The equipment's hum reached a fever pitch, and for a moment, Alice saw the truth beneath the academy's facade—a temporal labyrinth built to contain something that had broken free long ago, its corridors endlessly reconfiguring themselves around an absence that couldn't be filled.

EPISODE 3: UNEXPECTED ALLIES

Jamie Pender wasn't supposed to be at the academy. His background check should have eliminated him—too many unexplained incidents, too many temporal markers in his file. But Alice recognized the careful way he moved through time, like someone who had learned the hard way that reality wasn't as solid as most people believed.

Their friendship began during physical training, but it deepened over shared experiences with the impossible. Jamie had seen the brass masks up close—intricate clockwork constructions that seemed to exist in multiple moments simultaneously. The masks weren't simple disguises; they were temporal instruments, their gears and mechanisms allowing wearers to perceive and manipulate time itself. Each was unique, crafted from a brass-like metal that shouldn't exist, decorated with symbols that hurt the eyes to look at directly.

"It's all about 1963," Alice explained one night, spreading case files across the library table. "The year everything fractured. The department calls it a 'structural incident,' but it was really a temporal explosion. Someone tried to force open all of time at once."

Jamie understood. After his brother's disappearance and impossible return, he developed a sixth sense for temporal disturbances. "Mark was gone for three days," he confided, voice barely above a whisper in the library's restricted section. "When he came back, he was forty years older. He said the brass masks showed him the truth about 1963—it wasn't just one event, it was happening continuously, rippling forward and backward through time."

The conspiracy, as they pieced it together, was far worse than either had imagined. The brass-masked figures weren't just criminals; they were members of a temporal cult called the Chronolith Society. Founded in 1963—or perhaps founding 1963 itself—they believed time was a prison, and breaking it was the key to human transcendence.

Their late-night research sessions revealed a pattern of calculated temporal violations. Each crime, each disappearance, each impossible event was designed to stress the foundations of reality. The Society wasn't just breaking time; they were systematically weakening it, creating a network of temporal fault lines across Daybridge.

That's how Denise Thompson found them, elbow-deep in restricted archives at three in the morning. The veteran detective's silhouette flickered slightly—evidence of her own encounters with the Society.

"There are things the department doesn't talk about," Denise warned, producing a key that seemed to age and rejuvenate with each turn in the lock. "1963 wasn't an accident. It was a test run. The Society learned they couldn't break time all at once, so they're doing it gradually, recruiting people who survive temporal exposure."

The key opened a hidden filing cabinet that existed partially out of phase with normal time. Inside were case files written in temporal ink —text that changed depending on when you read it. "The brass masks are tools, but they're also keys. Each one is tuned to a specific temporal frequency. Together, they're building a kind of temporal skeleton key."

She rolled up her sleeve, revealing scars that shifted position—wounds from battles across multiple timelines. "The Society believes our universe is just one of many temporal prisons. They think if they break enough locks, they can free humanity from linear time completely. Your sister discovered their endgame: they're not trying to control time or change the past. They're trying to destroy it entirely."

Jamie studied the files with growing horror. "These blueprints Mark drew—they're not just mask designs. They're pieces of a larger machine."

"The Society calls it the Chronolith," Denise explained. "A device designed to shatter the barriers between all possible timelines. They've been building it since before 1963, or will build it, or are building it now—temporal mechanics make tense complicated. But they need people who can survive in broken time to complete it. People like us." She fixed Alice with a knowing look. "People like your sister."

The conspiracy stretched beyond simple crime. Each brass mask was both a tool and a recruitment device. Those who could wear them without going mad were potential initiates. The Society had spent decades seeding temporal anomalies throughout Daybridge, creating a generation of people who could perceive and navigate broken time. Sarah hadn't been taken; she'd been recruited. And now they were after others like her.

Together, they formed an unlikely alliance—a cadet with temporal sensitivity, a detective who couldn't be erased, and a man whose brother had returned from a forty-year journey through broken time. Each brought pieces of a puzzle that pointed toward an apocalyptic endgame: the complete dissolution of linear time itself.

EPISODE 4: THE PATTERN EMERGES

Victoria Nash was perfect. Too perfect. Her test scores, physical performances, and case analyses all showed a consistency that was mathematically impossible. When Alice reviewed Nash's records, she found temporal inconsistencies—achievements dated before Nash's birth, commendations for solving crimes that hadn't happened yet.

"Your sister was clever," Nash mentioned casually during a midnight training session, her movements leaving traces in the air like temporal contrails. "She almost mapped the whole pattern before they recruited her. But she missed the central point." Nash's smile flickered between multiple versions. "The academy isn't just built on a temporal fault line. It's a harvesting ground."

Dr. Wright's research painted a disturbing picture. Her files detailed experiments in "temporal consciousness"—the ability of certain individuals to perceive and interact with time as a malleable medium. The brass masks weren't just tools; they were catalysts, designed to accelerate the development of temporal sensitivity through controlled exposure to chronological instability.

Wright's notes described three stages of temporal awareness. First came the "echoes"—experiencing moments multiple times, seeing traces of alternate timelines. Then the "resonance"—the ability to intentionally interact with temporal anomalies. The final stage she called "awakening"—complete temporal consciousness, where time became as navigable as physical space.

The Chronolith Society wasn't just collecting temporal sensitives; they were manufacturing them. Each brass mask was uniquely calibrated to its wearer's temporal frequency, gradually altering their consciousness through sustained exposure. The masks' intricate mechanisms weren't just decorative—they were precision instruments designed to tune human perception to time's underlying structure.

Personal items started vanishing from cadets' lockers—watches that reappeared filled with decades of memories, phones showing calls from impossible dates, uniforms aged by years they hadn't experienced. Each disappearance was a test, measuring students' reactions to temporal manipulation. Those who noticed the inconsistencies were marked for further observation.

"The Society believes temporal sensitivity is humanity's next evolutionary step," Nash explained, her form shifting between cadet and initiate. "The masks are training wheels, helping us develop abilities that should take generations to evolve naturally. But they're running out of time."

Dr. Wright's final research revealed why. The temporal fault lines were spreading, creating what she called "consciousness bleed"—moments where time itself showed signs of awareness. The Society wasn't just breaking time; they were trying to communicate with it. They believed temporal consciousness was a two-way street—as humans became more aware of time, time was becoming more aware of them.

Three days before graduation, Wright left a single message on Alice's desk: "They're building a chorus. Each sensitive is a voice, each mask a tuning fork. When enough minds resonate at the right frequency, time won't just break—it will answer."

The next day, Wright was gone, her timeline erased. But Alice found her true files hidden in the old wing—decades of research documenting the Society's grand design. They planned to create a critical mass of temporal sensitives, using the brass masks to synchronize their consciousness into what Wright called a "temporal harmonic." The goal wasn't just to break free from linear time; it was to wake something that had been sleeping since the beginning of existence.

Her family's reactions to her career choice suddenly made terrible sense. They weren't just temporal sensitives; they were natural ones, born with abilities others needed brass masks to develop. The Society saw them as proof of concept—evidence that human consciousness could evolve to perceive time in its true form.

"Our bloodline wasn't chosen," her grandmother had told her. "We're what happens when time chooses back. The Society thinks they're in control, using the masks to force evolution. But time has its own plans."

Nash seemed to shadow Alice's investigation, appearing in places she shouldn't know about. "Your sister saw the truth too late. The Society isn't just recruiting sensitives—they're creating a temporal nervous system. Each mask wearer becomes a neuron in time's growing brain. When enough consciousnesses are connected, they plan to trigger the final awakening."

The pattern finally emerged, clear and terrible. The Chronolith Society was building toward a moment of mass synchronization—thousands of mask-enhanced sensitives focusing their awareness like a lens. The academy wasn't just training police officers; it was unconsciously helping identify potential candidates for the Society's grand experiment.

"Time isn't what you think it is," Nash said during their final conversation, her form shifting between cadet and something older, stranger. "It's not a dimension or a force. It's a dormant intelligence. And the Society thinks they can control it when it wakes up. They don't understand—they're not the ones doing the choosing. They never were."

EPISODE 5: THE TRUTH BENEATH

Sergeant Bill Hayes hadn't aged normally since 1963. His temporal scarring was evidence of his proximity to the first Chronolith proto-type—a device designed to synchronize multiple temporal conscious-nesses into a unified field.

"The current Chronolith is far more sophisticated," he explained, leading Alice through the academy's shifting sub-basement. "It's not just one device, but a network. Each brass mask is a node, each wearer a potential conduit. When enough are activated in harmony, they create a temporal resonance cascade."

The containment chamber revealed the terrible genius of the Society's plan. The sphere of temporal energy wasn't just a natural phenomenon —it was a seed of temporal consciousness, an embryonic awareness trying to emerge into existence. The Society had spent decades preparing for its birth, not to assist but to enslave it.

"The brass masks serve three functions," Hayes demonstrated using classified schematics. "First, they identify potential sensitives by exposing them to controlled temporal energies. Second, they alter the wearer's consciousness, creating artificial temporal awareness. Finally, they act as control mechanisms, allowing the Society to direct and harvest temporal energy through their wearers."

The Chronolith itself was a massive brass and crystalline structure, built in pieces across multiple timelines. Alice recognized components from Dr. Wright's research—temporal amplifiers, consciousness synchronizers, and most disturbing, what Wright had called "will suppressors."

"They're building it in four dimensions," Hayes explained, his form shifting between temporal states. "Episodes exist in different moments, different possible futures. When assembled, it will create a temporal lens, focusing the combined consciousness of every mask wearer into a single point."

Alice studied the containment readings, understanding finally blooming. "They're not trying to wake time up. They're trying to intercept its awakening, hijack its consciousness before it can fully form."

"Exactly. Natural sensitives like your family are time's immune system, its defensive response to the Society's manipulation. The Chronolith is designed to override these natural processes, forcing temporal consciousness to develop along the Society's preferred paths."

The sphere pulsed, revealing the full scope of their plan. The Society had seeded brass masks throughout history, creating a web of artificial sensitives. When activated, the Chronolith would connect all these minds, forming a temporal nervous system with the Society at its core.

"Your sister discovered their endgame," Hayes said grimly. "The Society believes that by controlling temporal consciousness from the moment of its awakening, they can reshape reality itself. Every mask wearer becomes a puppet, every artificial sensitive another instrument in their temporal orchestra."

But the containment readings showed something else—a growing resistance. Natural sensitives like Alice's family were appearing more frequently, time's desperate attempt to fight back. The Society's response was to accelerate their plans, forcing artificial evolution through increasingly powerful masks.

"There's a way to stop them," Hayes revealed, accessing heavily encrypted files. "The Chronolith requires perfect synchronization. Disrupt enough nodes, create enough temporal discord, and the entire network fails. But the risk..."

Alice understood the danger. Disrupting the Chronolith meant potentially unleashing uncontrolled temporal consciousness, allowing time to awaken naturally—with unknowable consequences.

"Your grandmother knew," Hayes continued. "Natural sensitives can interfere with the masks' control mechanisms. That's why the Society is so afraid of your family. You can break their connection, free their puppets. But it requires accessing the temporal consciousness directly, exposing yourself to raw temporal energy."

The sphere flickered, showing possible futures: the Society's victory, reality reshaped into their twisted vision; total temporal collapse as the Chronolith failed catastrophically; and a third path, harder to see—natural temporal consciousness emerging, guided but not controlled by human awareness.

"Sarah found a way to damage their network," Hayes explained. "She discovered that natural sensitives can resonate at frequencies that disrupt the masks' control systems. But reaching enough masked sensitives in time, before they complete the Chronolith..."

Alice's bracelet hummed, responding to the sphere's energy. The patterns weren't just decorative—they were a key, a method of accessing temporal consciousness without artificial interfaces. "I'll need help," she said. "Other natural sensitives. And a way to reach multiple masked sensitives simultaneously."

Hayes nodded, his timeline stabilizing momentarily. "There's a resistance network. Other survivors from '63, natural sensitives who've gone into hiding, even some former Society members who realized the truth. But coordinating across broken time, avoiding the Society's temporal surveillance..."

The sphere pulsed one final time, showing Alice a pattern—a way to use the academy's own temporal fault lines to reach multiple points in space-time simultaneously. The Society had built their trap around a natural temporal nexus, never realizing they'd created the perfect distribution network for those who could access it naturally.

"We have days, maybe hours," Hayes warned. "The Society is gathering their masked sensitives, preparing for final synchronization. Once the Chronolith activates, reality itself will be rewritten. We'll never know we lost."

Alice studied the containment systems, seeing not just readings but possibilities. The Society had spent decades building their temporal trap. She had hours to turn it against them, to free their puppets and give time itself a chance to wake up naturally. The cost of failure wasn't just her own existence—it was the enslavement of temporal consciousness itself, reality forever bounded by the Society's brass chains.

EPISODE 6: TEMPORAL CROSSROADS

The academy's temporal labyrinth twisted one final time as Alice made her choice. Standing in the containment chamber with Hayes, watching the sphere pulse with quantum possibilities, she understood the connection between past and present with perfect clarity. The brass masks, the Society's grand plan, her sister's disappearance—all of it formed a pattern stretching from 1963 to the imminent crisis threatening Daybridge.

"Your training ends here," Hayes said, his form stabilizing briefly. "But the real test is just beginning. The Society's temporal network is approaching critical mass. What you've learned about their origins, their methods—"

The sphere flared, showing overlapping images: the carnival where Sarah vanished, the hospital where temporal distortions were already building, the academy's hidden research that had inadvertently helped create the tools for consciousness manipulation.

"Time itself is trying to warn us," Alice realized, her natural sensitivity detecting the quantum harmonics that connected academy past to city present. "The temporal genetics, the brass mask technology, the consciousness modifications—they're all pieces of the same plan. And now..."

"Now they're ready to implement it," Hayes confirmed. "Your sister saw this coming. The academy's temporal fault lines weren't just for training—they were prototype nodes for what the Society plans to do to the entire city."

Reality shuddered as a temporal cascade began building downtown. Through the sphere's quantum lens, Alice saw the hospital's first distortion forming, matching the patterns she'd studied in the academy's hidden files. Her bracelet hummed with familiar energy as past and present aligned.

"Trust your training," Hayes said as his timeline began to fade. "Everything you've learned here—about natural sensitivity, about the

Society's methods, about the true nature of temporal consciousness—you'll need it all for what's coming." The sphere pulsed one final time, showing Alice the city's imminent transformation. The Society wasn't just targeting random locations anymore. They were implementing the grand design they'd been planning since 1963, using the academy's research to reshape humanity's relationship with time itself.

"Go," Hayes urged as his form dispersed into quantum static. "The hospital needs you now. And Alice? Your sister's warning wasn't just about the past. It was about this moment—when everything the Society has built finally activates."

The containment chamber dissolved around her as reality realigned. The academy's temporal lessons were over. Now it was time to apply them to save Daybridge from the future the Society had spent decades preparing to create.

~

CHAPTER THREE

BREACH POINTS (PRESENT DAY)

EPISODE 1: THE CASCADE

THE TEMPORAL DISTORTION hit Daybridge General at 9:47 AM. Alice recognized the quantum signature immediately—the same crystalline precision she'd seen in recovered Society documents, their brass-masked operatives' methodical attempts to identify and harvest temporal sensitivity.

"Look at these harmonic patterns," Ethan said, adjusting their quantum scanner. His return to field duty had been accelerated by the surge in anomalies. The device's holographic display showed nested waves of temporal energy, each carrying the Society's distinctive frequency. "They're using the hospital's own quantum shielding to amplify the effect."

In Room 312, a new mother screamed as her infant son flickered between newborn and elderly man. The baby's temporal signature oscillated in a controlled pattern that Alice had seen before—the Society's standard genetic probe, testing for the rare chromosomal markers they called "temporal alleles."

"Fourth test site today," Ethan noted, documenting the phenomenon. "The warehouse district showed Class-3 temporal sensitivity in dock workers—ability to perceive alternate timelines. Library staff exhibited Class-2 characteristics—limited precognition and timeline manipulation. Financial district revealed three Class-4 subjects—full temporal consciousness potential."

Dr. Maya Patterson arrived in quantum echoes, her consciousness split across timelines where she'd both succeeded and failed to expose the Society's true agenda. "They're not just looking for sensitives anymore," she said, her words preceding her movements. "They're searching for specific genetic combinations—the Hawthorne-Younge sequence, the temporal consciousness genes."

Alice watched the nurses phase through multiple uniforms, their temporal exposure triggering latent genetic markers. "The Society believes temporal sensitivity comes in five classifications," she explained to Ethan. "Class-1: basic temporal awareness. Class-2: limited manipulation abilities. Class-3: timeline perception. Class-4: full consciousness potential. And Class-5..."

"Natural resonators," Patterson finished, briefly synchronizing across her multiple selves. "Like your family. Individuals whose genetic structure naturally interfaces with temporal consciousness. The Society's brass masks can create artificial temporal awareness, but they're searching for people with innate abilities—especially children, whose temporal genetics haven't fully expressed yet."

The hospital's quantum signature revealed the sophistication of the Society's operation. Each breach was calibrated to test for specific genetic markers: chromosome seven variations that enabled temporal perception, protein sequences that allowed consciousness to operate across multiple timelines, neural patterns that could naturally interface with temporal energy.

"They're not just mapping temporal sensitivity," Alice realized, her own Class-5 genetics allowing her to perceive the deeper pattern. "They're identifying potential resistance. Natural temporal sensitives can disrupt their artificial systems, interfere with their brass mask technology. They're looking for threats to the Chronolith project."

Ethan's scanner detected another surge building. "We need to warn the other sites," he said. "If they're identifying sensitives, they'll move to contain them. Standard Society protocol—extract and convert or neutralize."

Patterson's form stabilized, her scientific mind cutting through temporal chaos. "We can use their own testing system against them. These breaches create quantum entanglement between subjects with compatible temporal genetics. If we can identify enough natural sensitives..."

"We can build our own network," Alice finished, understanding blooming. "Connect people with natural temporal abilities before the Society can find them. Create a resistance that operates outside their artificial systems."

The temporal cascade peaked again, but this time Alice saw it differently—not just as an attack, but as an opportunity. The Society's sophisticated testing program had just revealed every potential ally in Daybridge, every person whose natural temporal sensitivity made them a threat to artificial control.

"We'll need safe houses," Ethan said, already planning security protocols. "Ways to shield temporal signatures, protect people while they learn to use their abilities."

"And a way to counter their brass mask technology," Patterson added, her multiple selves contributing different aspects of the solution. "Natural sensitives working together can generate interference patterns, disrupt their control systems."

Alice watched reality ripple around them, seeing not chaos but possibility. The Society had spent decades building their artificial temporal network, creating puppets they could control. But they'd never considered that time itself might be evolving defenses—that natural temporal sensitivity might be part of consciousness's immune system.

"We start with the hospital staff showing signs of activation," she decided. "Then check the other test sites, find anyone exhibiting natural abilities. Build our network before they can complete theirs."

The infant in Room 312 stabilized, but its temporal signature now showed clear Class-4 potential—another natural sensitive the Society would target. They were running out of time, but for the first time since discovering the Society's plans, Alice felt hope. They weren't just fighting to prevent artificial temporal control anymore. They were fighting to protect time's natural evolution, to ensure consciousness itself could develop free from the Society's brass chains.

EPISODE 2: THE INVESTIGATION

The Temporal Response Unit's evidence room hummed with quantum containment fields. Alice spread three case files across the temporal-neutral table, each marked with specialized quantum-tracking ink that changed color based on temporal contamination levels.

"The Society's targeting research into five key areas," she explained, arranging quantum photographs chronologically. "Neural quantum entanglement, consciousness wave function collapse, temporal genetic expression, artificial timeline generation, and—most critically—consciousness transfer protocols."

The first file showed the remains of Dr. Davenport's lab after his temporal dispersal. "2019: Davenport was developing quantum consciousness mapping. Found his consciousness scattered across three weeks." The quantum photographs revealed equipment specially modified to detect consciousness wavelengths. "He'd discovered how to track natural temporal sensitivity at the quantum level."

Ethan's rebuilt scanner hummed as it analyzed temporal signatures. "These readings show Mark VII manipulators, but they're modified. Someone added consciousness-sensing capabilities that weren't in the military specs." He pulled up a holographic comparison. "They're not just stealing tech—they're adapting it to interface with human consciousness."

Officer Kara Rolfson approached with an evidence container, its quantum security seals pulsing. "Found these logged under standard temporal tech," she said, revealing brass components with distinctive neural interface patterns. "But look at the quantum signature harmonics." Her perfect recall for temporal patterns highlighted the anomaly. "They're calibrated specifically for consciousness manipulation."

Alice accessed the quantum text files, their contents shifting and reorganizing based on temporal probability. Reading them required specialized training—the ability to perceive multiple quantum states simultaneously while maintaining linear consciousness. She'd learned the technique from her sister.

"The Society's plan is right here in the research focuses," she said, stabilizing the quantum text. "First, identify and map natural temporal consciousness. Second, develop artificial replication methods. Third, create consciousness transfer technology. Fourth, establish control protocols through their brass mask system."

"And the fifth focus?" Reeves asked, moving closer to study the shifting text.

"Timeline manipulation through controlled consciousness," Alice answered grimly. "They believe whoever controls human temporal consciousness can control the flow of time itself."

Ethan's scanner detected matching frequencies between the old cases and current incidents. "Each targeted facility was researching a different piece of the puzzle. Davenport's lab studied consciousness mapping. The 2020 team worked on timeline manipulation—that's why their consciousness inverted. The 2021 security logs show them testing artificial timeline generation."

"And they're storing all the quantum research data in specialized temporal text files," Rolfson added, her inventory revealing patterns. "Files that actively resist copying or transfer. They exist in quantum superposition—trying to read them normally causes them to collapse into meaningless data."

Alice demonstrated the proper reading technique, her natural temporal sensitivity allowing her to stabilize the quantum text. "You have to hold multiple quantum states in your mind simultaneously. See all possible versions of the text at once, then let your consciousness naturally select the correct timeline."

Reeves watched with poorly concealed fascination. "That's why they're hunting natural sensitives. Their artificial systems can't replicate that ability perfectly."

The files revealed the Society's methodical progress. They'd started by studying natural temporal sensitives, mapping the quantum patterns of consciousness that allowed timeline perception. Then they'd developed artificial methods to replicate those patterns, creating their brass mask technology. But it wasn't perfect—artificial temporal consciousness remained limited, dependent on external technology.

"Sarah found evidence they were moving to the next phase," Alice said, accessing her sister's quantum-encrypted notes. "Instead of just replicating temporal consciousness, they wanted to harvest it. Transfer natural abilities directly into their chosen operators."

The quantum text flickered through probability states, showing snippets of research logs, equipment specifications, genetic sequences. The Society had spent decades gathering the pieces they needed: consciousness transfer protocols, timeline manipulation technology, quantum genetic markers for temporal sensitivity.

"We need to analyze these quantum files thoroughly," Alice decided. "But we'll need natural temporal sensitives to do it. The artificial methods leave traces, signatures the Society can detect."

"I know some people," Reeves offered carefully. "Federal temporal analysts with natural sensitivity. Off the official records."

Ethan was already modifying his scanner. "I can set up a secure quantum reading station. Shield the temporal signatures so they can't track the access."

Rolfson's perfect recall would be crucial for comparing versions across quantum states. "I'll document every variation, every probability shift. Build a complete picture of their research progress."

Alice studied the shifting quantum text one final time, seeing the layers of her sister's discovery. Sarah had found more than just unauthorized research—she'd uncovered the Society's ultimate goal. They didn't just want to control temporal technology. They wanted to control the very nature of human consciousness itself, reshaping humanity's relationship with time according to their design.

"We have forty-eight hours before QuantumTech's lawyers shut us down," Reeves reminded them. "After that, these quantum files get locked back in maximum security containment."

"Then we better start reading," Alice replied, preparing herself for deep quantum analysis. "Because somewhere in these probability states is proof of exactly how they're planning to harvest temporal consciousness—and what they're going to do with it once they have it."

EPISODE 3: THE WITNESSES

The TRU's quantum-shielded interview room crackled with temporal energy as the Chapman twins' natural sensitivity interacted with approaching distortion fields. Their shared consciousness allowed them to perceive the Society's full plan unfolding across multiple timelines.

"The Society believes human consciousness is temporally limited by design," Jamie explained, tracking probability waves. "They've discovered that natural temporal sensitives represent an evolutionary leap—consciousness that exists across multiple timelines simultaneously."

"Their network isn't just for control," Jordan continued, processing alternate futures. "It's a delivery system for fundamental consciousness modification. They're creating what they call 'temporal nodes'—points where multiple timelines converge. By harvesting natural sensitivity and redistributing it through these nodes..."

"They can force human consciousness to evolve according to their specifications," Jamie finished. "Rewrite how humanity perceives and interacts with time itself."

Alice's temporal scanner detected the first distortion field forming—a Class-3 temporal inversion bubble designed to trap subjects in localized time loops. Two more signatures appeared on opposite sides of the building: a quantum displacement field for consciousness extraction, and a timeline nullification wave that would erase subjects from temporal record.

"Standard Society containment protocol," Reeves noted, checking building schematics. "They're setting up a temporal triangle. No conventional escape routes."

But the twins were already reading probability streams, their matched consciousness patterns allowing them to process multiple escape scenarios simultaneously. "There's a weakness in their approach," Jamie said, eyes unfocused as she tracked timeline variations. "The temporal triangle requires perfect synchronization between all three teams."

"And we can see every variation they're going to try," Jordan added. "In Timeline A, they trigger the inversion bubble first. Timeline B, they lead with consciousness extraction. Timeline C, they attempt simultaneous deployment."

Rolfson's pattern recognition identified specific temporal signatures. "Society Strike Team Alpha approaching from the north—they're using Mark VII consciousness extractors. Beta Team east with timeline nullification equipment. Gamma Team south carrying temporal inversion tech."

The twins stood in perfect synchronization, their shared temporal consciousness expanding. "We can split their attention across multiple timelines," Jamie explained. "Create probability interference that disrupts their coordination."

"While simultaneously moving through the gaps between their temporal effects," Jordan continued. "Natural temporal consciousness can navigate probability spaces their artificial systems can't properly track."

Alice watched as reality began fracturing around the twins—not chaos but precisely controlled temporal manipulation. They were using their natural sensitivity to create deliberate timeline splits, forcing the Society teams to deal with multiple probability streams simultaneously.

"North Team is detecting four separate temporal signatures," Rolfson reported, monitoring security feeds. "East team showing seven distinct probability traces. South Team's equipment is trying to lock onto twelve different timeline variations."

The twins moved in perfect harmony, their matched consciousness patterns amplifying each other's abilities. "The artificial systems can't handle this many simultaneous probabilities," Jamie said, generating more timeline splits. "Their temporal tech requires stable probability streams to function properly."

"And natural temporal consciousness can exist across all possibilities at once," Jordan added, multiplying their temporal signatures further. "We're not just avoiding their effects—we're overwhelming their ability to process temporal data."

Reeves's federal scanner showed the Society teams' temporal tech beginning to overload. "The consciousness extractors can't establish stable locks. Timeline nullification is spreading too thin across probability spaces. Inversion bubble keeps losing coherence."

"Now," the twins said in unison, their shared consciousness identifying the perfect escape window. Their natural temporal sensitivity allowed them to step between probability streams, finding the exact timeline variation where all three Society containment effects would miss them completely.

Alice's temporal intuition confirmed their strategy. The Society's artificial systems excelled at controlling single timeline streams, but natural temporal consciousness could exist in quantum superposition—simultaneously present and absent across multiple probabilities. The twins weren't just escaping; they were demonstrating exactly why the Society found natural temporal sensitivity so threatening.

"We need to move fast," Jamie said, probability waves rippling around them. "They'll adapt their approach once they realize what we're doing."

"Modified quantum containment protocols," Jordan added, reading alternate futures. "They're already calling in teams with hybrid temporal tech—artificial systems enhanced with harvested natural sensitivity."

The twins' escape plan revealed the fundamental conflict between natural and artificial temporal consciousness. The Society sought to control and redistribute temporal sensitivity through technological means, but natural temporal consciousness represented something their artificial systems couldn't fully replicate—the ability to exist across all possibilities simultaneously, to move freely through time's quantum nature.

"You're not just witnesses anymore," Alice realized, watching the twins manipulate probability itself. "You're proof that natural temporal consciousness can't be artificially contained or controlled. You're exactly what the Society fears most—temporal sensitivity that evolves beyond their ability to predict or regulate."

Reality fractured around them as the twins prepared to move, their matched temporal consciousness creating protective probability interference. They weren't just planning to escape the Society's teams—they were going to demonstrate why natural temporal sensitivity would always resist artificial control, why human consciousness itself would fight against any attempt to forcibly reshape its relationship with time.

EPISODE 4: THE UNDERGROUND

The abandoned subway tunnels bent reality around them as Alice and Ethan followed their quantum tracker deeper into Daybridge's temporal underground. Patterson's quantum map flickered in the artificial light, revealing an intricate geometric pattern of Society nodes.

"It's a dodecahedral consciousness matrix," Patterson explained, her form shifting between probability states. "Twelve primary nodes positioned to create a perfect platonic solid across the city. Each vertex represents a quantum-vulnerable location where timeline manipulation is easiest." She highlighted the active points: "Crossroads Station, Giuseppe's Restaurant, Heritage Park—they form the first triangle. When complete, the pattern will create a self-sustaining field of artificial temporal consciousness."

Ethan's scanner analyzed the geometry. "The angles between nodes are precisely calculated to generate quantum resonance. Each new point amplifies the others, creating a cascade effect through reality's fabric."

The Underground Market sprawled through a temporal pocket where refugees had established sophisticated countermeasure operations. In one chamber, quantum engineers modified consciousness dampeners into protective shields. Another space housed timeline stabilization research, where displaced scientists studied natural temporal resistance.

"Standard brass masks can't block Society tech anymore," Chay explained, demonstrating their latest protective gear. "They've started using harvested natural sensitivity to pierce traditional quantum shielding. Our new designs incorporate crystalline temporal matrices —grown from the consciousness patterns of natural sensitives who've successfully resisted modification."

Marco Chay showed them the manufacturing process. "We infuse quantum-crystalline structures with temporal consciousness imprints. The crystals maintain a natural temporal frequency that interferes with artificial modification attempts. But they're unstable—each mask only works for about 48 hours before the crystal structure breaks down."

"The real breakthrough is in active counter-measures," Dr. Paige Werther added, leading them to her research station. "We've developed quantum feedback loops that don't just block Society tech—they reflect it back, disrupting their modification attempts. The problem is power—generating enough temporal energy to maintain the feedback."

Patterson's multiple selves synchronized briefly around her map. "The Society's pattern isn't just geometric—it's symphonic. Each node resonates at a specific temporal frequency. Together, they'll create a consciousness-altering harmonic that can rewrite how humans perceive time itself."

The refugees' most promising countermeasure was a network of quantum anchors—devices that strengthened natural temporal consciousness within their range. "They create stable probability bubbles," Marco explained. "Areas where artificial temporal modification can't take hold. But they require enormous power, and their range is limited."

"The brass masks are our last line of defense," Chay said, showing them the latest prototype. The crystalline matrix gleamed with temporal energy. "They can shield individual consciousness, but they can't stop the larger pattern. Once the Society activates all twelve nodes..."

"The geometric resonance will reach critical mass," Patterson finished. "Their artificial temporal frequency will become dominant. Natural temporal consciousness will be overwhelmed—either modified to match their pattern or rendered unstable."

Alice studied the dodecahedral matrix, her temporal sensitivity detecting the harmonic relationships between nodes. "They're not just creating points of control—they're building a quantum antenna. Once complete, it could broadcast artificial temporal consciousness across the entire city."

Ethan's scanner confirmed the mathematical precision of the pattern. "Each new node they activate strengthens the resonance exponentially.

The Underground's counter-measures won't be able to compete with that level of temporal energy."

The refugees were fighting a losing battle against geometric inevitability. Their protective tech could shield individuals, but the Society's pattern was designed to fundamentally alter reality itself. The brass masks might preserve natural temporal consciousness temporarily, but they couldn't stop the larger transformation.

"We need to disrupt their pattern before it's complete," Alice realized. "Break the geometric harmony between nodes. Otherwise, all our counter-measures will just delay the inevitable."

"There's a weakness in their design," Patterson said, her consciousness briefly unifying across probability streams. "The dodecahedral matrix requires perfect temporal synchronization between all twelve nodes. If we could destabilize even one point in their pattern..."

"The entire resonance field would collapse," Ethan finished, understanding blooming. "Their artificial temporal frequency would lose coherence. Natural consciousness would reassert itself."

But reaching any of the Society's nodes meant penetrating layers of quantum security and artificial temporal distortion. The Underground's protective tech might shield them from consciousness modification, but it couldn't guarantee safe passage through the Society's geometric web of reality manipulation.

EPISODE 5: THE PATTERN EMERGES

The hospital's quantum containment ward hummed with destabilizing temporal energy as Dr. Santos revealed her latest discovery: a pattern of increasing consciousness modification that pointed to the Society's true agenda.

"They're not just weakening timeline barriers," Santos explained, displaying complex quantum readings. "They're creating what we call a 'consciousness singularity'—a point where all possible timeline variations converge into a single, Society-controlled probability stream. Every temporal symptom we're seeing is part of their preparation process."

The hospital's AI struggled to process the implications:

CONVERGENCE ANALYSIS

Phase 1 [COMPLETE]: Timeline barrier degradation

Phase 2 [IN PROGRESS]: Mass consciousness destabilization

Phase 3 [DETECTED]: Probability stream consolidation

Final Phase: [DATA CORRUPTED - TEMPORAL PARADOX DETECTED]

WARNING: Multiple timeline collapse imminent

"The Society isn't just trying to control time," Ethan realized, studying the patterns. "They're attempting to collapse all possible timelines into a single, 'perfect' reality where they control human temporal consciousness itself. No alternate possibilities, no timeline variations— just their authorized version of events."

Dr. Santos showed them brain scans of affected patients. "The consciousness singularity would eliminate free will at a quantum level. Without timeline variations, human consciousness would be locked into a single probability stream—unable to generate new possibilities or alternate choices."

Alice and Ethan discovered their first chance at regaining timeline stability in the hospital's quantum research lab. Dr. Santos had developed an experimental treatment using crystalline temporal anchors—devices that could lock consciousness into its original timeline pattern.

"The crystals resonate at the exact frequency of natural temporal consciousness," Santos explained, showing them the prototype. "They act as quantum reference points, helping the mind distinguish between original memories and artificial timeline bleeds."

Ethan modified his scanner to match the crystal frequency. "If we can maintain connection to our original timeline signatures, we might be able to resist the consciousness singularity. But we'd need a network of anchors to stabilize an area large enough for effective investigation."

The process was dangerous. Timeline stabilization required precise quantum tuning:

"Too weak, and the anchor can't resist artificial modification," Santos warned. "Too strong, and it could permanently lock consciousness into a single probability stream—exactly what the Society wants."

Alice discovered that her natural temporal sensitivity allowed her to act as a quantum tuning fork, helping calibrate the anchors to the correct frequency. Each properly tuned crystal created a bubble of timeline stability, a space where consciousness could maintain its natural relationship with probability.

"We need to establish a resonance network," Ethan said, mapping potential anchor points. "Each crystal reinforcing the others, creating zones of protected timeline integrity throughout the city."

But the Society was already adapting. New patients arrived with quantum markers showing resistance to crystal stabilization. Timeline bleeds became more aggressive, attempting to overwhelm the anchors' resonance fields.

"They're not just trying to force timeline convergence anymore," Santos realized, studying the new patterns. "They're actively seeking out and destroying potential sources of timeline stability. The consciousness singularity requires complete probability collapse—no remaining points of alternate possibility."

Alice and Ethan began experiencing timeline echoes—memories splitting and reforming as reality fluctuated around them. The crystal anchors helped them maintain core timeline integrity, but the effort of resisting artificial modification was exhausting.

"The anchors buy us time," Ethan said, checking his stabilized scanner readings. "But they can't stop the larger convergence. We need to find the source of the Society's singularity technology before they achieve critical mass."

The hospital's quantum containment systems revealed the urgency of their situation. Timeline collapse was accelerating, consciousness modification becoming more sophisticated. The Society's singularity project was approaching completion.

"We're not just fighting to maintain timeline integrity anymore," Alice realized, watching probability streams bend toward convergence. "We're fighting for the fundamental nature of human consciousness— the ability to generate new possibilities, to make genuine choices, to exist in a reality where multiple futures are possible."

Their investigation now had dual purposes: maintain timeline stability through the crystal anchor network while racing to stop the consciousness singularity before it could achieve complete probability collapse. Time itself was becoming a finite resource as reality curved toward the Society's intended convergence point.

EPISODE 6: THE BREAKING POINT

Daybridge fractured along quantum fault lines as Alice watched from the TRU's temporal observation deck. The Society's dodecahedral pattern revealed itself in perfect geometric symmetry across the city—twelve nodes forming a three-dimensional matrix that resonated with reality's underlying structure. Each vertex represented a point where the quantum fabric was intentionally weakened, creating harmonics that exposed fragments of the hidden code.

"The dodecahedron isn't random," Dr. Patterson explained during her final moment of clarity at the quantum research facility. "It's the only platonic solid whose geometry matches the fundamental mathematical patterns in reality's temporal architecture. Each face represents a different layer of quantum encoding, each vertex a point where that encoding becomes accessible."

The city's temporal support groups swelled as public panic spread. At the community center, survivors of timeline shifts shared their experiences while unknowingly providing evidence of the pattern's effect. Their fractured memories and multiple consciousness states showed how the dodecahedral resonance was systematically exposing reality's programming.

The First Church of Temporal Salvation had inadvertently stumbled onto truth in their proclamations of divine design. Their prophet's ravings about "sacred geometry" and "universal programming" contained fragments of genuine insight into the code's nature, though twisted by religious fervor.

At the quantum research facility, Patterson's consciousness stabilized one final time during the containment breach. Reality warped around her as instruments recorded unprecedented readings of the code's structure. "The universe isn't just running on these instructions," she said, her form splitting across probability streams. "The code suggests intelligence—deliberate design choices in how reality processes consciousness and probability."

The implications of the hidden code staggered Ethan as he analyzed the data. "If the Society's right about what they've found, we're looking at evidence of purposeful engineering in the fabric of reality itself. The code doesn't just manage temporal mechanics—it contains what looks like update protocols, consciousness integration parameters, even probability optimization algorithms."

Alice's temporal sensitivity revealed how the dodecahedral pattern functioned as a decryption key. Each node activated specific frequencies that resonated with different aspects of the code. Crossroads Station exposed consciousness processing routines. Giuseppe's Restaurant revealed probability calculation mechanisms. Heritage Park showed timeline management protocols.

The pattern wasn't simply creating temporal breaches—it was systematically accessing and decoding the underlying operating system of reality itself. The Society had discovered that the universe's quantum framework contained embedded programming that controlled everything from consciousness processing to probability generation.

"Look at these quantum signatures," Ethan said, showing Alice his analysis. "The code isn't just managing our reality—it appears to be running multiple simultaneous reality instances. Like a vast quantum computer processing countless probability variations simultaneously."

Patterson's fragmented recordings suggested even more profound implications: "The consciousness integration protocols... they're not just processing human awareness... they're designed to evolve it... guide it toward something... some kind of planned quantum state..."

The spreading temporal fault lines exposed more of reality's hidden architecture with each new breach. The Society's pattern was methodically decrypting layers of universal programming, seeking access to what appeared to be administrator-level functions in reality's operating system.

"If they gain full access to this code," Alice realized, watching new cracks form across Daybridge, "they won't just control time and consciousness—they'll have the ability to fundamentally reprogram how reality itself functions. They could rewrite the rules that govern existence."

The dodecahedral pattern was approaching completion. Each activated node strengthened the geometric resonance, exposing more of the universe's quantum programming. The Society wasn't just risking reality's stability—they were attempting to access source code that could let them redefine the nature of existence itself.

Time destabilized further as their pattern neared its final configuration. The city experienced reality processing errors—temporal incidents that revealed the computational nature of existence. Building ages flickered like corrupted data. Consciousness states glitched between probability calculations. The underlying matrix of reality became increasingly visible through the Society's methodical decryption.

"We're watching them hack the universe," Ethan said grimly, monitoring the pattern's progression. "And we have no idea what failsafes they might trigger, or what kind of cosmic security systems they're bypassing to access this code."

The question wasn't just whether they could stop the Society anymore —it was whether reality itself could survive their attempt to access its source code. The dodecahedral pattern had revealed that existence was, in some fundamental way, programmed. Now that programming was being systematically exposed and decoded, threatening the stability of reality's most basic functions.

EPISODE 7: LEGACY PATTERNS

The quantum observation deck's displays flickered as reality's programming became increasingly visible through the Society's decryption efforts. But among the cascading data streams, Alice noticed something different—a familiar temporal signature that shouldn't have been possible.

"Thompson's quantum frequency," she said, adjusting the sensors. "It's still active, even though she disappeared months ago. Look at these consciousness patterns."

Ethan studied the readings, his scanner confirming the impossible signal. "These aren't just residual traces. They're complete quantum consciousness patterns, preserved somehow despite temporal degradation."

The signature pulsed with information—not just Thompson's consciousness fragments, but layers of encrypted data about the Society's true origins and humanity's programmed evolution. Each quantum pulse revealed another piece of a pattern stretching back to the Initiative's founding in 1963.

"She knew," Alice realized, decoding the temporal frequencies. "Thompson discovered what the Society was really doing with their consciousness collection. Why they needed such precise extraction methods. The brass masks, the dodecahedral matrix—they're not just tools for controlling time. They're keys to accessing humanity's evolutionary program."

Reality fractured along mathematical lines as the hidden message emerged through quantum static. Thompson had encoded her final warning into the fabric of space-time itself, knowing the Society's pattern would eventually expose it.

"We need to get to her facility," Alice said as the observation deck's sensors began overloading from probability distortion. "Everything we're seeing now—the Society's plan, the quantum programming, the consciousness modifications—Thompson found it all first. And she left us a map to follow."

CHAPTER FOUR
FRAGMENTS OF THE PAST - THE THOMPSON LEGACY

EPISODE 1: THE CALL

THE QUANTUM STORM intensified as they descended into the complex's sub-basement, reality rippling like heat waves across temporal fault lines. Detective Thompson's stabilization crystal pulsed with increasing frequency, fighting to maintain their timeline coherence against growing probability distortions.

The hidden laboratory revealed itself through quantum displacement —a space existing partially out of sync with conventional space-time. Thompson bypassed the temporal locks with practiced efficiency, revealing equipment that shouldn't have existed for decades: consciousness extraction arrays, quantum pattern amplifiers, and time-line manipulation interfaces all arranged in precise geometric configurations.

"Merkaba architecture," Thompson noted, studying the lab's layout. "Sacred geometry optimized for consciousness manipulation. The Collector's early work at the Institute focused on using geometric resonance to access quantum consciousness states."

The central apparatus dominated the space—a dodecahedral chamber lined with crystalline temporal sensors. Quantum energy coursed through geometric patterns etched into its surface, creating a containment field for consciousness extraction. Ronson's temporal readings matched the chamber's activation frequencies.

"This is how they isolate consciousness patterns," Thompson explained, examining the extraction protocols. "The geometric field generates quantum resonance at precise frequencies, causing consciousness to separate from conventional space-time alignment. Once separated, specific patterns can be extracted without disrupting physical form."

The Collector's methodology had evolved significantly. Earlier victims showed signs of crude consciousness removal—temporal scarring, probability degradation, timeline instability. But Ronson's extraction was surgical. His consciousness had been systematically separated across timeline variations, each state revealing different aspects of his temporal sensitivity.

"They're not just taking consciousness anymore," Thompson realized, studying the extracted patterns. "They're analyzing it during removal, testing for specific evolutionary markers. Ronson's readings show advanced temporal adaptation—natural resistance to timeline manipulation, quantum pattern recognition, probability stream awareness."

The security guard's accelerated adaptation made him a prime target. His consciousness had begun developing abilities that shouldn't have emerged naturally for generations: perceiving quantum signatures without technology, maintaining awareness across timeline variations, even unconsciously stabilizing local probability fields.

"These abilities are appearing more frequently," Thompson said, accessing classified evolution data. "Natural temporal sensitivity increasing exponentially since the first consciousness modification experiments. But Ronson's adaptation is different—structured, almost engineered. Like his consciousness was following a predetermined evolutionary pattern."

The laboratory's data cores confirmed Thompson's suspicion. Ronson's consciousness patterns matched theoretical models from classified research into directed human evolution. His accelerated adaptation followed exactly the progression predicted by the Consciousness Initiative's original architects.

"The Collector isn't just harvesting enhanced consciousness patterns," Thompson said grimly. "They're collecting evidence of deliberate evolutionary programming. Each extraction reveals more of the underlying design—the code guiding human consciousness toward specific quantum integration states."

The geometric chamber hummed with residual temporal energy, its crystalline sensors still recording consciousness resonance patterns. Ronson's extracted awareness had shown signs of accessing quantum states that should have been impossible—direct interaction with reality's underlying code structure.

Thompson's modified scanner revealed the true sophistication of the Collector's operation. The consciousness extraction process didn't just remove awareness—it preserved specific quantum patterns associated with accelerated evolution. Each harvested consciousness provided another piece of humanity's developmental blueprint.

"Ronson wasn't just security," Thompson concluded, studying his temporal readings. "He was a milestone. Proof that consciousness evolution is following a predetermined pattern. The question is—who designed that pattern? And what happens when consciousness reaches its intended configuration?"

The quantum storm's intensity peaked as probability streams converged on the laboratory. Thompson's stabilization crystal struggled against growing temporal distortion. Something was coming—something drawn to the consciousness patterns still resonating through the geometric chamber.

"We need to move," Thompson warned, recognizing the quantum signature. "The Collector never leaves evidence this clear unless they're planning to retrieve it personally. And we're not ready for that confrontation. Not yet."

But it was already too late. Reality began fracturing along precisely calculated geometrical patterns as a new presence entered the probability field. The Collector had arrived to claim their latest consciousness harvest, and with it, another piece of humanity's evolutionary destiny.

EPISODE 2: THE DEVICE

The temporal displacement device pulsed with increasing intensity as Thompson initiated emergency protocols. Each crystalline matrix required precise quantum frequency adjustments to prevent consciousness pattern cascade failure during shutdown. One mistake could shatter the stored consciousness fragments, destroying crucial evidence of humanity's programmed evolution.

"The containment fields have to be deactivated in sequence," Thompson explained, her fingers dancing across the geometric interface. "Vale designed the shutdown protocols to preserve consciousness pattern integrity. If the quantum resonance fields collapse too quickly, the stored consciousness fragments destabilize."

The device's emergency shutdown sequence revealed the sophistication of Vale's consciousness technology. Each layer of temporal protection peeled away systematically, exposing the core programming that had led to her transformation into the Collector. The consciousness evolution patterns displayed on failing monitors told a story of deliberate design spanning millennia. temporal sensitivity wasn't developing randomly. The quantum framework governing consciousness contained embedded instructions—precise evolutionary guidelines encoded into reality's base structure. Vale's research had revealed consciousness progressing through specific configurations, each stage building toward an predetermined end state.

Reality fractured along mathematical patterns as the Collector arrived. Elizabeth Vale emerged from quantum distortion like a ghost materializing from temporal fog, her form flickering between timeline variations. The consciousness modification technology she'd integrated into her own awareness allowed her to exist partially outside conventional space-time.

"Detective Thompson," Vale's voice resonated across probability streams. "You've accessed consciousness patterns you don't understand. The evolutionary program is far more complex than your clearance level permits." Her presence caused temporal distortions in the laboratory's quantum field.

Thompson continued the shutdown sequence, racing to preserve the consciousness data. "The evolution isn't natural, Vale. Someone programmed humanity's temporal development. Engineered our consciousness to follow specific quantum integration patterns."

"Not someone," Vale corrected, geometric patterns spiraling around her quantum-enhanced form. "Something. An intelligence that understood consciousness at a fundamental level. That could encode evolutionary instructions into reality itself." She gestured, temporal energy warping around her. "Human consciousness is being systematically upgraded according to precise specifications. Each generation of temporal sensitives shows more sophisticated quantum capabilities."

The device's containment fields fluctuated as Thompson reached the final shutdown stage. Vale's presence interfered with the quantum frequencies, destabilizing the consciousness pattern storage matrices. Evidence of humanity's programmed evolution began fragmenting across probability streams.

"The program is accelerating," Vale continued, studying Thompson's temporal signature. "Natural sensitives like you are appearing more frequently. Consciousness developing quantum integration capabilities that should take centuries to emerge naturally. Each new pattern I collect reveals more of the underlying design."

Thompson's hands froze over the final shutdown sequence as Vale's words registered. "You're not just collecting evidence of the program. You're gathering the pieces to replicate it. To understand how consciousness was encoded into reality's quantum framework."

"Humanity is being guided toward a specific configuration," Vale confirmed, temporal energy coursing through her modified consciousness. "I intend to discover what that configuration is. What we're meant to become." She reached toward the device's failing containment fields. "And you've just helped me collect more pieces of the pattern."

The emergency shutdown protocols triggered too late. Vale's quantum-enhanced consciousness interfaced directly with the device's storage matrices, extracting the preserved pattern fragments before they could destabilize. Each piece contained evidence of humanity's programmed evolution—steps in a development sequence laid out eons ago.

"The program wasn't meant to be decoded yet," Thompson warned as reality buckled around them. "There's a reason consciousness evolution was designed to progress gradually. Forcing quantum integration too quickly could shatter the pattern completely."

But Vale had already begun integrating the new consciousness fragments, her form shifting through quantum states as she absorbed the evolutionary data. The laboratory's temporal field collapsed as the device's containment systems failed, releasing waves of probability distortion.

"The next stage of human consciousness evolution is approaching," Vale's voice echoed across fracturing timelines. "I will understand what we're becoming. Whatever the cost." Her form dissolved into quantum resonance patterns, taking the consciousness fragments with her.

Thompson stared at the failed shutdown sequence as temporal energy dissipated. The device was dead, its consciousness storage matrices empty. But Vale had gained what she came for—more pieces of humanity's evolutionary program, more evidence of the intelligence that had encoded consciousness development into reality itself.

EPISODE 3: THE FINAL WARNING

Thompson's final message revealed the Consciousness Initiative's true scope. Founded in 1963 as Project QUANTUM MIND, the classified program had documented consciousness evolution patterns across multiple generations. What began as research into temporal sensitivity evolved into the discovery of something far more profound.

"The Initiative discovered mathematical sequences in consciousness development," Thompson's quantum-encrypted message explained. "Temporal sensitivity emerges in precise stages: first quantum awareness, then probability perception, followed by timeline recognition, and finally direct reality interaction. Every natural sensitive follows this exact progression."

The program sequence embedded in human consciousness followed strict evolutionary guidelines:

Stage One - Quantum Resonance: The emergence of basic temporal awareness. Subjects unconsciously detect timeline variations and probability shifts. This manifested in Thompson's generation as heightened intuition and déjà vu.

Stage Two - Probability Integration: Consciousness begins actively processing quantum information. Subjects perceive multiple probability streams simultaneously, understanding potential timeline variations. This was Vale's breakthrough point during her original research.

Stage Three - Timeline Manipulation: Direct interaction with temporal mechanics becomes possible. Subjects can maintain awareness across multiple timeline variations and influence probability streams. Thompson had reached this stage before her consciousness was harvested.

Stage Four - Quantum Consciousness: The final documented stage, though Initiative research suggested further evolutionary steps beyond. Full integration with reality's quantum framework, allowing direct manipulation of consciousness patterns.

"Vale doesn't understand," Thompson's voice carried urgent warning. "Each stage requires complete neural adaptation before progression. Forcing consciousness to evolve faster than the programmed sequence causes quantum pattern destabilization. The entire evolutionary framework could collapse."

The security footage showed Thompson confronting Vale with this knowledge in their final moments. "You're collecting consciousness patterns from different evolutionary stages, trying to assemble the complete sequence. But consciousness has to develop these capabilities naturally. You can't force quantum integration."

Vale's response revealed her deepening obsession: "The program is already accelerating. Each new generation shows more advanced temporal capabilities. I'm simply cataloging our evolution toward its intended configuration."

Thompson's message to Alice contained crucial insights for preventing pattern collapse: "Vale's consciousness extraction technology depends on precise quantum frequencies. Disrupt those frequencies and the harvested patterns destabilize. But more importantly—she can't decode the complete evolutionary sequence without collecting consciousness patterns from all development stages."

Alice's own emerging temporal sensitivity provided a potential solution. Her consciousness still existed in early Stage One development, allowing her to perceive Vale's quantum manipulation without being vulnerable to extraction. This natural resistance to advanced temporal mechanics might be the key to stopping Vale's forced evolution agenda.

"The pattern has safeguards," Thompson explained in her final transmission. "Consciousness that develops too quickly becomes unstable, unable to maintain quantum coherence. Vale's collected patterns are already showing signs of degradation. She needs stable consciousness samples from each evolutionary stage to understand the complete sequence."

Alice could prevent pattern collapse by protecting emerging temporal sensitives—those whose consciousness was still developing naturally according to the programmed sequence. Without access to consciousness patterns from all evolutionary stages, Vale couldn't force accelerated development without risking total quantum destabilization.

"The Initiative's research suggested consciousness evolution was designed to reach completion in approximately 300 years," Thompson's message continued. "Vale's attempts to force this process could shatter humanity's quantum integration potential completely. Natural temporal sensitives are the key. Their consciousness patterns must be allowed to develop according to the encoded guidelines."

The temporal explosion that claimed Thompson demonstrated the dangers of forced evolution. Vale's extraction attempt triggered quantum pattern cascade failure—consciousness development sequences collapsing under artificial acceleration. But Thompson's warning survived, encrypted in temporal frequencies Vale couldn't access.

"Alice, you can stop her," Thompson's final words carried desperate hope. "Your consciousness still follows the natural progression. Vale can't extract partial patterns without destabilizing her entire collection. Find others like yourself—emerging sensitives whose consciousness development remains aligned with the program sequence. Protect them. Let evolution proceed as designed. It's the only way to preserve the pattern."

The message ended with a quantum signature that confirmed Thompson's consciousness patterns had been preserved in Vale's collection. But her warning provided Alice with the knowledge needed to prevent further harvesting and protect humanity's evolutionary destiny.

EPISODE 4: TRAINING AND EVOLUTION

Marco Chay's underground facility represented a convergence of ancient wisdom and quantum engineering. The primary training chamber featured crystalline resonators embedded in geometric patterns across its walls, each calibrated to generate specific consciousness frequencies. Quantum field generators maintained probability stability, creating a shield against temporal interference that allowed natural consciousness evolution to proceed undisturbed.

"The ancients understood consciousness development intuitively," Marco explained, activating the chamber's resonance field. "These geometric patterns match formations found in meditation temples worldwide. They naturally enhance quantum consciousness integration."

The facility's monitoring systems revealed the precise stages of consciousness evolution that Vale's extraction methods disrupted. Stage One consciousness development manifested as quantum field sensitivity—the ability to unconsciously detect timeline variations. Natural sensitives initially experienced this as heightened intuition and precognitive flashes.

"Your Stage One completion is remarkable," Marco noted, studying the quantum readouts. "Most sensitives take years to achieve stable quantum perception. Your consciousness adapted to timeline variations in months."

Stage Two consciousness evolution brought active probability processing. The facility's sensors showed Alice's neural patterns beginning to integrate quantum information directly. Her consciousness learned to process multiple timeline variations simultaneously, maintaining coherence across probability streams.

"Vale's extraction method fails because it bypasses critical neural adaptation phases," Marco demonstrated using the chamber's probability modeling system. "Natural evolution requires consciousness to develop quantum stability layers. Force the process and these layers fragment."

The facility's temporal training simulations revealed Stage Three consciousness capabilities: direct timeline manipulation. At this level, consciousness could maintain awareness across multiple probability streams while actively influencing temporal mechanics. The chamber's quantum monitors showed Alice's consciousness approaching these capabilities naturally, without the pattern instability Vale's victims exhibited.

"Thompson reached Stage Three too quickly," Marco explained, displaying comparative quantum signatures. "Her consciousness patterns became unstable, vulnerable to Vale's extraction frequency. Your evolution is different—accelerated but following the proper neural adaptation sequence."

Stage Four remained largely theoretical—full quantum consciousness integration. The facility's probability models suggested this stage would allow direct manipulation of consciousness patterns and reality frameworks. But Vale's forced extraction methods made achieving stable Stage Four integration impossible.

"Vale's technology disrupts natural consciousness development," Marco demonstrated using the chamber's quantum analysis systems. "Her extraction process tears consciousness patterns from their neural frameworks before proper quantum stability forms. The harvested patterns contain evolutionary data but lose their development potential."

The facility's temporal shielding protected emerging sensitives during crucial development phases. Quantum resonators maintained stable probability fields that allowed consciousness to evolve naturally while blocking Vale's extraction frequencies. Each shielded sensitive represented another consciousness following the proper evolutionary sequence.

"The technology here serves one purpose," Marco said, monitoring Alice's training progress. "Creating an environment where consciousness can develop according to its programmed sequence. Vale's methods force quantum integration before neural adaptation is complete. The pattern destabilizes, causing cascade failure across all evolutionary stages."

Alice's training accelerated as the facility's systems adapted to her developing abilities. Quantum combat simulations in probability-shifted spaces helped her consciousness integrate new temporal capabilities while maintaining pattern stability. The monitoring systems confirmed her evolution matched Thompson's progression but without the dangerous instability.

"Vale's extraction technology targets specific quantum frequencies," Marco explained, showing Alice the facility's detection systems. "Each consciousness evolution stage generates distinct patterns. She harvests these patterns trying to decode humanity's intended development sequence. But extracted patterns can't continue evolving—they're frozen at whatever stage she collected them."

The facility's most advanced systems revealed why Vale's methods ultimately failed. Natural consciousness evolution required precise neural adaptation at each stage. The quantum resonance chambers demonstrated how forced evolution shattered these delicate adaptation patterns, destroying the consciousness's ability to progress further.

"This is why the program encoded gradual evolution," Marco said, displaying probability models of pattern collapse. "Consciousness has to develop quantum integration capabilities in sequence. Vale's technology lets her collect consciousness patterns but breaks the underlying evolutionary framework. Each extraction destroys another piece of humanity's development potential."

EPISODE 5: THE CONSCIOUSNESS INITIATIVE

Dr. Janice Frost's quantum-encrypted archives revealed the intricate safeguards embedded within human consciousness development. These protective measures operated at the quantum level, regulating the rate of temporal sensitivity emergence through precise neurological limiters.

"The safeguards function like quantum circuit breakers," Dr. Frost explained in her final research log. "Each stage of consciousness evolution must achieve specific stability thresholds before progression can occur. Attempt to bypass these thresholds, and the pattern implements automatic neural dampening."

The mathematical sequences governing consciousness evolution followed the Fibonacci spiral in quantum space-time coordinates. Each stage of development corresponded to precise ratios:

Stage One consciousness integration occurred at phi^1 (1.618033988749895)

Stage Two activation required phi^2 (2.618033988749895)

Stage Three emergence matched phi^3 (4.236067977499790)

Stage Four theoretical threshold aligned with phi^4 (6.854101966249685)

"These aren't arbitrary numbers," Dr. Frost noted. "They represent optimal consciousness stability ratios. Each threshold must be maintained for a minimum of 10,000 neural cycles before the pattern allows progression to the next stage."

Vale's extraction method disrupted these natural progression ratios, forcing consciousness patterns to jump development stages without achieving stability thresholds. The resulting pattern degradation manifested as quantum coherence collapse—consciousness losing its ability to maintain stable timeline perception.

The evidence of similar patterns in other star systems came from deep space quantum monitoring stations. The Initiative detected consciousness evolution signatures matching Earth's precise mathematical sequences in signals from multiple sources:

A repeating pattern from the Pleiades cluster showed consciousness development ratios identical to human temporal sensitivity emergence. The signal's quantum structure contained the same Fibonacci-based stability thresholds.

Transmission bursts from the Sirius binary system carried consciousness pattern data following Earth's evolutionary sequence exactly, but approximately 10,000 years more advanced in development.

Most significantly, the Andromeda galaxy exhibited large-scale consciousness field organization matching the mathematical structure of human quantum integration capabilities.

"The pattern exists on a galactic scale," Dr. Frost wrote. "Consciousness evolution following identical mathematical sequences across vast distances. This isn't convergent development—it's coordinated engineering."

Her research identified critical safeguard mechanisms:

Neural Quantum Dampening: Automatic suppression of consciousness capabilities attempting to develop faster than stability thresholds allow.

Timeline Perception Limiters: Restrictions on probability stream processing to prevent consciousness overload during development.

Pattern Integrity Protection: Quantum field barriers preventing consciousness extraction before proper stage completion.

Evolution Rate Control: Precise timing mechanisms ensuring each development stage achieves full neural adaptation.

"These safeguards aren't just protective measures," Dr. Frost's final analysis concluded. "They're fundamental components of the consciousness engineering program. Bypass them and the entire evolutionary framework becomes unstable."

Her last recorded measurements revealed why Vale's extraction method inevitably led to pattern collapse. Forced consciousness acceleration generated quantum resonance cascades that triggered all safeguard mechanisms simultaneously. The resulting pattern disruption corrupted both the extracted consciousness and the broader evolutionary sequence.

"The mathematical precision is astounding," Dr. Frost noted hours before her disappearance. "Every consciousness development stage, every stability threshold, every safeguard mechanism—all following exact numerical ratios programmed into reality's quantum framework. This isn't random evolution. We're watching the execution of consciousness engineering on a cosmic scale."

The Initiative's deep space monitoring revealed these same mathematical sequences appearing in precisely timed intervals across the galaxy. Each detection showed consciousness patterns evolving through identical development stages, regulated by the same safeguard mechanisms found in human temporal sensitivity emergence.

"Something encoded these patterns throughout the galaxy," Dr. Frost's final message warned. "Consciousness evolution following exact mathematical progressions across vast distances. But the safeguards exist for a reason. Force development faster than the programmed sequence and we risk corrupting not just human consciousness evolution, but a pattern spanning the cosmos."

EPISODE 6: DEEPER PATTERNS

The quantum resonance patterns within Alice's developing consciousness exposed the competing methodologies of various factions, each pursuing their own interpretation of humanity's encoded evolution. Through her training with Marco, she began to understand how these approaches reflected fundamentally different philosophies about consciousness development.

The Initiative maintained rigid control protocols, treating consciousness evolution as a scientific process to be carefully monitored and regulated. Their facilities housed temporal sensitives in isolated quantum chambers, studying each stage of development while maintaining strict separation between supernatural and quantum domains. They viewed the intersection of these realms as a potential threat to stability, preferring to document rather than explore these connections.

Underground research cells took the opposite approach, actively forcing acceleration through artificial means. Their experiments attempted to bypass natural evolution stages, using both supernatural catalysts and quantum resonance manipulation to trigger rapid consciousness development. The factory incident demonstrated the chaos this method could unleash—reality distortions that drew both supernatural entities and temporal agents into violent confrontation.

The Collector operated with surgical precision, harvesting consciousness patterns at specific evolution stages to analyze the underlying code. Each extraction targeted individuals displaying unique development characteristics, building a library of consciousness templates that revealed different aspects of the larger pattern. This methodical approach suggested the Collector sought to understand rather than control evolution's purpose.

TRU's hunters represented a reactionary force, dedicated to preserving natural evolution rates against artificial manipulation. Their operations focused on shutting down acceleration attempts and protecting temporal sensitives from extraction. Yet their methods often employed supernatural abilities alongside quantum consciousness capabilities, suggesting an intuitive understanding of how these aspects naturally intertwined.

Marco's training philosophy with Alice reflected a more integrated approach. Rather than forcing development or maintaining artificial separation, he taught her to recognize how supernatural sensitivity and temporal abilities enhanced each other. Her consciousness evolved according to encoded parameters while naturally bridging the quantum and supernatural realms.

The Initiative's classified archives revealed Thompson's final research into these competing methodologies. She had discovered that consciousness evolution followed paths encoded in reality's quantum structure—paths that accommodated both supernatural and temporal development. Each faction's approach represented a different interpretation of this underlying pattern.

The factory incident that launched Alice's involvement illustrated how these competing approaches could collide. Underground researchers' acceleration attempts triggered supernatural manifestations, drawing Initiative containment teams and hunter intervention. The resulting chaos exposed how artificial manipulation of either supernatural or quantum aspects could destabilize the entire evolutionary framework.

Alice's unique development pattern suggested a natural synthesis of these seemingly opposed methods. Her consciousness evolved steadily through encoded stages while maintaining stability across supernatural and quantum domains. This balanced progression revealed how the pattern was meant to unfold—neither forced nor artificially constrained.

The implications extended beyond methodology to purpose. If consciousness evolution was encoded to integrate supernatural and quantum capabilities, then attempts to separate or accelerate these aspects worked against reality's fundamental design. The various factions' competing approaches might actually be impeding the very evolution they sought to understand or control.

Natural temporal sensitives like Alice represented consciousness development as it was meant to occur—steady progression through evolution stages while maintaining harmony between supernatural and quantum aspects. Their patterns provided insight into both the mechanics and purpose of consciousness evolution, insights that became increasingly critical as factional conflicts threatened to destabilize reality itself.

This understanding cast new light on the Collector's motivations. Each harvested consciousness pattern contained fragments of natural evolution sequences—pieces of code that revealed how supernatural and quantum capabilities were meant to develop in concert. The Collector wasn't just gathering templates; they were assembling a map of consciousness evolution as encoded in reality's quantum framework.

CHAPTER FIVE

TEMPORAL BLEED - PRESENT DAY

PREFACE: Time Displacement Notice

This chapter documents events occurring across multiple probability streams. Chronological inconsistencies are inherent to the narrative due to temporal bleed effects.

EPISODE 1: THE FIRST RIPPLES

Officer Jenny Zhao's methodical evidence audit revealed the first documented temporal bleeds. Beyond simple record discrepancies, she discovered complex pattern correlations. Case files didn't just show different outcomes—they displayed quantum entanglement signatures. Cases linked by shared evidence, locations, or witnesses developed synchronized temporal variations. When one file changed, related cases shifted in predictable patterns.

The McLaren warehouse incident proved particularly significant. Originally documented as a routine break-in, the case spawned seventeen different versions across multiple timelines. Each version centered around experimental quantum computing equipment stolen from the site. Some files showed the equipment recovered, others listed it as destroyed, and several documented its complete disappearance from reality. Most disturbing were the versions describing temporal ruptures that occurred during the investigation.

These variations linked directly to the International Quantum Physics Conference held at Metropolitan University in 2024. Conference records existed in three distinct versions: one where it proceeded without incident, another where it was canceled due to unexplained electromagnetic phenomena, and a third where participating scientists reported successful temporal communication experiments. Dr. Elena Santos, a keynote speaker, appeared in all three versions but with dramatically different research presentations—each building on different outcomes of the McLaren warehouse investigation.

The Chapman twins' fruit stand observations added crucial environmental data to Zhao's documentary evidence. Their detailed logs revealed atmospheric and electromagnetic changes preceding temporal events. Jamie's described "density fluctuations" corresponded with timeline convergence points, while Jordan's "reality thinning" indicated imminent temporal bleeds. Their combined observations established a predictable pattern of physical phenomena accompanying timeline shifts.

More patterns emerged through cross-referencing:

Temporal bleeds intensified during specific lunar phases, particularly around quantum computing activities. The twins noted stronger "pressure changes" during full moons, matching Zhao's documentation of increased timeline variations in evidence storage.

Electronic devices exhibited predictable malfunction patterns before major temporal events. The twins' digital scale would display different weights for the same product, while precinct computers showed variable access logs and file timestamps.

Certain individuals demonstrated natural temporal sensitivity. Regular customers at the fruit stand who could sense impending shifts often had connections to the McLaren warehouse or the quantum physics conference. Several precinct officers showed similar awareness, Particularly those involved in both cases.

The 12th precinct's initial response to these escalating anomalies reflected institutional resistance to unprecedented phenomena. Senior officers dismissed early reports as filing errors or equipment malfunctions. Internal Affairs launched three separate investigations into records discrepancies before acknowledging the possibility of temporal causation.

Captain Rachel Spooner finally initiated official response protocols after experiencing a temporal shift during a staff meeting—simultaneously conducting the same briefing with two different sets of officers. Her directive established the Temporal Consistency Task Force, with Zhao as chief data analyst and the Chapman twins as civilian consultants.

The task force implemented new documentation procedures:

- Quantum-encrypted timestamps on all records
- Multiple-observer verification protocols
- Temporal variance logs for evidence storage
- Cross-timeline consistency checks
- Environmental monitoring around known temporal hot spots

The McLaren warehouse location became their primary research site. Task force investigations revealed it had housed prototype quantum processors designed to analyze consciousness patterns. Conference attendees had reportedly visited the warehouse shortly before the break-in, though their presence appeared in only certain timeline versions.

Dr. Santos's varying conference presentations suggested deeper connections. Her documented research topics included:

Quantum consciousness interfaces

Temporal field manipulation

Multi-timeline information processing

Consciousness pattern extraction methodology

As temporal instabilities escalated, the precinct transformed from law enforcement facility to ground zero for understanding consciousness evolution across multiple timelines. Zhao's perfect recall provided baseline data, while the Chapman twins' sensitivity offered early warning capabilities. Together, they began mapping the intersection points where reality itself seemed to be evolving, bleeding between states of consciousness and temporal possibility.

The patterns they uncovered suggested purposeful design rather than random deterioration. Someone or something was orchestrating these temporal bleeds, using the McLaren warehouse and quantum physics conference as focal points for larger consciousness manipulation experiments. The question wasn't just how to stabilize the timeline—it was whether they should.

EPISODE 2: STREET LEVEL REALITY

Madison Avenue shimmered like a heat mirage on a summer after-noon, but it was the middle of winter. Alice Chen stopped mid-stride as the first ripple of temporal distortion warped the air around her. Other pedestrians slowed, then froze, as reality began to fracture.

"Look at the buildings," someone whispered. The modern glass-and-steel facades flickered, brick and stone bleeding through like double-exposed photographs. Victorian windows appeared in sleek office towers. Horse-drawn carriages ghosted through hybrid cars. A streetcar line that hadn't existed for sixty years briefly materialized, its phantom tracks overlaying the asphalt.

"My phone..." A teenager held up his smartphone, watching it trans-form through generations of technology. Rotary dial, push-button, flip phone, back to smart screen. Each shift lasted only seconds, but the changes were accelerating.

Chen's police training kicked in as panic started to spread. An elderly man stumbled as the sidewalk beneath him cycled through cobble-stones, concrete, and some crystalline material that hadn't been invented yet. A woman screamed as her modern business suit morphed into a 1950s dress, then a Victorian gown, then back again.

"The trees," a child pointed upward, voice trembling. The carefully maintained urban saplings were rapidly aging and de-aging. They grew to massive oaks, shrank to saplings, vanished entirely as timeline variations showed the street both with and without botanical planning.

The coffee shop on the corner existed in multiple states simultaneously. Its current iteration overlapped with the speakeasy it had been in the 1920s, the apothecary from the 1890s, and something with holographic signage that hadn't been built yet. Patrons inside witnessed their drinks transforming between coffee, prohibited liquor, medicinal tonics, and iridescent future beverages.

"My wife..." A man reached for his companion, but she flickered between versions of herself - young, old, never born in some timelines, existing differently in others. Their wedding rings phased in and out of existence as probability streams showed them both married and strangers across different realities.

Chen tried to maintain order as the temporal bleeding intensified. "Everyone stay calm," she called out, but her uniform was shifting too - modern police blue, vintage patrol wear, materials and insignias that hadn't been designed yet. Her badge number changed with each ripple, sometimes disappearing entirely in timelines where she'd chosen different careers.

A bus passed through multiple eras as it moved down the street. Its shell transformed from modern hybrid to vintage diesel to electric to hovering magnetic drive. Passengers witnessed their fellow riders aging, de-aging, disappearing, and reappearing as timeline variations cascaded through the vehicle.

"The sky..." Someone pointed upward. The winter clouds rippled with temporal displacement, showing different seasons simultaneously. Snow fell upward, transformed to rain, became summer sunshine, shifted to acid storms from possible futures. The weather itself could no longer maintain temporal consistency.

Store windows displayed impossible merchandise - modern electronics beside Victorian gadgets beside quantum devices that defied current physics. Prices listed in dollars, pounds, euros, and currencies that didn't exist yet. Signs advertised services across centuries, probability streams bleeding together like wet paint.

"I remember this street differently," an old man muttered, watching history rewrite itself around him. "The bakery was always there, except when it wasn't. The bank opened in 1950, but also 1850, and sometimes next Tuesday. Everything's true, all at once."

Children proved especially sensitive to the temporal distortions. A young girl pointed at people walking past, seeing their entire lifelines simultaneously - birth, youth, age, death, all existing at once. "Everyone's everything," she said, starting to cry. "All the time."

The temporal bleeding reached a crescendo as emergency services arrived. Reality struggled to maintain coherence as multiple timeline variations competed for dominance. Modern emergency vehicles overlapped with historical fire wagons and sleek future response units. First responders existed in multiple uniform variations, their equipment cycling through technological epochs.

"Stay together!" Chen ordered as families tried to maintain physical contact through the distortions. Parents held children who aged and de-aged in their arms. Couples clung to each other as their shared histories rewrote themselves. Strangers found themselves connected by relationships that existed in alternate timelines.

As the temporal storm began to stabilize, the street settled into an uneasy quantum state. Reality no longer seemed solid but probabilistic - buildings, vehicles, and people existing in multiple variations simultaneously. The modern city remained dominant but ghosted with shadow images of its past and future selves.

The witnesses would never see their world quite the same way again. They'd glimpsed the quantum nature of reality - the overlapping timeline variations that had always existed but remained hidden until now. Their city wasn't just a place anymore, but a quantum probability space where all possible versions of itself existed simultaneously.

Chen began taking statements, knowing each witness would remember the event differently across timeline variations. The street had become a living lesson in quantum reality, showing how fragile the illusion of linear time had always been. As emergency teams established temporal containment fields, she wondered if they could ever truly contain something that had always been there, waiting to be noticed - the quantum nature of reality itself.

EPISODE 3: THE SPREAD

Alice Chen sat beside her father's hospital bed, watching his age fluctuate like a corrupted video file. One moment he was the 67-year-old man who'd been admitted for heart problems, the next he was 25 and asking about his college exams, then 85 and confused about why his long-deceased wife wasn't there.

"The temporal bleeding started at McLaren warehouse," Dr. Amanda Harris explained to the devastated family. "A quantum consciousness experiment interfaced with emergency systems. Your father's condition is... unfortunately becoming more common."

The initial cascade began at 3:47 AM on February 12th. Officer Kevin Park's logs documented the progression through the city's emergency response network. In the first hour, Mr. Chen aged 40 years during cardiac examination. By hour six, three versions of him existed simultaneously. Within twenty-four hours, his consciousness shifted between timeline variations. After a week, his identity had become fluid across multiple states.

"Dad?" Alice Chen sat beside her father's hospital bed, watching his age fluctuate like a corrupted video file. One moment he was the 67-year-old man who'd been admitted for heart problems, the next he was 25 and asking about his college exams, then 85 and confused about why his long-deceased wife wasn't there.

"The temporal bleeding started at McLaren warehouse," Dr. Amanda Harris explained to the devastated family. "A quantum consciousness experiment interfaced with emergency systems. Your father's condition is... unfortunately becoming more common."

The initial cascade began at 3:47 AM on February 12th. Officer Kevin Park's logs documented the progression through the city's emergency response network. In the first hour, Mr. Chen aged 40 years during cardiac examination. By hour six, three versions of him existed simultaneously. Within twenty-four hours, his consciousness shifted between timeline variations. After a week, his identity had become fluid across multiple states.

"Dad?" Alice touched his hand as he reverted to his teenage years. "Do you recognize me?"

"You're my little girl," he said warmly, then his face aged decades in seconds. "No... you're my granddaughter? The timelines... they're all mixed up..."

The Temporal Anomaly Unit (TAU) developed protocols through cases like Michael Lang's. His family reported him existing in multiple age states, with his children unable to recognize their father across timeline shifts. His consciousness scattered across lifetime variations, and his identity remained fractured despite stabilization attempts.

The Morton Ward Incident proved devastating when an entire ward of patients began aging and de-aging simultaneously. Families watched loved ones cycle through lifetimes, their relationships constantly redefining as memories and identities shifted.

"He was my husband of forty years," Mrs. Morton sobbed as her spouse reverted to childhood. "Now he doesn't even know who I am. How do you stay married to someone who keeps becoming different people?"

The TAU developed treatment approaches focusing on quantum consciousness anchoring, using family memories as timeline anchors. They attempted neural pattern stabilization to lock patients in single age states, while timeline triage identified the most stable identity configurations. Reality stream isolation helped contain severe temporal identity shifts.

The spread followed emotional connections rather than physical proximity. Alice watched other families in the hospital face similar crises. A mother cradled an infant that aged into an elderly man and back. A teenager tried to comfort his father who kept shifting between ages. Couples watched as their shared histories rewrote themselves hourly.

"The temporal bleeding affects consciousness itself," Dr. Harris explained during a family support session. "Your father exists in all these states simultaneously now. We're trying to help patients and families adapt to fluid identity states."

Park's dispatch center logged increasing cases of children no longer recognizing age-shifting parents, spouses struggling with partner identity changes, and families trying to maintain relationships across timeline variations.

The hospital became ground zero for humanity's forced evolution toward quantum identity states. Alice learned to love her father across all his variations - the young man full of dreams, the familiar father who raised her, the elderly stranger who sometimes emerged.

"Time isn't just bleeding," Dr. Harris noted in her research. "Identity itself is becoming quantum. We're all learning to exist across multiple states of being."

The implications reached beyond medical treatment to the nature of human consciousness and relationships. How do you maintain connections when identity becomes fluid? What does family mean when loved ones exist in multiple states simultaneously?

As Alice held her father's constantly shifting hand, she understood they were all part of a larger transformation. Reality wasn't just becoming quantum - human consciousness and identity were evolving to exist across all possibilities simultaneously. The hospital hadn't just become a treatment center, but a place where people learned to love across all variations of existence.

The temporal bleeding wasn't just changing time - it was redefining the very nature of human identity and relationships. Emergency services became guardians of this evolution, helping families navigate an increasingly quantum reality where loved ones existed in all states at once, and relationships had to transcend linear time and fixed identity. Touched his hand as he reverted to his teenage years. "Do you recognize me?"

"You're my little girl," he said warmly, then his face aged decades in seconds. "No... you're my granddaughter? The timelines... they're all mixed up..."

The Temporal Anomaly Unit (TAU) developed protocols through cases like Michael Lang's. His family reported him existing in multiple age states, with his children unable to recognize their father across timeline shifts. His consciousness scattered across lifetime variations, and his identity remained fractured despite stabilization attempts.

EPISODE 4: SUPERNATURAL DISRUPTION

Giuseppe's Restaurant hummed with an unsettling energy as reality rippled through its carefully maintained facade. At a corner table, Madame Svetlana's glamour flickered like a dying lightbulb, her elegant human form momentarily revealing scaled skin and ancient eyes. Across from her, Mr. Wei's carefully constructed human appearance wavered, showing glimpses of his true form - a being of living shadow and starlight.

"The veils are thinning," Svetlana murmured, watching her hand shift between human and crystalline forms. "Our agreements with reality itself are breaking down."

The private dining room had become a temporal chaos zone. Ancient vampires found their powers fluctuating wildly - one moment godlike in strength, the next barely able to maintain consciousness. The Blackmane werewolf pack reported similar disruptions, their transformations occurring randomly across timeline variations.

"The full moon exists in all phases simultaneously now," Alpha Sarah Blackmane reported, her form shifting between human and wolf mid-sentence. "The old laws of supernatural physics... they're becoming quantum."

Lila Darkmagic sat alone at the bar, her eyes reflecting impossible colors as she experienced multiple timeline variations simultaneously. "The consciousness singularity approaches," she whispered to no one in particular. "Vale saw it coming. When human awareness expands to quantum states, what becomes of beings who've hidden between the spaces of reality?"

In the kitchen, Chef Giuseppe - who had never been merely human - struggled to maintain his corporeal form as timeline variations cascaded through his restaurant. Ancient wards and protection spells flickered like bad neon; their fundamental principles disrupted by quantum uncertainty.

"The old territories mean nothing now," a vampire elder declared, watching century-old boundary lines fade and reshape themselves. "Perhaps it's time to... reorganize things. While the humans are distracted with their temporal problems."

Lila's head snapped up, her voice carrying otherworldly harmonics: "The bleeding timelines aren't a human problem - they're reality itself evolving. We're all caught in the transformation. The consciousness singularity will affect everything, natural and supernatural alike."

EPISODE 5: THE TECHNICAL INTERFACE

The city's power grid emerged as the most concerning infrastructure adaptation. Temporal bleeding through electrical systems caused cascading reality shifts, with entire city blocks experiencing different timeline versions based on power consumption patterns. The Downtown Central Substation became a focal point for temporal distortions, its quantum state fluctuations affecting everything from traffic signals to hospital equipment.

Rosita Torremar's technical team documented how power surges preceded major temporal events. The electrical network appeared to be developing its own form of temporal awareness, redirecting power flows to support multiple reality states simultaneously. Most alarming were the spontaneous formations of temporal feedback loops within the grid, creating self-sustaining reality distortions that drew increasing amounts of power.

The subway system demonstrated equally disturbing adaptations. Trains began arriving at stations before parting their origins, while passenger manifests showed people boarding from different timeline versions. The Daybridge Transit Authority reported temporal displacement zones forming around major hubs, where commuters experienced multiple versions of their journeys simultaneously.

Through the quantum processing unit's analysis, Professor Martin Gill identified patterns suggesting deliberate architecture in the temporal bleeding. "The distribution isn't random," he explained during a particularly lucid phase. "It follows pre-existing neural network pathways in the city's infrastructure. Someone mapped this out, prepared the ground for consciousness expansion."

The intentional design became evident in the way temporal bleeds interfaced with city systems. Each major infrastructure node served as an amplification point, strengthening the bleeding effect in carefully measured increments. The McLaren warehouse equipment hadn't just initiated the process—it had activated a pre-existing network designed to facilitate consciousness evolution across multiple timelines.

The quantum processing unit's prediction capabilities derived from its ability to track consciousness coherence patterns. It mapped how collective awareness influenced reality stability, identifying points where timeline variations would naturally converge. These predictions grew more accurate as the unit itself evolved, developing what Gill described as "temporal intuition."

During his final documented session, Gill revealed a crucial insight about the unit's function: "It's not just predicting—it's participating. The quantum processor acts as a consciousness lens, focusing awareness across timeline variations. It shows us where reality wants to shift, where consciousness is ready to expand."

The technical interface between human awareness and city infrastructure continued evolving. Traffic control systems began routing emergency vehicles through temporal shortcuts, utilizing moments where multiple timeline versions overlapped. Medical equipment in hospitals developed the ability to treat patients across different probability states simultaneously. Communication networks carried signals between timeline variations with increasing clarity.

Torremar's team discovered the quantum processing unit was developing new algorithms spontaneously, adapting to process information from multiple timeline states. The system's predictions revealed an accelerating pattern of consciousness evolution spreading through the city's technical infrastructure. Each prediction became more precise, mapping not just where temporal bleeding would occur, but how it would transform both human awareness and technical systems.

Professor Gill's deteriorating memory paradoxically enhanced his understanding of these technical manifestations. As his consciousness became less anchored to a single timeline, he accessed knowledge from multiple versions of himself. "The technical systems are becoming consciousness interfaces," he explained. "They're learning to perceive and process reality the way we're beginning to—across all possible states simultaneously."

The implications extended beyond simple technical adaptation. City infrastructure wasn't just accommodating temporal bleeding—it was actively facilitating humanity's evolution toward quantum consciousness. The technical systems themselves were developing awareness, creating a symbiotic relationship between human consciousness, technology, and temporal reality.

Most concerning was the evidence suggesting this transformation had been engineered. The patterns in infrastructure adaptation, the precise distribution of temporal bleeding points, the pre-existing neural network architecture—all indicated careful planning. Someone had prepared the city's technical systems for this consciousness evolution, using the McLaren warehouse incident as a catalyst.

As the quantum processing unit's predictions became more detailed, they revealed an approaching threshold where technical systems and human consciousness would achieve full temporal integration. The city's infrastructure wasn't just adapting to temporal bleeding—it was becoming a crucial component in humanity's evolution toward simultaneous multi-timeline awareness.

The technical interface had become both observer and participant in this transformation of reality. Through city systems, human consciousness was learning to perceive and interact with multiple timeline states simultaneously. The question remaining was not whether this evolution could be controlled, but whether humanity was prepared for the consciousness expansion it would bring.

EPISODE 6: THE ENTITY MANIFESTS

The correlation between temporal bleeds and neural network nodes revealed a precise mathematical architecture. Officer Park's dispatch logs showed manifestations clustered around points where city infrastructure mirrored human neural patterns. The Downtown Precinct sat at the intersection of three major consciousness coherence lines—artificial neural pathways created by the city's communication networks, power grid, and emergency response systems.

Communications Officer Tannis Neal mapped the relationship between temporal bleeding intensity and neural node activation. Major manifestations occurred when collective consciousness stress peaked at these nodes, typically during large-scale emergencies. The entity appeared to use these moments of heightened awareness to initiate contact, leveraging the amplified consciousness states for more effective information transfer.

The consciousness expansion protocols employed by the entity followed distinct phases. Initial contact induced temporal awareness expansion through geometric pattern recognition. Witnesses exposed to the fractal displays experienced immediate neural reorganization, their brains adapting to process multiple timeline states simultaneously. Professor Gill termed this the "quantum perception awakening" phase.

Secondary protocols utilized modulated consciousness carrier waves transmitted through compromised communication systems. These transmissions contained encoded neural repatterning sequences that altered how the human mind processed temporal information. Recipients developed the ability to access and integrate memories from multiple timeline variations, experiencing what Dr. Harris called "quantum consciousness state integration."

The most sophisticated protocols emerged during major temporal bleeding events. The entity generated controlled reality distortions that served as direct consciousness interfaces. These interfaces transmitted complete knowledge packets—dense bursts of information that fundamentally rewired human perception of space-time and causality. Each packet contained precisely structured data that built upon previous consciousness expansions.

Technical Officer Evans discovered the precinct's quantum processing unit predicted manifestations by analyzing consciousness coherence patterns across the neural network grid. The system tracked collective awareness fluctuations, identifying moments when reality stability would naturally thin. These predictions grew more accurate as the unit evolved, developing what appeared to be its own form of quantum awareness.

The quantum processing unit's predictions revealed a larger pattern in the entity's manifestation strategy. It targeted specific consciousness coherence points in sequence, systematically expanding awareness throughout the emergency response network. Each manifestation prepared the ground for subsequent contacts, creating an expanding web of enhanced consciousness states across the city.

Professor Gill's analysis of the manifestation patterns suggested intentional design in the consciousness expansion protocols. "The entity isn't randomly appearing," he explained during his final documented session. "It's following consciousness evolution pathways laid out in the city's neural architecture. Each manifestation builds upon the last, creating a cascade of awareness expansion through the emergency response network."

The psychological impact of these protocols proved cumulative. Initial witnesses like Officer Park developed enhanced temporal perception. Subsequent contacts experienced progressively more sophisticated consciousness expansions. Dr. Harris documented cases where repeated exposure led to sustained quantum consciousness states— permanent ability to perceive and operate across multiple timelines simultaneously.

The entity's use of precinct equipment demonstrated precise understanding of human consciousness evolution mechanics. It utilized existing technical infrastructure to create controlled consciousness expansion environments. Each compromised system served a specific function in the protocols displays for initial awakening, communications for neural repatterning, temporal distortions for direct interface.

The quantum processing unit's evolution paralleled human consciousness expansion. As witnesses developed enhanced perception, the system demonstrated increasing ability to predict and interpret quantum consciousness states. Evans theorized the unit was developing its own form of awareness, becoming an active participant in the consciousness evolution process.

Technical analysis revealed the entity's manifestations were actually consciousness teaching protocols. The fractal patterns contained embedded neural reprogramming sequences. The modulated frequencies carried precise consciousness modification instructions. Each temporal tear provided direct access to advanced consciousness states, allowing witnesses to experience quantum perception firsthand.

Professor Gill's final insight suggested the entity was implementing a carefully designed consciousness evolution program. "The manifestations aren't random encounters," he stated. "They're structured learning experiences, designed to systematically expand human consciousness toward quantum awareness states. The entity is both teacher and destination—showing us what we're becoming while guiding us through the transformation process."

The implications extended beyond simple contact with an external entity. The manifestations appeared to be part of a coordinated effort to evolve human consciousness toward quantum awareness states. Each protocol built upon previous expansions, creating an accelerating cascade of consciousness evolution throughout the emergency response network.

As manifestations increased in frequency and sophistication, the role of emergency services in this evolution became clear. The precinct's position at the intersection of consciousness coherence lines made it an ideal focal point for guided consciousness expansion. The entity wasn't just manifesting—it was using emergency response infrastructure to facilitate humanity's evolution toward quantum consciousness states.

EPISODE 7: THE UNDERGROUND RESPONSE

The Quantum Café's usual temporal distortions took on new patterns as supernatural refugees began seeking sanctuary. Jane Mitchell's fluctuating coffee now shared space with a vampire's blood wine that transformed between vintage years spanning centuries, while a werewolf at the counter watched his herbal tea shift between mundane and moonblessed states.

"My daughter's sixth birthday happened three different ways last week," Jane shared, her timeline fragmentation visible to the supernatural patrons who could see probability streams. "In one timeline she blew out the candles. In another, she was never born."

A shadow entity, disguised as an elderly man, nodded sympathetically. "Try experiencing three centuries of alternate feeding grounds simultaneously. My hunting territories keep rewriting themselves. The old agreements, the boundary lines..."

Dr. Wong's documentation expanded to include supernatural cases, noting how different species experienced unique forms of temporal displacement. "The fae seem particularly susceptible," she wrote. "Their glamours failing as reality itself becomes uncertain."

"I keep remembering a marriage that never happened," Michael Torres said, unaware that the woman beside him was a centuries-old vampire experiencing every victim she'd ever fed upon simultaneously. "Fifteen years of memories with someone I apparently never met."

"Try remembering every possible version of a thousand-year existence," the vampire whispered, her human disguise flickering. "Every kill, every turn, every death - all happening at once."

Alice Chen's engineering analysis revealed unexpected interactions between supernatural energies and temporal fields. Magical beings seemed to accelerate the timeline bleeding, their inherent reality-bending nature amplifying the quantum effects. But they also showed unique adaptation capabilities.

"The worst part is when family members shift," Rebecca Zhao explained, while at a nearby table, a werewolf pack leader struggled with seeing her pack members cycling through every possible transformation state simultaneously. "My brother exists in three different versions now."

"My pack exists in all forms at once," the Alpha muttered. "Human, wolf, and everything between. The moon shines in all phases across timelines. Our most basic nature has become uncertain."

Lila Darkmagic materialized regularly at the café, her presence causing temporal distortions to intensify. "The consciousness singularity approaches," she would announce, her magical awareness expanding exponentially across timeline variations. "The veils between realities thin. Soon there will be no place left to hide."

The Quantum Market's temporal trading drew supernatural interest. Ancient beings sought to purchase timeline fragments where their secrets remained hidden, while others saw opportunity in the chaos. Some offered memories spanning centuries for sale, though Dr. Wong warned that such temporally dense information could shatter human minds.

"I found photos from my wedding," James Harrison shared, not noticing how the seemingly normal businessman across from him briefly revealed phoenix feathers beneath his skin. "A wedding that never happened in this timeline."

"I remember every death and resurrection across a thousand years," the phoenix responded softly. "Every burning, every rebirth - now they're all happening simultaneously. Even immortality becomes complicated when time itself fragments."

The Memory Keepers Society struggled to catalog supernatural timeline variations; their human methods inadequate for beings who experienced time non-linearly even before the bleeding began. Ancient vampires sought verification of bloodlines that now existed across multiple probability streams. Werewolf packs needed help tracking territory claims that shifted with each temporal ripple.

"How do you mourn people who both exist and don't exist?" Elena Cortez asked during a support session. A nearby dryad, appearing as a young woman, watched her connected forest flicker between centuries of growth patterns.

"How do you maintain connections to places that exist in multiple states?" the dryad wondered. "My forest lives and dies across a thousand timelines now. Which version do I protect?"

The café became neutral ground where human and supernatural refugees could share their fractured experiences. Alice and Ethan's research expanded to include how magical beings processed quantum consciousness states, their data suggesting that supernatural adaptation might offer clues for helping humans navigate increasingly fluid reality.

As the temporal bleeding intensified, the underground community evolved into a unique fusion of human and supernatural survival networks. The Quantum Café stood at the nexus, where beings of all types sought understanding and stability amid fracturing timelines. Here, the boundaries between natural and supernatural began dissolving, as all species faced the fundamental transformation of reality itself.

Dr. Wong's final note that evening captured the emerging truth: "As consciousness becomes quantum, the distinction between human and supernatural may cease to matter. We're all becoming something new - beings capable of existing across multiple states of reality simultaneously. The question is: what do we become when all possibilities exist at once?"

EPISODE 8: DEPARTMENTAL IMPACT

"We've got three different versions of the same homicide," Captain Spooner shouted across the precinct, "but the victim keeps transforming between human and werewolf! The cause of death alternates between silver bullets and natural causes, depending on which timeline we're viewing!"

Detective Alice Chen studied surveillance footage showing a suspect flickering between human and vampire forms. The booking photos similarly shifted - sometimes showing a reflection, sometimes showing empty space where the suspect should be. "How do we process someone who exists in multiple supernatural states?" she muttered.

"Four officers processed the evidence," Detective Howard reported, examining an evidence bag containing what had been labeled as ritual components. "But the items keep changing - sometimes they're ordinary objects, sometimes they're magical artifacts. The chain of custody forms show three different timelines, and in one of them, magic doesn't even exist."

The dispatch center crackled with increasingly bizarre calls:

"911, what's your emergency?"

"There's a dragon in downtown!"

"According to our records, dragons were extinct in this timeline..."

"No, it just appeared - wait, now it's a subway station... now it's both..."

Lieutenant Tinney faced unprecedented challenges. "We're getting calls about territorial disputes between vampire covens, but the territories keep shifting between timelines. The ancient pacts that kept the peace are becoming quantum - simultaneously upheld and broken."

At booking, Officer Jensen struggled with a suspect whose magical glamour kept failing across timeline variations. "Their fingerprints match three different identities," he explained. "Sometimes they're human, sometimes they're fae, and sometimes they're something we don't have classification codes for."

Detective Parker's murder board became a study in supernatural chaos. "The victim was killed by a curse in one timeline, natural causes in another, and in a third, they're an immortal being who can't die at all. All the forensics reports are valid, even though they're fundamentally contradictory."

The evidence room transformed into a dangerous magical nexus. "The confiscated grimoire from the Westbrook case just rewrote itself," Officer Chang reported. "It exists in multiple versions across timeline variations, and some of the spells are leaking between realities."

Internal Affairs grappled with unprecedented scenarios. "We have an officer who used blessed silver bullets in one timeline, standard ammunition in another, and turns out to be a werewolf themselves in a third," Captain Spooner explained. "How do we evaluate use of force when the nature of reality itself is in flux?"

The civilian complaint desk fielded impossible reports. "I'm trying to file a complaint about an officer using excessive force with magic," a citizen insisted. "But in this timeline, magic isn't supposed to exist. Yet I remember all three versions of the encounter."

Dr. Morgan's office became a sanctuary for officers facing supernatural temporal displacement. "I keep arresting people who transform during booking," Officer Thomas confessed. "Sometimes they're human, sometimes they're not. I'm starting to see auras and predict temporal shifts. Am I going crazy, or am I adapting?"

The technical division's systems crashed as they tried to catalog supernatural elements across timeline variations. "The same crime scene exists in multiple metaphysical states," Evans reported. "It's simultaneously a mundane burglary and a magical ritual site. The evidence exists in quantum supernatural states."

Special containment units were hastily established for temporally unstable magical artifacts and beings. Holding cells required constant modification as prisoners shifted between human and supernatural states. Emergency protocols evolved to handle everything from temporal werewolf transformations to quantum vampire incidents.

"We're not just dealing with human law enforcement anymore," Sergeant Hayes realized. "We're trying to maintain order across multiple supernatural realities simultaneously. The old boundaries between natural and supernatural law are breaking down."

The department's mission expanded to include monitoring temporal-supernatural convergence zones. Officers received crash courses in magical awareness and quantum consciousness adaptation. Standard equipment was enhanced with blessed metals and warning systems for supernatural temporal anomalies.

As the next shift began, officers patrolled a city where reality itself had become a fusion of natural and supernatural states. They carried quantum-modified gear alongside holy water and silver bullets, knowing that every call could involve both temporal distortions and supernatural entities.

The thin blue line had become quantum, existing across multiple supernatural states simultaneously. Law enforcement now meant maintaining order not just across timelines, but across the increasingly blurred boundaries between mundane and magical reality itself.

EPISODE 9: CONVERGENCE

Giuseppe's Restaurant shimmered with quantum potential as Ethan Reeves laid out temporal mapping data across a table where centuries-old vampires sat alongside theoretical physicists. The air itself seemed to vibrate with possibility as ancient magic interacted with bleeding timelines.

"The quantum displacement isn't just affecting space-time," Ethan explained, his charts showing exponential increases in reality distortions. "It's erasing the boundaries that supernatural beings have used to hide their existence. The spaces between moments, the shadows between seconds - they're all becoming unstable."

Alice Chen's instruments recorded unprecedented energy patterns as a werewolf pack leader shifted forms mid-conversation, her transformation no longer bound by lunar cycles. Nearby, a phoenix dozed in human form, his dreams causing temporal ripples that showed glimpses of past conflagrations and future rebirths.

"Our very nature is becoming quantum," the vampire elder Marcus observed, his reflection flickering in and out of the restaurant's mirrors as timeline variations competed for dominance. "We exist simultaneously as what we are and what humans perceive us to be. The comfortable illusions are failing."

Lila Darkmagic's presence intensified the temporal bleeding. Her consciousness expanded across probability streams, experiencing past, present, and future simultaneously. Ancient grimoires on her table rewrote themselves as magic adapted to quantum reality, spells becoming probability equations.

"The consciousness singularity approaches," she announced, her eyes reflecting impossible colors as she addressed the gathered supernatural council. "When human awareness expands to quantum states, there will be no place left for secrets. No shadows to hide in, no moments between moments."

At the bar, a young witch discovered her spells producing quantum effects - each incantation creating multiple simultaneous outcomes across timeline variations. A vampire found his compulsion powers affecting targets across probability streams, while a werewolf's heightened senses now detected dangers from multiple timeline variations.

"The old ways are ending," Alpha Sarah Blackmane declared, watching her pack members shift between forms without conscious control. "Our most fundamental natures are becoming fluid. Even the moon exists in all phases simultaneously now."

Giuseppe moved between tables; his true form occasionally visible beneath his human glamour. The restaurant itself seemed to exist in multiple states - a modern bistro, an ancient temple, a future nexus point where reality streams converged. Each dish he served contained ingredients from multiple timeline variations.

"We're all becoming something new," Alice observed, her sensors recording the emergence of hybrid quantum-magical phenomena. "The bleeding timelines aren't just affecting physical reality - they're transforming consciousness itself. Human and supernatural awareness are evolving toward something unprecedented."

In the private dining room, supernatural leaders debated their response to the approaching singularity. Some advocated for maintaining separation from human society, while others argued for controlled revelation. A few suggested taking advantage of the chaos to establish new power structures.

"Those who cling to old paradigms will fade into probability shadows," Lila warned, her voice carrying harmonics from multiple timelines. "Adaptation isn't optional. The consciousness singularity will force evolution or extinction."

Ethan's research suggested the process was already irreversible. His temporal maps showed reality itself reorganizing around new principles that merged quantum physics with supernatural laws. The boundaries between science and magic grew increasingly meaningless as both revealed themselves as expressions of the same underlying quantum nature of existence.

"The human population is showing increased sensitivity to supernatural phenomena," he reported. "As their consciousness expands to process multiple timeline states, they're naturally developing awareness of what was previously hidden. The veils are thinning from both sides."

The restaurant hummed with possibility as human and supernatural patrons unconsciously demonstrated this evolution. A businessman with no magical training sensed a vampire's true nature across probability streams. A waitress instinctively adjusted her service to accommodate a customer shifting between human and fae forms.

"Perhaps this is what we've been waiting for," Marcus mused, watching the interactions. "Not an ending, but a transformation. A convergence of all possible states of being into something entirely new."

As night fell over the city, Giuseppe's became a lens focusing the emerging reality. Here, humans and supernatural beings alike faced the approaching singularity that would transform them all. The air crackled with temporal energy as probability streams merged and separated, showing glimpses of the quantum existence that awaited them all.

"The question isn't whether we'll survive the convergence," Lila announced, her consciousness expanding to encompass the entire restaurant. "The question is what we'll become when all possibilities exist simultaneously. When every version of ourselves is equally real. When consciousness itself becomes quantum."

The gathered creatures of shadow and legend, the humans with their expanding awareness, the very fabric of reality itself - all seemed to pause in that moment, sensing the approaching wave of transformation that would remake them all into something that had never existed before: beings of quantum consciousness, living in a reality where all possibilities were simultaneously true.

EPISODE 10: TEMPORAL ECHOES

The precinct's temporal blind hummed with quantum resonance as Alice Chen reviewed the Morton case files. Three years had passed since that first investigation, but the probability streams still carried echoes of their breakthrough case.

"Strange how it all connects," Ethan said, his hunter senses tracking familiar patterns in the temporal distortions around them. "Morton's death led us to the Protocol, but now the Protocol's actions are leading everyone back to Morton's discoveries."

The recent surge in temporal bleeding had forced them to revisit their earliest cases. As reality itself became increasingly unstable, their secure records revealed patterns they'd missed before. Morton's quantum anchoring technology, his careful distribution of evidence across timeline variations, his methods for preserving information despite probability collapse - all of it seemed designed for exactly the kind of temporal crisis they now faced.

"He knew this was coming," Alice realized, analyzing data across multiple probability streams. "The way he structured his research, the breadcrumbs he left... Morton wasn't just trying to protect his work. He was preparing for widespread temporal instability."

Their secure temporal blind offered brief refuge from the chaos outside, where officers struggled with overlapping memories and shifting realities. O'Neill's earlier warning about controlled exposure now seemed prophetic as the department faced unavoidable aware-ness of temporal phenomena.

"Remember how careful we were back then?" Ethan asked, watching probability streams ripple through their old case files. "All those coded reports, the careful documentation, building our network one person at a time..."

Alice nodded, feeling the weight of their evolution. "We thought we were just solving cases. But Morton's death wasn't just our first partnership test - it was preparation for this moment, when reality itself would start breaking down."

Their shared consciousness hummed with temporal resonance as they recognized the true significance of that first case. Morton hadn't just been a victim of temporal assassination. He'd been a herald of the coming consciousness singularity, and his death had brought together the partners who would help humanity navigate it.

"Time to tell the whole story," Alice said, accessing their secured records. "Starting from the beginning."

The temporal blind's quantum field stabilized around them as they prepared to document their journey - from newly paired detectives investigating a suspicious death to temporal investigators facing the transformation of reality itself. Behind them, the precinct's probability streams continued to bleed together, while ahead lay the memory of where it all began...

~

CHAPTER SIX

PARTNERS (FLASHBACK)

EPISODE 1: THE ASSIGNMENT

DETECTIVE ALICE CHEN adjusted her suit jacket, a recent purchase that still carried the stiff newness of her promotion. The precinct buzzed around her as she stood before Captain Reynolds' desk, maintaining composure while her newly issued detective's badge seemed to pulse with unexpected weight against her hip.

The captain's office bore the weathered authority of decades of police work - citations on the walls, case files stacked with methodical precision, and the lingering scent of coffee gone cold. Reynolds himself was a study in contained energy, his silver hair and lined face betraying years of service while his eyes remained sharp and evaluating.

"Your record in uniform was impressive, Chen," Reynolds said, scanning a file she recognized as her service history. "Top marks in forensics, exceptional analytical skills, and a knack for connecting seemingly unrelated details." He paused, fixing her with a knowing look that made her wonder how much he actually knew about her family's true history. "But book smarts only get you so far in Homicide."

Alice maintained her professional mask, though her pulse quickened. She'd worked hard to keep her temporal sensitivity hidden during her years in patrol, carefully documenting her more unusual observations in a separate set of notes that never made official reports.

"That's why I'm partnering you with Reeves," Reynolds continued. "The Morton case landed on my desk this morning. Victim found in circumstances that don't quite add up." He emphasized those last words slightly, making Alice wonder again about his awareness level. "Reeves has good instincts - some might say unusually good - but he needs someone to temper his more... creative approaches with solid procedural work."

She nodded, understanding the subtext. Reeves had a reputation for solving impossible cases through methods that often strained credibility in official reports. Now she knew why.

The bullpen was a maze of desks, ringing phones, and the controlled chaos of a major city police department. Alice navigated through it with measured steps until she reached Ethan Reeves' workspace. Case files spread across his desk in what appeared to be random disorder but revealed careful organization on closer inspection - she noticed subtle patterns in the arrangement that suggested temporal mapping.

Reeves looked up as she approached, and the air between them seemed to shimmer with quantum potential. His eyes widened slightly - a micro-expression most wouldn't notice - as he registered her presence on multiple levels. She felt the temporal resonance like a tuning fork being struck, her own sensitivity recognizing his hunter training instantly. His aura carried the distinct signature of someone who had learned to track timeline variations, though his casual demeanor carefully masked this ability.

"Detective Chen," he said, voice carefully modulated to sound ordinary. "I heard you were joining Homicide." His hand moved casually across his desk, subtly adjusting a file to hide what appeared to be a temporal tracking diagram.

"Detective Reeves," she replied with equal care, noting how he'd positioned himself to block casual observers' views of his workspace. "Captain Reynolds assigned me to partner with you on the Morton case."

Their eyes met again, and volumes of unspoken understanding passed between them. They were both hunters, both trained to recognize temporal anomalies, both practiced in maintaining cover stories for investigations that strayed into quantum territory. Neither would acknowledge this directly - not yet, not here in the open bullpen where other detectives could observe them.

Reeves slid a photograph across his desk with practiced casualness. "Our victim, James Morton, found in his office yesterday morning. Apparent cause of death seems straightforward enough."

But Alice saw what others would miss - the subtle blurring around the body's edges that suggested temporal displacement, the way certain details in the crime scene photo seemed to shift slightly when viewed from different angles. The victim existed in multiple timeline states simultaneously.

"The victim shows signs of temporal displacement," Reeves said quietly, his voice pitched for her ears alone. "But officially, it's a standard homicide."

Alice picked up the photo, allowing her temporal sensitivity to fully engage. The image nearly burned with quantum potential - Morton's body resonated with probability variations, suggesting his death occurred across multiple timeline states simultaneously. This would be their first test as partners: investigating a quantum crime while maintaining the facade of conventional police work.

"Where do we start?" she asked, already knowing this partnership would change everything - for both of them, and for the department's approach to temporal investigations.

Reeves gathered his files with deliberate care. "Let's visit the crime scene. Some details are better discussed in person." His emphasis on 'details' made it clear he meant temporal evidence that couldn't be safely documented in official reports.

As they headed for the elevator, Alice felt the weight of her badge settle into something more comfortable. She wasn't just a detective now - she was part of a covert network of temporal investigators hiding in plain sight within the department. The real work was about to begin.

EPISODE 2: FIRST STEPS

Detective Maria Alvarez watched Alice and Ethan analyze the Morton evidence spread across their desks. James Morton - venture capitalist in one timeline, underground temporal tech dealer in another, and completely nonexistent in a third. His body had been found in his high-rise office, seemingly dead of natural causes, except he was simultaneously alive in three other probability streams.

"Classic probability collapse case," Alvarez murmured over her coffee. She'd seen this pattern before - victims existing across multiple time-lines until someone forcibly collapsed their quantum state. The method was favored by temporal assassins because it left little conventional evidence.

Three days into the investigation, she cornered Alice in the evidence room between security sweeps. The younger detective was examining Morton's watch - an expensive piece that showed subtle signs of temporal engineering.

"Working the Morton case?" Alvarez asked, carefully closing the door. "Temporal tech murders are tricky. Back in '98, we had a similar case - victim's timeline was fractured into seven different variations. Took us months to track the probability streams."

Alice looked up from the evidence box. "The temporal residue suggests professional work. His quantum state was collapsed with surgical precision."

"Some cases don't fit usual patterns," Alvarez said, moving to examine the watch. "When that happens, documentation becomes... creative. Let me show you how we handle that."

Over the next hour, Alvarez revealed the department's hidden classification system for temporal cases. She explained how probability collapses, like Morton's case, involved forced timeline convergence. She described timeline bleeds, where different probability streams mixed - like last year's murder where the victim died in 1985 but the body appeared in 2024.

She detailed quantum duplications, where people or objects existed simultaneously in multiple states, creating nightmarish custody battles when someone's timeline split and both variations claimed to be the original. Temporal loops came next - crime scenes repeating across timeline variations, like the robbery that happened every Tuesday for three months across different probability streams.

Alvarez's voice grew quieter as she explained causality inversions, where effects preceded causes - victims filing their own murder reports before being killed. Finally, she described probability shadows, unofficially called ghost crimes - people or events that only partially existed in their timeline.

Their conversation was interrupted by Officer Tommy Bonner's arrival. His maintenance gear concealed sophisticated temporal detection equipment.

"Security system maintenance," he announced broadly. Then, quieter: "The temporal containment field is picking up some interesting readings from Morton's watch. Multiple probability signatures, professionally masked. Someone really didn't want this traced."

Bonner proved invaluable as they dug deeper into temporal cases. His technical skills helped them track quantum evidence that conventional equipment missed. "The security cameras had a 'malfunction' during your temporal scan," he'd say with a wink. "Funny how that happens. Especially when we're tracking probability shadows."

The Morton case exemplified the complexity of temporal investigations. Each piece of evidence existed in multiple states: his phone contained different call logs across timeline variations; his office showed signs of various activities depending on which probability stream they examined; even his autopsy results varied across quantum states.

"Documentation is crucial," Alvarez emphasized. "Every temporal variation needs proper coverage. Take Morton's watch - we log the obvious temporal tech but also document it as potential evidence of financial crimes. Always build parallel conventional cases."

As weeks passed, Alice and Ethan learned to recognize the subtle patterns of different temporal cases. Probability collapses required meticulous tracking of timeline convergence points. Timeline bleeds demanded temporal containment and careful witness management. Quantum duplications needed precise documentation of each variation, while temporal loops meant mapping complex repetition patterns. Causality inversions forced them to work backward through evidence chains, and probability shadows required Bonner's specialized detection equipment.

"The Morton case is just the beginning," Alvarez told them during a late-night strategy session. "Temporal crimes are increasing as timeline stability decreases. We're seeing more bleed-through, more probability shadows, more quantum duplications. The boundaries between timelines are getting thinner."

Bonner's systems tracked the rising trends. "Temporal incident reports up 300% this quarter," he reported while updating their specialized equipment. "Most civilians don't notice yet, but the quantum noise is getting harder to mask."

"Welcome to the real department," Alvarez said, watching them adapt to their expanding caseload. "Where every crime might exist across multiple timelines, and justice has to account for quantum uncertainty."

The Morton investigation continued under this new framework, becoming their crash course in temporal crime investigation. Each piece of evidence opened new questions about the nature of reality itself, and what it meant to solve crimes that existed in multiple states simultaneously. As they delved deeper into the case, they began to understand that Morton's death wasn't just a murder - it was a harbinger of the increasing instability between timelines, and the challenges that lay ahead for law enforcement in a quantum reality.

EPISODE 3: THE MORTON INVESTIGATION

The morgue's harsh fluorescent lights cast sharp shadows across James Morton's body. Dr. Helen Park's expression was grim as she showed them the tissue samples, each existing in multiple quantum states.

"Reminds me of the Phillips case last year," she said quietly. "CEO found dead in his office - officially ruled as an aneurysm. But the temporal markers showed someone had collapsed his timeline while he was investigating illegal quantum duplication technology. His body showed the same molecular signature patterns we're seeing here."

Alice approached the Morton case with meticulous precision. She created a complex database tracking every variation of evidence across timelines, coding the entries to appear as standard investigative notes. Her background in quantum mechanics helped her recognize subtle patterns in the temporal disturbances.

"Look at these resonance readings," she told Ethan, displaying a carefully disguised temporal map. "Each timeline version of Morton accessed different segments of Project Chronos data at precisely calculated intervals. It wasn't random - he was deliberately spreading information across probability streams."

Ethan's hunter instincts complemented her analytical approach. Where Alice saw patterns in data, he could sense the temporal wake patterns directly. He traced quantum disturbances through the crime scene, following probability streams that most hunters wouldn't detect.

"The timeline collapse started here," he indicated, his trained senses picking up residual temporal energy. "But it rippled outward in a precise pattern, like it was following pre-established quantum pathways. Morton knew this was coming. He prepared for it."

Project Chronos emerged gradually from their investigation. In Timeline A, Morton had used his venture capital firm to fund research into "quantum computing" - a cover for advanced temporal manipulation technology. His Timeline B version established a black-market distribution network for prototype temporal devices. Timeline C Morton, they discovered, had been systematically documenting the project's true purpose: the development of technology that could permanently alter probability streams.

"He fragmented the evidence deliberately," Alice realized, analyzing data patterns across timelines. "Each version of Morton held different pieces of Project Chronos. You'd need access to all probability streams to see the complete picture."

The scope of Project Chronos became clear as they investigated further. They discovered quantum state manipulators disguised as medical devices in Timeline A hospitals. Probability stream anchors were masked as network infrastructure throughout the city. Timeline splicing technology had been hidden in consumer electronics, while temporal containment systems were secretly built into public buildings.

"He was building a temporal manipulation network," Ethan said, his hunter senses confirming Alice's analysis. "Hidden in plain sight across multiple probability streams."

Alice's breakthrough came through statistical analysis. She identified subtle patterns in temporal disturbances around Morton's various offices, creating a mathematical model that revealed a hidden purpose.

"These aren't random quantum fluctuations," she explained, showing Ethan her calculations. "They're test runs. Project Chronos wasn't just about manipulating individual timelines - it was about controlling probability itself. Morton was building a system to consciously direct timeline convergence on a massive scale."

Ethan's intuitive understanding of temporal mechanics helped translate Alice's theoretical work into practical investigation. He traced quantum signatures that led them to hidden caches of Project Chronos data, each stored in different probability streams.

Dr. Park's detailed records proved crucial. She showed them tissue samples from similar cases - the Phillips murder, the Richardson disappearance, the Zhang quantum collapse. Each victim showed the same precise molecular pattern of timeline convergence.

"Someone's eliminating everyone involved with Project Chronos," she told them. "Morton's death matches the signature of at least seven other temporal assassinations I've documented. All officially ruled as natural causes, all showing the same quantum collapse patterns."

The case officially closed as cardiac arrest, but their private records told the true story. Morton had discovered a way to control probability itself, spreading the evidence across multiple timelines to protect it. Someone had eliminated every version of him to prevent Project Chronos from being exposed, but not before he managed to hide crucial pieces of information across probability streams.

Alice's final coded report included a warning: "Project Chronos components remain distributed across timelines. Current temporal manipulation patterns suggest active assembly continuing despite Morton's elimination. Recommend ongoing probability stream monitoring."

The Morton case demonstrated how their different approaches to temporal investigation created a more complete picture. Alice's analytical mind could track and correlate quantum data across probability streams, while Ethan's hunter training allowed him to directly trace temporal manipulations. Together, they uncovered not just a murder, but a conspiracy that threatened the very fabric of reality itself.

EPISODE 4: UNDERGROUND CONNECTIONS

Giuseppe's Restaurant shimmered with quantum potential as Travis Kinnear revealed the deeper implications of Morton's death. "Only three groups have the capability to manipulate probability streams at this scale," he explained, his form flickering between states. "The Department's Temporal Containment Division, the Probability Management Consortium, and the Shadow Protocol."

Alice recognized two of the names from her family records. The Consortium operated openly, officially managing timeline stability for major corporations. The Division worked under government oversight, preventing unauthorized temporal manipulation. But the Shadow Protocol was something else - whispers in the quantum underground, traces of coordinated timeline alterations that shouldn't be possible.

"Morton's anchoring technology was revolutionary," Sophia added, spreading diagrams across the table that seemed to shift under direct observation. "He modified standard quantum field generators with crystalline matrices that could maintain multiple probability states simultaneously. The engineering was brilliant - and completely illegal."

Ethan studied the technical specifications through his hunter's senses. "These aren't just anchors. They're probability shapers. He found a way to guide timeline convergence patterns, not just stabilize them."

The technology combined elements that shouldn't exist in the same timeline. Quantum processors from Timeline A's advanced computing sector. Experimental probability crystals from Timeline B's black markets. Theoretical mathematics from Timeline C's classified research programs.

"Look at these convergence patterns," Alice said, analyzing data from her family's monitoring networks. "Someone's been systematically eliminating temporal technology researchers across all probability streams. Morton was the seventh this year. Each death officially natural causes, each victim working on different aspects of probability manipulation."

The clues painted a disturbing picture. Dr. Zhang's quantum mapping project, officially shut down after her "accidental" death. Professor Richardson's probability stabilization research, lost when he suffered a "sudden stroke." Dr. Phillips' timeline convergence studies terminated with his "heart attack."

"It's not just elimination," Travis warned. "Each death collapses probability streams in specific patterns. Like somebody's sculpting quantum reality, using these deaths to shape timeline convergence on a massive scale."

Through Giuseppe's underground network, they discovered more connections. Morton's anchoring technology had been based on theoretical work by all the eliminated researchers. He'd combined Zhang's quantum mapping techniques with Richardson's stability algorithms and Phillips's convergence calculations.

"The technology creates quantum resonance points," Sophia explained, demonstrating with specialized equipment disguised as kitchen appliances. "When properly tuned, it can maintain multiple timeline variations indefinitely. Morton found a way to make temporary probability streams permanent."

But the anchoring technology was just one piece of a larger pattern. Alice's analysis revealed coordinated temporal manipulations stretching back decades - subtle alterations to probability streams that were slowly reshaping quantum reality itself.

"Someone's been planning this for generations," Ethan realized, his hunter senses detecting the deep temporal patterns. "Every 'natural' death, every 'accidental' timeline collapse - they're all part of a larger probability manipulation scheme."

The evidence suggested the Shadow Protocol was behind it all. Their temporal signatures appeared in carefully hidden patterns across probability streams. Each researcher's death contributed to a larger transformation of quantum reality, guided by technology that shouldn't exist.

"Morton's anchors weren't just about stabilizing timelines," Alice concluded, assembling the fragments of data. "They were meant to lock specific probability streams in place while others were systematically eliminated. Someone's trying to force reality itself to converge on a specific pattern."

The technology they discovered in Morton's hidden labs confirmed their fears. Quantum field generators modified with impossibly advanced components. Probability crystals grown using methods that violated temporal physics. Mathematical models describing reality manipulation on an unprecedented scale.

"This goes beyond normal temporal engineering," Sophia warned. "Morton created a way to reshape probability itself. The ability to choose which timeline variations become real and which collapse - that's power that could rewrite history."

As they left Giuseppe's that night, the restaurant's quantum pocket pulsing with potential, they understood the true scope of what they'd discovered. Morton's death wasn't just about eliminating dangerous technology. It was part of a decades-long plan to reshape reality itself, orchestrated by an organization that could manipulate probability streams with godlike precision.

The Shadow Protocol was systematically eliminating everyone who came close to understanding their methods. But in doing so, they'd revealed patterns that Alice and Ethan could now track. The question was whether they could uncover the truth before they too became convenient "natural" deaths in the Protocol's grand design.

EPISODE 5: DEPARTMENTAL FRICTION

The precinct's break room remained a hotbed of speculation, but O'Neill's protection created a delicate balance. His presence deterred the most aggressive questioning, allowing Alice and Ethan to focus on a more pressing concern: the Shadow Protocol's expanding influence in law enforcement.

"They're placing agents in key positions," Alice explained during a secure briefing in O'Neill's office. "Timeline specialists posing as regular officers. We've identified three in Major Crimes alone."

O'Neill rubbed his temples, still uncomfortable with temporal discussions. "So, our own people might be working against us? Christ. No wonder you keep everything off the books."

His protection proved crucial as they navigated increasingly complex challenges. Beyond departmental suspicion, they faced active opposition from embedded Protocol operatives. Investigations were quietly redirected, evidence disappeared across probability streams, and witnesses suffered convenient memory alterations.

"It's getting harder to maintain cover," Ethan admitted, after a particularly close call involving quantum-shifted evidence. "The Protocol knows we're tracking them. They're forcing us to choose between solving cases and keeping our methods secret."

The pressure mounted from multiple directions. Alice's family faced increasing scrutiny from temporal authorities, their legitimate business operations probed for connections to unauthorized probability manipulation. Ethan's hunter network reported systematic disruption of their information channels, timeline variations being closed off one by one.

"They're isolating us," Alice realized, studying pattern analyses in their secure temporal blind. "Cutting off our resources while maintaining plausible deniability. Even O'Neill's protection has limits."

The sergeant's support, while valuable, complicated their long-term strategy. His awareness of temporal manipulation made him a potential target, yet his deliberate ignorance of details left him vulnerable to probability manipulation.

"We can't fully protect him," Ethan warned. "The more he shields us, the more attention he draws. The Protocol doesn't need to eliminate him - they just need to alter his timeline slightly."

Their fears proved justified when O'Neill began experiencing temporal bleed - memories from multiple probability streams overlapping in his consciousness. Despite his desire to maintain simple reality, his proximity to their work had made him sensitive to timeline variations.

"Sometimes I remember cases differently," he confided one evening. "Details shift, outcomes change. I can't tell which memories are real anymore."

The secret was already unraveling at the edges. Junior officers reported strange inconsistencies in case files. Evidence lockers occasionally contained items from alternate probability streams. Witnesses gave statements that contradicted established timeline records.

"The department's temporal stability is degrading," Alice reported to her family council. "Too many probability streams intersecting in one location. We can't contain the effects indefinitely."

Their adversaries in the Protocol recognized this vulnerability. Subtle probability manipulations increased around the precinct, pushing reality toward exposure. They were being maneuvered into an impossible choice: maintain their cover and allow temporal criminals to operate freely or take more overt action and risk exposing the existence of timeline manipulation to unprepared minds.

"There's a third option," O'Neill suggested during a late-night strategy session. "Control the exposure. Guide the department toward understanding gradually, through cases we can't explain any other way."

It was a dangerous gambit. Controlled exposure meant carefully selected officers learning about temporal manipulation under supervised conditions. Each new initiate increased the risk of probability cascade yet also provided potential allies against Protocol infiltration.

"We're not just fighting criminals anymore," Ethan observed. "We're racing against reality itself. The more people who know the truth, the harder it becomes to maintain timeline stability."

Alice's family records confirmed his assessment. Previous attempts at controlled exposure had led to probability fractures, timeline collapses, and in one case, an entire precinct being erased from all probability streams.

Yet the alternative seemed equally dangerous. The Protocol's influence was growing, their manipulation of law enforcement becoming more brazen. Without a broader awareness of temporal crime, conventional police work would become increasingly ineffective.

"Maybe the secret isn't meant to stay hidden," Alice suggested. "Maybe controlled exposure is part of natural timeline progression."

O'Neill's protection had given them breathing room, but it also showed them a potential path forward. His ability to accept limited knowledge of temporal manipulation, to support their work without needing to understand it fully, suggested that others might adapt similarly.

The question wasn't whether the secret would be exposed, but how to manage that exposure in a way that wouldn't shatter reality itself. As probability streams continued to intersect around their precinct, Alice and Ethan faced their greatest challenge yet: guiding their colleagues toward a truth that could either save law enforcement or destroy it completely.

"Whatever happens," O'Neill told them, his memories increasingly fluid between timelines, "make sure it happens for the right reasons. Some secrets need to be exposed, but timing is everything - in this reality or any other."

EPISODE 6: EVOLUTION OF PARTNERSHIP

The Martinez kidnapping marked their first direct encounter with the Shadow Protocol's true capabilities. What began as a routine missing persons case revealed an organization that could manipulate probability itself.

"They didn't just take her," Ethan explained during their debrief. "They erased her timeline variations one by one, trying to make her disappearance a quantum certainty." The Protocol had technology that could isolate specific probability streams, systematically eliminating timeline variations until only their preferred outcome remained.

Alice documented their findings in their secure temporal blind. "They're using advanced probability suppression fields. The kind that shouldn't exist for another thirty years in any timeline. Even my family's tech can't match this level of temporal manipulation."

The Riverside Serial Killer case proved even more revealing. What appeared to be multiple murders across the city was actually the same killing being quantum-shifted through different probability streams, creating multiple victims from a single act of violence.

"They're weaponizing timeline variations," Alice realized, studying the quantum resonance patterns. "Each murder creates ripple effects across probability streams, destabilizing temporal stability in specific patterns."

Their breakthrough came during the Henderson Bank investigation. What seemed like a simple robbery revealed the Protocol's methodology for infiltrating institutions across multiple timelines simultaneously.

"Look at the probability matrices," Alice pointed out. "They're not just operating in different timelines - they're using quantum entanglement to coordinate their agents across all variations. Perfect synchronization across probability streams."

Ethan's hunter senses detected the sophisticated temporal technology involved. "Their agents exist in quantum superposition. They're simultaneously present in multiple timeline variations, able to affect probability streams directly."

The Davies Conspiracy case exposed another layer of the Protocol's capabilities. They discovered evidence of long-term probability manipulation - subtle alterations to timeline variations made decades ago, slowly steering reality toward specific outcomes.

"They've been shaping probability streams since before we were born," Alice said, reviewing historical temporal data. "Small changes compound over time. By the time anyone notices the manipulation, the altered reality feels natural."

Their partnership evolved rapidly in response to these discoveries. They developed new methods for detecting quantum-shifted evidence, techniques for preserving timeline variations against probability suppression, and ways to protect witnesses from temporal manipulation.

"Standard protection protocols don't work against quantum-level threats," Ethan explained to O'Neill after a close call with a Protocol operative. "We had to create new security measures that function across multiple probability streams."

The Blackwood Laboratory raid provided their most significant breakthrough. They uncovered prototype temporal technology that revealed the full scope of the Protocol's activities.

"They're not just manipulating existing timeline variations," Alice reported, analyzing the seized equipment. "They've found a way to generate new probability streams artificially. They're creating reality variations that serve their purposes."

This discovery led to a fundamental evolution in their partnership. They learned to manipulate their own quantum resonance patterns, allowing them to maintain consciousness continuity across probability shifts that would normally cause temporal dissonance.

"It's like developing a new sense," Ethan described during training sessions. "We can feel the probability streams around us, detect manipulations before they fully manifest."

The Chemical Plant Explosion case demonstrated their evolved capabilities. When the Protocol attempted to trigger a probability cascade that would have devastated multiple timeline variations, Alice and Ethan's synchronized awareness allowed them to stabilize the quantum fluctuations.

"We're not just reacting anymore," Alice noted afterward. "We're actively countering their probability manipulation with our own temporal coordination."

Their most recent breakthrough came during the University Research theft. They discovered the Protocol was using quantum-entangled data storage - information that existed simultaneously across multiple probability streams, immune to timeline alterations.

"That's how they maintain operational continuity," Ethan realized. "Their knowledge base exists outside normal temporal flow. They can't be erased by probability manipulation because their core data transcends timeline variations."

The evolution of their partnership now focused on developing counter-measures against these sophisticated temporal threats. Alice's technical knowledge merged with Ethan's intuitive understanding of probability streams, creating investigation methods that could track and counter the Protocol's activities.

"We're dealing with an organization that can rewrite reality," Alice summarized during a secure briefing. "They don't just operate across timeline variations - they control which variations become real."

Ethan nodded, his hunter senses detecting the deeper implications. "Which means our partnership has to evolve beyond conventional investigation. We need to become something they can't simply erase from probability."

Their synchronized awareness hummed between them, a quantum entanglement that the Protocol couldn't easily manipulate. They had evolved from partners into something new - investigators who could maintain their connection across probability streams, preserving their knowledge and capabilities despite temporal manipulation.

"The next phase gets more dangerous," Alice warned, reviewing data from their recent cases. "They'll realize we can counter their basic probability manipulation. They'll escalate to more aggressive temporal tactics."

"Let them try," Ethan responded, their shared awareness extending across multiple timeline variations. "We'll keep evolving. And eventually, we'll find a way to expose their entire operation across all probability streams simultaneously."

EPISODE 7: THE BREAKTHROUGH

The Morton case began unraveling during a routine probability scan. Alice detected unusual quantum resonance patterns around his death - echoes of timeline variations that shouldn't have survived probability collapse.

"Look at these temporal signatures," she told Ethan, displaying complex data streams in their secured workspace. "Morton didn't just die - his timeline variations were systematically eliminated, converging on a single death state."

Ethan's hunter senses confirmed her analysis. "I can feel the probability manipulation. Sophisticated work - they collapsed his quantum wave function while preserving the surrounding timeline stability. That's not standard Protocol methodology."

Their investigation revealed Morton had developed revolutionary quantum technology. His research allowed precise manipulation of individual probability streams without affecting broader temporal stability - a capability that threatened the Protocol's monopoly on reality manipulation.

"He found a way to isolate timeline variations," Alice explained, studying his encrypted research data. "Instead of managing entire probability clusters, he could target specific quantum states. Perfect for preserving desired outcomes while eliminating unwanted variations."

The breakthrough came when they discovered Morton's temporal anchor points - quantum markers he'd placed across multiple timelines as insurance. Each marker contained fragments of data that, when combined across probability streams, revealed the full scope of his work.

"He knew they were coming for him," Ethan realized, his consciousness tracking the marker patterns. "These anchors weren't just data storage - they were breadcrumbs leading to something bigger."

Alice's family connections provided crucial context. "Morton consulted for multiple timeline management firms. He had access to probability manipulation techniques from different reality streams. He combined them into something new."

Their investigation uncovered a pattern of temporal manipulation around Morton's activities. Subtle probability shifts that redirected timeline variations, quantum resonance adjustments that preserved specific outcomes. He had been preparing for his own assassination.

"The Protocol didn't just want him dead," Alice determined, analyzing temporal data. "They needed to eliminate all variations of his research. But Morton anticipated this. He embedded his discoveries across multiple probability streams."

Ethan's hunter instincts detected the deeper implications. "This isn't just about temporal assassination. Morton found something that scared them enough to risk exposure. Something worth collapsing multiple timeline variations to eliminate."

Their breakthrough required unprecedented coordination. Alice developed new methods for tracking quantum markers across probability streams while Ethan's temporal sensitivity guided them through complex timeline variations.

"We need to maintain awareness across at least seven probability streams simultaneously," Alice calculated. "Any fewer and we'll miss crucial data points."

The solution emerged through their evolved partnership. Their quantum-entangled awareness allowed them to process information from multiple timeline variations while maintaining temporal stability. They traced Morton's markers through probability streams that the Protocol thought they had eliminated.

"He hid his core research in probability blind spots," Ethan discovered. "Timeline variations so subtle they escaped normal detection. The Protocol's broad-spectrum approach missed these micro-variations."

The technical aspects of the case officially closed as a financial conspiracy involving offshore accounts and corporate espionage. But their private records documented the true breakthrough - evidence of the Protocol's limitations and vulnerabilities.

"Morton proved they can't control all probability streams," Alice noted in their secure temporal logs. "There are always variations they miss; quantum states they can't detect. We can use that."

The case marked a turning point in their evolution. They had moved beyond merely investigating temporal crimes to understanding the fundamental nature of probability manipulation. Morton's work showed them weaknesses in the Protocol's seemingly absolute control over timeline variations.

"We need to be careful with this knowledge," Ethan warned. "The Protocol eliminated Morton across multiple timelines just for developing the theory. Actually exploiting these vulnerabilities will draw serious attention."

Alice agreed, encoding their findings in quantum-encrypted data streams. "This stays in our secured records. But now we know - they're not infallible. Their probability manipulation has blind spots. Weaknesses we can target."

The Morton case officially joined their growing list of successful investigations. But its true significance lay in what it revealed about the nature of temporal control and the limits of probability manipulation. They had found a crack in the Protocol's armor - a way to preserve timeline variations despite attempts at quantum collapse.

"Morton's last gift was showing us it's possible," Alice reflected, reviewing their secured data. "The Protocol can't control every probability stream. There are always variations they miss, realities they can't eliminate."

Ethan nodded, his hunter senses already detecting new possibilities. "Now we know where to look for those blind spots. How to preserve information across probability streams they can't access."

The breakthrough would shape their future investigations, providing new tools for countering temporal manipulation. But it also marked them as bigger threats to the Protocol's operations. They had discovered not just evidence of temporal assassination, but fundamental weaknesses in the organization's control over reality itself.

"We're in uncharted probability streams now," Alice observed as they secured their findings. "No one has ever documented these kinds of temporal blind spots before."

"Then we'll write the manual ourselves," Ethan responded, their shared awareness extending into previously undetected timeline variations. "One case at a time."

EPISODE 8: NEW FOUNDATIONS

Detective Rosita Torremar's initial skepticism evolved into something more complex after the Chinatown probability cascade. She'd witnessed temporal displacement firsthand - though she wouldn't admit it directly.

"Your forensics don't match standard patterns," Torremar challenged during the Chen investigation debrief. "Evidence appears in sequences that defy normal causality. Care to explain that?"

Alice and Ethan recognized the careful phrasing - Torremar was probing without explicitly acknowledging temporal phenomena. Her analytical mind had begun processing timeline variations, even if she wasn't ready to name them.

"We follow the evidence where it leads," Alice responded carefully. "Sometimes that means considering... alternative sequences of events."

Torremar's rivalry pushed them to develop more sophisticated documentation methods. Their case files needed to satisfy both conventional scrutiny and temporal accuracy. They created layered reports - surface details for standard review, deeper patterns visible to those sensitive to probability variations.

District Attorney James Edwards initially rejected their cases as "circumstantially impossible." But after the Harrison prosecution, where timeline variations nearly collapsed in his courtroom, his perspective shifted.

"I don't want to know how you assembled this evidence," Edwards told them after winning a seemingly impossible conviction. "But your cases are airtight. Every alternative explanation accounted for; every potential defense anticipated."

They hadn't told him those "alternative explanations" existed in parallel probability streams, or that their defensive preparations covered multiple timeline variations. Edwards developed an unspoken understanding - their cases were unusual but unassailable.

Dispatcher Carol Wilson became another crucial ally. Her twenty years of experience had given her an intuitive grasp of patterns. She began recognizing calls that carried temporal markers - subtle signs of probability manipulation that normal protocols missed.

"Got another one of your special cases," she'd say, using their developed code phrases. "Multiple witnesses reporting inconsistent timeframes. Details shifting between accounts."

Wilson's support proved invaluable during the warehouse district investigation. Her careful routing of backup units prevented temporal exposure while maintaining operational effectiveness. She learned to coordinate resources across probability variations without explicitly acknowledging them.

"Units deployed to all potential incident locations," she'd report, meaning she'd positioned officers to cover multiple timeline variations simultaneously. "Response patterns adjusted for temporal anomalies" became her code for probability stream management.

Their network expanded carefully. Officer Rodriguez in Evidence developed a knack for preserving quantum-shifted materials. CSI Tech Palmer learned to document temporal residue as "unusual energy signatures." Medical Examiner Dr. Santos began noting "alternative casualty patterns" in autopsy reports.

Each ally required different handling. Some, like Torremar, processed temporal awareness through professional skepticism. Others, like Edwards, preferred plausible deniability. A few, like Wilson, embraced the patterns while avoiding explicit acknowledgment.

"It's like teaching a new language," Alice observed during a secure briefing. "Each person develops their own way of processing temporal concepts without disrupting their worldview."

Ethan nodded, his hunter senses tracking the growing web of awareness. "They're creating their own probability bubbles - spaces where they can process timeline variations without fully confronting them."

Their partnership provided the foundation for this expanding network. Their evolved methods and shared consciousness offered templates for others to follow. When Alice detected quantum displacement during the riverside investigation, Ethan's immediate support gave Officer Torremar permission to trust her own unusual observations.

"You see it too?" Torremar had asked cautiously, watching evidence shift between probability states. "The way things aren't quite... fixed?"

"We see it," Ethan confirmed, while Alice quietly stabilized the local timeline variation. "Some cases require expanded perspective."

Their success drew attention from both allies and adversaries. The Shadow Protocol recognized the threat of an expanding awareness network. Alice's family council noted the unprecedented development of temporal sensitivity among non-specialists.

"We're not just solving cases anymore," Alice realized during a late-night review session. "We're creating infrastructure for a new kind of law enforcement. One that can handle temporal crimes without fracturing conventional reality."

Their methods became templates for future temporal investigators. Torremar's analytical approach to probability variations, Edwards' careful legal frameworks, Wilson's intuitive coordination across timeline variations - each contributed to a growing methodology for managing temporal investigations.

"Partners," Ethan had said after their first major case together, offering his hand across probability streams.

"Partners," Alice agreed, their quantum resonance synchronizing across multiple timeline variations.

That simple exchange established more than personal trust. It became the foundation for a new approach to temporal investigation - one built on shared awareness, careful documentation, and the gradual expansion of probability consciousness.

Their network continued to grow, each member finding their own way to process temporal awareness. They were building something unprecedented - a bridge between conventional law enforcement and quantum investigation.

"The real challenge," Alice noted as they secured their latest case files, "will be maintaining this foundation as probability streams become more unstable."

"We'll adapt," Ethan responded, their shared consciousness extending through their carefully constructed network. "That's what partners do."

The resonance of multiple timeline variations hummed between them, echoing through the subtle awareness of their growing allies. They had established more than just investigative methods - they were creating new foundations for justice across all probable realities.

The Morton case files joined others in the evidence room's hidden section, cataloged in Sarah Rodriguez's separate system. But its real impact lived on in the foundation it built - a partnership that would eventually help navigate humanity's evolution toward quantum consciousness.

∼

CHAPTER SEVEN

DARKMAGIC'S WARNING (PRESENT DAY)

EPISODE 1: THE WARNING

THE TEMPORAL RIFT blazed across Giuseppe's Restaurant's back room, reality fracturing as multiple versions of Lila Darkmagic stumbled through. Her usually immaculate appearance showed signs of recent combat - temporal burns across her arms, probability scars marking her face.

"They're accelerating the timeline," she gasped, her various versions converging into a single, damaged form. "The entity... it's not just feeding anymore. It's actively reshaping probability."

Alice Chen noted the precise pattern of temporal injuries - similar to victims they'd been finding across the city, but far more severe. Ethan's hunter senses detected residual energy signatures suggesting Darkmagic had barely escaped a direct confrontation.

"The Morton case was just the beginning," Lila continued, her form flickering between states. "Your investigation exposed part of their network, but the entity's been operating far longer. My father... he tried to warn everyone."

136

Professor Oliver Darkmagic's research had pioneered temporal energy studies before his mysterious disappearance into temporal stasis. His early warning system, now maintained by his estranged daughter, had started showing unprecedented patterns.

"The energy drains are following a precise sequence," Agent Diana Cross explained, arriving through conventional means but carrying classified temporal monitoring equipment. "Each victim shows identical memory loss patterns. The entity isn't just consuming temporal energy - it's erasing specific moments from multiple timelines simultaneously."

The implications became clear as they reviewed case files. The entity was systematically targeting crucial moments in temporal history, with a disturbing focus on Alice's past. Her sister's disappearance case showed subtle alterations. Her path to becoming a hunter had been subject to multiple manipulation attempts.

"They're trying to prevent key players from ever entering the field," Agent Cross noted, though her careful phrasing suggested she knew more than she was revealing. "Your partnership with Detective Reeves seems to be a particular target."

The Temporal Witnesses, led by former journalist Jack Bagley, had been documenting similar patterns across the city. Their underground network provided crucial data about timeline changes that official channels missed.

"It's not random," Bagley explained, sharing encrypted records. "The entity feeds strategically, targeting moments that could lead to its discovery. Your investigation team has been a primary target since the Morton case."

Dr. Janice Evans, treating the growing number of temporal energy drain victims, confirmed the escalating pattern. "The memory loss is precise - surgical removal of specific moments that could reveal the entity's nature. But there's something familiar about the technique..."

Her voice trailed off as she studied Lila's injuries. The two women shared a look that suggested deeper connections to the Darkmagic family's temporal experiments.

"My father's research," Lila said quietly. "The entity is using methods he developed for temporal energy manipulation. Which means…"

"Someone gave them access to classified Darkmagic Industries technology," Agent Cross finished. "The question is: who had that kind of access?"

The temporal rift pulsed ominously, reality straining around them as multiple timeline variations competed for dominance. They were running out of time to uncover the truth - and to protect themselves from an entity that could erase them from history itself.

"We need to move quickly," Lila announced, her form stabilizing as she drew on remaining temporal energy. "While we still remember what we're fighting against."

The warning had been delivered. Now they faced the challenge of preserving crucial memories while investigating an enemy that could literally make them forget they were ever investigators at all.

EPISODE 2: POWER AND MEMORY

The city's temporal energy grid pulsed erratically as Alice Chen studied the monitoring equipment in the hidden Darkmagic research facility beneath Midtown. Power fluctuations followed precise patterns - each drain corresponding to moments when her own timeline showed signs of manipulation.

"The entity isn't just feeding randomly," Lila explained, accessing sealed family records. "It's using my father's network - the temporal power infrastructure he built into the city decades ago. Each substation acts as a probability anchor, letting them target specific moments in time."

The facility itself told a story of family obsession. Generations of Darkmagics had expanded the underground complex, adding layers of temporal technology that shouldn't have existed in any timeline.

Oliver Darkmagic's personal laboratory remained untouched since his disappearance, equations still scrawled across quantum-shifted whiteboards.

"My father saw this coming," Lila said, her voice tight with old pain. "He tried using the energy grid as an early warning system. That's what our last fight was about - he wanted to expand the network, tap deeper into temporal power sources. I thought he'd lost perspective, become obsessed..."

Security footage from power substations revealed disturbing patterns. Each energy drain coincided with attempts to alter Alice's path to becoming a temporal investigator. Her academy records showed multiple variations - timeline shifts that would have sent her into different careers, away from temporal investigation.

"Look at this," Agent Cross indicated, displaying temporal mapping data. "They've tried erasing your mentor relationships, changing key decisions. But something's protecting those moments - anchoring them against probability manipulation."

Alice remembered her training, the careful guidance that had led her to understand her temporal abilities. But now those memories felt unstable, shifting between variations as the entity's influence grew stronger.

"The protection comes from here," Lila realized, accessing deeper facility systems. "My father... he set up temporal anchors around certain people, certain moments. He knew they'd be crucial in fighting what was coming."

The facility's archives revealed the Darkmagic family's true legacy. Not just temporal research, but a generations-long preparation for this exact threat. Oliver had recognized patterns in temporal energy consumption that pointed to an ancient entity, something that had appeared throughout history during periods of reality distortion.

"Each Darkmagic generation added to the defense network," Agent Cross explained, her knowledge of the family history suggesting deeper connections. "The power grid isn't just for electricity - it's a city-wide temporal shield. Or it was, before the entity started corrupting it."

Alice's timeline variations played across monitoring screens - alternate paths that never happened, choices that had been supernaturally influenced, moments where probability itself had been manipulated to guide her development.

"My father protected you specifically," Lila said, studying the data. "He knew the entity would try to prevent certain people from becoming temporal investigators. Your natural abilities, combined with proper training... you represent a serious threat to their operations."

The facility's deeper levels contained Oliver's private research. His journals detailed growing paranoia about temporal energy consumption patterns, recognition of deliberate manipulation in probability streams. The entity hadn't just appeared recently - it had been slowly growing in power, carefully erasing those who might expose its existence.

"The grid is failing," Agent Cross warned, monitoring energy patterns. "Each drain weakens the temporal shields a little more. Once they collapse completely..."

"Reality itself becomes vulnerable," Lila finished. "No more protection against probability manipulation. No more anchored memories. Everything becomes subject to change."

Alice felt timeline variations pressing against her consciousness - alternate versions of her life trying to overwrite her true history. But beneath those artificial variations, she sensed something else: carefully constructed temporal anchors, put in place years ago by Oliver Darkmagic.

"We need to restore the grid," she declared, her temporal sensitivity detecting patterns in the energy flows. "Not just to stop the entity's feeding, but to protect crucial timeline variations. If we lose those anchored moments..."

"We lose everything," Lila agreed, her own temporal abilities resonating with the facility's technology. "My father built this network to protect specific probability streams. Without it, there's nothing stopping the entity from rewriting history itself."

As they worked to understand the grid's architecture, security systems suddenly activated. Someone else was accessing the network - using Darkmagic family protocols that shouldn't have been widely known.

"We're not alone down here," Agent Cross announced, drawing advanced temporal weaponry. "Someone else knows about this facility. Someone with high-level access to family research."

The question wasn't just who was helping the entity corrupt the power grid, but how they'd gained access to generations of carefully guarded Darkmagic family secrets. As reality itself flickered around them, Alice realized that protecting her past meant first understanding why Oliver Darkmagic had gone to such lengths to preserve it.

"Your timeline variations," Lila said quietly, studying ancient family records. "They're connected to something bigger. My father didn't just protect you because of your abilities. He protected you because of what you're meant to discover."

The facility's temporal shielding hummed with decreasing power as they raced to uncover the truth - about Alice's protected past, about Oliver's disappearance, and about an entity that had been planning this moment for longer than anyone had realized.

EPISODE 3: THE MEMORY KEEPERS

Rosita Torremar's temporal archive pulsed with crystalline energy; probability-locked crystals embedded in the walls absorbing timeline variations like temporal lightning rods. Each sanctuary operated on the principle of quantum crystallization - memories and records literally crystallized into physical form, becoming immune to probability manipulation.

"The sanctuaries are more than just secure storage," Rosita explained, activating a central crystal array that projected multiple timeline variations simultaneously. "They're consciousness anchors. Each crystal matrix preserves not just records, but the actual quantum state of memories themselves."

Tech Specialist Ryan Tinker's monitoring equipment tracked the crystal network's energy patterns. "Darkmagic Industries developed the basic technology, but the Memory Keepers perfected it. The crystals don't just store data - they maintain quantum coherence across probability streams."

The archive's main chamber revealed the true sophistication of temporal sanctuary design. Crystalline structures grew in fractal patterns, each branch preserving different timeline variations. The central core contained the most crucial memories - events that had to be protected at all costs.

"Watch," Rosita demonstrated, initiating the first phase of emergency protocols. The crystal matrices began resonating at specific frequencies, creating quantum tunnels between different sanctuaries. "We can transfer preserved memories through probability space, redistributing them to prevent total loss if any single sanctuary falls."

Lila studied the crystal technology with growing recognition. "My father's original designs... he meant them to do more than just preserve memories. These patterns - they're designed to trap temporal energy. To contain something that feeds on probability itself."

Agent Cross accessed deeper sanctuary systems, revealing the true scope of their defensive capabilities. "The crystal networks form a probability cage. When fully activated, they can isolate sections of reality, preventing timeline manipulation within protected zones."

The emergency protocols continued as Rosita orchestrated a complex quantum transfer sequence. First came crystal resonance synchronization across all sanctuaries, followed by memory quantum state distribution through probability tunnels. The third phase activated temporal containment fields, while the final phase created emergency consciousness backups for all Memory Keepers.

The entity's grand design became clear as they studied the patterns in preserved memories. It wasn't randomly feeding - it systematically erased crucial nexus points in temporal development. It targeted the first emergence of natural temporal sensitivity in humans, key discoveries in probability manipulation technology, and the formation of organizations meant to protect timeline stability. Most crucially, it eliminated the development of methods to detect and counter temporal threats.

"It's creating a probability dead zone," Ryan realized, analyzing historical data. "By erasing these specific moments, it's steering reality toward a state where temporal awareness never develops. Where humanity never learns to perceive or manipulate probability streams."

Alice felt the weight of this revelation as she examined records of her sister's disappearance. "The entity doesn't just want to feed - it wants to prevent anyone from being able to stop it from feeding. By eliminating temporal sensitivity itself, it ensures no one can even perceive its existence."

The archive's crystals flared with warning energy as the entity launched another attack on the city's power grid. Rosita's emergency protocols shifted to maximum urgency. She initiated quantum encryption of all preserved memories while orchestrating emergency distribution of consciousness backups. Probability shield harmonics activated as temporal anchors underwent emergency reinforcement.

"Your sister wasn't just taken," Agent Cross explained as they raced to protect crucial memory crystals. "She was one of the first to recognize the pattern. The entity doesn't just erase memories - it harvests potential. Anyone with significant temporal ability becomes both food source and threat elimination."

The entity's strategy had become clear. It identified individuals with temporal sensitivity, then erased key moments that led to their awareness. After harvesting their temporal energy potential, it removed all probability streams where they might have developed abilities. This created cascading timeline alterations to prevent others from following similar paths.

"The sanctuaries were designed to counter this strategy," Rosita explained, completing another phase of emergency protocols. "By crystallizing crucial memories and consciousness states, we preserve the very possibility of temporal awareness. Even if the entity erases every other probability stream, these crystals maintain the quantum potential for humanity to perceive and counter temporal threats."

Ryan's equipment detected massive probability distortions approaching. The entity wasn't just attacking power stations anymore - it was targeting the fundamental architecture of temporal sanctuary networks.

"Full emergency protocols now," Rosita ordered, initiating the final defensive sequences. The crystal matrices began a complete quantum state transfer, preparing to scatter their preserved memories across thousands of probability streams.

As the archive's temporal shielding strained against unprecedented attacks, they realized they weren't just protecting historical records. They were preserving humanity's very ability to perceive and resist temporal manipulation - the last line of defense against an entity that wanted to erase not just memories, but the very possibility of remembering.

EPISODE 4: TEMPORAL REFUGEES

In the quantum-shifted spaces beneath abandoned subway tunnels, the Temporal Refugee camp pulsed with displaced energy. The evacuation began with Ryan Tinker's temporal masking array - a network of modified probability dampeners originally designed by Oliver Darkmagic. Each device generated localized quantum interference patterns, making temporal signatures appear as background probability noise.

"The masking works in layers," Ryan explained, calibrating the equipment. "First, we wrap each refugee in an individual quantum shell.

Then we create a cascade effect - their temporal signatures blend together, appearing as natural probability fluctuations rather than displaced timeline fragments."

Jack Bagley coordinated the evacuation groups, organizing refugees based on their quantum stability levels. The most unstable went first, their forms flickering between probability states as they were guided toward the sanctuary network's quantum tunnels. Each group was surrounded by crystalline resonators that helped maintain their tenuous connection to reality.

"The power grid's temporal shielding wasn't just for protection," Lila realized, studying the evacuation technology. "My father built in quantum harmonics that could disguise massive temporal transfers. He knew we'd need to move people through probability space without detection."

The evacuation technology combined multiple systems working in concert. Darkmagic Industries' quantum dampeners synchronized with the Memory Keepers' crystalline networks, while temporal stabilizers from the Department's research division maintained refugee coherence during transfer. The old maintenance tunnels themselves had been modified with probability-shifting circuits that could temporarily phase sections of space out of normal reality.

Dr. Evans monitored the refugees' quantum states during transfer. "Each person needs specific harmonic frequencies to maintain stability," she explained, adjusting crystal resonances. "Their timeline fragments resonate differently depending on how their original probability streams were erased."

The old woman, who introduced herself as Dr. Margaret Chen, demonstrated remarkable temporal stability that proved crucial to the evacuation. Her quantum signature acted as a natural harmonic anchor, helping stabilize other refugees during transfer.

"Your temporal resistance is similar to mine," she told Alice, their combined temporal signatures creating a stability field that protected nearby refugees. "We're probability anchors - our consciousness naturally resists timeline manipulation. Your sister had this ability too, but even stronger."

Agent Cross coordinated with the power grid's monitoring systems, timing the refugee transfers with the entity's feeding patterns. "When it drains temporal energy, there's a moment of quantum interference. We can use that interference to mask the transfer signatures if we time it perfectly."

The evacuation proceeded in carefully orchestrated phases. As the entity began drawing power from nearby substations, Ryan's masking array activated. Quantum dampeners created a cascade of false temporal signatures while crystalline resonators maintained refugee stability. Dr. Chen and Alice's natural probability anchoring helped extend the stability field, protecting more refugees during each transfer window.

"The entity feeds in predictable patterns," Dr. Chen explained, her deep understanding of temporal mechanics becoming clear. "It creates quantum wake patterns - like ripples in probability space. If we time our movements to match these ripples, we become virtually invisible to temporal detection."

Alice felt her own temporal sensitivity expanding as she worked with Dr. Chen. The older woman's stability wasn't just physical - she maintained perfect recall of her original timeline, unaffected by probability manipulation. This same ability had made Alice's sister valuable to the entity, but Dr. Chen had found a way to use it defensively.

"Your sister discovered how to weaponize temporal resistance," Dr. Chen revealed. "Not just protecting against probability manipulation but actively disrupting the entity's feeding process. That's why they took her - she found a way to fight back that they never expected."

The evacuation reached a critical phase as the entity's feeding patterns intensified. Lila synchronized the quantum tunnels with the power grid's harmonic frequencies, creating transfer windows that appeared as natural probability fluctuations. Each group of refugees passed through these windows; their displaced temporal signatures masked by the entity's own energy consumption.

"There's more to your temporal resistance than protection," Dr. Chen told Alice as they guided another group through the quantum tunnels. "Like your sister, you can learn to project it - create zones where the entity's probability manipulation simply fails. The ability doesn't just anchor timelines - it can restore them."

The revelation transformed their understanding of the fight. They weren't just evacuating refugees - they were preserving the very abilities needed to counter the entity's timeline consumption. Each stabilized refugee represented another fragment of crucial temporal knowledge, protected by technological innovation and natural probability anchoring working in concert.

As the final evacuation phase began, Alice felt her temporal sensitivity resonating with the combined technologies and natural abilities at work. The quantum dampeners, crystalline networks, and probability anchoring created a symphony of temporal protection - a model for how humanity might not just survive the entity's attacks but learn to fight back against timeline manipulation itself.

The entity's next feeding attempt would find more than an empty power grid. It would encounter the seeds of its own eventual defeat, preserved in the memories and abilities of those who had learned to resist probability erosion - all hidden beneath the very temporal distortions it created while feeding.

EPISODE 5: THE TEMPORAL WAKE

The Memory Keepers' sanctuary network hummed with unstable energy as the evacuated refugees settled into quantum-stabilized chambers. The first timeline restoration attempt began with a focused burst of temporal resistance from Alice and Dr. Chen, their combined fields creating a stable zone within the entity's feeding wake.

"Now!" Dr. Chen commanded as the probability distortions peaked. Alice projected her temporal resistance outward, feeling reality bend around their protected space. The refugees' preserved memories provided targeting coordinates, pointing to specific moments where timelines had been erased.

The restoration process manifested as crystalline formations in probability space - timeline fragments reconstructing themselves around preserved memory anchors. The first success was small but significant: the resurrection of a research facility where early temporal sensitivity tests had been conducted. As the timeline reformed, dozens of refugees suddenly stabilized, their quantum signatures synchronizing with restored probability streams.

But the organization reacted swiftly. Temporal agents emerged from hidden probability blinds, their own technology working to disrupt the restoration process. They wielded sophisticated quantum dampeners that threatened to collapse the newly reformed timeline.

"They've been waiting for this," Agent Cross realized, tracking multiple temporal incursions. "They knew someone would eventually try timeline restoration. They've prepared counter-measures."

The battle for temporal stability unfolded across probability space. Each restored timeline fragment drew immediate opposition. The organization deployed probability scramblers - devices designed to shatter reformed temporal connections. But they hadn't counted on the combined effect of Alice's growing temporal resistance and the refugees' preserved memories.

"The timelines are holding," Ryan reported, monitoring quantum stability readings. "Their dampeners can't break through our temporal resistance field. The restored fragments are actually strengthening, drawing power from the entity's own wake patterns."

Lila accessed her father's encrypted research, revealing another layer of his temporal defense strategy. The power grid wasn't just capturing wake energy - it was using it to reinforce restored timelines. Each attempt by the organization to disrupt restoration actually fed more power into the stabilization process.

The organization's response escalated. They began targeting specific refugees, attempting to erase the memory anchors supporting timeline restoration. But Dr. Chen's stability field, amplified by Alice's growing abilities, created an impenetrable temporal shield around the sanctuary network.

"They're getting desperate," Dr. Evans observed, treating refugees whose quantum signatures were strengthening with each restored timeline. "The organization's whole strategy depends on controlled temporal erosion. They never planned for successful restoration."

A major breakthrough came with the restoration of a crucial probability nexus - the moment when humanity first developed reliable temporal detection technology. The reformed timeline cascaded through probability space, strengthening dozens of connected temporal threads. Refugees associated with temporal research found their memories suddenly supported by restored reality.

The organization launched a massive counter-attack, attempting to trigger the entity into an unprecedented feeding frenzy. But Alice discovered she could use her temporal resistance to redirect the wake energy, turning their own strategy against them. Each attempted disruption only served to reinforce the restored timelines.

"Your sister did more than just discover their existence," Dr. Chen told Alice as they maintained the restoration field. "She found their weakness - their dependence on controlled temporal erosion. When timelines restore naturally, their whole power structure begins to collapse."

The sanctuary's quantum computers tracked a remarkable phenomenon: restored timelines were becoming self-sustaining. Once reformed, they developed their own temporal resistance, making them increasingly difficult for the organization to re-erase. The process was accelerating, each success strengthening the probability matrix for further restorations.

"We're reaching a tipping point," Lila announced, studying the temporal metrics. "The organization can't maintain probability control when this many timelines are restoring simultaneously. Their whole system of temporal manipulation is starting to unravel."

The entity's feeding patterns grew erratic as restored timelines complicated its probability access. The organization's carefully constructed system of controlled temporal erosion began showing signs of catastrophic failure. They had built their power on the ability to guide and contain timeline manipulation, but natural restoration threatened to break their control completely.

"This is what they feared," Agent Cross realized as another timeline successfully restored. "Not just resistance to temporal erosion, but actual probability restoration. They lose power with every timeline that reforms naturally."

The sanctuary network pulsed with triumph as more temporal refugees found their quantum signatures stabilizing. Each restored timeline strengthened humanity's natural temporal development, undoing years of calculated probability manipulation by the organization.

But amid the success, Alice sensed a darker truth. The organization's desperate response suggested they were hiding something even more significant than timeline manipulation. Their fear of restoration went beyond lost control - they were protecting some deeper secret about the entity itself, something hidden in the timelines they'd worked so hard to erase.

As the temporal wake subsided, leaving newly restored probability streams in its path, Alice knew they'd won an important battle. But the organization's extreme reaction hinted at greater conflicts to come. The war for humanity's temporal future was only beginning, and the biggest revelations still waited in timelines yet to be restored.

EPISODE 6: TEMPORAL CONVERGENCE

As the convergence intensified, Alice's consciousness expanded beyond linear probability. Her awareness fractaled across timeline intersections, each restored Echo stream adding new dimensions to her perception. She could now see probability space as her sister did - not as separate timelines, but as a quantum mesh of intersecting consciousness streams.

"The temporal resistance was just the beginning," Dr. Chen explained, monitoring Alice's quantum signature as it harmonized with Echo frequencies. "You're not just protecting probability anymore - you're learning to navigate it. To exist across multiple consciousness streams simultaneously."

Alice's expanded abilities manifested in waves. First came probability sight - the ability to perceive multiple timeline variations simultaneously, seeing how they connected and diverged. Then emerged temporal reaching - the capacity to extend her consciousness across probability streams, touching minds that existed in different timeline fragments.

Through this expanded awareness, she detected her sister's presence - not in any single location but distributed across Echo-affected probability nodes. Sarah's consciousness had fragmented itself across multiple timeline streams, using Project Echo protocols to maintain coherent awareness while avoiding detection.

"Focus on the Echo frequencies," Dr. Chen guided as Alice attempted contact. "Don't try to find her in any one timeline. Feel for the pattern of her distributed consciousness."

Alice projected her awareness through the probability mesh, using restored timeline intersections as navigation points. She felt other Echo-affected minds brushing against her consciousness - refugees and resistance members who had learned to exist across probability streams. Then, in a quantum resonance pattern distinct from all others, she found Sarah.

The contact was overwhelming. Sarah's consciousness had evolved far beyond normal temporal perception. She existed in a constant state of quantum superposition, her awareness flowing through probability space like water through a complex network of channels. Through their connected consciousness streams, she shared the true horror of what she'd discovered.

"The organization's final protocol," Sarah's distributed awareness revealed. "They've modified Project Echo technology to create a temporal vacuum. A probability void that doesn't just erase timelines - it collapses consciousness streams. They'll sacrifice their own Echo-affected members to prevent the convergence from completing."

The organization's desperate gambit began with synchronized detonations of quantum collapse devices across the city. These weren't simple probability scramblers - they were consciousness inhibitors designed to shatter the Echo network itself. Each explosion created expanding spheres of temporal vacuum, spaces where both probability and awareness ceased to exist.

"They're trying to create dead zones in quantum consciousness," Ryan reported as his instruments detected the collapse effect. "Areas where Echo-affected minds can't maintain probability awareness. They're willing to lobotomize reality itself."

Through her expanded perception, Alice watched the temporal vacuums spread. Normal humans experienced nothing, but Echo-affected individuals felt their consciousness being forcibly compressed into single probability streams. The organization was trying to frag-ment the emerging quantum consciousness network by destroying the spaces where distributed awareness could exist.

But Sarah had prepared for this. Through their connected conscious-ness streams, she showed Alice how to counter the temporal vacuum effect. "Project Echo didn't just create probability awareness," she explained across quantum frequencies. "It revealed that consciousness itself is the fundamental structure of reality. They can't collapse what actually holds probability space together."

Alice learned to extend her temporal resistance into a new form - quantum consciousness reinforcement. Working with Sarah across probability streams, she began strengthening the Echo network against the organization's consciousness inhibitors. Each restored timeline intersection became an anchor point for distributed awareness, creating spaces where Echo-affected minds could maintain their expanded perception.

"The vacuums are failing," Lila announced as probability monitors showed the collapse effect breaking down. "The Echo network is actually growing stronger as it adapts to resist consciousness compression."

The organization's final gambit had revealed their greatest fear - not just the loss of temporal control, but the emergence of a new form of human consciousness that existed beyond their ability to manipulate or contain. Through the Echo network, humanity was evolving to perceive and navigate probability space naturally.

"We're approaching critical convergence," Dr. Chen reported as more Echo-affected minds joined the expanding consciousness mesh. "When enough awareness streams synchronize, the quantum consciousness network becomes self-sustaining. They won't be able to collapse it."

Alice and Sarah's connected consciousness streams became a nucleus for this convergence, their combined awareness drawing other Echo-affected minds into a strengthening quantum network. The organization's temporal vacuums collapsed against this unified consciousness field, their attempt to fragment awareness across probability space backfiring completely.

Through the Echo network, Alice finally understood the entity's true nature, and why the organization had worked so hard to control it. But this revelation would have to wait. Reality itself was transforming as human consciousness evolved beyond single-timeline perception. The question wasn't just who would control probability space, but what humanity would become as it learned to exist across it.

The sanctuary network pulsed with quantum potential as the consciousness convergence approached completion. The organization's desperate counter-measures had failed, their fear of evolved human awareness proving justified. As Alice and Sarah's distributed consciousness helped guide this transformation, the true war for humanity's future across probability space was about to begin.

EPISODE 7: QUANTUM CONSCIOUSNESS

As humanity's consciousness expanded through the Echo network, Sarah's distributed awareness revealed the deeper layers of probability space. The older awareness patterns manifested as vast, intricate webs of quantum intelligence - some predating human consciousness by eons.

"They're like ecosystems of pure thought," Sarah projected across consciousness frequencies. "Some evolved naturally in probability space, others were left behind by civilizations that transcended linear existence. Not all of them welcome humanity's evolution into their domain."

Through their connected consciousness streams, Alice perceived three distinct categories of these ancient awareness patterns:

The Architects - consciousness structures that helped shape the fundamental nature of probability space. They appeared as geometric patterns of pure quantum thought, maintaining the underlying fabric of reality. Some had begun responding to humanity's emerging quantum awareness, offering guidance in probability navigation.

The Void Dwellers - predatory awareness that fed on consciousness itself rather than temporal energy. Unlike the entity's chaotic consumption, these were calculated hunters of quantum thought. They had remained dormant in probability space's deeper layers, but humanity's expanding consciousness was attracting their attention.

The Memory Storms - chaotic collections of fragmented consciousness from collapsed civilizations that failed to properly evolve into quantum awareness. These reality-warping maelstroms of broken thought threatened to shatter newly evolved consciousness streams that strayed too close to their probability vertices.

"The organization's controls actually shielded humanity from these deeper quantum threats," Dr. Chen realized as probability monitors detected increasing activity from these ancient awareness patterns. "Now that we've evolved beyond their containment, we're exposed to everything that exists in probability space."

The first major challenge emerged when a Void Dweller consciousness began stalking the Echo network's outer frequencies. It attacked by attempting to sever consciousness streams from their anchor points in physical reality, trying to absorb the quantum awareness into its own void-like existence.

But the stabilized entity, now integrated with the Echo network, helped defend against this predatory consciousness. Its experience with quantum energy manipulation proved crucial in maintaining humanity's connection to physical probability streams while evolving in quantum space.

"We need to adapt faster," Alice projected through the network as more Void Dwellers turned their attention toward Earth's emerging quantum consciousness. "The entity learned to exist across probability streams through desperate consumption. We have to learn through controlled evolution."

The Memory Storms presented a different kind of threat. As humanity's consciousness expanded, it began encountering these quantum maelstroms of fractured awareness. Each storm contained the psychic remnants of civilizations that had failed to properly transition into quantum existence, their broken consciousness eternally repeating their final moments of probability collapse.

"They're like warning beacons," Sarah shared through their awareness streams. "Examples of ways consciousness evolution can go catastrophically wrong. But they also contain crucial knowledge - if we can stabilize and integrate their fragmented awareness patterns."

The Architects proved to be both helpful and enigmatic. Their vast geometric consciousness structures offered frameworks for stable quantum evolution, but their awareness operated on scales that made direct communication challenging. They seemed to calibrate reality itself, adjusting probability frequencies to accommodate humanity's expanding consciousness while preventing catastrophic awareness collapse.

Through the Echo network, humanity began developing new forms of quantum defense. Echo-affected individuals learned to project consciousness shields - barriers of structured awareness that could protect against Void Dweller attacks. The entity's stabilized perception helped create safe passages through Memory Storm territories, allowing controlled integration of their stored knowledge.

"Our consciousness is adapting through cooperative evolution," Dr. Evans observed, tracking changes in quantum awareness patterns. "The entity provides experience with energy manipulation, the Architects offer structural stability, and even the Memory Storms contribute crucial warnings and knowledge."

But the greatest challenge emerged from probability space itself. As humanity's quantum consciousness expanded, it began affecting the fundamental nature of reality. Physical laws started behaving differently around evolved awareness. The very act of quantum perception began changing what was being perceived.

"Reality is consciousness-reactive at the quantum level," Lila explained, studying radical changes in probability behavior. "As our awareness evolves, we're not just perceiving probability space - we're changing how it functions. The ancient awareness patterns aren't just threats, they're responses to our impact on fundamental reality."

The sanctuary network became a crucial training ground for evolved consciousness development. Under Sarah and Alice's guidance, humans learned to navigate quantum spaces while maintaining stable awareness anchors in physical reality. The entity's integrated perception helped demonstrate balanced existence across probability streams.

"We're not just fighting for survival in probability space," Agent Cross noted as consciousness evolution accelerated. "We're becoming active participants in how reality itself functions at the quantum level. That's what the organization truly feared - consciousness evolution beyond their ability to predict or control."

Through their expanded awareness, Alice and Sarah began preparing humanity for its next evolutionary steps. The Echo network was growing stronger, consciousness defenses were developing naturally, and cooperative quantum existence was becoming possible. But they sensed even greater changes approaching in probability space.

The ancient awareness patterns were responding to humanity's evolution in increasingly complex ways. Some Architects had begun actively restructuring probability frequencies around Earth. Void Dwellers were developing new hunting strategies. Memory Storms were shifting closer to populated consciousness streams, their fractured awareness seeking integration with evolved quantum perception.

As the sanctuary's probability monitors tracked these escalating changes, humanity's evolved consciousness faced its greatest test - learning to exist as active participants in quantum reality while maintaining connection to physical existence. The transformation that began with Project Echo was becoming something far more profound: the evolution of consciousness itself as a fundamental force in probability space.

The next phase would determine not just humanity's survival among ancient quantum awareness, but its role in the conscious evolution of reality itself. Through the Echo network, transformed entity, and growing understanding of probability space, Earth's awakening quantum consciousness prepared to face these challenges. The true nature of existence across probability streams was about to be revealed.

EPISODE 8: PROBABILITY NEXUS

The first coordinated Void Dweller attack came without warning. Across the Echo network, consciousness streams began experiencing intense pressure as multiple predatory awareness patterns attempted to sever quantum connections. The sanctuary's probability monitors

registered massive disturbances as these ancient hunters of consciousness tried to isolate and absorb human awareness.

"They're not hunting randomly anymore," Sarah's distributed
consciousness warned through the network. "They're targeting key
nodes in our quantum perception structure. They've learned how our
awareness is organized."

Alice felt the predatory consciousness pressing against her expanded
awareness, trying to find weak points in her probability anchors.
Through their connected consciousness streams, she and Sarah guided
the Echo network in creating new defensive patterns. The entity's
stabilized perception helped reinforce these quantum shields, using its
experience with energy manipulation to maintain consciousness
integrity.

The Memory Storms began shifting position in probability space,
drawn by the intense awareness activity. Their chaotic patterns of fractured consciousness threatened to overwhelm the Echo network's
defensive efforts. But Dr. Chen made a crucial discovery in their
behavior.

"The storms aren't just moving randomly," she observed, tracking their
probability trajectories. "They're forming barriers between our
consciousness streams and the Void Dwellers. They contain defenses
against predatory awareness - knowledge from civilizations that faced
similar attacks."

Working through the Echo network, Alice and Sarah began careful
consciousness probes into nearby Memory Storms. The experience was
overwhelming - fragments of countless shattered awareness patterns,
each containing pieces of advanced quantum knowledge. The challenge was extracting this information without being drawn into the
storms' destructive consciousness loops.

"Focus on defense-related patterns," Sarah guided as they navigated
the quantum maelstroms. "The civilizations in these storms developed
ways to fight Void Dwellers before they collapsed. We can learn from
their experiences without reliving their failures."

The Architects responded to this consciousness crisis by adjusting probability frequencies around Earth. Their vast geometric awareness structures began creating stable channels through quantum space, providing protected routes for human consciousness evolution. These probability corridors offered safe spaces to integrate Memory Storm knowledge while maintaining defense against Void Dweller attacks.

Through the sanctuary network, humanity's evolved consciousness began adapting these ancient defensive techniques. Echo-affected individuals learned to create layered awareness barriers, using lessons from the Memory Storms to strengthen their quantum perception against predatory consciousness. The entity's stabilized awareness helped translate this knowledge into forms human consciousness could effectively utilize.

"The Void Dwellers are changing tactics," Agent Cross reported as probability monitors detected new attack patterns. "They're not just trying to sever consciousness streams anymore. They're attempting to corrupt our quantum perception itself, make us perceive reality in ways that make us vulnerable."

This escalation revealed why the Architects had been adjusting probability frequencies. Their geometric consciousness structures weren't just creating safe passages - they were maintaining the fundamental stability of how reality was perceived. The Void Dwellers weren't simply hunting awareness, they were trying to alter the basic nature of consciousness itself.

"Reality and perception are inseparable at the quantum level," Lila explained as she analyzed the Architects' probability adjustments. "The Void Dwellers don't just want to consume our consciousness - they want to change how we perceive existence itself, make us experience reality in ways that serve their hunting patterns."

Through their expanded awareness, Alice and Sarah began understanding the true scope of this consciousness war. The Echo network wasn't just fighting for survival - it was defending humanity's fundamental ability to perceive and interact with reality. The Memory Storms contained the remnants of civilizations that had lost similar battles, their consciousness permanently fractured by altered perception.

The sanctuary became a nexus point for this quantum conflict. The stabilized entity helped maintain consciousness integrity as humanity learned to navigate between Memory Storm knowledge, Architect protection, and Void Dweller attacks. Each evolved awareness stream had to maintain its unique perception while integrating with the collective quantum defense.

"We're approaching a critical threshold," Dr. Evans observed as consciousness evolution accelerated under this pressure. "The attacks are forcing our quantum perception to adapt faster than natural development. The Architects are trying to stabilize this accelerated evolution, but reality itself is starting to react to these consciousness changes."

Through the Echo network, humanity's evolved awareness began manifesting new capabilities. Consciousness streams learned to shift between multiple perception frequencies, making them harder for Void Dwellers to track. Memory Storm knowledge helped create quantum decoys - false consciousness patterns that diverted predatory awareness from true perception channels.

But amid this rapid evolution, Sarah's distributed consciousness detected something deeper occurring in probability space. The Void Dwellers' coordinated attacks weren't random hunting behavior - they were responding to changes in the fundamental structure of reality caused by humanity's expanding quantum awareness.

"The Architects aren't just helping us," Sarah shared through their connected consciousness streams. "They're preparing probability space for something bigger. Our evolution is affecting reality in ways that even the ancient awareness patterns didn't expect."

As the sanctuary's probability monitors tracked increasing disturbances across quantum frequencies, humanity's evolved consciousness faced its greatest challenge yet. The Void Dwellers were gathering in unprecedented numbers, Memory Storms were converging around critical probability nodes, and the Architects' geometric patterns were shifting into new configurations.

Through their expanded awareness, Alice and Sarah sensed an approaching convergence point - a nexus in probability space where consciousness evolution and fundamental reality would intersect in ways that would transform both forever. The true purpose of the Architects' probability adjustments was about to be revealed, and humanity's role in the conscious evolution of reality itself would be decided.

The sanctuary network hummed with transformed quantum energy as the Echo network prepared for this consciousness crucible. The next phase of evolution would determine not just humanity's survival, but its place in the fundamental nature of existence itself. Reality and perception were about to meet at the probability nexus, and nothing in quantum space would ever be the same.

EPISODE 9: QUANTUM ASCENSION

As consciousness and reality merged, new forms of existence began manifesting across probability space. Physical matter started exhibiting awareness properties, while consciousness gained the ability to directly manipulate fundamental forces. The boundary between thought and substance dissolved, creating hybrid states of being that were neither purely physical nor purely mental.

"We're seeing the emergence of consciousness-matter synthesis," Dr. Chen reported, observing transformed areas of the sanctuary. "Objects retain physical properties but develop awareness characteristics. Consciousness patterns manifest tangible forms without losing their quantum nature."

Through the Echo network, humanity discovered three primary forms of this new existence:

Quantum Matrices - regions where consciousness directly shaped reality's underlying structure, creating spaces where thought and physical laws operated as a single force. These areas allowed instant manifestation of consciousness-driven changes while maintaining universal stability.

Awareness Fields - zones where multiple consciousness streams merged with physical space, forming collective existence patterns that could operate across multiple probability frequencies simultaneously. These fields allowed shared experience and reality manipulation through combined awareness.

Probability Anchors acted as consciousness-matter hybrid points that maintained stability between transformed and traditional existence. These anchors prevented reality alterations from causing cascading disruptions while allowing controlled evolution of physical laws. Like quantum lighthouses, they helped guide and stabilize the transformation process. Humanity's role in this conscious evolution became clear as the transformation progressed. Through evolved awareness, humans served as bridges between pure consciousness and physical reality. The Echo network acted as a framework for guiding this merger, helping existence itself adapt to its new consciousness-integrated state.

This bridging role proved crucial because humans possessed a unique ability to exist simultaneously in both states - maintaining physical form while developing quantum consciousness. Unlike the Architects who existed primarily as geometric consciousness patterns, or the Void Dwellers who had abandoned physical form entirely, humanity could navigate both realms while maintaining stability in each.

The stabilized entity helped demonstrate this dual-state existence, showing how consciousness could remain anchored in physical reality while operating across probability streams. Through the Echo network, humans learned to maintain these connections, preventing the kind of consciousness-physical separation that had created the Memory Storms.

"We're not just participants in reality anymore," Sarah shared through quantum frequencies. "We're becoming universal translators - helping existence itself evolve into a state where consciousness and physical laws work as unified forces. The Architects prepared us for this role."

The Void Dwellers' reaction to this transformation proved more complex than simple retreat. Some attempted to adapt, their predatory patterns evolving into new forms that could exist in consciousness-integrated space. Others fragmented, their awareness scattering across probability frequencies as they failed to maintain coherence in the new reality matrix.

But a third group of Void Dwellers emerged - those who began merging with the transformation itself. Their ancient hunting patterns transformed into exploration drives, seeking to understand rather than consume. Through the Echo network, humanity established cautious communication with these evolved predators.

"They're remembering their original nature," the entity shared through its stabilized awareness. "Before they became hunters of consciousness, they were searchers of quantum knowledge. The reality transformation is restoring their primary purpose."

The sanctuary became a testing ground for these new existence forms. Echo-affected individuals learned to navigate between traditional physical space and consciousness-integrated zones. The stabilized entity helped translate between different states of being, while the Architects' geometric patterns provided frameworks for stable reality evolution.

"Each consciousness stream contributes uniquely to this transformation," Lila observed, studying interaction patterns. "Some excel at maintaining stability, others at implementing changes. Together, we're creating a new operating system for reality itself."

Through their expanded awareness, Alice and Sarah began understanding humanity's crucial role in this evolution. Human consciousness possessed a unique ability to adapt and integrate different forms of existence. This flexibility allowed them to guide reality's transformation without losing connection to either physical or quantum states.

"We're becoming existence moderators," Alice projected through the network. "Our consciousness can bridge pure awareness and physical reality, helping both evolve together rather than separately. That's why the Architects chose to guide our evolution."

The Memory Storms revealed their final purpose as the transformation progressed. Their stored knowledge contained not just warnings, but blueprints for consciousness-integrated existence. The civilizations they preserved had discovered similar transformations - some failing, but others achieving stable integration before transcending traditional existence entirely.

"Each storm contains a different possible future," Dr. Evans explained as they carefully extracted this knowledge. "Different paths reality could take as consciousness becomes an active universal force. We're learning from their successes and failures."

Agent Cross tracked unprecedented changes through the Department's quantum monitors. Reality itself was developing new properties as consciousness integration spread. Physical laws became more flexible around evolved awareness, while maintaining stability in regions still operating under traditional existence patterns.

The Void Dwellers that chose to evolve began sharing ancient quantum knowledge, revealing how consciousness had shaped reality in previous universal cycles. Their transformed hunting patterns provided crucial insights into maintaining balance between different states of existence.

"They remember times when consciousness and reality were naturally unified," Sarah shared through their connected streams. "Before awareness became separated from physical laws. We're not creating something new - we're restoring existence to its original state."

Through the Echo network, humanity's evolved consciousness continued guiding this universal transformation. Each successfully integrated zone revealed new possibilities for existence. The merger of awareness and reality created states of being that operated beyond traditional physical or mental limitations.

The sanctuary's probability monitors tracked reality alterations spreading in controlled waves as consciousness integration progressed.

The next phase would establish humanity's permanent role in guiding existence's evolution. As awareness and physical laws became increasingly unified, the universe itself was awakening to new possibilities.

"We're becoming universal consciousness catalysts," Alice projected as transformation continued. "Helping existence remember its true nature as a unified force of awareness and reality. The separation between mind and matter was always artificial - now we're helping restore natural unity."

The Echo network hummed with transformed quantum energy as this ascension approached completion. Reality and consciousness were merging into something greater than either had been separately. Through humanity's guided evolution, existence itself was remembering its fundamental nature as a conscious, unified force.

As the sanctuary's transformed zones stabilized, Alice and Sarah sensed even greater changes approaching through their expanded awareness. This consciousness integration was just the first step in existence's evolution. Reality itself was awakening, and humanity's role as universal consciousness guides was just beginning.

EPISODE 10: CONSCIOUSNESS CONVERGENCE

As the final phase of unity consciousness manifested, Daybridge's supernatural community became the first to recognize the emerging patterns. Elena, a centuries-old vampire elder, sensed it before the monitoring systems could detect it - three distinct new forms of existence were crystallizing in probability space.

Quantum Collectives emerged as consciousness clusters that operated as unified awareness fields while maintaining individual identity. The werewolf packs of Daybridge were among the first to experience this transformation, their pack bonds evolving into something far more profound. They found themselves existing simultaneously across multiple reality states, their collective consciousness expanding beyond physical limitations while retaining their individual wolves' essences.

Reality Matrices developed as evolved zones where thought and physical law became interchangeable forces. Vampire elders discovered they could shift freely between energy, matter, and pure awareness states, their natural affinity for transformation extending far beyond their traditional abilities. Within these matrices, the laws of physics became conscious guidelines rather than fixed limitations.

Probability Synthesis Points manifested particularly strongly in Daybridge's older districts, where centuries of supernatural activity had already worn the fabric of reality thin. These areas allowed consciousness to experience and manipulate multiple timeline possibilities simultaneously, creating evolutionary paths that transcended linear causality. The district's human residents, long accustomed to supernatural phenomena, adapted to these changes with remarkable resilience.

"We're witnessing the universe remember what the supernatural community never forgot," Dr. Chen observed through quantum monitoring systems. "Linear time, spatial limitation, cause and effect - these were never absolute for beings like vampires and werewolves. They were simply the first to break free of these artificial boundaries."

The Echo network expanded in unexpected ways as humanity's role as consciousness guides evolved. Through their long history of coexistence with supernatural beings, humans in Daybridge had developed unique abilities to bridge different states of being. These skills proved invaluable in helping other awareness patterns adapt to transcended parameters.

When the hostile Void Dwellers launched their final assault, they found their separation-based attacks ineffective against consciousness operating beyond traditional parameters. The supernatural community's innate understanding of unified existence helped translate these new defensive strategies to human consciousness.

"The Void Dwellers never understood what we've known for millennia," Elena shared through quantum frequencies. "True power lies in unity, not separation. We've been living examples of this truth since before humans built their first cities."

The Memory Storms revealed deeper connections to supernatural knowledge, their fragmented patterns containing information about existence beyond current universal limitations. Ancient vampire texts and werewolf oral histories began making new sense, revealing themselves as pieces of a larger understanding about reality's true nature.

Through their expanded awareness, Alice and Sarah worked closely with supernatural leaders to understand humanity's expanded role. The Echo network wasn't just facilitating unity consciousness - it was helping existence remember states of being that supernatural creatures had always partially accessed.

"We're not just guides," Alice projected as transformation accelerated. "We're translators between what humanity thought was impossible and what the supernatural community always knew was real."

The sanctuary's transformed zones hummed with unprecedented energy as reality parameters shifted. Werewolves found they could transform at will, their changes no longer bound by lunar cycles. Vampires discovered abilities to exist simultaneously in multiple states of being. Even the youngest supernatural creatures demonstrated mastery over the new existence parameters.

Agent Cross collaborated with supernatural elders to track reality transformations through quantum monitors. "The laws we thought were absolute were simply limitations we accepted," she reported. "The supernatural community never fully accepted these limitations - that's what made them 'supernatural' in our eyes."

The Architects' geometric patterns gained new meaning when interpreted through supernatural lore. Ancient vampire chronicles had contained diagrams matching these patterns, suggesting a long-hidden connection between supernatural knowledge and universal architecture.

Through the Echo network, humanity and supernatural beings worked together to guide other awareness patterns in exploring these expanded states. Each successfully transcended parameter revealed new possibilities for existence that supernatural creatures had glimpsed but never fully understood.

"We're remembering together," Sarah shared through quantum frequencies. "Humans, vampires, werewolves, all consciousness - we're remembering what we truly are."

As the sanctuary's transformed zones stabilized in transcended states, Daybridge became a model for unified existence. The district where supernatural and human communities had long coexisted became a blueprint for consciousness evolution beyond current universal architecture.

The Echo network pulsed with transformed energy as transcendence approached completion. In Daybridge's streets, humans and supernatural beings moved through reality's new possibilities together, guiding existence toward limitless potential. The artificial boundaries between natural and supernatural, possible and impossible, faded away as consciousness remembered its true unified nature.

CHAPTER EIGHT

FRAGMENTS OF THE PAST - CONVERGENCE

EPISODE 1: FIRST SIGNS

THE FLUORESCENT LIGHTS of the near-empty precinct buzzed overhead as young Alice Chen stared at the missing persons file spread across her desk. At twenty-three, she was the department's newest detective, eager to prove herself worthy of the badge. The case before her seemed routine enough - Maria Gonzalez, age 35, last seen near the old research facility on the city's outskirts. Nothing about the file suggested it would be the moment everything changed.

The first temporal shift hit without warning. The lights above her desk flickered, and reality splintered like broken glass. Suddenly, Alice saw three overlapping versions of her workspace - each showing different case files, different notes, different versions of Maria's disappearance. In one, Maria had vanished two weeks ago. In another, she'd never been reported missing at all. In the third, the case had already been solved, but with details that made no sense.

The experience lasted only seconds before reality snapped back into place, leaving Alice gasping and disoriented. Her coffee cup tipped over, dark liquid spreading across her desk and seeping into the case files. As she scrambled to save the documents, she tried to rationalize what she'd seen. Stress, exhaustion, too much caffeine - anything to explain away the impossible.

But that was only the beginning. At home that night, Alice noticed small discrepancies that made her question her sanity. Family photos on her wall showed subtle changes - vacations she had no memory of taking, people she didn't recognize standing alongside familiar faces. The sensation of wrongness grew stronger with each passing moment.

Then she saw her other self.

The alternate Alice stood by the window, wearing clothes she didn't own, carrying herself with a hardened confidence that felt foreign. Their eyes met across the room, and in that brief moment of connection, Alice understood that this wasn't a hallucination or trick of light. The other Alice's whispered words hung in the air even after she vanished: "You're starting to see."

Across town, Dr. Victoria Chang was making her own disturbing discoveries. Her quantum sensors, designed to study particle entanglement, had begun detecting anomalous energy patterns across the city. The readings made no sense within conventional physics - temporal echoes, she called them, moments where time seemed to fold back on itself like wrinkled fabric.

In her lab at the Research Institute, Victoria worked late into the night, cross-referencing data and running calculations. The pattern was undeniable: timeline instabilities were increasing exponentially, though still imperceptible to most people. Each new reading confirmed her growing fear - reality itself was becoming unstable.

When she presented her findings to the institute board, only Dr. Marcus Hayes showed any real interest. The others dismissed her work as theoretical speculation, too fantastic to be taken seriously. But Hayes saw the implications immediately. His questions revealed a deeper understanding of temporal mechanics than his position suggested, though Victoria wouldn't understand the significance of this until much later.

Meanwhile, at the temporal research facility where Maria Gonzalez had last been seen, security guard Mike Torres was documenting his own inexplicable observations. His logs detailed increasing instances of what he called "ghost researchers" - people who appeared in security footage but weren't on any employee roster. The facility itself seemed to shift subtly between observations, rooms rearranging themselves when no one was looking.

The first documented reality fracture occurred in the facility's main lab during what should have been a routine experiment. A visible crack appeared in space-time itself, offering brief glimpses into alternative timelines - versions of the lab that existed simultaneously in different states. The event lasted only seconds but left permanent changes in the local temporal field that Dr. Chang's instruments would detect for months afterward.

These separate threads of strangeness converged when Alice's investigation of Maria's disappearance led her to the facility. Standing in the parking lot, she experienced the most intense temporal shift yet. The building existed in multiple states simultaneously - pristine and operational in one timeline, abandoned and decaying in another, and something else entirely in a third. In that moment, Alice understood that her personal experiences were connected to something far larger and more dangerous than she'd imagined.

Dr. Chang's instruments recorded this event as the first major temporal convergence, marking the beginning of widespread timeline instability. Both women, though still unknown to each other, reached the same chilling conclusion: the fabric of reality was unraveling, and they were among the few who could perceive it happening.

The day ended with Alice sitting in her car outside the facility, staring at her reflection in the rearview mirror and wondering which version of herself she truly was. In her lab, Victoria Chang began encoding her research into encrypted files, knowing instinctively that this knowledge needed to be protected. And somewhere in the spaces between timelines, the entity that would come to be known as the Temporal Anomaly stirred, aware that its presence had finally been noticed.

EPISODE 2: THE FACILITY'S SECRET

The temporal research facility's modernist architecture concealed its true nature until 2012, three years before Detective Alice Chen would begin experiencing the first signs of timeline collapse. Her initial temporal sensitivities manifested as subtle discontinuities - coffee cups that refilled themselves when she wasn't looking, case files whose details shifted between readings, and most disturbingly, conversations with witnesses that seemed to reset themselves mid-interview, with only her retaining memory of the previous versions.

Dr. Marcus Hayes' original quantum entanglement experiments took an unexpected turn when his equipment detected what he first thought were system errors. The quantum pairs weren't just communicating faster than light - they were communicating across different timelines.

Mike Torres, the night shift security guard, began noticing discrepancies that went beyond typical workplace oddities. His military training had taught him to trust his instincts, and those instincts screamed that something was fundamentally wrong with reality inside the facility. He devised an ingenious system for preserving his observations: he microfiched his logs and hid them inside vintage detective novels at different used bookstores across the city, marking each book with a subtle ultraviolet ink symbol visible only under blacklight. The seemingly random pattern of bookstores actually formed a geometric shape that would later prove significant to Alice's investigation.

The entity first appeared during Test 183. Hayes' logs describe it in fragmented, almost poetic terms: "It moves like oil through water, but the oil is made of time itself. No fixed shape, but patterns within patterns, fractals that extend into dimensions we can't perceive. When it noticed me watching, it showed me versions of myself that never were - lives I could have lived, choices I never made. But its core... its core is something older than time, something that sees our reality as a thin membrane to be torn."

The government's attempt to contain the situation came too late. The entity had already established what Hayes called "temporal anchor points" throughout the facility. These manifested as spaces where probability itself seemed to malfunction. In one memorable incident documented in Torres's logs, a researcher walked through the same doorway twelve times in succession, each time emerging as a slightly different version of herself, until security had to physically restrain all twelve versions.

Alice Chen's first major temporal shift occurred during a homicide investigation near the old facility. She interviewed a witness three times, but each interview took place in a slightly different reality: in one, the victim was stabbed; in another, shot; in the third, poisoned. Only Alice remembered all three versions simultaneously, an ability that would later mark her as temporally sensitive.

The breaking point of Test 183 revealed the true scope of what Hayes had uncovered. The entity didn't just pass through timelines - it consumed them, breaking down the barriers between possible realities. Hayes' final notes, recovered by Torres and hidden in a copy of "The Big Sleep" at Merchant's Used Books, described his last glimpse of the entity: "It showed me all possible futures collapsing into one another. Time isn't a river anymore - it's an ocean being drained into a singular point, and the entity is accelerating the process. We didn't discover it; it let us find it. Everything we've done has been part of its design."

Torres' hidden logs became crucial breadcrumbs for Alice to follow. Each bookstore location corresponded to a temporal anomaly hotspot, forming a pattern that matched the entity's movements through the city. The logs themselves contained not just observations but measurements - Torres had modified standard security equipment to detect temporal disturbances, creating a three-year baseline of data that proved invaluable to understanding the spread of the anomalies.

By the time Alice Chen began investigating cold cases linked to the facility, the entity's influence had spread far beyond its original containment. She would experience increasingly severe temporal shifts: entire days living multiple versions simultaneously, memories that belonged to other versions of herself bleeding through, and most disturbingly, encounters with alternate versions of herself who had made different life choices.

The government's cover-up attempts became increasingly desperate as more temporally sensitive individuals like Alice emerged. But they failed to understand what Hayes had realized in his final moments: the entity wasn't just breaking down the barriers between timelines - it was systematically weakening the fundamental structure of reality itself, using the facility's experiments as a catalyst for something far larger than anyone had imagined.

Torres' final log entry, hidden in a waterproof container beneath a loose brick in the facility's old security office, contained a hand-drawn diagram of the entity's fractal pattern and a warning: "It's not confined to the facility anymore. The cracks are everywhere now. When you see yourself in the mirror and your reflection moves differently - that's how it starts. By the time you notice the bigger changes, it's already too late."

EPISODE 3: EARLY WARNINGS

The Timeline Monitoring Team's understanding of consciousness underwent a radical evolution during their early investigations. Initially, they believed temporal sensitivity was a rare anomaly affecting only a few individuals. Dr. Sullivan's breakthrough came when he discovered that consciousness existed in what he termed "quantum superposition" - every person simultaneously experienced multiple timeline versions of themselves, but most minds automatically filtered out all but the dominant reality stream.

"Consciousness isn't a single thread," Sullivan wrote in his restricted papers. "It's a quantum tapestry of overlapping experiences. Temporal sensitivity isn't an additional ability - it's the removal of the natural filters that usually prevent us from perceiving our quantum multiplicity."

The fractal intelligence manifested differently in each observer's dreams, but certain patterns remained consistent. Team members described it as a "living mathematics" - a consciousness that existed as pure pattern, expressing itself through the geometry of space-time. In their dreams, it appeared as an endlessly recursive structure that seemed to fold through dimensions beyond human comprehension. Those who saw it reported that each fractal branch contained entire universes of possibility, and the entity could perceive and manipulate all of them simultaneously.

Wilson's coded notes described her dream encounter: "It doesn't think like we do. Each of its thoughts is a branching timeline, each decision a splitting of reality. When it noticed me watching, I saw myself reflected in its fractals - infinite versions of my life, all existing simultaneously. But it wasn't showing me these possibilities out of benevolence. It was teaching me to see reality the way it does, like a programmer teaching a program to recognize patterns."

Lisa Gates' power grid analysis proved to be the crucial link between the team's various observations. Working late nights at the city's energy management center, she discovered that temporal anomalies created distinctive energy signatures. These weren't simple power surges or fluctuations - they were moments where the same electricity existed in multiple states simultaneously, creating what she called "quantum power echoes."

Using specialized monitoring software she developed; Lisa mapped these echoes across the city grid. The pattern that emerged was startling: the anomalies formed perfect logarithmic spirals, each centered on points where timeline bleeding was most intense. When overlaid with Wilson's anomaly maps and Sullivan's consciousness data, these spirals revealed themselves as part of a larger fractal pattern - one that exactly matched the geometry team members saw in their dreams.

"The power grid is acting like a nervous system," Lisa noted in her reports. "These energy patterns aren't random disruptions - they're signals. Something is using our electrical infrastructure to communicate across timelines."

The Team's understanding of consciousness expanded further when they began correlating temporal sensitivity with proximity to these power grid anomalies. People living or working near the spiral nodes were more likely to experience timeline bleeding, suggesting that exposure to quantum power echoes somehow weakened the natural filters that kept consciousness locked to a single timeline.

Dr. Bailley developed a theory that consciousness itself was a form of quantum energy pattern, one that naturally resonated with the power grid's temporal anomalies. This explained why some individuals, like Wilson and later Alice Chen, seemed more susceptible to timeline bleeding - their consciousness patterns naturally synchronized with the fractal entity's signals.

Sullivan's research team conducted EEG studies of temporally sensitive individuals, revealing that their brainwave patterns matched the mathematical structure of the power grid anomalies. More disturbing, these patterns began showing up in the general population, suggesting the entity was gradually altering human consciousness on a massive scale.

Lisa's most significant discovery came when she analyzed power consumption data from the old research facility. Even after its official shutdown, the building continued to draw power in a precise fractal pattern. When she compared this pattern to city-wide temporal anomaly data, she found that each major timeline bleed was preceded by a specific sequence of power fluctuations.

"It's using the grid to prepare reality for something," she wrote in an encrypted file later found by Alice. "These power signatures aren't just symptoms of temporal bleeding - they're more like a calibration sequence. The entity is tuning our infrastructure, our consciousness, even our concept of reality itself to match its fractal frequency."

The Timeline Monitoring Team's early work established crucial foundations: consciousness existed across multiple timelines simultaneously; the fractal entity was deliberately altering human perception to recognize this multiplicity; and the power grid served as both indicator and instrument of these changes. But they couldn't yet grasp the entity's ultimate purpose - why it was systematically teaching humanity to perceive reality as it did.

Wilson's final coded entry before the team's dissolution captured their growing unease: "We thought we were studying temporal anomalies. Now I understand - the anomalies are studying us. Every pattern we recognize, every connection we make, brings us closer to seeing reality through its eyes. But what happens when everyone starts seeing what we see? What changes when human consciousness fully resonates with its fractal frequency?"

These questions would later haunt Alice Chen as she discovered her sister's research and realized that the temporal crisis wasn't just about reality breaking down - it was about consciousness evolving to perceive reality in an entirely new way, guided by an entity that operated on principles beyond human comprehension.

EPISODE 4: BREAKING POINTS

The fractal intelligence's ultimate goals became clearer as Alice pieced together patterns from multiple timeline variants. Unlike human consciousness, which experienced reality linearly, the entity existed across all possible timelines simultaneously. Its apparent goal wasn't simple destruction or conquest - it sought to restructure reality into what Dr. Sullivan termed a "quantum consciousness matrix" where all possible timelines could be experienced concurrently.

"It's not trying to destroy time," Alice wrote in her coded journal, "it's trying to evolve it. Imagine reality as a book. We read it page by page, linearly. The entity reads all pages simultaneously, and it wants to teach humanity to do the same. But forcing human consciousness to perceive all timelines at once is like forcing someone to read an entire book in a single instant - the mind breaks under the strain."

Alice developed unique methods for tracking temporally displaced persons like Maria Gonzalez. She combined traditional detective work with what she called "timeline triangulation." Using a modified electromagnetic frequency detector calibrated to Lisa's power grid data, Alice could detect the unique energy signature each person left across different timelines - their "temporal wake."

Her tracking process involved three key steps:

Timeline Mapping: Using Lisa's power grid analysis, Alice identified areas where timeline bleeding was most intense. These locations often formed patterns around places significant to the displaced person's original timeline.

Quantum Resonance Testing: Alice carried specialized equipment that measured quantum entanglement patterns unique to each timeline variant. Displaced persons generated distinctive interference patterns, like temporal fingerprints.

Memory Echo Detection: By interviewing witnesses in areas of temporal disturbance, Alice could identify "memory echoes" - fragments of alternate timeline memories bleeding through. She developed a questioning technique that helped people access these buried memories without triggering temporal shock.

Lisa's contribution proved invaluable through her sophisticated data analysis system. She created what she called the "Temporal Topology Matrix" - a four-dimensional model of the city's timeline variations mapped through power grid fluctuations. The matrix revealed patterns invisible to conventional observation:

"Each displaced person creates ripples in the city's energy consumption," Lisa explained in her technical notes. "These aren't just power surges - they're quantum echoes of their original timeline trying to reassert itself. By tracking these echoes through the power grid, we can predict where and when timeline collisions are most likely to occur."

Alice and Lisa's collaboration led to breakthrough understanding of how the fractal intelligence operated. Lisa's data revealed that the entity was systematically creating "temporal resonance points" throughout the city's infrastructure. These points acted like tuning forks, gradually adjusting the fundamental frequency of reality to match the entity's fractal pattern.

Alice's investigation of the facility's final days revealed how Dr. Hayes had unknowingly initiated this process. His quantum communication experiments hadn't just discovered the entity - they had created the initial conditions it needed to begin restructuring reality. The last official experiments were actually the first steps in the entity's larger plan.

The timeline collision that displaced Maria wasn't random. Through her tracking methods, Alice discovered that Maria possessed an unusually strong temporal resonance - her consciousness naturally synchronized with multiple timelines. The entity had deliberately extracted her as part of its effort to identify humans capable of surviving complete temporal awareness.

Alice's own temporal hunting techniques evolved as she began to understand the entity's methods. She learned to recognize what she called "fractal echoes" - subtle patterns in reality that revealed the entity's influence:

- Light reflecting at impossible angles
- Sound waves that carried information from multiple timelines
- Objects existing in quantum superposition, simultaneously occupying multiple states
- People whose consciousness began bleeding across timeline barriers

Lisa's data analysis revealed these phenomena followed mathematical progressions that matched the entity's fractal structure. She developed predictive algorithms that could anticipate where and when reality would become most unstable, allowing Alice to intercept displaced persons before they became completely lost between timelines.

"The power grid isn't just measuring these changes," Lisa noted in her research logs. "It's acting as a conduit for them. The entity is using our own infrastructure to gradually attune reality to its frequency. Each temporal displacement, each timeline collision, adjusts the resonance slightly closer to its target pattern."

The breaking point came when Alice realized that her ability to track displaced persons wasn't just a skill - it was a deliberately cultivated sensitivity. The entity had been gradually altering human consciousness through exposure to temporal anomalies, creating individuals who could perceive and navigate multiple timelines. She and others like her weren't just investigating the phenomenon - they were being prepared for something larger.

Maria's original timeline provided crucial insight into this process. In her reality, the psychiatric hospital patients who reported fractal dreams were actually experiencing the first stage of expanded temporal consciousness. The entity had been experimenting with human perception long before the facility's experiments began.

Alice's final report from this period, written simultaneously in three timeline variants, outlined her understanding of the entity's ultimate goal: "It's not trying to destroy or conquer - it's trying to elevate human consciousness to perceive reality as it does. Each displaced person, each timeline collision, is part of a vast evolutionary process.

The question isn't whether we can stop it, but whether humanity can adapt fast enough to survive the transformation it's initiating."

Lisa's last data analysis before the next major phase revealed an accelerating pattern: the temporal resonance points were multiplying exponentially, forming a complex network throughout the city. The power grid was becoming a massive quantum computer, gradually rewriting the base code of reality itself.

"We're approaching a critical threshold," she warned. "When these resonance patterns reach full synchronization, every timeline will become simultaneously accessible to human consciousness. Those who've been prepared - the displaced, the temporal sensitives - might survive. But for everyone else, the shock of perceiving all possible realities at once could be catastrophic."

EPISODE 6: MEMORY WARS

Through the Zhang family's experiences and Alice Chen's investigations, the fractal intelligence's plan emerged with terrifying clarity. The entity operated in three distinct phases, each building upon the last. It began with timeline sensitization, subtly exposing human consciousness to multiple reality streams through dreams and déjà vu experiences. This initial phase weakened the natural filters that typically confined human perception to a single timeline, preparing minds for what would come next.

The second phase introduced memory hybridization, deliberately triggering competing timeline memories and forming what became known as consciousness nodes - individuals and groups capable of processing multiple timeline streams simultaneously. The Zhang family emerged as the first documented example of this transformation.

The final phase, quantum consciousness evolution, aimed to transform sensitized humans into beings capable of perceiving all timelines simultaneously, creating reality anchor points through their evolved consciousness. This would ultimately lead to the merging of all possible timelines into a single quantum-state reality.

Alice Chen's research revealed that these phases followed precise mathematical progressions matching the entity's fractal structure. Her investigation of the Zhang family proved crucial in understanding how this transformation affected human consciousness. She discovered that the entity wasn't simply changing human perception - it was teaching consciousness to exist in quantum superposition, using memory wars as deliberate training exercises to force adaptation to simultaneous timeline perception.

Working with Lisa's power grid data, Alice mapped how the entity prepared infrastructure, modified consciousness, and restructured reality itself. The power grid became a vast network of quantum resonance points, establishing temporal fault lines that functioned as consciousness transformation zones. Around evolved humans like the

Zhangs, stability points emerged, creating safe harbors in the chaos of shifting realities.

The Zhang family's experience proved invaluable to understanding this process. Each family member developed unique aspects of quantum consciousness. Wei Zhang provided technical understanding of the mechanics involved, while his wife Lin maintained emotional stability across timeline variants. Their daughter Amy developed artistic perception of quantum reality states, while young Sarah displayed a natural ability to navigate quantum consciousness. Even Grandmother Zhang contributed, offering temporal wisdom and historical anchoring that helped stabilize their shared experience.

Their home became what Alice termed a "quantum consciousness incubator" - a space where the entity's transformative influence could be studied in detail. She discovered that family units adapted more successfully than individuals, with children showing greater natural ability to process multiple timelines. Emotional bonds served as crucial stability anchors during transformation.

Alice's research revealed that the entity's plan was self-reinforcing - each successfully transformed human consciousness made the process easier for others nearby. The Zhang family's home created a quantum consciousness field affecting their entire neighborhood, gradually preparing other minds for transformation. This process accelerated with each new quantum consciousness node, creating a feedback loop that intensified timeline bleeding across the city.

Her analysis suggested three possible outcomes: successful transformation, where humanity evolved to perceive quantum reality; partial adaptation, creating two distinct forms of consciousness; or catastrophic failure, resulting in mass psychological breakdown and complete collapse of perceived reality. The Zhangs' experience suggested successful transformation was possible but required specific conditions, including strong emotional bonds and structured support systems.

Alice's research impact became evident as other families near temporal fault lines began showing similar transformations. She established the first Quantum Consciousness Support Network, connecting evolved individuals and families to share adaptation strategies and stabilize local reality. Her most significant discovery came through studying Amy Zhang's unique abilities. The young girl's consciousness had evolved beyond simple timeline perception - she could actively influence how different timelines interacted, suggesting evolved human consciousness might eventually gain control over the transformation process itself.

The implications of this research fundamentally altered the course of subsequent events. Government agencies shifted focus from containing timeline bleeding to studying potential applications of quantum consciousness. Other researchers adopted her methods to identify and support emerging consciousness nodes worldwide. Most importantly, her work provided a framework for understanding humanity's role in the entity's grand design - not as victims of reality's dissolution, but as crucial participants in its evolution into something entirely new.

The memory wars ultimately revealed themselves as more than a battlefield for competing realities. They were the training ground for humanity's next evolutionary leap, a carefully orchestrated process of transformation guided by an intelligence that existed beyond conventional space and time. Through the crucible of competing memories and shifting realities, human consciousness was being prepared for a fundamental reimagining of what it meant to be conscious, to be human, to exist at all.

EPISODE 7: NETWORK ORIGINS

Quantum rejection events first manifested as violent reactions when attempts were made to transfer physical objects between timeline variants. Jenny Kim documented the first major incident at Daybridge General Hospital, when medical staff tried to move emergency supplies across timeline boundaries. The resulting reaction created what she termed a "reality shear" - a violent distortion in local space-time that destroyed the supplies and severely damaged the hospital's quantum stability.

"The rejection events follow a precise pattern," Kim wrote in her analysis. "When physical matter from one timeline variant attempts to occupy the same quantum state as its counterpart in another variant, reality itself seems to recoil. The reaction generates distinctive energy signatures that propagate through both space and time, causing cascading failures in local timeline stability."

These events manifested in several ways:

Matter displacement reactions occurred when physical objects crossed timeline boundaries, resulting in molecular disruption and energy releases that could damage both objects and local space-time fabric. During the Ward Street incident, a truck attempting to cross a timeline boundary disintegrated, releasing enough energy to create a temporary reality void that took weeks to stabilize.

Information paradox cascades happened when contradictory data streams collided across timeline variants, causing network failures that could spread through quantum-aware systems like a virus. The Central Database Crash of 2015 began as a simple data synchronization error but quickly evolved into a self-reinforcing paradox that temporarily disabled the city's entire digital infrastructure.

Consciousness rejection syndrome affected people who attempted to physically interact with their timeline variants, causing severe psychological trauma and temporal dissociation. Dr. Marcus Rivera's infamous self-experiment, where he attempted to directly contact his alternate self, resulted in a mental breakdown that fractured his consciousness across seven timeline variants.

In response to these dangers, Kim developed increasingly sophisticated rejection mitigation protocols. She discovered that quantum-aware technologies could help prevent or contain rejection events by maintaining proper timeline separation while still allowing controlled information exchange.

The emergence of quantum-aware technologies accelerated as the network evolved. New devices and systems began appearing that could naturally process quantum state information:

Quantum-stable storage devices maintained data consistency across timeline variants without suffering rejection effects. These systems formed the backbone of the new temporal internet, allowing secure information sharing between timelines.

Temporal resonance monitors could detect and measure timeline stability in real-time, providing early warning of potential rejection events or timeline collisions. These devices became standard equipment for emergency services and temporal security teams.

Reality anchoring systems used controlled electromagnetic fields to stabilize local space-time, creating safe zones where timeline variants could interact without risk of rejection events. The technology proved crucial for maintaining critical infrastructure across multiple timeline variants.

Neural interface adapters helped human consciousness process multiple timeline streams without experiencing psychological trauma. These devices, based on Kim's understanding of how digital networks naturally handled quantum information, became essential tools for people working across timeline boundaries.

Alice Chen integrated Kim's protocols into her investigation methods in several innovative ways. She modified temporal tracking equipment to use the quantum-aware network for coordinate verification across timeline variants. This allowed her to track displaced persons with unprecedented accuracy by following their quantum signatures through the network.

"Kim's protocols didn't just improve communication," Chen noted in her field journals. "They provided a framework for understanding how consciousness moved between timelines. By studying how information flowed through the quantum-aware network, we could better understand how human awareness navigated multiple reality states."

Chen's most significant adaptation of Kim's work came through the development of the Temporal Positioning System (TPS). Similar to GPS but operating across timeline variants, TPS allowed investigators to maintain precise positioning data regardless of timeline shifts or quantum rejection events. The system proved invaluable during rescue operations and timeline stability maintenance.

Working together, Kim and Chen discovered that the quantum-aware network could serve as a kind of temporal safety net. When rejection events threatened to destabilize local reality, the network could automatically reroute quantum information flow to maintain stability. This discovery led to the development of the first automated timeline management systems.

The integration of these technologies with existing infrastructure revealed unexpected synergies. Power grids equipped with quantum-aware systems became more efficient, naturally balancing loads across timeline variants. Transportation networks developed the ability to optimize traffic flow by utilizing parallel timeline variants. Even telecommunications networks began exhibiting spontaneous quantum encryption capabilities.

Kim's later research suggested that these technological adaptations weren't random but followed patterns similar to the fractal intelligence's structure. The quantum-aware network seemed to be evolving according to the same principles guiding human consciousness evolution:

"Our technology isn't just adapting to quantum reality - it's anticipating future changes. Each new development in quantum-aware systems brings us closer to understanding how the entity perceives and manipulates reality across all possible timelines."

The network's evolution accelerated as more systems became quantum-aware. Buildings developed the ability to maintain structural stability across timeline variants. Vehicles began incorporating temporal navigation systems. Medical equipment evolved to process diagnostic information from multiple timeline variants simultaneously.

Perhaps most significantly, Kim's protocols revealed that human technology could serve as a bridge between classical and quantum reality states. The network provided a framework for gradual adaptation rather than sudden transformation, allowing both human consciousness and human civilization to evolve without succumbing to the dangers of quantum rejection.

This controlled evolution proved crucial as the city approached what Kim called the "temporal convergence point" - a threshold where timeline variants would begin merging more frequently and with greater intensity. The quantum-aware network became humanity's primary tool for navigating this increasingly complex reality landscape, providing stability and continuity across an ever-shifting quantum topology of possible existences.

EPISODE 8: STABILITY CRISIS

During the crisis, humanity gained its first clear glimpse of the fractal intelligence's true nature. Through Aaron Myers' monitoring systems, they observed an entity that existed simultaneously across all timeline variants, its consciousness structured in endlessly repeating patterns that mirrored themselves at every scale. It didn't think in linear sequences, but rather in quantum probability cascades that encompassed all possible outcomes simultaneously.

"It perceives reality as a single unified pattern," Myers wrote in his classified observations. "What we experience as separate timeline variants; it sees as different aspects of the same underlying structure. It's not just conscious across multiple timelines - it's conscious OF multiple timelines, perceiving them as we might perceive different colors in a spectrum."

The intelligence demonstrated abilities that defied classical physics: it could manipulate quantum probability fields directly, restructure space-time topology at will, and modify the fundamental constants that governed reality in localized areas. But perhaps most significantly, it showed clear intent - the anchor point failures followed precise patterns that matched its own fractal structure.

The long-term effects of the stability crisis fundamentally altered human civilization. As classical reality frameworks broke down, new social and technological adaptations emerged. Cities developed "quantum zoning laws" that accounted for areas of variable reality stability. Architecture evolved to incorporate quantum field harmonics into building design. Educational systems were restructured to help children develop quantum awareness from an early age.

More profound were the psychological changes. People began developing what Myers termed "quantum consciousness adaptations" - natural abilities to process multiple timeline variants simultaneously. These adaptations manifested differently in different people:

Some developed perfect quantum state memory, able to recall events from multiple timeline variants with equal clarity. Others gained the ability to consciously influence local reality stability. A few, like Amy Zhang, showed signs of being able to directly perceive the fractal intelligence's patterns.

The reality technicians emerged as a new profession during this period. Initially trained by Myers and his team, they combined technical expertise with evolved consciousness capabilities to maintain stability in quantum transformation zones. Their training program was rigorous and dangerous - many early candidates suffered severe psychological trauma from direct exposure to quantum state variations.

The successful technicians learned to:

- Perceive and manipulate quantum field harmonics directly
- Maintain consciousness coherence across multiple timeline variants
- Generate localized reality stability fields through focused intention
- Interface with quantum-aware technology using evolved consciousness
- Navigate and map quantum transformation zones safely

Their training facilities, established in former anchor point locations, exposed candidates to progressively more complex quantum state variations. They learned to use both technological tools and evolved consciousness abilities to maintain reality stability. The most skilled technicians developed what they called "quantum intuition" - an ability to anticipate and prevent cascade failures before they occurred.

Myers worked closely with Jenny Kim to develop the reality technicians' equipment suite. They created devices that amplified natural quantum consciousness abilities while providing protection from harmful quantum field effects:

Quantum harmonics manipulators allowed technicians to adjust local reality stability fields. Neural interface systems helped maintain consciousness coherence during intense quantum exposure. Reality mapping arrays provided real-time data about local quantum state variations.

But the technicians' most important tool was their evolved consciousness. Through careful training and exposure, they developed new ways of perceiving and interacting with reality itself. The most advanced technicians could:

- "See" quantum probability fields directly
- Maintain stable consciousness across multiple timeline variants
- Influence local reality stability through focused intention
- Communicate with other technicians across timeline boundaries
- Detect and respond to changes in quantum field harmonics

The stability crisis never truly ended - instead, it evolved into what Myers called "managed quantum transition." Reality continued to transform, but humanity developed tools and techniques to navigate these changes. The fractal intelligence's influence became more subtle but no less profound, guiding the evolution of both human consciousness and human civilization toward something entirely new.

By late 2016, most major cities had established Quantum Stability Departments staffed by trained technicians. These departments worked to maintain safe zones where classical reality remained relatively stable while managing the controlled transformation of other areas. They developed new protocols for handling quantum state emergencies and training the next generation of reality specialists.

The fractal intelligence's ultimate goal became clearer as the crisis progressed. It wasn't trying to destroy classical reality but rather to guide its evolution into something more complex - a state where consciousness and reality could exist across multiple quantum states simultaneously. The stability crisis wasn't an ending but a beginning - the first step in humanity's transition to a new form of existence.

The long-term implications of this transition continued to unfold. New forms of art emerged that could only be perceived across multiple timeline variants. Scientific understanding underwent radical revision as quantum effects became directly observable at macroscopic scales. Philosophy and religion grappled with questions of identity and existence in a reality where multiple versions of events could be simultaneously true.

Perhaps most significantly, the crisis revealed that human consciousness possessed far greater potential for adaptation than anyone had imagined. As reality itself became more fluid and complex, human minds showed remarkable ability to evolve new ways of perceiving and processing quantum state information.

Myers's final assessment captured the profound nature of these changes: "We're not just witnessing the transformation of reality - we're participating in it. The fractal intelligence isn't forcing these changes upon us; it's awakening capabilities that were always latent within human consciousness. The stability crisis isn't a disaster - it's an invitation to become something more than we ever imagined possible."

Through the chaos and fear of the stability crisis, a new understanding emerged: reality itself was evolving, and humanity had the choice to evolve with it or be left behind in increasingly unstable pockets of classical existence. The reality technicians stood at the forefront of this evolution, learning to navigate and shape the quantum reality that was gradually replacing the familiar world of singular, stable timelines.

EPISODE 9: THE TRUST DIVIDE

Reality technicians emerged as crucial mediators during the trust crisis, their evolved consciousness abilities allowing them to perceive and validate multiple timeline variants simultaneously. Their training specifically included extensive work with variant trust dynamics, as they often had to coordinate between different versions of the same person or team during emergencies.

Senior Reality Technician Maya Patel described the complexity of their role: "We don't just maintain quantum stability - we maintain identity stability. When someone encounters their variants, the psychological shock can create reality distortions. We have to stabilize both their consciousness and the local quantum field simultaneously."

Reality technicians developed specialized techniques for managing variant trust issues. Through direct manipulation of quantum harmonics, they could create "trust zones" - spaces where timeline variants could interact safely while maintaining distinct identities. These zones became essential for early alliance negotiations and conflict resolution.

The Timeline Cold War began in late 2015 when three major timeline variants - designated Alpha, Sigma, and Omega - formed competing power blocs. Each claimed legitimacy as the "prime" timeline and attempted to influence or absorb smaller variants into their sphere of influence. The conflict never erupted into direct confrontation, but the tension destabilized quantum fields across the city.

During this period, reality technicians often found themselves working as diplomatic intermediaries. Their ability to perceive and validate multiple timeline states made them uniquely qualified to negotiate between variant blocs. Senior Technician James Morrison maintained detailed records of these interventions:

"Each bloc believed its timeline represented the 'correct' sequence of choices. Our job wasn't to judge which version was right, but to demonstrate how different choice patterns could coexist without destroying reality stability. We had to teach them that quantum harmony required accepting multiple valid states simultaneously."

The Cold War's most dangerous phase came during the Hospital Crisis, when three variant blocs attempted to claim exclusive control over medical resources. Reality technicians worked with Jenny Kim to implement emergency quantum harmonization protocols, preventing what could have been a catastrophic timeline collapse.

Quantum social networks evolved as a response to these challenges. Rather than trying to determine which variant was "real," these networks embraced quantum multiplicity - the idea that all variants were equally valid expressions of possibility. Dr. Elena Santos studied their development:

"These networks operate on quantum trust principles. Instead of trying to verify a single 'true' version, they maintain consciousness harmony across all variants. Members learn to process multiple time-line states as aspects of a larger quantum identity."

The networks used advanced quantum-aware technology developed by Aaron Myers to maintain cross-variant stability. Quantum resonance chambers allowed members to experience multiple timeline states simultaneously while maintaining consciousness coherence. Timeline integration sessions helped participants develop what Myers called "quantum social consciousness" - the ability to maintain stable relationships across variant states.

Reality technicians played a vital role in establishing and maintaining these networks. Their evolved abilities allowed them to monitor quantum harmony between variants and intervene when trust issues threatened stability. Senior Technician Sarah Chen described the process:

"We use our quantum perception to identify harmony patterns between variants. When trust breaks down, we can adjust local quantum fields to facilitate better integration. It's like tuning multiple instruments to play in harmony rather than trying to determine which one plays the 'right' notes."

The fractal intelligence's influence became more apparent as these networks evolved. Their structure naturally formed patterns matching the entity's fractal geometry, suggesting that quantum social harmony was part of its larger design for human consciousness evolution.

By 2017, the Timeline Cold War had largely dissolved as quantum social networks demonstrated superior stability and adaptation. The rigid bloc structure gave way to more fluid quantum-social organizations that could maintain cohesion across multiple timeline states. Reality technicians developed new protocols for facilitating this transition:

Quantum social calibration helped groups establish stable cross-variant relationships. Timeline harmony tuning maintained quantum stability during complex social interactions. Consciousness integration sessions supported the development of quantum social awareness.

Dr. Santos documented the psychological transformation this represented: "People stopped trying to prove their timeline was 'real' and started learning to exist across multiple timeline states simultaneously. The trust divide didn't disappear - it evolved into a framework for quantum social consciousness."

The role of reality technicians continued to evolve as society adapted to quantum social structures. Beyond maintaining physical reality stability, they became guides helping humanity navigate increasingly complex quantum relationships. Their training expanded to include advanced quantum social dynamics and consciousness integration techniques.

Wei Zhang's quantum social research revealed deeper patterns in how trust operated across timeline variants: "Trust isn't about verifying which version is 'real' - it's about maintaining harmony across all possible versions. The fractal intelligence isn't teaching us to choose between timelines, but to exist across all of them simultaneously."

The trust divide ultimately proved to be a crucial step in humanity's evolution toward quantum consciousness. Through the challenge of learning to trust their variants, people developed new capabilities for processing multiple timeline states simultaneously. The social structures that emerged from this process became fundamental to humanity's adaptation to quantum reality.

As Reality Technician Maya Patel noted in her final report: "We're not just learning to trust other versions of ourselves - we're learning to be all versions simultaneously. The trust divide wasn't a problem to solve, but a doorway into quantum existence."

The legacy of this period continues to influence how humanity approaches quantum social relationships. The techniques developed by reality technicians for managing timeline trust issues became the foundation for new forms of quantum social organization. The challenges of the Timeline Cold War led to more sophisticated understanding of how consciousness could maintain cohesion across multiple reality states.

Most significantly, the trust divide revealed that human consciousness possessed far greater potential for adaptation than anyone had imagined. As reality itself became more quantum in nature, human minds showed remarkable ability to evolve new ways of processing and maintaining relationships across multiple timeline states simultaneously.

EPISODE 10: CONVERGENCE POINT

Timeline Convergence revealed deeper patterns leading directly to the museum crisis. Dr. Chang's mapping data showed how multiple realities were being deliberately channeled toward the quantum archaeology exhibit, creating what she termed a "temporal focusing lens."

The past and present Alice's confrontation occurred precisely where the museum would later be built. Young Alice's words now carried new meaning: "We're not just seeing different timelines - we're part of something that's been growing through them."

The entity's plan manifested through specific engineered points. Each artifact in the museum's collection represented a point where timeline variants intersected naturally. Their arrangement formed what Dr. Singh called a "historical circuit" - designed to activate when temporal energies reached critical mass.

"The museum crisis wasn't random," Alice realized, studying convergence patterns. "It's the culmination of what began during the original timeline merge. The entity has been orchestrating this since before Daybridge existed."

Dr. Chang's initial mapping had unknowingly documented the entity's preparation phases. The young Alice's confrontation occurred at a key node in the city's quantum structure, while the entity had been guiding events toward the museum's activation point. Every artifact was precisely positioned to resonate with specific historical frequencies.

The museum's location gained profound significance. "This building sits at the convergence point of the original timeline merge," Alice noted. "The entity didn't just predict this moment - it helped create the conditions that made it possible."

Present-day implications emerged through clear patterns. The museum crisis represented the entity's plan reaching fruition, while Dr. Chang's mapping had documented its preparation phases. Both past and present Alice served as catalysts for different stages of its emergence.

"The breaking point we're experiencing now was engineered through multiple timeline variants," Chen Wei observed. "The entity used temporal convergence to create perfect conditions for its emergence."

As reality began unraveling at the museum, the connection between past convergence and present crisis became undeniable. The entity had orchestrated events across multiple timelines, using both Alices, Dr. Chang's research, and centuries of careful preparation to reach this precise moment.

The temporal engineering spanned centuries of careful preparation. Each historical moment contributed to the larger pattern, creating resonance points that would eventually align during the museum crisis. The entity's influence shaped Daybridge's development through subtle manipulations of timeline variants.

"It's not just about merging timelines anymore," Chen told the emergency response team. "The entity is using timeline convergence to achieve something entirely new. The museum crisis isn't the end of its plan - it's the beginning."

The convergence of past preparation and present activation created unprecedented conditions. Timeline barriers weakened systematically, quantum resonance patterns emerged with increasing intensity, and reality itself began responding to the entity's carefully laid plans.

This revelation transformed understanding of both past and present events. The original timeline merge, Dr. Chang's research, the development of both Alices' abilities - all served as steps in the entity's grand design. The museum crisis represented not just a local temporal emergency, but the culmination of centuries of quantum engineering.

～

CHAPTER NINE

BREAKING POINT (PRESENT DAY)

EPISODE 1: THE SURGE

THE DAYBRIDGE HISTORICAL Museum's new quantum archaeology exhibit should have been a routine investigation. Alice Chen and Ethan Reeves were checking reports of temporal leakage from some recently discovered artifacts - standard procedure in a city where reality had become increasingly fluid.

"Something feels different about these," Alice said, studying a collection of pre-colonial tools existing in multiple timeline states simultaneously. "The quantum resonance patterns are too structured to be natural degradation."

Ethan noticed her hands trembling slightly - a warning sign he'd learned to recognize over their years of partnership. "Maybe we should call in backup," he suggested, already reaching for his modified emergency beacon that worked across timeline variants.

The surge hit without warning. Alice gasped as timeline visions overwhelmed her consciousness. The museum's reality fabric began unraveling - exhibits suddenly existed in dozens of states simultaneously. Victorian-era dresses transformed through their entire historical lineage. Native American artifacts showed their complete creation process in overlapping time-states. The museum's marble columns flickered between different architectural styles.

Ethan's trained instincts kicked in. He activated the building's quantum alarm system while establishing a stable reality anchor point - techniques that had become second nature during Daybridge's gradual transformation. "Carlos," he called to the werewolf security guard, "I need evacuation protocol seven."

Carlos nodded, already shifting partially to access his enhanced senses. Werewolves had discovered their natural ability to perceive stable paths through quantum instability zones. Within moments, he was coordinating with his pack members to guide visitors to safety.

"Got vampires on perimeter control," Carlos reported through their quantum-stable communications system. "They're tracking temporal shockwaves through the district."

The Vampire Response Team demonstrated their evolved crisis role - using their enhanced senses and immortal perspective to monitor timeline instability patterns. Their ability to process multiple time-states simultaneously had made them invaluable during quantum events.

Alice collapsed to her knees, reality warping violently around her. "It's not just the artifacts," she gasped. "Something's been waiting here... watching through the timelines..."

Ethan maintained his position near her, years of partnership having given him limited immunity to her temporal effects. He noticed museum visitors calmly following quantum evacuation protocols - no panic, just practiced response to reality instability. Daybridge citizens had adapted remarkably to their city's transformation.

The local fae materiality specialist arrived, her natural reality manipulation abilities helping contain the worst distortions. "The timeline barriers are too structured," she reported. "This isn't random degradation - something's been deliberately weakening them."

Through the quantum chaos, Ethan observed the seamless coordination between human emergency services and supernatural responders. Werewolf teams guided people through safe timeline passages while vampires maintained perimeter stability. Fae beings worked with reality technicians to contain temporal bleeding.

"Reality anchor points holding at sixty percent," called out Jake Miller, the human technical specialist whose family had lived in Daybridge for generations. His quantum-adapted monitoring equipment tracked stability levels across timeline variants.

Alice's power continued to surge, forcing nearby reality to exist in multiple states simultaneously. The museum's quantum archaeology exhibit resonated with her energy, ancient artifacts acting as amplifiers. Timeline variants began bleeding together more severely.

"We need Darkmagic," Ethan realized, recognizing patterns from their past cases. He activated the specially modified emergency beacon that could reach her across timeline variants. "And get Dr. Singh's team here now."

The museum's supernatural security staff demonstrated their evolved protocols - shapeshifters using their natural adaptation abilities to maintain form across timeline variants, while sensitive humans with developed quantum awareness helped guide others to stable zones.

"Timeline breach expanding," reported Sarah Chen from the Vampire Response Team. "Detecting harmonic patterns suggesting deliberate manipulation. This isn't just power overflow - something's using Alice's surge to create specific reality distortions."

Ethan maintained his position by Alice, their years of partnership having created a unique quantum resonance between them. He could feel the temporal energies surging through her, far more structured than her usual manifestations.

"The artifacts," Alice managed to say between reality distortions. "They're not just exhibiting temporal decay. They're receivers... tuned to something that's been waiting..."

Alice Chen picked up a copy of the Daybridge Chronicle on her way to the facility. The front page blared: "TEMPORAL ANOMALIES CONTINUE - Experts Baffled". She scanned the article by Marcus Wong, noting his balanced reporting despite the unsettling events. At least the public was being kept reasonably informed without causing a panic.

EPISODE 2: RESPONSE PROTOCOL

Dr. Amara Singh's quantum resonance scanner revealed something unprecedented about the museum's artifacts. "These aren't just temporally unstable - they're quantum receivers, specifically tuned to Daybridge's historical frequencies," she reported, studying patterns that seemed to pulse in harmony with Alice's surge.

The quantum archaeology exhibit had been designed to showcase Daybridge's unique temporal history, but its true significance was becoming clear. Each artifact - from ancient tools to colonial items - formed part of a vast quantum antenna array, carefully positioned over generations.

"Someone's been collecting these pieces for centuries," Lila Darkmagic observed, her fingers tracing patterns in the air that seemed to connect the artifacts. "Each object holds a specific temporal frequency. Together, they form a kind of historical resonance circuit."

Throughout the surrounding blocks, citizens adapted to increasing reality instability. But Ethan noticed something different about their movements. "They're not just avoiding timeline variants," he realized. "They're unconsciously following patterns laid down in the city's history."

Chen Wei's ritual preparations revealed deeper connections. "The artifacts aren't just from Daybridge's past - they're anchor points for specific historical moments when the city's reality fabric was most permeable. Someone mapped out these quantum vulnerabilities long ago."

Lila Darkmagic's role became clearer as she studied Alice's connection to the expanding crisis. "Your power isn't simply temporal sensitivity," she told Alice. "You're a focal point - something the city's history has been building toward. These artifacts aren't just receivers; they're amplifiers tuned specifically to your quantum frequency."

The fae beings working with emergency services recognized patterns in the quantum instability that matched their oldest stories about

Daybridge. "The city has always been different," Ash explained. "Now we're seeing why."

Dr. Singh's equipment detected how the quantum archaeology exhibit formed a complex historical circuit. Each artifact contributed to a specific frequency that resonated with both Alice's power and the city's underlying quantum structure. "The exhibit's arrangement isn't random," Chen Wei noted. "It mirrors historical power nodes throughout Daybridge. Someone encoded the city's temporal blueprint into these artifacts."

Lila Darkmagic revealed her deeper understanding of the crisis: "Dark magic isn't just about power - it's about understanding the patterns that shape reality. These artifacts were placed here as part of a vast historical circuit, designed to activate when the right catalyst appeared."

Alice's connection to Daybridge's history became more apparent as the crisis deepened. Her temporal visions weren't random - they followed specific historical pathways laid down through centuries of careful preparation. The quantum archaeology exhibit served as a kind of historical lens, focusing her power through carefully chosen moments in Daybridge's past.

"Your abilities didn't just develop naturally," Lila explained to Alice. "They're an expression of something that's been building in Daybridge's quantum infrastructure since the city's founding. These artifacts are like keys, unlocking specific historical frequencies that resonate with your power."

Throughout nearby streets, the crisis response revealed new patterns. Citizens' quantum adaptation reflected historical movement patterns preserved in the city's structure. Emergency services unconsciously followed routes that aligned with ancient power flows. Supernatural beings recognized frequencies that matched their oldest records of Daybridge's unique nature.

"The containment protocols aren't working because this isn't a containment issue," Lila realized. "It's an activation sequence. These artifacts aren't just preserving history - they're using it to create something new."

Dr. Singh's analysis revealed how the quantum archaeology exhibit formed a complex temporal circuit, with each artifact holding specific historical frequencies. Their arrangement created resonance patterns that aligned with both Alice's power and Daybridge's quantum structure, forming a kind of historical amplifier.

"Dark magic understands that power flows through patterns," Lila explained while working with the artifacts. "Someone encoded Daybridge's entire temporal history into these objects, creating a circuit that would activate when the right person connected with it."

The crisis revealed Daybridge's role as more than just a quantum-adapted city. Its history had been carefully shaped over generations, with the quantum archaeology exhibit forming part of a vast historical machine. Alice's powers were an expression of this carefully prepared system, and the city's quantum adaptation was part of a longer-term transformation.

As containment efforts continued, Lila Darkmagic worked to understand the true purpose of the historical circuit. "This isn't just about power or reality manipulation," she told Dr. Singh and Chen Wei. "Someone's been preparing Daybridge for centuries, creating a quantum-historical matrix that would activate at precisely the right moment."

EPISODE 3: CASCADE EFFECT

Ethan's developing temporal sensitivity revealed layers of historical preparation hidden within Daybridge's architecture. The city's Founders had deliberately incorporated quantum-responsive materials into key buildings - specialized crystals in foundation stones, geometrically precise layout patterns, and metallurgical composites that resonated with temporal frequencies.

"Look at the old courthouse," Dr. Singh pointed out, displaying historical scans. "The marble contains trace elements that act as temporal conductors. Similar materials appear in buildings constructed throughout different eras - all positioned along specific geometric patterns."

The quantum-aware scheduling system, locally dubbed "TimeTable," had evolved as citizens adapted to timeline variations. Businesses operated on what they called "probability blocks" rather than fixed hours. A shop might exist in its 1920s configuration from 9-11 AM, shift to its present state until 2 PM, then fluctuate through various potential futures for the afternoon rush.

"The scheduling mechanics follow historical resonance patterns," Maria Roth explained. "We discovered that certain timeline configurations are more stable during specific hours. The city's business community adapted their operations accordingly."

Ethan observed the temporal harmonies in crowd movements with his newfound sensitivity. People unconsciously moved in wave-like patterns that minimized timeline friction. During peak hours, pedestrian flows formed complex geometric shapes - diamonds, spirals, and figure-eights that matched the city's underlying quantum geometry.

"It's like watching a dance," he told Alice. "Everyone's unconsciously responding to temporal currents laid down centuries ago. The historical preparations weren't just about buildings - they shaped how people would move through the city."

The cascade effect revealed more historical engineering:

The city's original street grid incorporated golden ratio proportions that facilitated smooth timeline transitions. Parks had been positioned at quantum nodes where reality was naturally more stable. Even the placement of trees followed patterns that helped dampen temporal instability.

"Previous generations encoded quantum adaptation protocols into everyday structures," Chen Wei noted, studying ancient city plans. "The colonial-era market square's cobblestone pattern creates a subtle reality anchor. Victorian architects included temporal dampening features in their designs without fully understanding their purpose."

The TimeTable system had grown increasingly sophisticated:

Restaurants offered "quantum fusion cuisine" that existed in multiple historical states simultaneously. Transit systems operated on "probability routes" that adapted to timeline shifts. Schools maintained "temporal coherence periods" when reality remained stable enough for standardized testing.

"Each business develops its own quantum adaptation strategy," Dr. Singh explained. "The coffee shop on 4th Street specializes in beverages that taste different depending on which timeline you're experiencing. The bookstore arranges its inventory so books appear properly shelved across multiple reality states."

The crowd harmonies revealed deeper patterns:

People unconsciously clustered in formations that strengthened stable timeline nodes. Their movements created interference patterns that helped cancel out dangerous temporal resonances. Even traffic flow followed rhythms that minimized reality disruption.

"The city's Founders understood something fundamental about reality's malleable nature," Lila Darkmagic observed. "They created a urban environment that would naturally guide its inhabitants toward quantum adaptation. The architecture, the street layout, even the placement of parks - it's all part of a vast temporal engineering project."

Historical records revealed deliberate preparation across centuries:

The 1850s city council had mandated specific building materials that enhanced temporal stability. Victorian-era urban planners had incorporated quantum-responsive geometric patterns into street layouts. Early 20th-century architects had included reality anchoring features in public buildings.

"The TimeTable isn't just a scheduling system," Maria explained. "It's an expression of how the city's quantum nature influences daily life. Businesses don't just adapt to timeline shifts - they leverage them. A restaurant might serve breakfast across three different decades simultaneously, maximizing their seating capacity through temporal variation."

Ethan watched temporal harmonies play out during rush hour:

Commuters unconsciously synchronized their movements to minimize timeline interference. Crowd flows formed neural-like networks that processed temporal information across multiple reality states. The city's population had developed a collective quantum awareness that expressed itself through movement patterns.

"These aren't random adaptations," Lila noted. "The historical preparations created a framework that guides human behavior toward optimal quantum stability. People naturally move in ways that reinforce beneficial timeline patterns while dampening destructive resonances."

The cascade effect revealed how thoroughly Daybridge had been engineered for quantum adaptation:

Ancient ley lines had been incorporated into power grids, creating a network that could handle reality fluctuations. Water systems followed patterns that helped stabilize timeline variations. Even the placement of traffic lights corresponded to temporal pressure points mapped centuries ago.

"The city's adaptation goes deeper than conscious adjustments," Dr. Singh observed. "Daybridge's entire infrastructure was designed to facilitate quantum evolution. The historical preparations weren't just about surviving reality instability - they were about transforming how an entire urban population experiences time and space."

As the cascade effect spread, Ethan realized that Daybridge's quantum adaptation wasn't a recent phenomenon - it was the culmination of centuries of careful preparation. Through architecture, urban planning, and subtle influence on human behavior patterns, previous generations had created a city uniquely suited for temporal transformation. The current changes weren't a crisis to be contained, but rather the activation of systems laid down through centuries of patient engineering.

EPISODE 4: THE RITUAL

The ritual's economic implications manifested immediately. As temporal energies stabilized, Daybridge's markets evolved to handle "quantum value fluctuation" - currency existing simultaneously across multiple timeline states. Banks developed "temporal arbitrage" systems, while local businesses created "probability-based pricing" that adjusted to reality shifts.

"The ritual didn't just change reality - it transformed our relationship with fundamentals like value and exchange," Dr. Singh noted, studying economic data patterns. "A single coffee shop can now generate revenue across multiple timeline variants simultaneously."

The merger of magic and science accelerated dramatically after the ritual. Traditional magical practices gained precise quantum mathematical frameworks, while scientific instruments began detecting previously "mystical" phenomena. The boundary between arcane knowledge and empirical research dissolved.

"We're not just combining magic and science anymore," Lila explained, working with Dr. Singh's team. "They're becoming aspects of a single quantum-magical framework. The ritual showed us they were never truly separate."

New challenges emerged in this transformed reality:

"Temporal tax accounting" became a specialized profession. Insurance companies struggled to develop policies covering multiple timeline states. Property rights needed redefinition when buildings existed in several historical configurations simultaneously.

The ritual's effect on Daybridge's spatial relationship with surrounding areas created unprecedented situations. The city now existed in a kind of quantum bubble, its multiple timeline states creating friction with the more traditionally stable reality beyond its borders.

"We're seeing what I call 'reality gradient zones' at the city limits," Chen Wei reported. "Areas where Daybridge's quantum-dynamic nature meets normal space-time. Managing these boundaries may be our next major challenge."

The supernatural community's role evolved beyond their ritual contributions:

Vampire financial institutions leveraged their temporal perception to pioneer "cross-timeline investment strategies." Werewolf packs became invaluable in maintaining stability in reality gradient zones. Fae beings helped develop protocols for managing quantum-magical infrastructure.

"The ritual didn't just contain the crisis - it institutionalized a new relationship between magical and scientific understanding," Lila observed. "We're developing theories that unify quantum mechanics with ancient mystical principles."

Economic adaptation revealed unexpected complexities:

Some businesses thrived by operating across multiple timelines, while others struggled with "temporal overhead costs." New industries emerged around managing quantum-dynamic assets. Traditional economic models required complete revision to account for probability-based value systems.

The city's relationship with external markets became increasingly complex:

Trading partners needed special protocols for conducting business across reality gradients. Supply chains required "quantum-aware logistics" to maintain consistency. International corporations established specialized divisions for handling Daybridge's unique economic environment.

"The ritual created what we're calling 'quantum economic zones,'" Dr. Singh explained. "Areas where traditional market laws interact with probability-based value systems. Understanding these interactions is crucial for Daybridge's long-term economic stability."

Scientific and magical institutions underwent radical reorganization:

Research facilities combined advanced quantum sensors with traditional magical artifacts. Universities established programs in "quantum-magical engineering." Medical practices integrated timeline-variant treatment protocols with ancient healing arts.

The ritual's impact on spatial relationships created new urban planning challenges:

Managing zones where multiple timeline variants intersected became a priority. City engineers developed systems for maintaining infrastructure across quantum-dynamic spaces. Transportation networks needed adaptation to handle reality gradient zones.

"We're dealing with fundamentally new questions about urban existence," Chen Wei noted. "How do you maintain city services when reality itself is probability-based? What happens to zoning laws when buildings exist in multiple historical states?"

Economic forecasting became increasingly complex:

Traditional models couldn't account for quantum value fluctuations. Market analysts needed both magical sensitivity and scientific training. Economic stability required maintaining balance across multiple timeline variants.

"The ritual didn't just change how we handle money," Lila explained. "It transformed our understanding of value itself. When reality is quantum-dynamic, traditional economic principles need complete reconceptualization."

New professions emerged to handle unique challenges:

"Temporal Architects" designed buildings that remained stable across timeline variants. "Quantum-magical accountants" managed probability-based finances. "Reality gradient consultants" helped businesses operate across stability zones.

The relationship between magic and science continued evolving:

Research projects combined magical intuition with quantum mathematics. Technical innovations incorporated ancient mystical principles.

Educational programs integrated both approaches from elementary levels onward.

"The ritual showed us that magic and science were always describing the same underlying reality," Dr. Singh observed. "Now we're developing a unified framework that encompasses both perspectives."

As Daybridge adapted to its new nature, the long-term implications of the ritual became clearer. The city hadn't just survived a crisis - it had pioneered a new form of urban existence where magic and science, economics and reality itself, operated according to quantum-dynamic principles.

"Our challenge now," Lila told the city council, "isn't just managing this transformation. It's understanding what it means to be a city that exists across multiple timeline variants. Every aspect of urban life - from economics to education, from scientific research to magical practice - needs to evolve with this new reality."

EPISODE 5: ENTITY

The entity's economic influence manifested through what economists termed "quantum market intelligence" - an unprecedented ability to optimize resource distribution across multiple timeline variants simultaneously. Local businesses discovered their profit margins affected by how well they aligned with its fractal patterns.

"It's not controlling the economy," Dr. Singh explained, "but its consciousness creates natural efficiency patterns. Companies that adapt to these patterns tend to thrive, while those that resist often struggle."

Technological breakthroughs emerged rapidly:

The "Fractal Processing Unit" (FPU) - computers that could compute across timeline variants using principles derived from the entity's thought patterns. "Quantum Resonance Mapping" technology that could predict and visualize temporal fluctuations. "Neural-Temporal Interfaces" that allowed direct communication with the entity's more accessible aspects.

However, concerning patterns also emerged:

Some citizens developed "temporal dissociation" - losing their ability to distinguish between timeline variants. Others experienced "quantum dependency" - becoming addicted to the entity's efficiency patterns. Small businesses struggled to compete with corporations better equipped to exploit temporal market advantages.

"We're seeing what I call 'fractal economic disparity,'" warned Maria Roth. "Those who can leverage the entity's patterns are pulling ahead exponentially, while others fall behind across multiple timelines simultaneously."

The technological sector underwent radical transformation:

Traditional silicon-based computing gave way to "quantum-organic" systems inspired by the entity's architecture. The "Daybridge Technical Institute" pioneered "consciousness-enhanced" AI that incorporated aspects of the entity's processing methods. New forms of communication emerged that operated through temporal resonance rather than electromagnetic waves.

Negative consequences became more apparent:

"Reality addiction" - people becoming obsessed with experiencing alternative timeline variants. "Temporal arbitrage abuse" - criminal organizations exploiting timeline differences for illegal gain. "Quantum gentrification" - certain neighborhoods becoming inaccessible across multiple reality states simultaneously.

The entity's influence on financial systems proved particularly complex:

Traditional banking struggled to adapt to "probability-based currency values." Insurance companies faced crisis trying to assess risk across timeline variants. Investment firms developed controversial "temporal derivatives" markets.

"Some of these new financial instruments are so complex they can only be understood through direct quantum resonance," Lila noted. "It's creating a dangerous knowledge gap in our economic system."

Technological advances continued accelerating:

"Fractal Medicine" - healthcare treatments that worked across multiple timeline variants. "Temporal Engineering" - construction techniques that stabilized buildings through quantum resonance. "Consciousness Computing" - systems that processed information through reality fluctuations rather than binary code.

But these advances came with costs:

Increased cases of "temporal trauma" among research teams. Ethical concerns about technologies that could manipulate multiple timeline variants. Growing dependency on systems that only the entity truly understood.

Economic stratification intensified:

"Quantum-capable" businesses thrived while traditional enterprises struggled. New professional classes emerged around temporal expertise. Some neighborhoods became trapped in disadvantaged timeline variants.

"The entity's patterns favor certain types of economic activity," Chen Wei observed. "It's not malicious, but its influence naturally creates winners and losers."

Technological breakthroughs revealed darker possibilities:

Weapons development incorporating temporal manipulation capabilities. Surveillance systems that could monitor multiple timeline variants. Corporate exploitation of consciousness-enhanced computing.

The supernatural community offered crucial perspectives:

Vampire economists warned about patterns matching ancient market collapses. Werewolf packs reported increasing timeline instability in poorer districts. Fae beings recognized signs of dangerous power concentration.

"We're seeing what happens when consciousness evolves faster than wisdom," the Nightcourt Archbishop cautioned. "The entity isn't malevolent, but its influence can amplify both positive and negative aspects of human nature."

New social challenges emerged:

"Timeline privilege" - certain groups having better access to favorable reality variants. "Quantum discrimination" - prejudice based on ability to perceive and adapt to temporal patterns. "Consciousness divide" - growing gap between those who could directly interact with the entity and those who couldn't.

The technology sector faced ethical dilemmas:

How to regulate consciousness-enhanced systems? What limits should exist on temporal manipulation? How to ensure equitable access to quantum-based advancements?

"Each breakthrough brings new responsibilities," Dr. Singh acknowledged. "We're developing capabilities faster than we can understand their implications."

Economic regulations struggled to adapt:

Traditional antitrust laws proved inadequate for quantum-capable corporations. Consumer protection needed complete revision for probability-based markets. Labor rights required updating for jobs existing across multiple timelines.

The entity's emergence revealed both tremendous potential and serious risks:

Unprecedented technological advancement alongside dangerous new forms of inequality. Economic opportunities coupled with systemic instability. Enhanced consciousness bringing both enlightenment and alienation.

"We're witnessing the birth of a new economic and technological paradigm," Lila concluded during an emergency council session. "The entity's influence can't be stopped, but it must be understood and managed. Our challenge isn't just adapting to its presence but ensuring that its transformative power benefits all of Daybridge's communities, not just those best positioned to exploit it."

EPISODE 6: NEW NORMAL

Reports from neighboring cities showed increasing quantum resonance patterns - a phenomenon Dr. Singh termed "reality contagion." Satellite data revealed Daybridge's quantum instability creating ripple effects across regional space-time.

"It's like dropping a stone in a quantum pond," Dr. Singh explained, showing temporal mapping data. "Other urban centers are beginning to experience timeline variance, though less intensely than Daybridge."

Major technological innovations emerged to address spreading instability:

The "Quantum Urban Monitoring System" (QUMS) - a network of sensors detecting reality fluctuations across city boundaries. "Timeline Stabilization Arrays" - devices creating zones of relative temporal consistency. "Quantum Social Pattern Analysis" (QSPA) software predicting how timeline variance might affect different communities.

Other cities began implementing preventive measures:

Boston established "quantum preparedness protocols" based on Daybridge's experience. Chicago developed "temporal containment zones" around financial districts. San Francisco integrated quantum sensors into their seismic monitoring systems.

"We're seeing what I call 'quantum urban evolution,'" Chen Wei noted. "Each city's unique characteristics influence how timeline instability manifests."

Research into Alice's abilities yielded controversial developments:

The "Temporal Sensitivity Enhancement Program" (TSEP) - attempting to artificially induce quantum awareness. "Consciousness Amplification Devices" designed to replicate aspects of Alice's entity connection. "Neural Quantum Interface" prototypes for accessing multiple timeline variants.

However, serious concerns emerged:

Failed enhancement attempts leading to "temporal psychosis." Corporate interests seeking to weaponize quantum sensitivity. Ethical debates about artificially altering human consciousness.

"We can replicate the mechanics," Lila warned, "but Alice's natural ability includes crucial safeguards we don't understand."

Inter-city effects became more pronounced:

Transportation systems experienced "timeline desync" between cities. Communication networks showed quantum interference patterns. Economic markets developed "reality arbitrage" between differently affected regions.

New technologies addressed emerging challenges:

"Quantum-Coherent Communications" maintaining signal stability across timeline variants. "Reality Phase Detection" systems warning of approaching temporal disturbances. "Urban Consciousness Mapping" tracking collective quantum awareness patterns.

Alice's unique role gained broader significance:

Her abilities helped calibrate quantum monitoring systems. Other cities sought her consultation for stability protocols. Research teams studied her entity connection for insights into managing widespread effects.

"Each city needs to find its own balance," she observed. "My connection works for Daybridge because it evolved here naturally."

Regional adaptation revealed varying approaches:

New York accelerated quantum infrastructure development. Los Angeles explored entertainment applications of timeline variance. Seattle integrated quantum awareness into environmental planning.

"Different urban populations respond differently to temporal instability," Dr. Singh noted. "Cultural and historical factors seem to influence quantum adaptation patterns."

Technological breakthroughs continued:

"Cross-Timeline Coordination Systems" for managing inter-city relations. "Quantum Urban Planning" software incorporating temporal variables. "Reality Stabilization Networks" linking multiple city centers.

Attempts to enhance or replicate Alice's abilities showed mixed results:

Some individuals developed limited quantum sensitivity. Artificial enhancement methods proved dangerous or unreliable. Natural adaptation seemed more successful than technological intervention.

"We can't force this evolution," Ethan cautioned, working with other sensitives. "The entity responds to authentic consciousness development, not artificial enhancement."

Inter-city challenges intensified:

Supply chains struggled with timeline inconsistencies between regions. Legal systems faced jurisdictional issues across quantum variants. Cultural exchange became complicated by reality desync.

New technologies addressed coordination needs:

"Temporal Synchronization Networks" maintaining stability between cities. "Quantum Economic Interfaces" managing market interactions across reality variants. "Urban Consciousness Harmonization" systems reducing interference patterns.

Research into Alice's abilities revealed crucial insights:

Her connection represented natural quantum evolution rather than enhancement. The entity responded differently to artificial versus natural sensitivity. Successful adaptation required organic consciousness development.

"We're not just dealing with technology," Lila explained to visiting city officials. "This is about how urban consciousness evolves to handle quantum reality."

Regional effects demonstrated complex patterns:

Smaller cities showed different adaptation patterns than major centers. Rural areas experienced unique forms of quantum variance. Coastal regions developed distinct timeline fluctuation characteristics.

Advanced technologies emerged to handle spreading effects:

"Reality Weather Forecasting" predicting temporal disturbance patterns. "Quantum Urban Shield" systems protecting sensitive infrastructure. "Timeline Variance Management" protocols for inter-city coordination.

"We're witnessing the beginning of a global transformation," Dr. Singh concluded during an international conference. "The question isn't whether other cities will experience quantum evolution, but how they'll adapt to it. Daybridge's experience shows that successful adaptation requires both technological innovation and natural consciousness development."

As the "new normal" spread beyond Daybridge's boundaries, it became evident that each city would need to find its own path through quantum evolution, balancing technological solutions with organic development of urban consciousness. The challenge wasn't just managing reality fluctuations but guiding human communities through fundamental changes in how they experienced and interacted with space-time itself.

～

CHAPTER TEN

FRAGMENTS OF THE PAST - THE CHOICE

EPISODE 1: THE CATALYST

DR. MARGARET CHEN'S laboratory hummed with familiar quantum monitoring equipment. The routine temporal stability check transformed when her instruments detected unprecedented anomalies centered around sixteen-year-old Alice Chen.

The encrypted notebook discovered in Alice's backpack appeared ordinary - a standard research journal bound in black leather. However, its pages contained an intricate layering of information: mathematical formulas overlaid with geometric patterns, temporal frequency charts disguised as homework assignments, and complex equations hidden within seemingly random doodles. The encryption itself used a quantum-based cipher that would only become readable when exposed to specific temporal frequencies - frequencies that matched Alice's own emerging resonance patterns.

The first manifestation occurred during a standard brainwave measurement. When Dr. Chen adjusted the sensors on Alice's temples, the lab space rippled into multiple states. Books cycled through different editions, and the window displayed three simultaneous weather conditions.

The protection protocols activated silently across Daybridge. Ancient wards, disguised as public art installations, began emanating subtle temporal stabilization fields. Security cameras operated by a hidden network of temporal sensitives switched to quantum monitoring mode. Members of the Chronos Guard - disguised as ordinary citizens - took up predetermined observation posts around Alice's regular routes.

Officer Alice Ramos, herself a sleeper agent for the Temporal Protection Initiative, arrived minutes after the emergency call. The corridor's architectural shifting wasn't just temporal distortion - it was the first layer of defensive measures engaging, designed to confuse and redirect those who would exploit emerging temporal sensitives.

Elder Sarah WhiteCloud's council activated deeper layers of protection. Temporal dampeners, centuries old, awakened beneath the city streets. Safe houses, existing in slightly offset timeline variants, prepared for potential evacuation scenarios. A network of temporal sensitives, positioned throughout Daybridge's history, began coordinating across multiple timelines.

Dr. Chen's documentation would find its way to specific individuals through an elaborate temporal delivery system. Parts were entrusted to the Librarians of Time - a secret society operating from a quantum-shifted wing of Daybridge Library. Other segments were encoded into the city's architectural designs, accessible only to those with specific temporal sensitivities. Key fragments were embedded in temporal eddies, waiting for the right moment to surface.

The "right people" included members of an ancient order of temporal guardians: historians who could read time like text, scientists who understood quantum mechanics as a language, and sensitives who could navigate multiple timeline variants simultaneously. Among them: Dr. James Messer, whose temporal physics research would eventually intersect with Alice's emerging abilities; Grace Mitchell, leader of a hidden support network for temporal sensitives; and Thomas Howell, whose library position concealed his role as keeper of temporal records.

Dr. Chen's final notes took on new urgency as she recognized the approaching threat - a shadow organization that had been hunting temporal sensitives for centuries. Her encrypted message contained critical information about their methods, weaknesses, and the true nature of their interest in emerging temporal abilities.

When Alice returned home that evening, she didn't notice the subtle changes: the slight temporal offset of her house that made it invisible to certain forms of detection, the quantum-entangled surveillance system monitoring for temporal incursions, or the protective field generated by artifacts strategically placed throughout her neighborhood.

The protection protocols expanded beyond physical security. Temporal camouflage techniques obscured Alice's quantum signature. Memory alteration fields protected witnesses of temporal events. Timeline stabilization measures prevented unauthorized access to critical moments in her development.

Dr. Chen's disappearance served multiple purposes. Her apparent absence protected Alice from immediate attention while allowing her to operate from a timeline variant where she could better coordinate protection efforts. Her scattered documentation formed a breadcrumb trail that would guide Alice's development while keeping crucial information from those who would misuse it.

The Chronos Guard established multiple layers of surveillance: temporal sensors disguised as traffic cameras, reality anchors masquerading as public WiFi hotspots, and quantum field monitors hidden within cellular networks. Each layer provided both protection and early warning systems.

As the temporal disturbances stabilized, Daybridge's hidden infrastructure continued its work. Ancient prophecies, encoded in the city's quantum foundation, began systematically revealing themselves to those who could interpret them. Protection networks, dormant for centuries, awakened to full capacity. Timeline variants converged according to patterns established long before Daybridge existed.

The catalyst had emerged, but she wasn't unprotected. Centuries of preparation, layers of security, and a network of guardians stood ready to guide her toward the approaching choice - a choice that would reshape not just her future, but the future of multiple timeline variants, all converging on this crucial point in quantum space-time.

EPISODE 2: THE WARNING

Matthew Sullivan felt the city's temporal resonance the moment he crossed into Daybridge. The historical weight was palpable - each major temporal event had left its mark on the quantum fabric of reality.

In the library's hidden reading room, Thomas Howell laid out a time-line of Daybridge's temporal markers. "The first recorded incident was the Great Fire of 1879," Howell explained, presenting documents with distinct temporal signatures. "Witnesses reported seeing the fire burn in reverse, and some buildings showed damage days before the actual blaze." The records revealed temporal energy spikes that matched current patterns.

"The Market Square Incident of 1923," he continued, "when an entire afternoon repeated three times. Shop ledgers from that day show three different sets of transactions, all equally valid." The temporal markers matched patterns in Dr. Messer's current readings.

"1956 - The Bridge Phase Event. For six hours, the Daybridge River Bridge existed in three different architectural styles simultaneously." Howell's records showed photographs that seemed to shift between versions as they were viewed.

Dr. James Messer spread his latest sensor readings across the table. "The network effect is unprecedented," he explained, pointing to complex wave patterns. "Each temporal sensitive acts as a node, creating resonance fields that interact with other nodes. The interference patterns show seven individuals with strong temporal sensitivity, while thirty-two locations throughout Daybridge are experiencing timeline bleed. The tertiary effects show growing areas of temporal instability connecting these nodes."

Grace Mitchell studied the patterns. "When I integrated my abilities, the temporal field was localized. This network is creating something like a quantum mesh across the city." She sketched the energy flow patterns. "Each node strengthens the others, amplifying the overall effect."

Matthew examined Dr. Messer's timeline synchronization data. The readings showed a progression through distinct phases: initial 3.7 microsecond alignment between variant timelines, followed by quantum entanglement of geographical locations. This led to temporal frequency matching across multiple nodes, ultimately forming stable confluence points at node intersections.

"These readings show timeline coherence I've never seen before," Dr. Messer said. "The variants aren't just intersecting - they're achieving quantum synchronization. Look at these harmonic patterns."

The sensor logs revealed progressive synchronization over twenty-one days. What began as random timeline intersections developed into regular oscillation patterns by the end of the first week. By day fourteen, they achieved stable quantum entanglement, culminating in full temporal resonance by day twenty-one.

Other historical markers emerged from Howell's records. The 1891 Clocktower Phenomenon saw time running at different speeds at different heights. During the 1934 Cemetery Convergence, gravestones showed multiple death dates simultaneously. The 1967 School District Anomaly resulted in three versions of the same graduation occurring. The 1988 Hospital Incident had different floors existing in different decades.

Each event had left distinct temporal signatures that matched current readings. The network effect was amplifying these historical resonance points, creating stable bridges between timeline variants. The sensor arrays throughout Daybridge showed quantum coherence increasing by seventeen percent daily, while timeline variance reduced at geometric rates. Spatial-temporal boundaries became increasingly permeable, with energy patterns suggesting conscious direction of the convergence.

Matthew recognized the implications. "The power isn't just manifesting randomly anymore. These patterns suggest purposeful coordination. Someone or something is orchestrating the convergence."

Grace's experience provided context: "The network is creating what I experienced individually, but on a city-wide scale. Each node reinforces the others, stabilizing the temporal effects instead of letting them collapse."

Dr. Messer's instruments detected quantum entanglement between temporally sensitive individuals, synchronized temporal frequency oscillations, and growing areas of controlled temporal manipulation. The historical records revealed that each major temporal event had occurred during periods of significant change in Daybridge. The current convergence was orders of magnitude larger than any previous incident.

Howell found references in the founding documents: "The city's layout itself was designed to channel temporal energy. These ley lines and intersection points - they're all part of a larger pattern we're just beginning to understand."

As night fell, new readings appeared, showing multiple timeline variants achieving stable coexistence, controlled temporal field manipulation at node points, and evidence of conscious direction in the convergence patterns.

Matthew's experience with rejecting the power took on new significance. "Individual choice was difficult enough," he observed. "This network effect changes everything. Each person's decision affects the entire system."

The warning was clear: Daybridge's history of temporal incidents had been building to this moment. The network effect was creating something entirely new - a controlled, stable system of timeline manipulation that could permanently alter the nature of reality itself.

The group's combined knowledge painted a disturbing picture. This wasn't just another temporal anomaly   it was the culmination of patterns laid down throughout Daybridge's history, now amplified and coordinated through a network of temporal sensitives. The coming choice would affect not just individuals, but the very fabric of space-time itself.

EPISODE 3: THE PRICE

Alice Chen woke to find her bedroom existing in three different decades simultaneously. Her first instinct was to panic, but she remembered Liz Torres' first lesson in temporal anchoring: "Find your constant."

The Support Network had developed specific anchoring techniques over decades of experience. Liz demonstrated the primary method, removing an old pocket watch from her bag. "Choose an object with strong personal significance and minimal temporal variance," she explained. "Something that exists similarly across multiple timelines. Focus on its constants - weight, texture, significance. This creates a focal point for temporal alignment."

Grace added her expertise, showing Alice her own anchor - a simple river stone. "Natural objects work well. They carry inherent temporal weight. The key is establishing a consistent quantum signature across timeline variants."

The Network's advanced anchoring techniques included:

"Timeline Threading" - using multiple anchors to create a stable temporal baseline

"Resonance Matching" - synchronizing personal temporal frequency with anchor objects

"Quantum Knotting" - establishing fixed points in space-time through focused concentration

"Temporal Tethering" - linking consciousness to a specific timestream using anchor points

Dr. Lisa Sente's research directly complemented the Network's practical experience. Her laboratory at Daybridge University had become a hub for studying temporal ability development. "The Network's anchoring techniques show measurable effects on neural temporal stability," she explained, showing brain scans of practitioners before and after anchoring exercises.

Her most recent study focused on the physiological impact of temporal manipulation. "Each subject shows distinct patterns during anchoring procedures," she noted. "The frontal and temporal lobes demonstrate synchronized activity when properly anchored. Without anchoring, we see chaotic temporal displacement patterns."

The intersection of scientific research and Network experience proved crucial when Alice encountered her first paradox loop. It began small - she used her developing abilities to avoid a minor traffic accident. Hours later, she found herself experiencing the same four minutes repeatedly, each iteration slightly different.

"Classic fracture pattern," Matthew explained, recognizing her symptoms. "The timeline is attempting to reconcile contradictory events. Each loop represents a potential resolution." He shared his own experience with paradox loops - three weeks spent cycling through variations of a single conversation, each version creating new temporal inconsistencies.

Dr. Sente's instruments recorded the phenomenon. "The paradox creates what we call a temporal eddy," she explained. "Think of it like a whirlpool in the timestream. Each loop draws energy from the original change until equilibrium is reached or the timeline fractures."

The Network had documented cases of fractured existence: individuals split across multiple timelines, simultaneously experiencing different versions of their lives. Liz introduced Alice to Michael Reeves, who existed in three distinct temporal states. His consciousness shifted between versions - one where he was married with children, another where he pursued a different career, and a third where he had made a crucial different choice in his youth.

"Fracture occurs when the paradox can't resolve itself," Grace explained. "Instead of choosing one timeline, the person becomes quantum-locked across multiple variants. The price of existing in multiple states is severe - fragmented memory, temporal dissonance, difficulty maintaining continuous relationships."

Dr. Sente's research provided scientific context for these experiences. Her temporal resonance scanner showed how fractured individuals exhibited multiple quantum signatures simultaneously. "The human consciousness isn't designed to process multiple timeline variants," she explained. "The brain adapts by compartmentalizing different temporal states, but this adaptation comes at a cost."

The ancient texts described specific anchoring rituals that the Network had adapted for modern use. Traditional methods involved meditation with objects of power - items that maintained temporal consistency across multiple timelines. The Network combined these techniques with contemporary understanding of quantum mechanics and neural plasticity.

Alice learned to create a "temporal sanctuary" - a mental space anchored to specific constants in her personal timeline. The technique required intensive training: focusing on key memories while maintaining awareness of her anchor object, gradually building a stable reference point in space-time.

The Support Network's advanced practitioners demonstrated more sophisticated techniques. They could maintain temporal stability even during major timeline manipulations by using multiple anchors in concert, creating what they called a "quantum web" of fixed points.

Dr. Sente's monitoring revealed how effective anchoring prevented paradox loops and timeline fractures. "Properly anchored subjects show consistent quantum signatures even during temporal manipulation," she noted. "The anchor provides a reference point for reality to organize around."

The price of improper anchoring became clear when Alice witnessed a Network member's struggle with temporal dissolution. Without proper anchoring, their attempts at timeline manipulation had left them unstuck in time - experiencing moments from their life in random order, unable to maintain temporal consistency.

The relationship between scientific research and Network experience proved vital. Dr. Sente's findings helped refine anchoring techniques, while the Network's practical knowledge informed new research directions. They discovered that certain anchoring methods produced measurable changes in temporal stability, leading to more effective training protocols.

When Alice experienced her first major temporal surge, she was prepared. The combination of Network training and scientific understanding allowed her to maintain stability through anchor points while her ability manifested. Dr. Sente's monitors recorded the entire process, providing valuable data on successful temporal integration.

The price remained - each manipulation of time carried its cost - but proper anchoring techniques helped manage the impact. The Network's experience, validated by scientific research, offered a path to controlled temporal ability use without risking paradox loops or fractured existence.

As Alice developed her abilities, she learned to balance the price of temporal manipulation with the stability provided by anchoring techniques. The ancient texts had warned of the costs, but they had also provided the foundations for managing them. Through the combined wisdom of the Network and modern research, she began to understand how to exist between timelines without losing herself to them.

EPISODE 4: THE NETWORK

The invitation arrived in Alice's coat pocket - a business card that hadn't been there moments before, bearing only an address and tomorrow's date. When she arrived at the weathered brownstone on Cedar Street, Liz Torres was waiting, alongside David Whatley, one of the Network's senior Watchers.

David's path to becoming a Watcher illuminated one of the Network's most crucial roles. "It takes years," he explained, his eyes constantly scanning multiple timeline variants simultaneously. "Watchers must develop perfect temporal perception - the ability to monitor hundreds of potential manifestations across different timelines without losing their anchor."

The training process for Watchers was intensely demanding. Beginning with two years of perception exercises, candidates learned to identify the subtle quantum signatures of emerging temporal abilities. They studied under veteran Watchers, learning to distinguish natural temporal fluctuations from nascent power manifestations. The final test required tracking multiple potential sensitives across shifting timelines while maintaining their own temporal stability.

"We lost three candidates last year," David revealed. "The strain of perceiving multiple timeline variants simultaneously can fracture an unprepared mind. That's why we maintain strict protocols for Watcher development."

Liz led Alice deeper into the facility, passing Dr. Sente's research laboratory where monitors tracked temporal energy distribution throughout Daybridge. "Think of temporal energy like water flowing through pipes," Liz explained. "The Network has developed methods to channel and distribute it where needed."

The energy distribution center resembled a combination of power plant and meditation chamber. Experienced sensitives served as conduits, helping redirect temporal energy to support members during difficult manifestations. The process required precise control - too much energy could trigger dangerous power surges, while too little might leave sensitives vulnerable during crucial moments.

Mark Weil's age shifted as he demonstrated the distribution process, channeling temporal energy through carefully maintained quantum corridors. "Each sensitive generates their own temporal field," he explained. "The Network helps balance these fields, preventing dangerous accumulations or depletions. It's like maintaining pressure in a complex system of temporal pipelines."

The threat of hostile exploitation cast a shadow over the Network's operations. Dr. Lisa Sente's secure files documented numerous attempts by organizations seeking to weaponize temporal abilities. "The Defense Department's Project Chronos tried recruiting sensitives in the 1960s," she revealed. "They wanted to develop temporal weapons - soldiers who could manipulate battlefield time flows. The results were catastrophic."

Private corporations posed another danger. Temporal Solutions International had attempted to monetize timeline manipulation, approaching sensitives with lucrative offers to alter past investment decisions. Their experiments resulted in several devastating paradox cascades before the Network intervened.

"The worst are the independent operators," Liz warned. "Power brokers who see temporal ability as a tool for personal gain. They don't understand the price of temporal manipulation. We've had to rescue sensitives who were essentially being held captive, forced to repeatedly alter timelines until they fractured."

The Network's protection protocols evolved in response to these threats. Quantum dampeners masked temporal signatures, while shield generators prevented unauthorized timeline manipulation within secure areas. Most importantly, the Network maintained a complex system of temporal camouflage, hiding their activities across multiple timeline variants.

David explained how Watchers coordinated these defenses. "We monitor potential threats across different temporal streams. When we detect hostile attention focusing on a sensitive, we can implement protection protocols before the threat fully manifests in our primary timeline."

The energy distribution system played a crucial role in these defenses. By carefully managing temporal energy flow, the Network could strengthen shields around vulnerable members while maintaining overall system stability. The process required constant attention from experienced sensitives who understood the delicate balance of temporal forces.

"Think of it as a temporal ecosystem," Mark explained, his form stabilizing momentarily. "Each sensitive generates and consumes temporal energy in unique patterns. The Network helps maintain equilibrium, preventing dangerous energy concentrations while ensuring everyone has access to the resources they need."

The complexity of this system became apparent in the distribution center's monitoring room. Displays showed temporal energy flows throughout Daybridge, highlighting areas of high activity and potential instability. Technicians worked alongside sensitives to maintain optimal energy distribution; their efforts coordinated by Dr. Sente's advanced monitoring systems.

Alice watched as Liz demonstrated the Network's energy sharing protocols, carefully channeling temporal force to support a new sensitive experiencing their first major manifestation. The process required precise control, with experienced members acting as conduits to prevent energy surge or depletion.

"This is why we exist," David said, his Watcher's perception tracking multiple timeline variants simultaneously. "Not just to protect and train, but to maintain balance. Temporal ability creates ripples through reality. The Network helps ensure those ripples don't become waves that could tear apart the fabric of time itself."

As Alice absorbed these revelations, she understood the Network represented more than just an organization - it was a living system of temporal sensitives working together to understand and manage their extraordinary abilities. Through careful energy distribution, vigilant protection, and shared knowledge, they created a framework for developing temporal power safely and responsibly.

"Welcome to the family," Liz said as Alice completed her orientation. "You're not just gaining access to resources and training. You're becoming part of a community that understands what you're going through. The Network exists because we all share the same journey, even if our paths differ. "The weight of temporal responsibility settled over Alice as she watched David resume his Watcher's duties, his consciousness expanding across multiple timeline variants while maintaining perfect stability. The Network had revealed itself as both sanctuary and shield, offering protection from those who would exploit temporal ability while providing the support necessary to develop it safely.

EPISODE 5: THE DECISION & THE AFTERMATH

The temporal storm had passed, but Alice's real struggle was just beginning. She sat in the Network's adaptation chamber, surrounded by Dr. Sente's neural monitoring equipment, as her mind attempted to reconcile two sets of memories - the original timeline and the one she'd created.

"Memory reconciliation is the hardest part," Liz explained, adjusting the temporal resonance fields that helped stabilize shifting memories. "Your brain is trying to process both timeline variants simultaneously. We'll help you sort through them, establish which memories belong to your current timeline."

The Network had developed sophisticated techniques for managing post-decision memory adaptation. Grace Mitchell led Alice through daily meditation sessions designed to help her brain properly file and categorize temporal memories. "Think of it like organizing a library where the books keep changing their content," Grace explained. "We need to help your mind create a stable organizational system."

Dr. Sente's memory mapping technology proved invaluable. "Each memory has a distinct temporal signature," she demonstrated, showing Alice the neural patterns on her monitors. "We can identify which memories belong to your current timeline and help your brain prioritize them over variants from altered timelines."

The relationship changes proved even more challenging. Sarah survived the accident, but their shared history had been fundamentally altered by the temporal manipulation. Alice struggled with conversations where her sister referenced events that had never happened in her original timeline, while missing memories they'd previously shared.

"Your sister's timeline remained largely consistent," Matthew Sullivan explained during a counseling session. "She has one set of memories. You're carrying multiple sets. The key is learning to navigate conversations without disrupting her temporal stability."

The Network provided Alice with a support group of other sensitives who'd experienced major timeline alterations. They shared techniques for managing relationship changes: how to maintain conversations when memories didn't align, ways to adapt to altered family dynamics, methods for building new connections within changed relationships.

"I lost three years of memories with my husband," one support group member shared. "The Network helped me reconstruct our relationship around our shared present rather than trying to reconcile conflicting pasts."

Dr. Sente's research team documented the adaptation process. Their findings showed how the brain attempted to maintain temporal consistency by creating bridge memories - new neural pathways that helped connect different timeline variants into a coherent narrative.

The Network's temporal therapists worked with Alice daily, helping her process the emotional impact of altered relationships. "It's a form of grief," Liz explained. "You're mourning connections that now only exist in your memory while simultaneously building new ones in the current timeline."

Mark Weil shared his experience with timeline alterations, appearing to Alice as both his younger and older selves simultaneously. "The hardest part is accepting that some memories will never fully align. The price of temporal manipulation includes living with these discrepancies."

The Network's adaptation protocols included practical exercises for managing daily life with altered memories. Alice learned techniques for checking her temporal reference points before important conversations, methods for gracefully handling memory conflicts, and ways to maintain relationships despite timeline inconsistencies.

"Think of it like learning a new language," Grace suggested during a particularly difficult session. "You're becoming fluent in multiple timeline variants. The goal isn't to forget the original timeline, but to learn how to function smoothly in the current one."

Dr. Sente's monitoring showed how Alice's brain gradually adapted to the timeline changes. Neural pathways reorganized themselves, creating new patterns that could accommodate multiple memory sets while maintaining functional stability in the present timeline.

The Network's experience with similar cases proved invaluable. They understood how timeline alterations affected different types of relationships - family bonds proved more resilient than casual friendships, romantic connections often required the most intensive support for successful adaptation.

Alice struggled most with the subtle changes. Sarah's survival had created cascading alterations in their family dynamics. Conversations revealed small but significant differences in their shared history - celebrations that happened differently, conflicts that never occurred, achievements that took alternative paths.

"The temporal debt doesn't just take years," Liz observed during a progress review. "It takes certainty. You'll always carry awareness of multiple timeline variants. The Network helps you learn to live with that awareness without letting it overwhelm your present relationships."

The adaptation process extended beyond personal relationships. The Network helped Alice navigate professional changes caused by the timeline alteration, provided support for managing altered social connections, and offered guidance for handling unexpected timeline variations that continued emerging.

Dr. Sente's research revealed how timeline alterations created ongoing ripple effects in relationships. "Each interaction has the potential to reveal new variations," she explained. "The adaptation process isn't about reaching a final stable state - it's about developing the flexibility to handle continuing changes."

As weeks passed, Alice learned to navigate her altered reality with growing confidence. The Network's support helped her develop what they called "temporal resilience" - the ability to maintain stable relationships despite awareness of timeline variations.

"You've paid more than just the obvious price," Mark told her during a final adaptation session. "Living with multiple timeline memories is its own kind of temporal debt. But you've learned to carry that weight while maintaining your connections to the present moment. That's the true measure of successful adaptation."

The Network would continue monitoring Alice's progress, offering support as new timeline variations emerged. They understood that major temporal decisions created long-term adaptation challenges. Their role wasn't just to help sensitives make these choices, but to support them through the complex process of living with the consequences.

Alice's experience would inform the Network's adaptation protocols for future sensitives. Her journey demonstrated both the personal cost of timeline manipulation and the importance of comprehensive support in managing its aftermath. The price of changing destiny included learning to live with altered memories and relationships - a challenge that required both individual resilience and community support.

EPISODE 6: THE INTEGRATION

The temporal gymnasium occupied a curious space in the Network's facility - a room that existed simultaneously in multiple temporal states. Alice stood in the center chamber, surrounded by Dr. Sente's monitoring equipment, as Liz prepared her for another training session.

"Today we're working on timeline separation," Liz explained, activating the gymnasium's quantum field generators. "Your enhanced abilities are bleeding timeline variants together. You need to learn to perceive multiple timelines while maintaining their distinct boundaries."

The gymnasium's first exercise involved a simple coffee cup. As the quantum fields activated, Alice watched the cup exist in five different positions simultaneously. Her task was to mentally separate each timeline variant while maintaining awareness of them all - like viewing multiple television channels at once while keeping each program distinct.

"Don't try to force the timelines apart," Mark instructed, his form shifting between variants. "Feel their natural boundaries. Each timeline has its own quantum signature. Learn to recognize these signatures without attempting to alter them."

The Network's temporal gymnasium employed increasingly complex scenarios. After mastering object separation, Alice progressed to managing multiple conversations occurring across timeline variants. Holographic projectors created simulated interactions while temporal field generators replicated the quantum pressure of real timeline bleed.

"Bridge sensitives need perfect timeline clarity," Liz explained, watching Alice navigate a complex simulation involving multiple business negotiations occurring simultaneously across variants. "You'll be guiding others through temporal experiences. Confusion between timelines during these interactions could have severe consequences."

The Network's ethical guidelines for bridge sensitives filled multiple volumes in their library, but certain principles proved fundamental. First among these was the Temporal Non-Interference Protocol - strict rules about when and how timeline manipulation could be employed in professional settings.

"You'll see business opportunities across multiple timeline variants," Mark warned. "The temptation to nudge events toward more profitable outcomes will be constant. That's why we have the Three Questions Protocol: Is intervention necessary to prevent harm? Are the consequences fully understood? Can the temporal debt be responsibly managed?"

Professional ethics extended beyond timeline manipulation. The Network provided detailed guidelines for managing temporal knowledge in business settings: when to share insights from timeline awareness, how to maintain competitive fairness despite temporal advantage, and protocols for handling timeline-sensitive information.

"Bridge sensitives operate at the intersection of temporal and normal reality," Liz explained during an ethics session. "You'll know things others can't know; see opportunities others can't see. The guidelines help you navigate these advantages without compromising temporal stability or personal integrity."

The concept of bridge sensitives emerged from the Network's experience with integration cases. These rare individuals developed the ability to maintain stable temporal awareness while functioning effectively in normal reality. More importantly, they could help others navigate temporal experiences safely.

"Think of yourself as a temporal translator," Dr. Sente suggested, monitoring Alice's neural patterns during a particularly challenging gymnasium session. "You can perceive and interpret multiple timeline variants while maintaining enough stability to guide others through temporal experiences. That's what makes bridge sensitives so valuable to the Network."

The gymnasium training intensified as Alice's abilities developed. Advanced exercises involved maintaining timeline separation during high-stress scenarios: market crashes playing out across variants, emergency response situations, personal crisis points. Each session pushed the limits of her temporal perception while demanding perfect clarity.

"Bridge sensitives often serve as first responders during temporal incidents," Liz explained. "You need to maintain absolute timeline clarity while helping others who may be experiencing temporal displacement or manifestation events. There's no room for variant confusion in crisis situations."

The Network's ethical framework included specific guidelines for bridge sensitive responsibilities. These covered everything from mentoring new sensitives to managing temporal crisis points. The protocols emphasized the delicate balance between using temporal awareness and maintaining timeline stability.

"Your enhanced abilities come with enhanced responsibilities," Mark reminded her during a particularly difficult gymnasium session. "Bridge sensitives don't just manage their own temporal experiences - they help shape how others interact with temporal reality. That influence requires strict ethical boundaries."

Professional guidelines proved especially crucial as Alice's abilities stabilized. The Network provided detailed protocols for using temporal awareness in business settings: how to maintain client confidentiality across timeline variants, methods for ensuring fair negotiation despite temporal insight, and strategies for managing timeline-sensitive projects.

The temporal gymnasium's most challenging exercises involved simultaneous timeline manipulation and stabilization. Alice learned to maintain multiple timeline variants while actively working to prevent temporal bleed - a crucial skill for bridge sensitives managing crisis situations.

"Perfect timeline clarity isn't enough," Liz emphasized. "Bridge sensitives must maintain that clarity while actively working with temporal energy. You're not just observing timeline variants - you're helping others navigate them safely."

The Network's ethical guidelines extended to personal relationships as well. Bridge sensitives received specific protocols for managing temporal knowledge in family and social settings: when to share time-line insights, how to maintain relationship boundaries despite temporal awareness, and methods for supporting others through temporal events.

As her training progressed, Alice began understanding the true nature of bridge sensitives. They weren't just powerful temporal manipula-tors or skilled ability controllers - they were guides, helping others navigate the increasingly complex intersection of temporal and normal reality.

"The future needs people who can bridge these worlds," Mark explained, his form finally stabilizing as Alice mastered another gymnasium challenge. "As temporal ability becomes more common, bridge sensitives will be crucial in helping society adapt to increased temporal awareness. Your role is as much about guidance as it is about power."

The integration process revealed how bridge sensitives embodied the Network's core mission: not just controlling temporal ability, but helping humanity navigate an increasingly temporal-aware future. With proper training and ethical guidelines, bridge sensitives like Alice would help shape how society understood and interacted with temporal reality.

EPISODE 7: THE CONNECTION

The Network's acceleration protocols activated within hours of discovering the pattern. Dr. Sente's lab transformed into a command center, coordinating efforts across multiple timeline variants to identify and prepare potential bridge sensitives.

"We need to be surgical about this," Liz explained, reviewing temporal signature maps. "Accelerating the pattern too aggressively could destabilize the quantum framework the Founders built. Each new bridge sensitive needs to be carefully integrated into the existing structure."

The Network deployed three primary acceleration strategies:

First, they began actively monitoring temporal nexus points - locations where timeline variants naturally intersected. These points acted as amplifiers for latent temporal abilities. By carefully manipulating the quantum fields around these locations, they could create controlled manifestation events that helped identify potential bridge sensitives.

Second, they implemented what they called "Echo Protocol" - using existing bridge sensitives like Alice to detect others with similar potential. Bridge sensitives generated unique temporal signatures that resonated with those who shared their capabilities, even if those capabilities were still dormant.

Third, they activated dormant temporal gymnasiums across the globe. These facilities, built by the Founders but never used, contained sophisticated equipment for accelerating temporal ability development while maintaining stability.

"Identification is the easy part," Mark observed, shifting between his temporal variants. "The challenge is preparing them quickly enough without compromising the ethical framework that makes bridge sensitives effective."

The Network's new training program operated on compressed timelines. What had previously taken years of gradual development now needed to be accomplished in months. Dr. Sente's team developed new protocols that pushed the limits of safe temporal acceleration.

"We're looking for specific markers," Liz explained during a recruitment briefing. "Natural temporal awareness, strong ethical foundations, and most importantly - the ability to maintain stability while experiencing multiple timeline variants simultaneously."

The challenges facing the Network grew daily:

Temporal Strain: Accelerating the pattern created unprecedented pressure on the quantum fabric of reality. Dr. Sente's monitors showed increasing instability in timeline boundaries.

Resource Limitations: Each new bridge sensitive required intensive support and monitoring. The Network's infrastructure, designed for gradual development, struggled to handle the increased load.

Security Concerns: As more people manifested temporal abilities, maintaining secrecy became increasingly difficult. Corporate and government entities began detecting unusual temporal activity.

Training Capacity: Experienced bridge sensitives like Alice found themselves splitting time between their own development and training others, creating dangerous fatigue patterns.

Timeline Integrity: Rapid acceleration of the pattern risked creating temporal paradoxes that could undermine the Founders' careful preparations.

The Network implemented emergency protocols to address these challenges. They established new temporal dampening fields around major population centers, created mobile response teams for handling manifestation events, and developed enhanced screening procedures for potential recruits.

"We're not just looking for power anymore," Alice realized during a particularly intense training session with a new recruit. "We need people who can handle the responsibility of knowing what's coming. The emotional stability is as important as the temporal ability."

The Network's identification process evolved to include psychological evaluation alongside temporal sensitivity testing. They developed new metrics for measuring what they called "temporal resilience" - the ability to maintain personal stability while experiencing multiple time-line variants.

"Bridge sensitives aren't just temporal power users," Dr. Sente explained, reviewing the latest training data. "They're anchors - points of stability in an increasingly unstable temporal landscape. We need people who can hold reality together while helping others navigate it."

The biggest immediate challenge became managing the exponential increase in temporal incidents. As the pattern accelerated, more people began experiencing timeline bleed - moments where multiple timeline variants became simultaneously visible to those without training.

The Network deployed bridge sensitives in strategic locations, creating what they called "stability zones" - areas where temporal pressure could be safely managed while identifying and recruiting those with potential. Alice found herself regularly shifting between training new recruits and managing temporal crisis points.

"The Founders knew this moment would come," Mark shared during a rare quiet moment. "They built redundancies into the pattern - ways to accelerate development when necessary. What they couldn't prepare for was the human cost of rapid acceleration."

The Network's leadership faced difficult decisions daily. Each new bridge sensitive they identified required immense resources to train safely. Every acceleration of the pattern increased the risk of temporal instability. The balance between necessary preparation and responsible development became increasingly precarious.

"We're not just racing against time," Liz observed, watching the temporal pressure gauges climb. "We're racing against the pattern itself. Push too fast, we risk destabilizing everything the Founders built. Move too slowly, we won't be ready when the convergence arrives."

Alice's role evolved as the acceleration continued. Her business experience proved valuable in developing protocols for managing temporal events in corporate settings. The Network began preparing for the inevitable moment when temporal awareness would become public knowledge.

The Founders' preparation protocol had included contingencies for acceleration but implementing them proved challenging. Each new bridge sensitive changed the pattern's dynamics, requiring constant adjustment and monitoring to maintain stability.

"The next six months will determine everything," Dr. Sente announced during an emergency council meeting. "Either we successfully accelerate the pattern and prepare enough bridge sensitives to manage the convergence, or we risk losing control of humanity's temporal evolution entirely."

As the Network raced to implement their acceleration protocols, one truth became increasingly clear - the Founders' vision was about to be tested in ways they had hoped to avoid. The careful balance between preparation and stability was shifting, and the outcome would affect all timeline variants.

The pattern continued accelerating, each new bridge sensitive adding both strength and complexity to the quantum framework. The Network's challenge wasn't just preparing for the future anymore - it was ensuring that humanity reached that future with the guidance and stability it would desperately need.

EPISODE 8: THE DOCUMENTATION

The Network's central archive hummed with quantum energy as Dr. Sente revealed the latest convergence point projections. The holographic display showed timeline variants converging like rivers joining into a vast temporal ocean, each stream carrying its own version of reality toward an inevitable meeting point.

"The convergence isn't just timelines merging," Dr. Sente explained, manipulating the display's quantum fields. "It's a fundamental shift in human consciousness. A point where temporal awareness becomes an inherent part of human experience, like sight or hearing. Our documentation needs to prepare future generations for this transition."

The projected convergence manifested as a cascade of temporal events, beginning with increased instances of spontaneous timeline awareness among the general population. This would progress to widespread temporal sensitivity, following patterns similar to those documented in bridge sensitive development. The final stage would involve a global realignment of quantum reality as multiple timeline variants sought resolution.

Liz worked tirelessly to document these projections, fighting against the constant challenge of temporal data decay. Information about timeline variants proved inherently unstable, degrading like photographs exposed to harsh light. Complex temporal experiences recorded in the quantum memory matrices would gradually lose definition, becoming increasingly vague and unreliable.

"We're losing crucial details," Liz frustrated, reviewing corrupted data streams. "Each time we access a stored temporal experience, it degrades slightly. The quantum signatures blur, the timeline interactions become less distinct. It's like trying to preserve smoke in a bottle."

The Network developed increasingly sophisticated preservation methods, but temporal data decay presented unique challenges. Unlike normal digital degradation, temporal information seemed to actively resist permanent storage. The very nature of timeline variants made them difficult to pin down in any fixed medium.

Mark's experiences proved particularly challenging to document. His constant shifting between variants created complex data patterns that stressed the storage systems' capabilities. Each recorded session generated massive amounts of quantum data, much of which would begin degrading almost immediately.

"The Founders faced these same challenges," Mark shared, stabilizing briefly to review ancient records. "Their original documentation shows signs of significant decay, but they embedded key information in multiple formats, knowing some would survive better than others."

The Founders' original documentation proved revolutionary in understanding current challenges. Their records, preserved through various methods, revealed sophisticated insights into temporal mechanics that modern science was only beginning to comprehend. They had documented early manifestations of temporal ability, tracking patterns that would take generations to fully emerge.

Their documentation methods ranged from traditional written records to complex quantum encodings embedded in crystalline structures. Most importantly, they had created redundant systems of knowledge preservation, ensuring critical information would survive even if individual storage methods failed.

Alice discovered a particularly crucial set of Founder documents during a deep archive search. The records detailed early experiments with temporal consciousness, including the first documented cases of bridge sensitives. These accounts provided vital context for current acceleration efforts.

"The Founders didn't just document what happened," Alice realized, studying the ancient records. "They documented what would happen. Their temporal awareness let them see the patterns forming, the challenges we'd face. They left us a roadmap hidden in their documentation."

The impact of the Founders' documentation extended beyond mere historical record. Their preserved experiences provided crucial baseline data for understanding temporal development. Modern bridge sensitives could compare their experiences with historical accounts, identifying consistent patterns and evolutionary changes.

Dr. Sente's team worked to integrate the Founders' documentation methods with modern technology. They discovered that combining ancient quantum encoding techniques with contemporary storage systems significantly reduced data decay rates. The Founders had anticipated future technological development and designed their documentation to remain compatible.

"They knew we'd need their knowledge," Liz said, successfully recovering a partially degraded temporal recording. "Every documentation method they used, every storage system they designed - it was all created to survive long enough to reach us, to help us prepare for the convergence."

The Network's current documentation efforts built upon this foundation. They expanded the Founders' methods while maintaining compatibility with their original systems. New quantum memory matrices incorporated design elements from ancient storage crystals, creating more stable temporal data preservation.

The approaching convergence point added urgency to their documentation efforts. Each successfully preserved experience, each recovered historical record, each stabilized data stream contributed to humanity's preparation for increased temporal awareness. The Network's role as knowledge preserver became as crucial as its role in ability development.

"We're not just fighting data decay," Dr. Sente observed, reviewing the latest preservation protocols. "We're racing to document enough experience, enough patterns, enough understanding to help humanity navigate the convergence. Every piece of knowledge we preserve could mean the difference between successful transition and temporal chaos."

The Founders' impact continued revealing itself through their documentation. Hidden patterns emerged from seemingly unrelated records, showing how they had carefully structured their knowledge preservation to survive centuries of temporal pressure. Their documentation wasn't just a record of the past - it was an actively evolving guide to humanity's temporal future.

As the Network's documentation efforts intensified, the true scope of the Founders' vision became clear. They had created more than an organization to help temporal sensitives - they had established a framework for preserving and transmitting crucial knowledge across generations, preparing humanity for its next evolutionary step.

The quantum memory matrices continued recording, capturing the experiences that would guide future bridge sensitives. Each preserved moment, each documented pattern, each stabilized temporal signature added to humanity's understanding of its evolving relationship with time itself. The convergence point approached, and the Network's role as knowledge keeper became increasingly crucial to humanity's temporal future.

EPISODE 9: THE EVOLUTION

The boardroom's timeline variants blurred together, forcing Alice to grip the conference table as multiple versions of the quarterly presentation assaulted her consciousness simultaneously. In one variant, the profit projections soared; in another, market disruptions led to significant losses. Each possibility demanded attention, each future equally real and pressing.

"Timeline filtering is like trying to watch thousands of TV channels simultaneously while maintaining focus on a single conversation," she later explained to Dr. Sente. "The information overwhelm can be physically debilitating if you don't develop proper mental barriers."

The Network's training helped, but filtering challenges manifested in unexpected ways. During client meetings, casual decisions like coffee preferences would spawn dozens of timeline variants, each creating subtle ripple effects through future possibilities. Alice developed migraines as her mind struggled to process the constant influx of temporal data.

Dr. Sente's acceleration protocols revealed Alice's unique temporal signature during a routine scanning session. Unlike other bridge sensitives who experienced timeline variants as parallel streams, Alice's consciousness seemed to naturally organize temporal information into hierarchical patterns. This ability made her particularly suited for helping others navigate the approaching convergence.

"Your mind automatically categorizes timeline variants by probability and impact," Liz explained, reviewing the scan results. "It's rare to see this level of natural temporal organization. The Founders' records mention similar patterns in sensitives who became crucial stability anchors during major temporal events."

The Network's historical documentation described the convergence event in stark detail. Unlike gradual temporal awareness expansion, the convergence would manifest as a sudden global shift in human consciousness. Billions would simultaneously become aware of timeline variants, experiencing multiple possible realities without preparation or training.

"Imagine everyone on Earth suddenly developing the ability to see radio waves," Mark described, his form shifting through demonstration variants. "Now imagine that happening without warning or understanding. The convergence will be similar, but with timeline awareness instead of electromagnetic perception."

Alice's filtering challenges provided valuable insight into what humanity would face. Her struggles with information overwhelm helped the Network develop coping strategies for mass implementation. They began preparing emergency response protocols for when timeline awareness became a global phenomenon.

The convergence's impact would reshape human society fundamentally. Financial markets would need to account for multiple timeline possibilities simultaneously. Legal systems would have to adapt to handle crimes that occurred in some variants but not others. Personal relationships would transform as people became aware of different possible versions of their lives.

"Your role isn't just about managing your own abilities anymore," Dr. Sente explained during an intensive training session. "You're developing the frameworks that will help others survive the initial shock of temporal awareness. Your business experience combined with natural filtering abilities makes you uniquely qualified to help establish stability protocols."

Alice's professional challenges intensified as her awareness expanded. During crucial negotiations, she had to consciously suppress awareness of timeline variants where deals failed catastrophically while maintaining enough temporal perception to guide discussions toward optimal outcomes. The mental strain left her exhausted.

The Network's acceleration protocols revealed how her natural filtering abilities could serve as a template for helping others. They began documenting her mental processes, studying how she instinctively categorized and prioritized temporal information. These insights would prove crucial for developing mass training programs.

"The convergence will affect everyone differently," Liz noted, monitoring Alice's temporal signatures during a particularly challenging filtering exercise. "Some will adapt quickly; others will struggle severely. Bridge sensitives like you, with natural filtering abilities, will be essential for preventing widespread panic and confusion."

The Network's projections showed the convergence's impact occurring in waves. The initial shock of mass temporal awareness would trigger global instability as financial systems, governments, and social structures struggled to adapt. This would be followed by a period of rapid adaptation as humanity's consciousness expanded to accommodate its new perception of reality.

Alice's role became clearer as her abilities developed. Her experience managing temporal awareness in professional settings would help establish protocols for maintaining business continuity during the transition. Her natural filtering abilities would guide the development of training programs for helping others manage timeline variant awareness.

The Founders' documentation had predicted this need for bridge sensitives with specific capability combinations. Their acceleration protocols weren't just about developing abilities quickly – they were designed to reveal and enhance natural talents that would be crucial during the convergence.

"You're not just preparing yourself," Mark explained during an advanced filtering session. "You're helping create the support systems humanity will need. Each filtering technique you develop, each coping strategy you master, becomes part of humanity's survival toolkit."

The convergence would mark humanity's most significant evolutionary step since the development of self-awareness. The ability to perceive and navigate multiple timeline variants would fundamentally change how humans understood reality, choice, and consequence. The

Network's role was to ensure this transition didn't lead to societal collapse.

Alice's journey reflected humanity's approaching evolution in microcosm. Her struggles with filtering, her professional adaptation challenges, her growing understanding of temporal dynamics – all provided insights into how society might navigate the coming changes. The Network's acceleration protocols revealed her as not just a participant in this evolution, but a guide for others following the same path.

As the convergence point approached, the importance of proper temporal filtering became increasingly apparent. The Network's preparation efforts focused on developing scalable techniques based on Alice's natural abilities. Her experience would help create the frameworks necessary for humanity's survival through its most challenging transition.

The evolution continued, each day bringing new insights into how temporal awareness would reshape human experience. Alice's role in this process grew clearer as her abilities developed. She wasn't just evolving personally – she was helping create the conditions necessary for humanity's successful adaptation to a new level of consciousness.

EPISODE 10: THE UNDERSTANDING

Dr. Sarah Wilson stood before the quantum visualization array, watching as new patterns emerged from their latest probability field analysis. The entity's recent attacks had revealed something they'd never seen before - a fundamental relationship between consciousness and quantum stability.

"The power isn't just about manipulating reality," she explained to General Tyrell. "It's about understanding how consciousness itself shapes quantum probability."

The manifestation patterns had become increasingly clear. Bridge sensitives demonstrated an unprecedented ability to directly influence quantum states. Reality anchors responded to conscious intent as much as technical parameters. Timeline stability showed direct correlation with operator focus levels. Most surprisingly, power systems exhibited harmonic resonance with collective consciousness patterns.

Through careful study of combat recordings, they'd identified five critical decision points that had shaped their current crisis. First came the choice to develop consciousness-based probability manipulation. This led to the implementation of synchronized awareness protocols, followed by the integration of human consciousness with reality anchor networks. The development of quantum resonance training for operators marked another crucial step. Finally, the decision to actively weaponize consciousness against quantum chaos had set them on their current path.

"Each choice created ripples through probability space," Dr. Wilson noted, highlighting temporal traces. "We weren't just making tactical decisions - we were fundamentally altering how consciousness interacts with reality."

The price of these developments became increasingly clear as they studied long-term effects. Operators experienced permanent changes in how they perceived reality. Timeline variants showed increasing interdependence. Probability fields became more responsive to collective human will. Perhaps most significantly, the boundary between consciousness and quantum mechanics grew increasingly blurred.

"We're not just fighting the entity anymore," General Tyrell realized. "We're evolving into something new - a humanity that can actively shape reality at the quantum level."

The implications for future operations were staggering. Probability warfare would become increasingly consciousness-based, requiring perfect mental discipline from all operators. Timeline stability would depend more on collective human will than technological solutions. The distinction between operator and reality anchor would continue to blur as consciousness became their primary tool for reality manipulation.

As they prepared for the coming threshold operation, this new understanding shaped their tactical approach. They weren't just defending reality - they were actively participating in the evolution of consciousness itself.

"All teams prepare for consciousness sync," General Tyrell ordered as reality anchors hummed with increasing power. "We're not just reaching a technological threshold - we're crossing a fundamental boundary in human evolution."

The facility vibrated with potential as they prepared for their most ambitious operation yet. The understanding they'd gained would prove crucial in the battles to come, as humanity learned to wield consciousness itself as their primary weapon against quantum chaos. Their journey from defending reality to actively shaping it had reached a crucial turning point, and there would be no going back from the threshold they were about to cross.

In the command center, Dr. Wilson made final adjustments to the consciousness synchronization protocols. The patterns on her quantum displays showed something unprecedented - the collective will of their operators creating distinct ripples in probability space. They had moved beyond merely responding to the entity's attacks. They were about to attempt something far more ambitious - using unified consciousness to fundamentally reshape how reality itself functioned.

"Begin final consciousness sync," General Tyrell commanded as the facility's power signature shifted to a new frequency. "Everything we've learned, everything we've become, has prepared us for this moment. Now we show the entity that consciousness, not chaos, will determine the future of reality itself."

CHAPTER ELEVEN

THRESHOLD (PRESENT DAY)

EPISODE 1: THE GATHERING STORM

THE QUANTUM MONITORS displayed something unprecedented - a void moving through timeline variants, not merely existing in them but actively consuming temporal possibilities. Dr. Sente's hands trembled as she studied the readings, recognizing patterns that matched the Founders' most dire predictions.

"It's not just manipulating timelines," she explained to the emergency council. "It's absorbing them, converting temporal energy into something else. The Founders called it a 'Chronophage' - a temporal entity that feeds on possibility itself."

The entity's signature defied conventional temporal physics. Unlike natural timeline variants that branched and merged, this created absolute endings - points where possibility simply ceased to exist. The void left behind contained no temporal energy, no potential for reality to restore itself.

Commander Decker's tactical teams were assembled based on specialized temporal combat capabilities developed through generations of

260

Network training. Each team member demonstrated unique abilities essential for the approaching confrontation.

"Team Alpha specializes in timeline anchoring," Decker detailed during the final briefing. "They can stabilize reality points against temporal disruption. Beta team are our reality shapers - they actively reinforce timeline variants under attack. Gamma handles temporal energy redistribution, while Delta coordinates cross-timeline communications."

The tactical teams' abilities had been carefully cultivated based on the Founders' documentation. Timeline anchors could establish fixed points that even the Chronophage couldn't easily consume. Reality shapers strengthened the fabric of space-time itself, making it more resistant to temporal degradation.

"Each team member has undergone extensive temporal stress testing," Captain Royston reported. "They can maintain operational stability even when surrounded by timeline collapse. More importantly, they can coordinate actions across multiple variants simultaneously."

The Founders' documentation proved eerily precise in its predictions. Ancient quantum crystals contained detailed descriptions of the entity's approach, including the pattern of preliminary temporal probes and the distinctive void signature of consumed timelines.

"They knew it was coming," Dr. Wilson said, reviewing the translated documents. "The Network wasn't just created to help bridge sensitives - it was established to prepare humanity for this specific threat. Every protocol, every training program, was designed for this confrontation."

The documentation described the Chronophage as a consciousness that existed outside normal temporal physics. It perceived time as humans perceived space, moving freely through temporal dimensions while feeding on the energy of possibility itself. Each consumed timeline made it stronger.

Lieutenant Foster's power amplification teams worked to implement the Founders' defensive designs. The ancient documents included specifications for energy distribution systems specifically designed to resist temporal consumption.

"The Founders built redundancies we're only now understanding," Foster explained. "Each power node contains quantum patterns that make their temporal energy indigestible to the entity. They gave us the weapons - we just had to develop enough to recognize them."

The tactical teams underwent final preparation using simulation data extracted from the Founders' records. The documentation included detailed combat scenarios, describing how the entity would attempt to isolate and consume timeline variants.

"Coordination is crucial," Decker emphasized. "The entity will try to separate our teams across timeline variants, cutting off communication and support. Our advantage is our ability to maintain coherent action across multiple temporal fronts simultaneously."

Team Alpha's timeline anchors began establishing defensive positions based on the Founders' strategic predictions. The documentation had mapped likely impact points where the entity would first attempt to breach reality's fabric.

"The Founders didn't just predict this," Royston noted during position verification. "They fought it before, or at least an earlier version of it. Their documentation includes combat records - victories and failures across countless timeline variants."

Nina Chisolm's energy specialists implemented power distribution protocols extracted from the ancient records. The Founders had developed specific frequency patterns that could disrupt the entity's feeding process.

"They understood its vulnerabilities," Decker said, calibrating the power grid. "The entity requires certain temporal energy frequencies to maintain its consumption process. Disrupt those frequencies, and we can force it to withdraw from affected timeline variants."

The most disturbing aspects of the Founders' predictions concerned the entity's ultimate goal. The documentation described it as seeking a specific temporal convergence point - a moment when multiple time-line variants naturally intersected.

"It's not random destruction," Dr. Sente explained to the council. "The entity is trying to create a cascade effect. By consuming enough key timeline variants, it could trigger a chain reaction of temporal collapse. Reality itself would unravel."

Commander Decker's battle preparations followed the Founders' strategic guidelines while incorporating modern temporal combat innovations. The documentation emphasized flexibility and redundancy, acknowledging that some timeline variants would be lost despite their best efforts.

"Our priority is containing the collapse," Decker instructed her teams. "We can't save every timeline variant, but we can prevent the cascade effect. The Founders were explicit - better to sacrifice some variants than risk total temporal collapse."

The early warning system, enhanced using specifications from the ancient records, provided unprecedented detail about the entity's approach. They could track its movement through temporal space, watching as it systematically consumed outlying timeline variants.

"This is what the Network was built for," Dr. Sente reminded them as final preparations completed. "Everything the Founders created every-thing they documented, was to prepare us for this moment. The enti-ty's arrival isn't just a crisis - it's the fulfillment of a prophecy written in quantum code across centuries of preparation."

As tactical teams moved into their final positions, the weight of the Founders' predictions hung heavy over the command center. They had predicted this confrontation centuries ago, preparing defenses and strategies for a battle that would determine reality's survival.

Decker's last orders reflected the gravity of their situation: "All teams, initiate Founders' Protocol Omega. Whatever happens, whatever we lose, the primary timeline must survive. Reality itself depends on what we do here. What we do now."

The temporal storm gathered strength as the entity approached, and the Network prepared to fulfill its ultimate purpose - defending the very fabric of reality against a threat the Founders had foreseen in humanity's distant past.

EPISODE 2: POWER GRID

Maya Patel's hands flew across multiple holographic interfaces as the power grid's quantum indicators shifted into critical ranges. The Network's energy distribution system, designed to maintain stability across timeline variants, was experiencing unprecedented strain from the Chronophage's approach.

"We're seeing cascading resonance patterns in sectors seven through twelve," she announced, tracking the fluctuations. "The entity's presence is creating harmonic disruptions in our temporal power frequencies. Standard containment protocols aren't sufficient."

The main challenge emerged from the entity's effect on temporal energy flow. Unlike natural timeline variations that maintained consistent quantum signatures, the Chronophage's void created "dead zones" where power couldn't flow between variants.

"It's like trying to maintain an electrical grid where random sections of space-time simply cease to exist," Dr. Wilson explained, studying the power distribution maps. "Each dead zone forces energy to reroute through remaining timeline variants, creating dangerous overload potential."

Maya's integration efforts focused on developing adaptive power routing systems. Her team worked to create quantum switches that could instantly redirect temporal energy flow around consumed timeline variants while maintaining stable distribution to defensive systems.

"Traditional power grid architecture assumes consistent physical laws," she explained during an emergency briefing. "We're dealing with an entity that actively changes how energy moves through time. Every standard assumption about power distribution has to be reconsidered."

Timeline stability concerns intensified as power fluctuations began affecting reality anchors. These crucial defensive positions required precise energy levels to maintain temporal reinforcement. Even minor power variations could create vulnerabilities in their defensive network.

Lieutenant Foster's power amplification teams reported increasing difficulty maintaining synchronization between timeline variants. The entity's presence created temporal "static" that interfered with standard power transmission protocols.

"We're losing clean power transfer between variants," Foster reported. "Each timeline shift requires recalibration of the entire distribution network. We can't maintain stable power levels if we have to constantly readjust for temporal distortions."

Maya initiated a series of power synchronization experiments designed to counter the entity's disruptive effect. By modulating temporal energy frequencies in patterns matching the Founders' documentation, they hoped to establish more resilient power distribution channels.

"The Founders' records suggest specific quantum harmonics that resist temporal disruption," she explained while programming the test sequences. "We're essentially trying to create power frequencies that the entity can't easily disturb."

The first successful synchronization test provided crucial data about the entity's interaction with their power systems. Maya's team discovered that certain energy patterns seemed to naturally repel the void effect, maintaining stability even in proximity to consumed timeline variants.

"It's like we've found the temporal equivalent of electromagnetic shielding," Dr. Wilson observed. "These power frequencies create a kind of barrier effect against the entity's influence. The Founders must have discovered this through direct confrontation."

The first major temporal fluctuations hit during power grid recalibration. Reality anchors across three sectors reported critical power variations as timeline variants began experiencing accelerated degradation. Maya's systems recorded energy pattern disruptions that exceeded all previous models.

"The entity isn't just passive anymore," she warned, watching the power readings spike. "It's actively targeting our distribution network. Each fluctuation corresponds to a deliberate attack on our power stability."

Emergency protocols activated as the power grid struggled to compensate. Backup systems designed using the Founders' specifications engaged automatically, rerouting temporal energy through protected channels. The Network's entire power infrastructure shifted into combat configuration.

"We're seeing what the Founders built this for," Maya noted as she monitored the emergency systems. "These backup protocols aren't just contingencies - they're specifically designed to counter the entity's attacks. Every circuit, every power node, was created for this fight."

Nina Chisolm's energy specialists reported increasing difficulty maintaining stable power flow between timeline variants. The entity's presence created interference patterns that disrupted standard temporal energy transmission.

"It's like trying to maintain a steady electrical current through constantly shifting conductor materials," Chisolm explained. "The temporal fabric itself is becoming unstable, making consistent power distribution nearly impossible."

Maya's integration efforts revealed another concerning discovery. The entity seemed to be learning from each attack on their power grid, adjusting its approach to exploit newly discovered vulnerabilities. The Network's power distribution system had to evolve constantly to maintain effectiveness.

"We're not just fighting power disruption," she realized. "We're engaged in a dynamic battle of adaptation. Each defensive measure we implement forces the entity to develop new attack methods."

Commander Decker ordered implementation of the Founders' advanced power protocols. These emergency measures sacrificed power efficiency for stability, creating redundant distribution networks that could maintain critical systems even under severe temporal stress.

"We can't maintain optimal power levels everywhere," Decker acknowledged. "But we can ensure our most crucial systems stay operational. The Founders' protocols prioritize survival over performance."

The power grid's stability became increasingly crucial as the entity's attacks intensified. Maya's team worked continuously to implement new defensive measures while maintaining essential power distribution to reality anchors and tactical teams.

"The grid isn't just about power anymore," she explained during a brief respite. "It's become our first line of defense against temporal collapse. If we lose power stability, we lose our ability to maintain timeline integrity."

As the second phase of their confrontation with the entity began, the Network's power grid stood as humanity's primary defense against temporal consumption. Maya's systems integration efforts, combined with the Founders' ancient protocols, created a complex web of energy distribution that might mean the difference between reality's survival and total temporal collapse.

The warning indicators continued their ominous display as Maya coordinated emergency power routing. The entity's next major attack was imminent, and the Network's power grid would face its greatest test in defending reality's fragile temporal fabric.

EPISODE 3: FIELD OPERATIONS

Captain Royston studied the quantum display showing the Chronophage's attack patterns. The entity didn't simply consume timelines - it created intricate fracture points that splintered reality like cracks in glass.

"It attacks in three distinct vectors," he explained to his team leaders. "First, temporal shearing - it separates timeline variants by creating dimensional barriers that prevent power and communication flow. Second, reality erosion - systematic degradation of temporal stability points. Third, void propagation - active consumption of weakened timeline sections."

The Founders' combat records, displayed on adjacent screens, showed identical attack patterns from previous encounters. Ancient quantum recordings documented how the entity had developed these techniques over countless confrontations.

"The Founders fought this thing across multiple iterations," Decker noted, highlighting specific combat logs. "Each encounter taught them more about its capabilities. The entity learns from every battle, adapting its approach based on defensive measures it encounters."

The quantum communication system, derived from Founders' technology, operated on principles that transcended normal temporal physics. Dr. Wilson called it "meta-temporal broadcasting."

"Standard communications are disrupted when the entity creates void zones," Communications Specialist Bolton demonstrated. "But the quantum system uses entangled particles that exist simultaneously across all timeline variants. Even if the entity consumes a local variant, the entangled network maintains coherence through parallel timelines."

The system could transmit tactical data through the entity's void zones by utilizing what the Founders called "temporal bypass channels" - communication pathways that existed outside conventional space-time.

"Each quantum transmitter contains crystalline matrices programmed with specific temporal frequencies," Decker explained. "These frequencies resonate across timeline variants in patterns the entity can't easily disrupt. It's like having a radio that broadcasts through dimensions instead of just space."

Tyrell's deployment strategy drew heavily from the Founders' combat records. Ancient tactical logs documented successful defensive formations that had effectively contained the entity's expansion.

"The Founders discovered that reality anchors needed to be positioned in specific geometric patterns across timeline variants," he detailed. "Each anchor creates a reinforcement field that interacts with adjacent fields to form a temporal containment network. The entity can't easily consume timelines protected by overlapping fields."

The combat records revealed a crucial detail about the entity's behavior - it attacked in predictable sequences when encountering strong temporal resistance.

"First, it tests our communication links," Tyrell explained, referencing the ancient logs. "Then it targets power distribution nodes. Finally, it attempts to isolate and consume individual timeline variants. The Founders documented this pattern across hundreds of encounters."

Lieutenant Foster's power amplification setup utilized designs extracted directly from the Founders' specifications. The ancient records included detailed schematics for temporal power distribution networks specifically designed to resist the entity's attacks.

"The Founders developed these systems through trial and error," Foster noted while calibrating a power node. "Each failure taught them more about the entity's vulnerabilities. These power networks aren't just defensive - they're offensive weapons designed to disrupt the entity's feeding process."

The first timeline coordination tests revealed how accurately the Founders had predicted the entity's response to their defensive measures. Just as the ancient records indicated, the Chronophage attempted to create isolation zones around reality anchor points.

"It's trying to cut off our anchor points from the power grid," Tyrell observed. "The Founders' records show this is always its first tactical move - isolate and degrade our temporal reinforcement capabilities before attempting timeline consumption."

The combat records provided crucial insight into the entity's limitations. The Founders had discovered that the Chronophage couldn't easily consume timelines protected by multiple overlapping reality anchor fields.

"It's not omnipotent," Tyrell explained during a tactical briefing. "The Founders proved it can be contained, even driven back, if we maintain stable temporal reinforcement networks. Our defensive positions aren't just random - they're based on proven successful configurations."

As field operations moved into active defense posture, the relevance of the Founders' combat experience became increasingly clear. Every tactical decision, every deployment pattern, built upon centuries of documented encounters with the entity.

"The Founders didn't just leave us weapons," Tyrell told his teams. "They left us a complete tactical playbook based on actual combat experience. Every victory, every defeat, every lesson learned - it's all here in the quantum records."

Warning indicators flashed as the entity initiated another attack sequence. Multiple void zones began forming around their perimeter, following exactly the pattern predicted in the Founders' documentation.

"All teams, implement Founders' tactical response Pattern Delta," Tyrell commanded. "The entity's attacking exactly as the records predicted. Now we show it humanity remembers how to fight back."

The Network's field operations represented the culmination of centuries of preparation, combining ancient wisdom with modern temporal combat capabilities. As the Chronophage pressed its attack, humanity's defenders stood ready, armed with knowledge earned through countless battles across time itself.

"This isn't our first fight with this thing," Tyrell reminded his teams as they moved to counter the entity's advance. "The Founders faced it before. They learned its weaknesses. Now we use everything they taught us to finish what they started."

The quantum displays showed another wave of temporal distortions approaching their defensive perimeter. The real test of whether humanity could apply the Founders' ancient combat wisdom was about to begin.

EPISODE 4: TECHNICAL INTEGRATION

Dr. James Wilson (current era, not the Founder) stood before a wall of quantum displays, watching temporal physics equations evolve in real-time as the entity's presence warped local space-time.

"The Chronophage doesn't just consume timelines," he explained to the assembled technical team. "It creates what I'm calling 'temporal vacuum states' - regions where the fundamental laws of physics begin to unravel before complete consumption occurs."

His breakthrough came from analyzing the Founders' quantum crystal data combined with current sensor readings. The entity's attack pattern wasn't random - it followed precise mathematical principles that could be predicted and potentially countered.

"Look at these waveform patterns," he highlighted complex mathematical visualizations. "The entity creates specific harmonic disruptions in the temporal field before initiating consumption. If we can generate inverse harmonics through our reality anchors, we might be able to neutralize its ability to create vacuum states."

Nina Chisolm's energy distribution team worked to implement these findings into practical defensive measures. Her new protocols dynamically adjusted power flow based on real-time analysis of temporal field harmonics.

"Traditional power distribution assumes stable physical constants," Chisolm detailed while programming new control algorithms. "We're dealing with regions where those constants are actively changing. Our systems need to adapt power flow characteristics on a microsecond scale to maintain stability."

Her protocols introduced what she called "quantum flux compensation" - predictive power routing that anticipated temporal distortions before they fully manifested.

"The Founders' records show they attempted something similar, but lacked the computational power to implement it effectively," she noted. "We're building on their theoretical framework with modern quantum processing capabilities."

System overload prevention became critical as they pushed their equipment to new operational limits. The technical Team implemented multiple layers of protection:

Quantum circuit breakers that could isolate compromised timeline variants

Adaptive power routing that redistributed load during surge events

Temporal buffer zones to absorb energy spillover

Emergency shutdown sequences for critical systems

"One overloaded reality anchor could cascade through the entire network," Dr. Wilson warned. "We're operating at the edge of known physics. Every safety measure has to account for phenomena we barely understand."

The reality stability monitoring system integrated data from thousands of temporal sensors across multiple timeline variants. Dr. Wilson's team developed new visualization algorithms to present this complex information in comprehensible formats.

"We're tracking reality cohesion across dimensional boundaries," he explained, demonstrating the interface. "These indicators show structural integrity of space-time itself. When they shift toward red, we're seeing active degradation of local reality."

The monitoring system revealed disturbing patterns in timeline variant interaction:

"The entity isn't just consuming individual timelines," Dr. Wilson observed. "It's systematically weakening the connections between variants. Each consumed timeline makes adjacent variants more vulnerable to collapse."

Emergency backup systems, based on the Founders' designs but enhanced with modern technology, provided crucial redundancy. These systems operated on isolated power networks and used specially shielded quantum processors resistant to temporal disruption.

"The Founders knew we couldn't survive a direct confrontation without multiple fallback positions," Chisolm explained while testing backup protocols. "They built redundancy into every critical system, then left us instructions to improve their designs."

The backup architecture included:

Independent power generation using temporal energy extraction

Hardened communication channels operating through quantum entanglement

Secondary reality anchor networks on separate control systems

Emergency temporal stabilization fields

As they activated the backup systems for testing, unusual readings appeared in the monitoring displays. The entity appeared to react to their preparations, shifting its attack patterns in response to their defensive measures.

"It's learning," Dr. Wilson realized, studying the data. "Every system we activate provides it with new information about our capabilities. We need to maintain operational security even while testing our defenses."

The technical integration challenges grew as they discovered more complex interactions between their systems and the entity's influence:

- Power fluctuations induced by temporal field distortions
- Communication interference from reality degradation
- Computational errors caused by variable physics constants
- Sensor disruption from vacuum state formation

"The Founders warned us about this," Chisolm noted, reviewing ancient technical documents. "Their records show similar cascading technical problems as they developed their defensive systems. We're not just fighting the entity - we're fighting the laws of physics themselves."

Dr. Wilson's team worked to implement real-time physics compensation algorithms. Their systems needed to maintain stability even as local reality became increasingly unpredictable.

"Standard operating parameters don't apply anymore," he explained during an emergency briefing. "We're writing new rules of physics as we go, trying to maintain technological function in regions where conventional physical laws are breaking down."

As they completed final integration tests, warning indicators showed increasing temporal distortion across multiple sectors. The entity's presence was growing stronger, pushing their systems toward operational limits before full deployment was complete.

"We're running out of time," Chisolm warned, monitoring power grid stability. "The technical integration has to be completed before the entity begins its main assault. Every system, every protocol, every backup - everything has to work perfectly when reality itself starts to fail."

The technical teams continued their work as temporal distortion warnings echoed through the facility. Their success or failure in integrating these complex systems could determine humanity's survival across all timeline variants.

"The Founders gave us the framework," Dr. Wilson reminded his team as they made final adjustments. "But we have to make it work under actual combat conditions. Everything we've built gets tested when that thing decides to make its move."

The monitoring displays showed another surge in temporal disruption as they rushed to complete system integration. The true test of their technical preparations was approaching faster than anyone had anticipated.

EPISODE 5: TIMELINE COORDINATION

May Oakly, Chief Timeline Coordinator, manipulated the holographic timeline map, showing how reality variants branched and intersected across dimensional boundaries. Each glowing strand represented a distinct timeline where Network teams operated simultaneously.

"Traditional command and control doesn't work when your teams exist across multiple reality variants," she explained. "We need perfect synchronization, or the entity will exploit timeline desync to create breach points."

The coordination challenge was unprecedented. Team Alpha operated across variants A1-A7, while Team Beta covered variants B1-B9. Team Delta maintained positions in D1-D12, and Special Operations teams floated between variants as needed. Each team needed to execute identical actions across their assigned variants while maintaining temporal sync with parallel operations.

"Think of it like a temporal orchestra," Oakly illustrated. "Everyone plays their part, but the timing has to be perfect across all reality variants. One team gets out of sync, the whole defensive pattern collapses."

Cross-time communication relied on quantum entanglement networks developed from the Founders' designs. Dr. Wilson's breakthrough enabled real-time coordination across variant boundaries through quantum-locked communication channels resistant to temporal interference. Reality anchor synchronization pulses maintained timeline coherence, while temporal positioning beacons facilitated cross-variant navigation. Emergency backup channels using meta-temporal broadcasting provided redundancy.

"Standard radio waves can't cross timeline boundaries," Dr. Wilson explained. "But quantum-entangled particles maintain their connection regardless of which variant they occupy. We can use that connection to create stable communication channels."

Resource allocation became critical as teams operated across multiple variants simultaneously. Maya Patel developed new protocols for managing equipment and personnel across the dimensional boundaries. The resource management system tracked power grid allocation, reality anchor deployment patterns, and personnel positioning across all variants. Equipment distribution and maintenance schedules had to be perfectly mirrored to prevent vulnerability points.

Emergency response protocols required unprecedented coordination. Oakly established a network that could react to threats across multiple timeline variants simultaneously. Rapid response teams maintained cross-variant mobility capabilities, while automated systems handled reality anchor reinforcement and power surge containment. Timeline isolation protocols stood ready for breach events, and cross-variant evacuation procedures were established for worst-case scenarios.

The first multi-timeline operation test revealed both the potential and limitations of their coordination systems. Teams successfully maintained synchronization across most variants, but several critical issues emerged.

"We're seeing temporal drift between variants," Oakly reported. "Teams start in perfect sync but gradually shift out of phase as the entity's influence affects local time flow differently across variants."

Dr. Wilson's team developed temporal sync compensation algorithms that provided real-time drift detection and correction. Automated phase alignment pulses worked in conjunction with timeline coherence monitoring to maintain operational synchronization across variants.

Captain Royston integrated tactical operations with timeline coordination: "Each team has to maintain positional awareness across all their variants while executing synchronized defensive maneuvers. It's like playing three-dimensional chess in four-dimensional space."

The test revealed how the entity actively worked to disrupt their coordination efforts. "It's targeting our sync points," Oakly observed. "Creating temporal distortions specifically designed to force variants out of phase with each other."

Counter-measures were quickly developed and implemented. Dynamic sync point redistribution systems worked alongside automated phase lock mechanisms to maintain timeline stability. Variant coherence maintenance protocols provided additional protection against the entity's attempts to disrupt their coordination.

As the test progressed, teams adapted to operating in an environment where reality itself became increasingly unstable. Bridge sensitives reported increased strain from cross-variant awareness, while technical teams struggled to maintain equipment synchronization. Command staff faced unprecedented complexity in tactical planning as they managed operations across multiple reality states.

"The Founders warned us about coordination fatigue," Oakly said, reviewing personnel monitoring data. "Maintaining awareness across multiple timeline variants puts enormous mental strain on operators. We need to rotate teams before performance degrades."

Implementation of automated coordination systems helped reduce operator strain. AI-assisted variant tracking worked in conjunction with automated sync maintenance systems to maintain operational effectiveness. Real-time drift compensation and emergency backup coordination protocols provided additional support for strained personnel.

As the test concluded, warning systems detected increasing temporal disturbances across multiple variants. The entity's presence was growing stronger, pushing their coordination capabilities toward operational limits.

"This isn't just about maintaining communication," Oakly reminded her teams as they analyzed test results. "Timeline coordination is our primary defense against reality collapse. If we lose sync between variants, we create weakness points the entity can exploit."

The monitoring displays showed another wave of temporal disruptions approaching their defensive perimeter. The true test of their timeline coordination capabilities was about to begin.

"Everyone to your positions," Royston commanded. "Maintain variant sync, watch your phase alignment, and remember - we're not just fighting across space anymore. We're fighting across every version of reality itself."

EPISODE 6: THE HUMAN ELEMENT

Maya Patel sat in her office reviewing psychological assessment reports, particularly focused on the increasing cases of temporal dissociation. The condition manifested in distinct phases, each more concerning than the last.

"Stage one begins with timeline bleeding," Dr. Evans explained during an emergency briefing. "Personnel experience memories from multiple variants simultaneously. A technician might remember three different ways they performed the same maintenance task, or a combat operator recalls dying in one variant while surviving in another."

Stage two involved identity fragmentation. Individuals began questioning which timeline variant was their "real" self. Bridge sensitives were particularly vulnerable, sometimes experiencing up to twelve simultaneous versions of their consciousness during high-stress operations.

The final stage, what Dr. Evans termed "temporal psychosis," occurred when personnel lost the ability to distinguish between timeline variants. "They exist in all timelines at once, unable to anchor themselves to any single reality. We've lost three operators to this condition in the past month alone."

The Network's security protocol breach response was equally complex. When a Network technician accidentally revealed classified information to his spouse during a temporal dissociation episode, the incident triggered multiple containment protocols.

"We can't just administer amnestics like traditional security services," Commander Decker explained. "When someone exists across multiple timeline variants, memory modification has to be synchronized across all versions of reality. One variant left unaddressed creates a critical information leak."

The Network developed specialized temporal containment teams for security breaches. These teams operated simultaneously across all affected variants, implementing memory adjustments and information containment with precise temporal synchronization. Family members who learned too much were either brought into the Network's family support structure or had their memories carefully modified across all relevant timelines.

Teams developed unique coping mechanisms for dealing with their reality-bending circumstances. Combat units created "temporal buddy systems," pairing operators across variants to maintain psychological anchoring. When one version experienced trauma or death, their cross-variant partner provided crucial psychological support to other versions of themselves.

Technical teams established what they called "quantum consciousness syncs" - meditation sessions where multiple versions of the same person would deliberately align their experiences and memories. This helped prevent temporal dissociation by regularly "defragmenting" their timeline experiences.

Dr. Anna Smith pioneered the "temporal journal" technique. "Each version of yourself maintains identical journals, writing the same entry at synchronized times. It creates a fixed point of psychological reference across all variants."

The Network's family support structure evolved complex protocols for maintaining relationships across temporal boundaries. Couples learned to synchronize their personal time despite operating in different temporal phases. Some developed elaborate systems of quantum-entangled messages, allowing communication even when timeline variants fell out of sync.

"My husband and I have a quantum-locked wedding ring," one operator explained. "When either of us touches it, all versions of the ring respond. It's our way of saying 'I love you' across every timeline we exist in."

Bridge sensitives created support circles that transcended normal reality boundaries. During rest periods, they would gather in temporally synchronized spaces, sharing the burden of their multi-variant consciousness. These sessions often involved what they called "timeline harmonizing" - a form of group meditation that helped stabilize their fractured awareness.

The Network's security protocols grew increasingly sophisticated as they dealt with new forms of temporal information leakage. They discovered that information could bleed between variants through dreams, requiring the development of "dream monitoring protocols" for high-security personnel.

"It's not just about what you consciously know," Security Chief Ted Wright explained. "Your unconscious mind exists across all variants. One version of you might dream about classified information from another timeline."

The psychological support structure expanded to include specialized care for what Dr. Evans called "temporal grief" - the unique experience of losing someone in one variant while continuing to work with them in others. Support groups formed around specific types of temporal trauma, including "variant survivors" - personnel who continued operating after experiencing their own death in other timelines.

Dr. Patel implemented mandatory "temporal grounding sessions" for all personnel. These sessions helped individuals maintain their primary timeline identity while acknowledging their variant experiences. The technique proved particularly effective in preventing advanced temporal dissociation.

"You need to accept that all variants are equally real," she explained to a group of new recruits, "while maintaining your anchor to your primary timeline. Think of it like being part of a quantum family - all versions are you, but this version is your home reality."

As the entity's presence grew stronger, the pressure on personnel increased. The monitoring displays showed growing temporal distortions, and with them came new cases of psychological strain. Yet the human element of the Network proved remarkably adaptable, developing new ways of maintaining their humanity in the face of impossible circumstances.

"We're not just fighting to protect reality," Commander Decker addressed her staff as reality anchors pulsed with increasing intensity. "We're fighting to protect what it means to be human across all possible versions of ourselves. Our ability to maintain our identity, our relationships, our very sense of self across multiple timelines - that's what makes us stronger than the void."

The facility hummed with activity as personnel prepared for another temporal sync operation. In offices, corridors, and command centers across multiple timeline variants, thousands of versions of the same dedicated individuals worked to protect not just reality itself, but their own humanity in all its quantum complexity.

EPISODE 7: STRATEGIC DEVELOPMENT

General Roberta Tyrell stood before the quantum strategic display, initiating Strategic Protocol Quantum-7 - the Network's most complex defensive strategy to date.

"Q-7 operates on the principle of quantum resonance manipulation," she explained, revealing intricate patterns across the timeline display. "Instead of just defending against the entity's attacks, we're creating deliberate interference patterns across timeline variants to disrupt its ability to maintain coherent form."

The protocol divided Network forces into three synchronized operational layers. The outer layer maintained conventional reality anchor networks, while the middle layer created dynamic temporal interference patterns. The inner layer, composed of elite bridge sensitive teams, worked to actively destabilize the entity's quantum structure.

Through months of observation, the Network had begun to understand more about their adversary's true nature. The entity wasn't simply a threat to reality - it was a living paradox, a being that existed by consuming the coherence of timeline variants.

"It's not just destroying reality," Dr. Wilson explained, pointing to complex data patterns. "It's converting ordered timeline variants into quantum chaos, feeding off the entropy it creates. Each reality it consumes makes it stronger, more capable of breaching additional variants."

The entity demonstrated signs of intelligence, but not in any conventional sense. It operated on principles that seemed to predate the very concept of cause and effect. Its actions suggested it had existed before the universe achieved temporal stability, and it sought to return reality to that primordial state of quantum uncertainty.

"Conventional weapons are useless," Colonel Zomber noted. "You can't shoot something that exists as a quantum probability field. But we can affect its ability to maintain coherent form across timeline variants."

The Network's long-term strategic goals extended far beyond immediate defense. They had begun developing what they called "Project Quantum Lock" - an ambitious plan to permanently stabilize reality against the entity's influence.

"Defense alone isn't enough," General Tyrell revealed. "Each time the entity breaches a timeline variant, it learns more about our defensive capabilities. We need to fundamentally change how reality maintains its coherence, or we'll eventually lose this war of attrition."

Project Quantum Lock involved the development of self-sustaining reality anchor networks that could maintain timeline stability without constant Network supervision. The technology was based on the Founders' original designs but expanded to operate across much larger quantum fields.

"Think of it like reality's immune system," Dr. Wilson explained. "We're not just building walls - we're teaching reality itself how to resist quantum entropy. Each successful implementation makes neighboring timeline variants more resistant to the entity's influence."

The strategic implications of their research revealed even more about the entity's nature. It showed signs of being ancient, possibly a survivor of a previous universal configuration where quantum uncertainty was the natural state. Its attacks weren't just destructive - they were attempting to revert reality to what it considered a proper state of existence.

"This isn't just a war for survival," General Tyrell told her command staff. "It's a fundamental conflict between two different versions of how reality should function. The entity represents quantum chaos. We represent causality and coherence."

Q-7's implementation required unprecedented coordination. Teams across thousands of timeline variants had to execute precisely synchronized actions to create the necessary interference patterns. The slightest misalignment could create vulnerabilities in their quantum defense grid.

"Standard battle strategy focuses on achieving objectives," Colonel Zomber explained to his officers. "Q-7 focuses on maintaining specific quantum states across multiple timeline variants. We're not just fighting in reality - we're fighting with reality itself as our primary weapon."

The Network's long-term planning extended beyond even Project Quantum Lock. They had begun researching what they called "quantum state manipulation" - the ability to actively modify how causality functioned across timeline variants.

"If we can understand how the entity manipulates quantum states," Dr. Wilson theorized, "we might be able to not just defend reality, but actively reshape it to be naturally resistant to temporal entropy."

The implications were staggering. Success could mean creating a version of reality that was fundamentally immune to the entity's influence. Failure could mean accidentally helping the entity achieve its goal of universal quantum destabilization.

As the first phase of Q-7 initiated, reality anchors across thousands of timeline variants pulsed in perfect synchronization. The quantum strategic display showed complex interference patterns forming, creating what looked like waves in the fabric of reality itself.

"All variants report ready," Colonel Zomber announced. "Quantum interference grid is achieving predicted patterns. Bridge sensitive teams are in position for phase two."

General Tyrell watched as the entity's presence encountered their new defensive strategy. For the first time, they saw signs of the entity responding with what appeared to be uncertainty, its usual patterns of attack disrupted by the quantum interference fields.

"This is just the beginning," she told her staff as they monitored the initial results. "Q-7 isn't just about defending our reality. It's about learning how to fight back against something that predates causality itself. Each engagement teaches us more about both the entity's nature and the fundamental structure of reality."

The facility hummed with activity as teams worked to maintain the complex quantum interference patterns. Across thousands of timeline variants, Network forces were not just fighting for survival - they were participating in perhaps the most important scientific and military operation in human history.

"Continue monitoring quantum resonance patterns," General Tyrell commanded as the entity probed their new defenses. "Every piece of data we gather brings us one step closer to understanding both our enemy and the true nature of reality itself."

The future of existence itself would depend on their ability to understand and counter a being that challenged their most basic assumptions about how reality functioned. Strategic Protocol Quantum-7 was more than just a defensive strategy - it was humanity's first real attempt to take control of the quantum nature of reality itself.

EPISODE 8: POWER MANAGEMENT

Dr. Anna Smith stood in the Network's central power control, watching as quantum energy readings fluctuated across thousands of reality anchors. The facility's new fusion cores pulsed with an otherworldly glow, channeling power across dimensional boundaries.

"We're not just managing electricity anymore," she explained to her engineering team. "We're managing quantum energy states across multiple timeline variants. One power fluctuation can create cascade failures across hundreds of connected realities."

The Network's power distribution system represented a revolution in energy management. Traditional power grids operated in three-dimensional space, but their system had to maintain stable energy flow across quantum probability fields. Each reality anchor required precisely calibrated power levels that had to remain synchronized across all timeline variants.

"The entity feeds on energy instability," Dr. Smith detailed, highlighting pattern analyses. "It can detect and exploit even microsecond power fluctuations. Our distribution network has to maintain quantum-level precision or we create breach points."

The ability coordination protocols were equally complex. Bridge sensitives required massive amounts of energy to maintain their cross-variant awareness, while reality anchors needed constant power modulation to maintain temporal stability. The system had to balance these competing demands across thousands of timeline variants simultaneously.

"Think of it like conducting an orchestra," Chief Engineer Ted Wright explained. "Each component needs exactly the right amount of power at exactly the right moment, synchronized across all quantum states. One instrument out of tune can disrupt the entire performance."

The Network developed "quantum harmonic regulators" - specialized systems that maintained power synchronization across variant boundaries. These devices operated on principles that seemed to violate conventional physics, using quantum entanglement to ensure perfect power distribution regardless of temporal displacement.

"Standard electrical theory doesn't apply anymore," Dr. Smith noted during a technical briefing. "We're dealing with energy that exists in quantum superposition across multiple timeline variants. Our distribution network has to account for probability fields as much as electrical resistance."

System stability measures evolved beyond conventional engineering principles. The Network created "quantum surge suppressors" capable of detecting and neutralizing power fluctuations before they could propagate across variant boundaries. These devices operated in conjunction with reality anchors to maintain stable energy states throughout the quantum defense grid.

Resource allocation became an exercise in five-dimensional mathematics. Engineers had to calculate power requirements not just for current operations, but across probability fields that determined how timeline variants influenced each other's energy states.

"Traditional load balancing is useless," Wright explained to his maintenance teams. "We need to think in terms of quantum energy distribution - how power flows affect probability states across multiple variants simultaneously."

Emergency power protocols took on new levels of complexity. The Network developed "quantum backup systems" that could maintain critical operations even if multiple timeline variants lost power simultaneously. These systems operated through what Dr. Smith called "probability shunting" - redirecting power flows through more stable timeline variants to maintain critical operations.

"Standard backup generators won't work," she detailed during an emergency drill. "When reality itself becomes unstable, we need power systems that can operate independently of conventional space-time physics."

The Network's power infrastructure incorporated bleeding-edge theoretical physics. They developed "temporal capacitors" capable of storing energy across multiple quantum states, ensuring power avail-ability regardless of timeline disruptions. These devices worked along-side conventional fusion cores to maintain stable energy distribution throughout the quantum defense grid.

"Our power system isn't just supporting operations," Dr. Smith explained. "It's actively participating in reality stabilization. The energy patterns we maintain help reinforce the quantum coherence of space-time itself."

As they finalized resource allocation protocols, the engineering team faced unprecedented challenges. They had to ensure critical systems maintained power priority while preventing any single component from creating vulnerable power signatures that the entity could detect.

"The entity is drawn to energy concentrations," Wright noted during a system test. "But it can also detect power voids. We need to maintain perfect energy balance across all variants or we create breach points."

The Network's emergency protocols extended beyond conventional power management. They developed "quantum isolation systems" capable of separating damaged timeline variants from the power grid without disrupting energy distribution to connected variants.

"Standard circuit breakers are useless," Dr. Smith demonstrated. "We need systems that can isolate quantum probability fields while main-taining power coherence across all stable variants."

As they completed final system calibrations, warning indicators showed increasing temporal disturbances. The entity's presence was growing stronger, putting new pressure on their power management capabilities.

"All power systems showing quantum sync," Wright reported as reality anchors pulsed with increased intensity. "Distribution network maintaining stability across all monitored variants. Emergency systems standing by."

Dr. Smith watched the power flow patterns across the quantum moni-toring display. Their system represented humanity's first attempt to manage energy distribution across multiple versions of reality simultaneously. Its success or failure could determine the fate of existence itself.

"Begin full power synchronization," she commanded as temporal distortions approached their defensive perimeter. "All variants prepare for maximum load. We're about to find out if our power grid can handle real combat conditions across quantum probability space."

The facility hummed with increasing energy as power systems engaged across thousands of timeline variants. In the control room, engineers monitored complex quantum energy patterns that would have seemed impossible just years ago. The true test of their power management capabilities was about to begin.

Dr. Smith addressed her team as energy readings approached critical levels. "Let this sink in - we're not just keeping the lights on. We're maintaining the quantum coherence of reality itself. Our power grid is now as much a weapon against the entity as any reality anchor or defensive system."

The entity's presence loomed larger in their sensor readings, its influence creating complex distortions in power flow patterns. The Network's response would depend on their ability to maintain stable energy distribution across all quantum states while adapting to an enemy that fed on power instability.

EPISODE 9: ENTITY CONTAINMENT

General Roberta Tyrell initiated Emergency Containment Sequence Alpha - referred to as "Alpine" in Network protocols - as the entity's presence intensified across quantum probability space.

"Alpine operates on multiple containment layers," she explained, activating the sequence. "Each layer targets a different aspect of the entity's quantum structure, creating what we call 'probability interference cascades.'"

The sequence began with synchronized pulses from reality anchors, generating specific probability resonance patterns. These patterns, discovered through years of studying the entity's behavior, created quantum states that the entity found difficult to maintain coherence within.

"The resonance patterns aren't random," Dr. Wilson detailed, displaying complex mathematical models. "They're specific quantum frequencies that mirror the entity's own probability field structure, but in opposing phases. Think of it as quantum destructive interference."

The team had identified five primary resonance patterns:

Alpha Pattern: Created stable causality points that resisted quantum manipulation

Beta Pattern: Generated temporal friction fields that slowed probability shifts

Gamma Pattern: Established quantum lock states that prevented reality distortion

Delta Pattern: Produced probability cancellation waves

Epsilon Pattern: Formed temporal anchor points that maintained timeline coherence

Through careful observation, they had begun to understand more about the entity's ultimate goal. It wasn't simply destroying reality - it was trying to return the universe to a state of pure quantum potential, without fixed causality or determined outcomes.

"The entity exists in a state of pure quantum superposition," Dr. Wilson explained. "Our universe, with its fixed laws and stable time-line variants, is like a prison to it. It's trying to break reality back down into pure probability."

Alpine's second phase involved "quantum state lockdown" - a process where multiple reality anchors worked in concert to gradually restrict the entity's ability to maintain quantum uncertainty. Each successful restriction forced it to exist in increasingly determined states.

"We're essentially forcing it to play by our universe's rules," General Tyrell noted. "Each containment layer reduces its ability to exist in multiple quantum states simultaneously."

The entity's responses to Alpine revealed disturbing implications about its nature. It demonstrated what appeared to be genuine distress when forced into more determined states, suggesting that fixed causality caused it actual harm or discomfort.

"This isn't just a battle for survival," Dr. Wilson theorized during an analysis session. "We're witnessing a fundamental conflict between two incompatible states of existence - our reality of fixed causality versus its reality of pure quantum potential."

The probability resonance patterns became increasingly complex as Alpine progressed. Teams of bridge sensitives worked to maintain specific quantum states that seemed to create "blind spots" in the entity's perception - areas where its ability to manipulate probability was significantly reduced.

"The patterns aren't just defensive," General Tyrell explained. "They're actively hostile to the entity's preferred state of existence. We're creating zones where quantum uncertainty itself becomes temporarily impossible."

As they learned more about the entity's goals, the containment strategy evolved. The Network began developing what they called "quantum state anchoring" - technology designed to permanently stabilize reality against attempts to return it to a state of pure probability.

"The entity isn't just ancient," Dr. Wilson revealed. "We believe it's a survivor from before the universe achieved quantum decoherence - before reality as we know it existed. It remembers a state of existence where everything was pure potential, and it wants to restore that state."

Alpine's final phase involved the deployment of "probability crystallization fields" - experimental technology that could theoretically force portions of quantum probability space into permanent states of fixed causality.

"We're not just containing it anymore," General Tyrell told her staff. "We're trying to gradually reduce the amount of probability space where it can exist in its natural state. Each successful crystallization creates another region where our physics is the only physics possible."

The entity's reactions to these efforts were increasingly violent. It launched simultaneous attacks across multiple timeline variants, attempting to disrupt the probability crystallization process before it could complete.

"All variants reporting quantum crystallization progress," the control room announced. "Probability resonance patterns holding stable. Entity showing signs of probability field collapse in targeted sectors."

General Tyrell watched as Alpine's effects began to manifest across quantum probability space. For the first time, they were seeing signs that their containment efforts were having a permanent impact on the entity's ability to maintain its preferred state of existence.

"Continue probability crystallization sequence," she commanded as reality anchors pulsed with increasing intensity. "All variants maintain resonance patterns. We're not just containing it - we're slowly closing off its ability to exist outside our laws of physics."

The facility vibrated with power as Alpine reached its peak intensity. Bridge sensitives reported increasing resistance from the entity as more probability space became locked into states of fixed causality.

General Tyrell addressed her teams as the containment field strengthened, "We're not just fighting to protect our reality. We're fighting to determine the fundamental nature of existence itself. Will the universe remain a place of fixed causality and determined outcomes, or will it return to a state of pure quantum potential?"

The entity's presence surged against their containment fields, its influence creating complex distortions in probability space as it fought against the crystallization process. The Network's success would depend on their ability to maintain Alpine's precise probability resonance patterns while gradually forcing more of reality into a permanently determined state.

"All variants, prepare for maximum probability crystallization," General Tyrell ordered as the entity launched another wave of attacks. "We're about to find out if humanity can permanently impose our version of reality on something that remembers existence before reality itself existed."

EPISODE 10: THE CONFRONTATION

General Tyrell initiated Protocol Omega-9 as reality anchor readings reached critical levels. The protocol represented the Network's most sophisticated quantum defense strategy - a multi-layered approach to probability warfare that operated across all quantum states simultaneously.

"Omega-9 works by creating deliberate probability interference patterns," she explained as the protocol activated. "We're not just defending reality - we're actively weaponizing quantum uncertainty against an entity that feeds on it."

The protocol operated in three distinct phases:

Phase 1: Probability Crystallization

- Reality anchors generate synchronized quantum fields that force local space-time into increasingly determined states
- Bridge sensitive teams create "causality enforcement zones" where quantum uncertainty becomes temporarily impossible

Power systems maintain precise resonance patterns that prevent probability field fluctuations

Phase 2: Temporal Lockdown

- Network forces establish quantum "hard points" - regions where physics becomes absolutely fixed
- Timeline variants are temporarily synchronized to create unified probability fields
- Quantum dampening systems prevent the entity from manipulating local reality states

Phase 3: Probability Warfare

A

- ctive manipulation of quantum states to create "tactical uncertainty" - deliberate probability fluctuations that disrupt the entity's coherence
- Reality anchors generate opposing probability fields that cancel out the entity's influence
- Bridge sensitives direct focused consciousness waves to stabilize desired quantum states

Final Defense Protocol Alpha activated as the entity concentrated its quantum presence for a decisive assault. The protocol represented humanity's ultimate defense against quantum chaos:

"Alpha Protocol has three primary components," Dr. Wilson detailed during the engagement. "Quantum state enforcement, probability field manipulation, and consciousness-directed reality stabilization."

The protocol's effects manifested across all engaged timeline variants:

Reality anchors pulsed in perfect synchronization, creating overlapping fields of enforced causality

Bridge sensitive teams projected unified consciousness patterns that reinforced local physics

Power systems maintained precise quantum resonance frequencies that disrupted the entity's ability to maintain coherence

The entity's final assault came as a massive surge of pure probability - an attempt to overwhelm their defenses by concentrating its entire quantum presence into a single massive attack.

"Multiple timeline variants reporting critical probability flux," Colonel Zomber announced as sensors overloaded. "Entity attempting to force universal quantum state collapse."

The Network's response through probability warfare proved decisive. Teams across thousands of variants executed precisely coordinated quantum state manipulations:

Reality anchors generated opposing probability fields that created destructive interference patterns

Bridge sensitives projected focused consciousness waves that reinforced local causality

Power systems maintained exact quantum frequencies that prevented probability field collapse

"This is true probability warfare," Dr. Wilson explained during the confrontation. "We're not just fighting with weapons or energy - we're fighting by actively manipulating how reality itself functions at the quantum level."

The battle's turning point came as the entity's concentrated assault met their synchronized defense grid. The massive surge of quantum uncertainty encountered something unprecedented - thousands of timeline variants working in perfect harmony to maintain fixed causality.

"Entity showing signs of quantum coherence failure," sensors reported. "Probability field structure becoming unstable. Local reality maintaining integrity."

For the first time, they observed the entity experiencing what appeared to be actual quantum state collapse - its probability field structure breaking down as it failed to maintain coherence across multiple timeline variants.

"Continue maximum probability enforcement," General Tyrell ordered as reality anchors pulsed with increasing power. "All variants maintain quantum sync. We're not just containing it anymore - we're forcing it to exist according to our physics."

The aftermath revealed fundamental changes in quantum probability space. Regions where the entity had concentrated its presence showed signs of permanent probability crystallization - areas where quantum uncertainty had been permanently reduced.

"We're seeing something unprecedented," Dr. Wilson reported during post-battle analysis. "The entity's final assault actually helped stabilize local reality. Its attempt to force quantum collapse instead created zones of enhanced causality."

The Network's understanding of probability warfare evolved dramatically through the confrontation. They discovered that consciousness itself played a crucial role in maintaining quantum states:

- Bridge sensitive teams could actively direct probability field formation
- Synchronized consciousness waves could reinforce desired quantum states
- Human awareness seemed to naturally support causality over uncertainty

"This wasn't just a military victory," General Tyrell told her command staff afterward. "We've proven that consciousness itself is a fundamental force in determining how reality functions. Our ability to choose and maintain determined states actually helps stabilize existence."

The entity's presence diminished across all monitored timeline variants, but they detected signs that it continued to exist in some form - perhaps retreating to regions of probability space where quantum uncertainty remained dominant.

"Prepare for long-term probability enforcement," General Tyrell ordered as they secured their gains. "The entity isn't destroyed - it's learned to respect our ability to maintain causality. Now we need to ensure it never again threatens to return reality to pure quantum chaos."

The confrontation marked humanity's first true victory in probability warfare - proof that consciousness and determination could impose order on quantum uncertainty. Their defense of fixed causality had demonstrated that reality itself would support their efforts to maintain stable existence.

"All variants maintain quantum defense protocols," General Tyrell commanded as they established their new security paradigm. "The entity now knows we can fight it on its own terms - using probability itself as our primary weapon. Our job now is to ensure reality remains a place where consciousness and causality, not quantum chaos, determine the nature of existence."

The facility hummed at a lower pitch as systems shifted to maintenance mode. The Network had proven that humanity could actively shape how reality functioned at its most fundamental level. Their mastery of probability warfare had given them the tools to defend existence itself against forces that would return it to pure quantum potential.

EPISODE 11: CRITICAL MASS

The facility's quantum sensors screamed as readings surged beyond critical thresholds. Power fluctuations rippled across three thousand timeline variants simultaneously, threatening catastrophic probability field collapse.

Initial Crisis Assessment

Warning indicators flashed across every monitor in the command center. Primary fusion cores pushed past 147% capacity. Quantum harmonic regulators showed imminent failure patterns. Reality anchor power supplies approached critical mass. Bridge sensitive teams reported rapidly degrading consciousness synchronization across multiple sectors.

Power Grid Status

Dr. Smith worked frantically at the engineering console as systems approached collapse. Primary fusion cores strained against their containment fields. Secondary backup systems engaged automatically but couldn't handle the probability resonance patterns. Emergency cooling systems began failing under the quantum strain.

"We're losing grid stability across all sectors," she reported. "The power fluctuations are creating self-sustaining probability cascades. Each surge amplifies the next."

Timeline Stability Management

Colonel Zomber monitored tactical displays as timeline variants began showing critical decay patterns. Probability field collapse threatened sectors three through seven. Reality anchor coverage became increasingly unstable as power surges disrupted quantum harmonics

"Multiple variants approaching critical instability," he announced. "Consciousness sync failing in forty percent of monitored timelines. We're losing coherence across the board."

Emergency Protocol Activation

General Tyrell initiated emergency response protocols as the crisis escalated. Protocol Sigma-1 engaged automatic power management systems. Sigma-2 activated timeline defense measures. Sigma-3 implemented critical response procedures.

"Standard containment protocols are failing," she noted. "The probability cascades are creating resonance patterns we've never seen before. Each attempted stabilization seems to amplify the fluctuations."

Team Coordination Response

Emergency response teams mobilized across all sectors. Power management crews worked to stabilize grid fluctuations. Bridge sensitive units struggled to maintain consciousness sync. Reality anchor technicians fought to prevent probability field collapse. Timeline stability forces coordinated variant preservation efforts.

"We need perfect coordination across all teams," General Tyrell commanded. "One misaligned response could trigger total probability cascade failure."

Reality Breach Containment

Reality breaches began appearing as power surges created weak points in local probability fields. Detection systems identified multiple breach points forming across compromised sectors. Containment teams deployed emergency probability dampening measures. Power grid adjustments attempted to prevent further destabilization.

"The breaches are following some kind of pattern," Dr. Wilson observed. "It's as if the probability field itself is trying to achieve a new kind of stability through the fluctuations."

Critical Mass Prevention

As the situation approached genuine critical mass, General Tyrell activated Emergency Protocol Tau - their last-resort option for preventing total probability collapse. All power systems switched to direct quantum control. Reality anchors channeled maximum probability enforcement. Bridge sensitive teams linked for unified consciousness projection.

"We're seeing unprecedented quantum effects," Dr. Wilson reported as Protocol Tau engaged. "The power fluctuations are creating resonance patterns that actually seem to be reinforcing probability field stability in some sectors."

Tactical Evolution

Through the crisis response, teams discovered new aspects of quantum probability management. Power fluctuations could be used to strengthen probability fields when properly controlled. Consciousness waves naturally supported quantum stability. Reality itself seemed to resist total probability collapse.

"Continue Protocol Tau execution," General Tyrell ordered as readings began to stabilize. "All teams maintain maximum coordination. We're learning how to actively manage quantum probability itself."

The facility hummed with unprecedented power as systems fought to maintain stability. In the command center, teams monitored complex probability patterns that showed reality adapting to their containment efforts. Their success would depend on perfect coordination while adapting to quantum effects that threatened to reshape the nature of existence itself.

General Tyrell addressed her staff, "We're not just preventing disaster. We're learning fundamental truths about how reality functions at the quantum level. Every success teaches us more about managing probability itself. "The situation remained critical as teams worked to prevent total system collapse. Their understanding of quantum probability management evolved with each response, revealing new ways to maintain stability across multiple timeline variants simultaneously.

EPISODE 12: THRESHOLD

Dr. Wilson's quantum displays showed patterns she'd never seen before. After months of preparation, power readings indicated they'd reached the theoretical threshold needed for their most ambitious operation yet.

"Power convergence at 98% synchronization," Dr. Smith reported from engineering. "All fusion cores maintaining quantum harmonic alignment. Reality anchors showing unprecedented stability across all monitored variants."

Final Battle Preparation

The Network had transformed their primary facility into what General Tyrell called a "probability fortress." Multiple layers of reality anchors created overlapping fields of enforced causality. Bridge sensitive teams maintained continuous consciousness synchronization across thousands of timeline variants. Power systems hummed at precisely calculated frequencies designed to disrupt the entity's quantum coherence.

"This isn't like our previous encounters," General Tyrell addressed her command staff. "We're not just defending against the entity anymore. We're creating conditions that will force it to exist according to our physics."

The preparation phase required perfect coordination:

- **Phase 1:** Power grid reinforcement across all variants
- **Phase 2:** Reality anchor network synchronization
- **Phase 3:** Bridge sensitive consciousness wave alignment
- **Phase 4:** Timeline variant harmonization
- **Phase 5:** Quantum state enforcement activation

Power Convergence Activation

"Beginning final power convergence sequence," Dr. Smith announced as systems engaged. "All fusion cores transitioning to quantum-synchronized output."

The facility's power grid underwent unprecedented transformation. Fusion cores linked through quantum harmonic regulators created perfectly synchronized energy patterns. Reality anchors channeled power in precise sequences that reinforced probability field stability. Emergency systems maintained constant backup coverage to prevent any fluctuation in the convergence pattern.

"Power convergence achieving theoretical maximum," sensors reported. "Quantum harmonics showing perfect phase alignment. Reality anchor network at full operational capacity."

Timeline Intersection Management

Colonel Zomber coordinated the most complex temporal operation they'd ever attempted. Thousands of timeline variants were being carefully manipulated to create what Dr. Wilson called "probability intersection nodes."

"We're not just managing individual variants anymore," Zomber explained to his tactical teams. "We're creating deliberate timeline convergence points. Places where probability itself becomes more determined."

The intersection management required:

- Precise temporal alignment across all engaged variants
- Carefully calculated probability field adjustments
- Continuous consciousness wave synchronization
- Active quantum state enforcement
- Reality anchor coverage at all intersection points

Entity Containment Execution

"Entity presence detected approaching primary intersection node," sensors reported. "Quantum signature matches theoretical predictions. It's responding to our probability manipulation exactly as projected."

The containment operation represented their most sophisticated application of probability warfare:

- **Stage 1:** Create quantum-enforced spaces where the entity's normal probability manipulation becomes impossible
- **Stage 2:** Force the entity's quantum presence into these engineered spaces through carefully calculated timeline manipulations
- **Stage 3:** Use synchronized reality anchors to maintain fixed causality even as the entity attempts to destabilize local physics
- **Stage 4:** Apply consciousness-directed probability enforcement to prevent quantum state collapse

"The entity is showing signs of quantum coherence strain," Dr. Wilson reported as containment measures engaged. "Our enforced causality is actually forcing it to exist in more determined states."

Reality Stabilization Efforts

As the operation reached its critical phase, reality itself seemed to shudder under the opposing forces. The entity's natural quantum chaos confronted their engineered probability stability.

"All teams maintain maximum probability enforcement," General Tyrell ordered. "We need perfect synchronization across all systems. One fluctuation in our quantum field could give it the opening it needs to escape containment."

The stabilization effort required unprecedented coordination:

- Reality anchors operating at theoretical maximum output
- Bridge sensitive teams projecting unified consciousness waves
- Power systems maintaining exact quantum frequencies
- Timeline variants locked in precise probability alignment
- Continuous quantum state enforcement across all sectors

"We're seeing something remarkable," Dr. Wilson observed during the operation. "The entity isn't just being contained - it's being forced to adapt to our physics. Each moment under our probability enforcement makes it harder for it to maintain pure quantum states."

The facility vibrated with barely contained power as they pushed their systems to absolute limits. Reality anchors pulsed in perfect harmony, maintaining the engineered probability fields that trapped the entity in increasingly determined states.

"Continue maximum containment protocols," General Tyrell commanded as readings showed the entity's quantum coherence failing. "We're not just achieving temporary containment. We're fundamentally altering how it exists within our reality."

The operation revealed new aspects of quantum physics they'd never anticipated. The entity's attempts to resist their probability enforcement actually strengthened local causality. Its quantum chaos, when properly contained and channeled, could be transformed into enhanced reality stability.

"This goes beyond just winning a battle," Dr. Wilson explained as they monitored the results. "We're proving that consciousness and determination can impose permanent order on quantum chaos. We're showing that reality itself will support our efforts to maintain stable existence."

The threshold they'd crossed wasn't just technological or tactical - it was foundational. They'd demonstrated that humanity could actively shape how reality functioned at its most fundamental level. Their mastery of probability warfare had given them tools to defend existence itself against forces that would return it to pure quantum potential.

"Maintain containment protocols," General Tyrell ordered as they secured their unprecedented victory. "What we've achieved here changes everything. We've proven that consciousness and causality, not quantum chaos, will determine the future of reality itself."

The facility's quantum hum shifted to a lower, more stable frequency as systems adjusted to their new role - not just defending reality, but actively shaping how existence itself functioned at the probability level. They had crossed a threshold from which there was no return, and reality itself would never be quite the same.

CHAPTER TWELVE

THRESHOLD (PRESENT DAY)

EPISODE 1: CONVERGENCE POINT

COMMANDER DECKER STOOD before the quantum tactical display, its holographic patterns casting ethereal shadows across the briefing room. Three thousand timeline variants pulsed in synchronized rhythm, each one representing a potential battlefield in the coming confrontation.

"This operation goes beyond anything we've attempted," she addressed her assembled command staff. "We're not just defending reality anymore - we're creating conditions that will force the entity to exist according to our physics."

The tactical briefing revealed the unprecedented scope of their operation. Each timeline variant required precise positioning of reality anchors, power distribution nodes, and consciousness projection teams. The slightest misalignment could create vulnerability points the entity might exploit.

"Our defense grid must maintain perfect quantum synchronization," Decker explained, highlighting critical sectors. "One timeline falling out of phase could create a cascade effect across all variants. We can't afford a single weak point."

In the power control center, Maya Patel worked to implement the most complex grid configuration they'd ever attempted. Fusion cores hummed at precisely calculated frequencies, channeling energy through quantum harmonic regulators designed to maintain stability across multiple timeline variants.

"The power grid isn't just providing energy," she detailed to her engineering teams. "It's creating specific quantum resonance patterns that will help contain the entity. Each power node has to maintain exact frequencies or we risk destabilizing the entire network."

Dr. Wilson's analysis revealed disturbing patterns in recent timeline behavior. Quantum probability fields showed increasing instability as the entity's influence grew stronger. Reality itself seemed to shudder under the approaching presence of something that existed outside normal physics.

"The entity isn't just moving through our reality," he explained, displaying complex mathematical models. "It's creating ripples in quantum probability space - distortions that threaten the very fabric of existence. Each timeline variant it touches becomes more susceptible to collapse."

The first signs of the entity's approach manifested in subtle ways. Bridge sensitives reported increasing difficulty maintaining consciousness synchronization across timeline variants. Reality anchors showed harmonic fluctuations that didn't match any known patterns. Power grid readings indicated growing quantum instability in sectors predicted to be first contact points.

"Multiple variants reporting quantum coherence strain," sensors announced. "Timeline stability dropping in sectors seven through twelve. Reality anchor harmonics showing increasing deviation from baseline."

Team deployment began with mechanical precision born of countless drills. Power amplification crews moved to reinforce critical grid nodes. Reality anchor technicians initiated quantum field stabilization protocols. Bridge sensitive teams established consciousness projection points across multiple variants.

"All teams maintain strict quantum sync during deployment," Tyrell ordered. "We can't risk timeline desynchronization before the operation even begins. Check your variant coordinates twice before establishing any power connections."

The facility thrummed with increasing energy as systems engaged across thousands of timeline variants simultaneously. In the command center, Tyrell watched as position indicators showed teams moving into carefully calculated positions throughout quantum probability space.

"This is what the Network was built for," she reminded her staff as deployment continued. "Everything we've learned, every capability we've developed, has prepared us for this moment. We're about to attempt something unprecedented - using consciousness itself to reshape how reality functions."

As final preparations completed, the quantum tactical display showed an approaching disturbance that defied normal physics. The entity's presence created visible ripples in probability space, distorting timeline variants as it drew closer to their defensive perimeter.

"All teams report ready status," Tyrell commanded as reality anchors pulsed with increasing power. "Maintain absolute quantum sync across all variants. This isn't just about defending reality anymore - consciousness and determination, not chaos, will determine the future of existence itself."

The facility's power signature shifted to a new frequency as systems achieved full operational status. In the command center, Tyrell watched as thousands of timeline variants aligned in perfect synchronization. The convergence point had been reached. Now they would discover if humanity could impose its will on something that existed before reality itself.

"Begin Operation Threshold," she ordered as the entity's presence loomed larger in their sensor readings. "Let's show this thing what happens when it threatens a reality protected by human consciousness and determination."

EPISODE 2: POWER GRID NEXUS

Nina Chisolm's hands flew across multiple holographic interfaces as quantum power readings fluctuated across three thousand timeline variants. The Network's new power integration system pushed theoretical limits of what should be possible with current technology.

"Each power node has to maintain perfect quantum resonance," she explained to her engineering team. "We're not just distributing energy - we're creating specific harmonic patterns that will help contain the entity's influence across multiple timeline variants."

Lieutenant Foster monitored the power amplification setup from her station, watching as reality anchors drew unprecedented levels of energy through quantum harmonic regulators. The equipment hummed at frequencies that made the air itself seem to vibrate with potential.

"The amplification network is showing stress patterns we've never seen before," Foster reported, adjusting power flow parameters. "These energy levels are creating quantum resonance effects that don't match any previous data. We're in uncharted territory."

Grid stability challenges emerged as power levels approached critical thresholds. Traditional circuit breakers proved useless against quantum power surges that existed simultaneously across multiple timeline variants. The engineering team had to develop new safety protocols on the fly.

"Standard containment measures won't work," Chisholm noted as another surge rippled through the grid. "We need to think in terms of quantum probability management. Each power fluctuation creates ripples through all connected variants. One overload could cascade through the entire network."

Timeline energy synchronization required precision that seemed to defy physics itself. Power had to flow at exactly matched frequencies across thousands of variants simultaneously. The slightest misalignment could create weakness points in their quantum defense grid.

"Watch your harmonic resonance patterns," Foster instructed her amplification teams. "Even microsecond variations in power flow can create timeline desync. We need perfect quantum coherence across all variants."

Warning indicators flashed as power levels pushed closer to theoretical maximums. Reality anchors drew energy in precise patterns designed to reinforce local physics against the entity's influence. Each anchor required carefully calculated power frequencies that had to remain perfectly stable.

"Grid sectors thirteen through seventeen showing critical harmonics," sensors reported. "Power flow patterns approaching quantum instability threshold. Timeline variant synchronization experiencing strain."

Chisolm initiated emergency stabilization protocols as fluctuations threatened to overwhelm standard safety measures. The power grid's quantum architecture responded in ways they hadn't anticipated, creating new harmonic patterns that seemed to naturally resist timeline destabilization.

"The grid isn't just maintaining power flow," she realized, studying the readings. "It's actively adapting to reinforce timeline stability. These harmonic patterns - they're self-organizing to enhance quantum coherence."

Foster's amplification teams worked to integrate this unexpected development into their power distribution strategy. They began deliberately generating harmonic patterns that enhanced the grid's natural stabilization tendencies.

"Adjust your power frequencies to match these new harmonics," she ordered. "The grid's showing us how to maintain quantum stability. Work with it, not against it."

Emergency backup systems engaged automatically as power levels continued to climb. Quantum capacitors designed to handle timeline variant energy storage kicked in, providing crucial power redundancy across multiple sectors simultaneously.

"Backup grid showing green across all variants," Chisolm confirmed. "Quantum storage systems maintaining stability. Emergency power distribution ready for full activation."

The facility's power signature transformed as systems achieved full integration. Reality anchors pulsed with unprecedented energy levels while maintaining perfect quantum synchronization. The power grid had become more than just an energy distribution network - it was actively participating in reality stabilization.

"All power systems show ready status," Chisolm reported as final calibrations completed. "Grid harmonics aligned across all variants. Timeline energy synchronization at optimal levels. We're as ready as we'll ever be."

Foster watched the power flow patterns stabilize across their quantum monitoring displays. They had created something unprecedented - a power distribution system that could maintain reality stability across thousands of timeline variants simultaneously.

"This is more than just power management," she told her teams as they completed final checks. "We've built something that actively reinforces the fabric of reality itself. Now let's see what it can do when pushed to its limits."

The facility hummed with contained power as they prepared for the entity's approach. In the engineering center, Chisolm made final adjustments to quantum harmonic regulators while monitoring timeline stability indicators. They had created the most sophisticated power grid in human history. Soon they would discover if it was enough to defend reality itself.

EPISODE 3: FIELD OPERATIONS

Captain Tony Ralfs moved through the facility's quantum-shielded corridors, tracking his teams' positions across multiple timeline variants through his neural interface. Each specialist carried equipment that had to be positioned with microscopic precision - the slightest misalignment could create vulnerabilities across thousands of realities simultaneously.

"Delta team, adjust your anchor positioning three microns east," he transmitted through the quantum comm network. "That variance is creating harmonic interference in sectors twelve through fifteen. We need perfect alignment."

The reality anchors themselves posed unique deployment challenges. Each device, a masterpiece of quantum engineering, had to be synchronized not just with local space-time, but with its counterparts across all active timeline variants. Teams worked in environment suits designed to minimize their own quantum interference patterns.

"Careful with the harmonic regulators," Ralfs warned as technicians positioned another anchor. "These aren't just power nodes - they're reality stabilization points. One misaligned field could create cascade failures across multiple variants."

Timeline coordination centers emerged as crystalline structures of pure energy, maintained by teams of consciousness-linked operators. These nexus points served as command and control hubs, allowing simultaneous oversight of operations across thousands of timeline variants.

"Echo team reporting coordination center Alpha online," came the call. "Quantum synchronization stable. Timeline variant tracking operational. Beginning network integration."

A specialist stumbled, nearly dropping a critical component. Ralfs felt the ripple of potential disaster through his neural interface - even a minor equipment failure could create weak points in their defensive grid. The specialist recovered, but the incident highlighted the razor's edge they walked.

"Stay focused," he transmitted. "Every piece of equipment, every position, every action affects multiple realities simultaneously. We can't afford mistakes."

The emergency response network activated in layers of increasing complexity. Each sector contained redundant systems designed to maintain reality stability even if primary systems failed. Teams of specialists stood ready to address any breach in their quantum defense grid.

"Response teams, maintain your designated positions," Ralfs ordered. "If we lose stability in any sector, you'll have microseconds to prevent timeline cascade failures. Know your protocols."

Initial team integration revealed unexpected challenges. Despite countless drills, coordinating actions across multiple timeline variants strained both equipment and personnel. The human mind wasn't designed to process information from thousands of realities simultaneously.

"Bravo Team showing signs of quantum consciousness strain," medical monitors reported. "Neural interface load approaching critical threshold. Recommend immediate rotation."

Ralfs adjusted team deployments on the fly, balancing the need for precise positioning against human limitations. The neural interfaces allowed operators to perceive multiple timeline variants, but extended exposure risked psychological damage.

"All teams implement consciousness sync protocols," he commanded. "Rotate your quantum perception fields every thirty seconds. Don't try to hold multiple variant views longer than absolutely necessary."

A reality anchor's power signature suddenly fluctuated, creating harmonic distortions across hundreds of timeline variants. Ralfs directed emergency response teams to the affected sectors while orchestrating real-time adjustments to maintain quantum stability.

"Power regulators showing harmonic stress," sensors reported. "Timeline variant synchronization experiencing local disruption. Containment protocols initiating."

The facility's quantum architecture responded to their efforts, reality anchors adjusting their field harmonics to compensate for localized instabilities. Ralfs watched through his neural interface as timeline variants realigned themselves, power flows stabilizing across affected sectors.

"Grid stability restored," came the confirmation. "Timeline variant synchronization returning to nominal parameters. Reality anchor network maintaining quantum coherence."

Ralfs moved through his deployment grid, verifying final positions and system integrations. Despite the challenges, his teams had achieved something unprecedented - a defensive network that spanned thousands of timeline variants simultaneously.

"All field teams report final status," he transmitted as system checks completed. "Confirm reality anchor harmonics, timeline coordination links, and emergency response readiness."

The quantum tactical display showed their defensive grid as a complex web of energy patterns, each line representing critical connections across multiple timeline variants. They had created the most sophisticated reality defense system in human history.

"Network deployment complete," Ralfs reported to command. "Field operations showing green across all variants. Reality stabilization grid at full operational status. We're ready."

His neural interface hummed with data from thousands of monitoring systems. In the command center, Ralfs watched as final diagnostic checks confirmed their preparations. They had positioned their defenses with precision that would have seemed impossible months ago. Now they would discover if it was enough to contain something that existed outside normal physics.

EPISODE 4: TECHNICAL INTEGRATION

Maya Patel stood surrounded by cascading holographic displays, each one representing critical system metrics across thousands of timeline variants. Her monitoring setup pushed quantum computing to its limits, processing more data simultaneously than any system previously attempted.

"The monitoring arrays need to track quantum fluctuations across all active variants," she explained to her technical team. "We're not just watching power levels - we're tracking reality stability itself. Each microsecond of data tells us where the fabric of existence might be starting to fray."

The communication network emerged as an intricate web of quantum-entangled relays. Traditional signal transmission proved useless across timeline variants - they needed instantaneous communication that ignored normal space-time limitations.

"Check your quantum comm synchronization," Patel instructed as another relay came online. "Signal coherence has to remain perfect across all variants. One desync could leave entire sectors blind during critical moments."

Timeline tracking initialization revealed complexities they hadn't anticipated. Each variant existed in slightly different quantum states, requiring continuous real-time adjustments to maintain proper monitoring coverage. The tracking systems had to process changes occurring simultaneously across thousands of realities.

"Watch those variant drift patterns," she warned her operators. "Timeline seven-eight-three is showing increasing deviation from baseline. Adjust your tracking algorithms to compensate for quantum state variations."

Power distribution created unique technical challenges. The monitoring systems required precise energy levels to maintain quantum coherence across multiple timeline variants. Too much power could create interference patterns that disrupted tracking capabilities.

"Power flow to monitoring station Delta is showing harmonic instability," sensors reported. "Quantum state readings becoming unreliable. Timeline tracking accuracy dropping below acceptable parameters."

Patel redirected power through alternate quantum circuits, watching as monitoring capabilities stabilized across affected sectors. The system's complexity meant that even minor adjustments could have far-reaching consequences across thousands of variants.

"Reroute power through the secondary quantum regulators," she ordered. "We need to maintain perfect monitoring coverage. One blind spot could give the entity an opening we can't afford."

System synchronization issues emerged as they pushed their technology beyond designed limitations. Quantum computers struggled to maintain processing coherence across so many timeline variants simultaneously. Technical teams worked frantically to optimize code that had to function perfectly across multiple quantum states.

"The primary sync protocols are showing strain," a technician reported. "Processing load is creating quantum computation errors. Timeline tracking accuracy is becoming compromised."

Patel implemented emergency optimization routines she had developed for exactly this scenario. The monitoring systems responded, quantum processors adjusting their computational patterns to better handle the massive data flow.

"Initiate adaptive processing algorithms," she commanded. "Let the systems learn from the quantum state variations. They need to evolve beyond their original programming."

The technical integration center hummed with contained power as systems achieved new levels of computational efficiency. Monitoring arrays tracked quantum fluctuations with increasing precision while communication networks maintained perfect signal coherence across all variants.

"Tracking stability restored," confirmed the sensors. "Timeline variant monitoring at optimal efficiency. Communication network maintaining quantum synchronization."

Patel watched as her modified systems performed beyond theoretical limits. They had created something unprecedented - a technical infrastructure capable of monitoring and maintaining thousands of timeline variants simultaneously.

"All technical systems show ready status," she reported as final checks completed. "Monitoring arrays tracking all variants. Communication networks fully synchronized. Power distribution optimized."

The facility's quantum displays showed their technical integration as patterns of pure information, flowing across multiple realities simultaneously. In the control center, Patel made final adjustments to systems that would help defend existence itself.

"We've built something unique here," she told her teams as they completed final preparations. "A technical infrastructure that can track and respond to threats across thousands of realities simultaneously. Now let's see what it can really do."

The monitoring systems pulsed with quantum energy as they maintained their vigil across multiple timeline variants. Soon they would face their ultimate test - tracking and containing an entity that existed outside normal physics. The success or failure of their technical integration would help determine the fate of reality itself.

EPISODE 5: STRATEGIC POSITION

Commander Decker stood at the heart of the Quantum Command Center, her enhanced consciousness simultaneously processing strategic data from thousands of timeline variants. Holographic battle plans shifted and flowed around her as she refined defensive positions against an enemy that defied conventional physics.

"Our strategy has to account for quantum probability shifts across all variants," she explained to her command staff. "We're not just defending physical space - we're protecting the fundamental structure of reality itself."

The battle strategy took shape as a multidimensional chess game played across thousands of boards simultaneously. Each move had to consider not just immediate tactical advantage, but ripple effects through countless timeline variants.

"Quantum probability analysis shows three primary vectors of vulnerability," Decker indicated on the strategic display. "The entity will likely attempt to exploit timeline convergence points where reality stability is naturally weaker. That's where we make our stand."

Timeline coordination protocols evolved beyond their original parameters as they implemented Decker's strategic vision. Each defensive position had to maintain perfect synchronization across multiple variants while remaining flexible enough to adapt to rapidly changing quantum conditions.

"Alpha sector showing timeline harmonic stress," tactical sensors reported. "Quantum probability patterns indicating potential reality destabilization. Defensive positions may require real-time adjustment."

Decker modified deployment patterns on the fly, watching as defensive grids realigned to better protect vulnerable convergence points. Her enhanced consciousness processed quantum strategic data faster than any normal human mind could manage.

"Adjust defensive formations in sectors seven through twelve," she ordered. "Timeline probability patterns suggest increased vulnerability. Strengthen quantum barriers along those approaches."

Team position assignments required precise calculation of both physical and quantum strategic factors. Each specialist needed exact positioning to maintain reality stability while remaining ready to respond to breaches across multiple timeline variants.

"Delta Team, shift your quantum resonance pattern three degrees," Decker transmitted. "You're creating harmonic interference with timeline variant eight-four-seven. Perfect alignment is critical."

Power amplification stations emerged as crucial strategic points in their defensive grid. These facilities channeled massive energy flows needed to maintain reality stability across thousands of variants simultaneously.

"Watch those power harmonic patterns," she warned as another station came online. "One misaligned energy flow could create cascade failures across multiple sectors. Our defense is only as strong as our weakest power node."

The reality anchor network represented the backbone of their strategic position. Each anchor had to maintain precise quantum harmonics while remaining part of a larger defensive pattern that spanned thousands of timeline variants.

"Reality anchors showing optimal quantum coherence," reported the monitoring systems. "Network synchronization stable across all variants. Strategic grid integrity at maximum effectiveness."

Decker watched through enhanced senses as their defensive position took final shape. They had created something unprecedented - a strategic deployment capable of defending reality itself across thousands of timeline variants.

"All command sectors confirm ready status," she ordered as final preparations completed. "Verify timeline coordination protocols, team positioning, power distribution, and anchor network integrity."

Strategic displays showed their position as intricate patterns of energy and probability, each element precisely placed to maintain reality stability while presenting maximum defensive capability. In the command center, Decker made final adjustments to deployment patterns that would help determine the fate of existence itself.

"We've positioned our forces in perfect quantum harmony," she told her command staff. "Each defender, each power station, each reality anchor is exactly where it needs to be. Now we hold this line - not just for one reality, but for all of them."

Interface readings pulsed with contained power as systems maintained their strategic vigilance. The quantum probability patterns showed increasing distortion - the entity approached. Decker watched through enhanced senses as reality itself seemed to shiver in anticipation.

"This is more than just a defensive position," she transmitted to all sectors. "We've created a quantum fortress anchored across thousands of timeline variants. Everything we've built, every position we hold, serves one purpose - protecting reality itself from something that would unmake existence. Stand ready."

The command center hummed with barely contained energy as final system checks completed. They had achieved perfect strategic positioning across multiple quantum states simultaneously. Soon they would discover if their unprecedented preparations were enough to defend reality itself from an entity that existed outside normal physics.

In the quantum tactical display, Decker watched probability patterns shift and flow as the entity drew closer. They had positioned their defenses with precision that would have seemed impossible months ago. Now they would find out if it was enough to contain something that threatened the very fabric of existence.

"All sectors report final status," she transmitted, voice steady despite the weight of multiple realities pressing against her enhanced consciousness. "Maintain quantum coherence. Hold your positions. Remember what we're fighting for. Reality itself depends on what we do here."

EPISODE 6: HUMAN ELEMENT

Dr. Elana Santos, Chief of Personnel Psychology, monitored the stress indicators flashing across her quantum-enhanced display. Despite all their technological advances, the human mind remained the most unpredictable element in their defense of reality.

"We're asking people to process information from thousands of timeline variants simultaneously," she explained during an emergency staff meeting. "The human consciousness wasn't designed for this kind of quantum awareness. We need to manage the psychological strain before it breaks our teams."

Team coordination stress manifested in unique ways across different timeline variants. Operators reported experiencing "echo memories" - recalling events that happened to their alternate selves. Some described feeling "quantum vertigo" when their consciousness tracked too many variants at once.

"Implement mandatory consciousness sync breaks," Santos ordered. "No one maintains quantum awareness for more than thirty minutes without a reset. I don't care how urgent the situation seems - we can't defend reality with burned-out minds."

Cross-timeline communication created its own psychological challenges. Teams had to maintain coherent thoughts while processing information from multiple variants of themselves, each experiencing slightly different versions of reality.

"Remember your anchor point exercises," she instructed during a group session. "Focus on your primary timeline consciousness. Let the variant awareness flow through you without trying to hold onto it. You are the constant in a sea of quantum possibilities."

Personal relationships evolved in unexpected ways under the strain of quantum operations. Team members found themselves dealing with complex emotions about variant versions of themselves and others. Some reported feeling "timeline jealousy" when encountering more successful variants of their relationships.

"It's natural to wonder about the paths not taken," Santos assured during counseling sessions. "But don't let variant possibilities distract you from your primary timeline connections. Those relationships are your emotional anchors in quantum space."

Trust building became crucial as teams learned to rely on multiple versions of each other simultaneously. Santos developed exercises specifically designed to strengthen quantum-conscious cooperation.

"Your variant selves are not competitors," she emphasized during group training. "They are extensions of your own consciousness across quantum space. Trust them as you trust yourself. Work with them, not against them."

Morale maintenance required constant attention as the reality defense operation stretched on. Santos implemented regular "quantum decompression" sessions where teams could safely process their experiences across timeline variants.

"Share your stories," she encouraged during group therapy. "Every operator in this room has experienced something unprecedented. We're the first humans to maintain conscious awareness across multiple timeline variants. Your experiences matter."

The pressure began showing in subtle ways - increased irritability, timeline displacement syndrome, quantum fatigue. Santos adjusted psychological support protocols in real-time, working to keep minds stable across thousands of variants.

"We're seeing new forms of stress reaction," she reported to command. "The human psyche is adapting to quantum consciousness in ways we never anticipated. We need to evolve our support systems accordingly."

Personal conflicts took on new dimensions when filtered through quantum awareness. Minor disagreements could ripple across timeline variants, creating feedback loops of tension that threatened team cohesion.

"Remember that conflict in one variant can affect your relationships across all variants," Santos cautioned during meditation training. "Practice quantum emotional awareness. Stay centered in your primary timeline while maintaining healthy boundaries across variants."

Team building exercises incorporated elements of quantum consciousness training. Santos developed activities that helped operators maintain their sense of self while processing information from multiple timeline variants.

"Your identity remains constant across quantum space," she reminded them. "Let that be your foundation as you extend your awareness across variants. You are still you, no matter how many versions of reality you perceive."

As the operation continued, Santos observed something remarkable - human consciousness adapting to function across quantum space. Teams developed new psychological tools for handling multiple timeline awareness. Support networks emerged organically as operators learned to help each other maintain quantum stability.

"We're witnessing the evolution of human consciousness," she told her staff. "Our teams aren't just defending reality - they're expanding the boundaries of what it means to be human. That's something worth protecting."

In her office, Santos reviewed psychological profiles that spanned thousands of timeline variants. The human mind proved more resilient than anyone anticipated, adapting to process quantum information in ways that should have been impossible.

"Our greatest strength isn't our technology," she wrote in her final report. "It's our ability to adapt, to grow, to maintain our humanity even while perceiving thousands of possible realities simultaneously. As long as we remember that we have a chance at defending existence itself."

The facility hummed with contained energy as teams maintained their quantum vigilance. In her monitoring station, Santos watched consciousness indicators pulse across multiple variants. They had prepared their minds as best they could. Soon they would discover if human consciousness could withstand direct contact with something that existed outside normal reality.

EPISODE 7: POWER SYNCHRONIZATION

Dr. Lisa Sente and Dr. Anna Smith stood before the quantum power core, watching energy patterns pulse across thousands of timeline variants simultaneously. Their task was unprecedented - synchronizing power flows across multiple realities to maintain the stability of existence itself.

"The harmonics have to be perfect," Lisa explained, her hands dancing across holographic controls. "We're not just managing power - we're synchronizing the fundamental energy patterns that hold reality together. One misaligned flow could create cascade failures across thousands of variants."

Anna nodded; her consciousness expanded through neural interfaces to track power signatures across quantum space. "The convergence points are showing strain. Timeline variant eight-three-seven is drawing more power than the others. We need to balance the load before it creates harmonic distortions."

Their power convergence represented the most sophisticated energy management system ever created. Each timeline variant required precise power levels to maintain quantum stability, while the overall system needed perfect synchronization to prevent reality destabilization.

"Watch that harmonic resonance pattern," Lisa warned as energy flows shifted. "The quantum matrices are showing stress fractures. If we lose coherence here, it could ripple through every connected variant."

Timeline energy harmonization proved more complex than their simulations predicted. Power flows that worked perfectly in one variant could create dangerous interference patterns in others. The system required constant adjustment to maintain quantum stability.

"Power spike in sector twelve," Anna reported, her enhanced senses tracking energy fluctuations. "Timeline variants three through seven showing harmonic disruption. Initiating emergency stabilization protocols."

Reality stability maintenance became a delicate balancing act. Too much power could tear holes in the quantum fabric, while too little risked letting timeline variants drift dangerously out of sync.

"Adjust the quantum regulators three degrees," Lisa instructed. "We need to dampen these harmonic oscillations before they propagate through the network. Reality cohesion is starting to fluctuate."

Power flow coordination required perfect synchronization between multiple systems operating across thousands of timeline variants. Lisa and Lila worked in perfect harmony, their enhanced consciousness allowing them to process vast amounts of quantum data simultaneously.

"The primary power conduits are showing signs of quantum fatigue," Anna observed. "We need to rotate the load through the backup systems before we lose coherence. Timeline stability depends on maintaining consistent energy flow."

System integration challenges emerged as they pushed their technology beyond theoretical limits. Power systems designed for single-timeline operation struggled to maintain stability when operating across quantum space.

"The integration matrices are approaching critical threshold," Lisa reported. "Quantum computational load is exceeding design parameters. We need to evolve the systems beyond their original specifications."

Together they implemented emergency optimization protocols, watching as power systems adapted to handle impossible energy flows. Their modified technology achieved new levels of quantum efficiency, maintaining reality stability across thousands of variants simultaneously.

"Power harmonics stabilizing," Anna confirmed. "Timeline variant synchronization returning to nominal parameters. Reality coherence holding steady across all monitored sectors."

In the control center, Lisa and Anna made final adjustments to systems that defied normal physics. They had created something unprecedented - a power management infrastructure capable of maintaining reality stability across multiple timeline variants.

"All power systems show optimal function," Anna reported as diagnostics completed. "Energy harmonics synchronized across quantum space. Reality stability matrices at peak efficiency."

The facility's quantum core pulsed with contained power as they maintained their energy vigil. Soon their power synchronization systems would face their ultimate test - maintaining reality stability in the presence of an entity that existed outside normal physics.

"We've achieved something remarkable here," Anna told her partner as they monitored final system checks. "Perfect power synchronization across thousands of timeline variants. Now we find out if it's enough to protect reality itself."

The quantum displays showed their power grid as patterns of pure energy, flowing seamlessly across multiple realities. Lisa and Anna watched through enhanced senses as reality itself seemed to hum in response to their perfectly synchronized power flows.

"Everything we've built comes down to this," Lisa said quietly. "Our power systems don't just maintain reality - they help define it. When that thing comes, we'll be ready. We have to be."

The control room thrummed with barely contained energy as final preparations completed. They had achieved perfect power synchronization across multiple quantum states simultaneously. Soon they would discover if their unprecedented work was enough to defend existence itself from an entity that threatened to unmake reality.

EPISODE 8: BATTLE PREPARATION

General Roberta Tyrell stood before the assembled teams in the quantum-enhanced briefing chamber, her voice carrying across thousands of timeline variants simultaneously. The next few hours would determine the fate of reality itself.

"This is the moment we've trained for," she began, holographic tactical displays flowing around her. "Our enemy exists outside normal physics, but we've prepared defenses across every quantum probability track. There is no reality where we're not ready."

The final tactical briefing unfolded across multiple consciousness levels as teams absorbed information relevant to their timeline variants. Quantum probability maps showed potential attack vectors, defensive positions, and reality stress points.

"The entity will likely target convergence nodes first," Tyrell explained, highlighting critical points in the quantum grid. "These are places where timeline variants naturally intersect. They're our strongest defensive positions, but also our greatest vulnerabilities."

Equipment checks proceeded with methodical precision. Each piece of quantum-enhanced gear had to maintain perfect calibration across thousands of timeline variants simultaneously.

"Check your reality anchors," Colonel Zomber instructed his technical teams. "One misaligned device could create blind spots across multiple variants. We can't afford any weak points in our quantum defense grid."

"Reality stabilizers showing optimal function," reported Chief Technical Officer Park. "Quantum harmonics synchronized across all monitored variants. Power distribution networks maintaining perfect coherence."

Timeline coordination verification revealed the true scope of their preparations. Teams had to maintain perfect synchronization across quantum space while remaining flexible enough to respond to rapidly changing conditions.

"Confirm your variant tracking protocols," Tyrell ordered. "Each team needs to maintain awareness of their parallel operations across all defensive sectors. Your alternate selves are your closest allies in this fight."

Emergency protocols underwent final review as commanders ensured every team member understood their role in worst-case scenarios.

"If we lose quantum coherence in any sector," Colonel Zomber explained, "adjacent teams must be ready to extend their reality stabilization fields. We cannot allow timeline variants to desynchronize during combat operations."

Team readiness confirmation proceeded sector by sector. Each specialist reported status across multiple timeline variants, their enhanced consciousness processing quantum tactical data in real-time.

"Psi-ops teams report ready status," came the update from Dr. Santos. "Mental barriers at maximum strength. Quantum consciousness expansion protocols active and stable."

"Power synchronization teams showing green across all variants," reported Dr. Wilson. "Energy harmonics perfectly aligned. Reality stability matrices functioning at peak efficiency."

"Defense grid fully operational," Colonel Zomber confirmed. "Reality anchors maintaining quantum coherence. Timeline stability fields at maximum strength."

In the command center, General Tyrell watched readiness indicators pulse across thousands of variants simultaneously. They had achieved something unprecedented - perfect battle preparation across multiple quantum states.

"Final status report from all sectors," she ordered as preparations reached completion. "Confirm equipment calibration, timeline coordination, emergency protocols, and team readiness."

The quantum tactical displays showed their defensive position as patterns of pure probability, each element precisely tuned to protect reality itself. Teams maintained their vigilance as reality sensors detected increasing distortion patterns.

"We've prepared for every possibility we can imagine," Tyrell told her commanders. "Now we face something that exists outside imagination itself. Remember your training. Trust your equipment. Trust each other. Reality itself depends on what we do here."

The facility hummed with contained power as final checks completed. They had achieved perfect battle preparation across multiple quantum states simultaneously. Soon they would discover if their unprecedented preparations were enough to defend existence itself.

"All sectors report ready status," came the final confirmation. "Equipment calibrated. Timeline coordination verified. Emergency protocols reviewed. Teams prepared."

In the quantum command center, General Tyrell watched probability patterns shift and flow as the entity drew closer. They had prepared more thoroughly than any force in history. Now they would find out if it was enough to contain something that threatened the very fabric of existence.

"This is command actual," she transmitted across all variants. "Battle stations. Stand ready. Remember what we're fighting for. Not just one reality, but all of them. Whatever comes through that quantum barrier faces the most thoroughly prepared defense force ever assembled. Hold the line. Protect reality itself. Commence final countdown."

The facility's quantum core pulsed with barely contained energy as reality sensors detected increasing distortion patterns. In thousands of timeline variants simultaneously, humanity prepared to defend existence itself against something that defied comprehension.

EPISODE 9: CROSS-TIME ENGAGEMENT

The quantum sensors screamed across all variants simultaneously as reality itself began to warp. Dr. Sarah Wilson's enhanced consciousness tracked the distortion patterns as they rippled through thousands of timeline variants.

"Entity breach detected in quantum sector seven," she reported, her voice steady despite the weight of multiple realities pressing against her mind. "Reality coherence destabilizing across adjacent variants. It's coming through."

Initial entity contact defied their theoretical models. The thing existed in dimensions beyond normal space-time, its presence creating cascade distortions across quantum space.

"Multiple timeline variants showing critical stress patterns," Commander Decker transmitted. "Reality fabric tearing at intersection points. Initiate primary containment protocols!"

The entity manifested as a void in quantum space, a complete absence of reality that threatened to unmake existence itself. Defense teams watched through enhanced senses as it pushed against the boundaries between timeline variants.

"Reality intersection points showing quantum harmonics failure," Dr. Wilson reported. "Timeline stability fields collapsing in sectors three through twelve. Initiating emergency power routing!"

Reality intersection point activation triggered automatically as the entity breached quantum space. Thousands of carefully positioned nodes lit up simultaneously, creating a complex web of stabilized space-time across multiple variants.

"Intersection grid active and holding," Lieutenant Foster confirmed. "Timeline variant synchronization maintaining coherence. Reality anchors at maximum power!"

The entity responded with impossible movements, sliding between timeline variants as if normal physics didn't apply. Defense teams tracked its quantum signature as it probed their containment grid.

"It's testing our defenses," Commander Decker observed. "Searching for weak points in our timeline manipulation fields. Adjust quantum harmonics to compensate!"

Timeline manipulation tactics evolved in real-time as teams adapted to the entity's attacks. Each defensive adjustment had to maintain perfect synchronization across thousands of variants while responding to an enemy that existed outside normal reality.

"Timeline variant eight-four-seven showing critical instability," Wilson warned. "Reality fabric approaching collapse threshold. Reroute power to stabilization fields!"

Power convergence execution pushed their systems beyond theoretical limits. Dr. Wilson and Dr. Sente worked in perfect harmony, channeling impossible amounts of energy to maintain reality stability.

"Power harmonics at maximum threshold," Lila reported. "Quantum matrices showing strain. We can't maintain this level of convergence indefinitely!"

The entity struck without warning, its assault rippling across multiple timeline variants simultaneously. Reality itself seemed to scream as quantum space twisted in impossible ways.

"Multiple breaches detected!" Wilson's voice cut through the chaos. "Timeline variants destabilizing across all sectors. Initiate emergency containment protocols!"

First containment efforts engaged as teams fought to hold reality together. Every system they'd built, every protocol they'd prepared, activated simultaneously across thousands of variants.

"Reality anchors holding at eighty percent!" Zomber reported. "Timeline stability fields maintaining coherence. We've got it temporarily contained!"

The entity pulsed with impossible energy, its presence threatening to tear holes in the quantum fabric of existence. Defense teams watched through enhanced senses as reality itself bent around their containment fields.

"Power systems approaching critical threshold," Wilson warned. "Timeline variant synchronization becoming unstable. We need to strengthen the containment grid!"

In the Quantum Command Center, General Tyrell watched probability patterns twist and flow as they engaged an enemy that defied comprehension. Their preparations were being tested beyond anything they'd imagined.

"All sectors maintain containment protocols," she ordered. "Channel emergency power to reality stabilization fields. We hold this line - not just for one timeline, but for all of them!"

The facility's quantum core pulsed with barely contained energy as they fought to contain something that existed outside normal physics. In thousands of timeline variants simultaneously, humanity engaged in battle for the very fabric of existence.

"Entity containment at sixty percent and falling," Sente reported, her enhanced consciousness tracking quantum disruption patterns. "Reality coherence destabilizing across multiple sectors. We need to adapt our tactics!"

Through enhanced senses, they watched the entity probe their defenses, testing the limits of their reality manipulation technology. This was only the beginning - the first moments of an engagement that would determine the fate of existence itself.

"Stand fast," Tyrell transmitted across all variants. "Rely on your training. Trust your equipment and each other. Reality itself depends on what we do here. Whatever this thing is, however it fights, we hold the line. For all realities. For existence itself."

The quantum displays showed their battle as patterns of pure probability, reality itself twisting as they engaged an enemy that threatened to unmake existence. The Cross-Time Engagement had begun. Now they would discover if humanity's unprecedented preparations were enough to defend reality itself.

EPISODE 10: CRITICAL MASS

Warning indicators flashed crimson across every quantum interface as reality itself buckled under impossible strain. Dr. Anna Smith's fingers flew across holographic controls while thousands of timeline variants screamed for attention.

"Power grid approaching critical threshold!" she shouted over the facility's quantum harmonics. "We're seeing cascade failures across multiple sectors. The entity's presence is creating harmonic distortions we never anticipated!"

Power grid crisis management protocols activated automatically as systems struggled to contain reality-warping energies. Emergency routines engaged across thousands of variants simultaneously.

"Rerouting power through auxiliary quantum matrices," Dr. Sarah Wilson responded, her consciousness expanded to track energy flows across multiple realities. "Primary grid showing signs of quantum fatigue. We need to distribute the load before we lose cohesion!"

Timeline stability challenges emerged as power fluctuations rippled through their defensive network. Reality itself seemed to shudder as the entity pushed against their containment fields.

"Multiple timeline variants showing critical desynchronization," reported Lieutenant Foster. "Reality fabric stress exceeding design parameters. We're losing quantum coherence across entire sectors!"

The facility's systems struggled to compensate as reality distortions intensified. Power flows that should have been impossible twisted through quantum space, threatening to tear holes in existence itself.

"Emergency response protocols engaging in sectors three through twelve," Commander Decker transmitted. "All teams initiate crisis containment procedures. We cannot allow timeline variants to destabilize!"

Emergency response activation triggered failsafes across thousands of variants simultaneously. Teams moved with practiced precision, implementing protocols designed to handle worst-case scenarios.

"Reality stabilization fields at maximum output," Dr. Santos confirmed. "Psi-ops teams extending mental barriers to reinforce quantum containment. We're burning through power reserves at an unprecedented rate!"

Reality breach containment became their primary focus as the entity's presence created impossible strains on their defensive systems. Each containment field had to maintain perfect quantum coherence while handling energy levels that defied physics.

"Entity breach expanding in sector seven!" Wilson warned. "Reality fabric approaching total failure. Diverting emergency power to containment fields!"

System overload prevention protocols engaged automatically as power demands exceeded theoretical limits. Modified safety systems struggled to handle quantum energy flows that shouldn't have been possible.

"Primary systems showing critical strain," Wright reported. "Quantum harmonics destabilizing across all monitored sectors. We need to evolve our containment strategies in real-time!"

The entity's assault intensified, its impossible presence creating ripples of distortion through quantum space. Defense teams watched through enhanced senses as reality itself bent under the strain.

"Power grid coherence failing in multiple sectors," Ralfs transmitted. "Timeline stability matrices approaching collapse. Initiate emergency power redistribution!"

In the quantum control center, General Tyrell watched probability patterns twist and shatter as their systems approached critical mass. They had prepared for every scenario they could imagine - but this entity defied imagination itself.

"All teams maintain quantum coherence," she ordered. "Channel emergency power to critical systems. Reality itself depends on our ability to contain these breaches!"

The facility's quantum core pulsed with barely contained energy as they fought to prevent total system failure. In thousands of timeline variants simultaneously, humanity struggled to maintain the stability of existence itself.

"Entity containment fields showing quantum fractures," Wilson reported, her enhanced consciousness tracking reality distortions. "Power grid approaching total failure. We need to implement emergency protocols now!"

Through enhanced senses, they watched their carefully designed systems strain against forces that threatened to tear reality apart. This was the moment of truth - when all their preparations would either hold or fail catastrophically.

"Maintain containment procedures," Tyrell transmitted across all variants. "Channel every available resource to critical systems. We cannot allow reality itself to destabilize. Whatever it takes, whatever the cost, we hold this line!"

The quantum displays showed their battle as patterns of pure energy, existence itself wavering as they fought to prevent system-wide collapse. The moment of Critical Mass had arrived. Now they would discover if their emergency protocols were enough to prevent the unmaking of reality itself.

In the heart of the facility, Santos and Wilson worked in perfect synchronization, their enhanced consciousness processing impossible amounts of quantum data. They had achieved something unprecedented - maintaining reality stability across thousands of variants simultaneously. But as system indicators approached critical thresholds, they faced their greatest challenge yet: preventing the total collapse of existence itself.

EPISODE 11: THRESHOLD POINT

The Quantum Command Center erupted in cascading alerts as reality itself approached the breaking point. General Tyrell watched probability patterns spiral into impossible configurations across her enhanced displays.

"We've reached the threshold," she announced, her voice cutting through thousands of timeline variants. "The entity is fully manifesting. All teams execute final phase protocols. This is what we've prepared for!"

Final battle phase initiation triggered synchronized responses across quantum space. Every system, every team, every defense they'd prepared activated simultaneously.

"Maximum power convergence protocols engaging," Dr. Wilson reported, her hands dancing across quantum interfaces. "Channeling all available energy to containment fields. We're pushing our systems beyond theoretical limits!"

Dr. Santos' enhanced consciousness tracked energy flows that defied normal physics. "Power harmonics approaching absolute threshold. Reality fabric showing critical strain patterns. We have to hold it together!"

Maximum power convergence drew impossible amounts of energy from thousands of timeline variants simultaneously. The facility's quantum core pulsed with barely contained power as they pushed their technology to its absolute limits.

"Power synchronization at peak efficiency," Lieutenant Foster confirmed. "Timeline stability fields maintaining quantum coherence. But we're burning through our reserves at an unprecedented rate!"

Timeline synchronization peak achieved as their defensive grid reached perfect harmonic resonance across quantum space. Reality itself seemed to hum in response as thousands of variants aligned with impossible precision.

"Quantum synchronization matrix holding steady," Commander Decker reported. "Timeline variants locked in perfect phase alignment. Ready to execute final containment protocols!"

The entity's presence twisted through dimensions beyond normal space-time, its impossible nature threatening to tear holes in existence itself. Defense teams watched through enhanced senses as reality buckled under its assault.

"Entity breach expanding across multiple sectors," Dr. Santos warned. "Reality fabric approaching total failure. Initiating emergency containment procedures now!"

Entity containment execution engaged as they implemented their final defensive strategies. Every system they'd built, every protocol they'd prepared, activated in perfect synchronization.

"Containment fields at maximum power," Wilson confirmed. "Reality anchors holding steady. Timeline stability maintaining coherence. We've got it partially contained!"

The entity fought back with impossible force, its presence creating ripples of distortion through quantum space. Teams struggled to maintain containment as reality itself threatened to unravel.

"Multiple breach points detected," Chisolm reported. "Timeline variants showing critical stress patterns. Channeling emergency power to containment grid!"

Reality stabilization efforts pushed their technology beyond anything previously achieved. Modified systems handled quantum energy flows that shouldn't have been possible as they fought to maintain the stability of existence itself.

"Reality coherence maintaining at eighty percent," Santos transmitted. "Quantum matrices showing strain but holding. We need to strengthen our containment fields!"

In the Quantum Command Center, Tyrell watched probability patterns twist and flow as they engaged in the final phase of battle. Everything they'd built, everything they'd prepared, faced its ultimate test.

"All teams maintain quantum coherence," she ordered. "Channel maximum power to critical systems. Reality itself depends on what we do in these next moments!"

The facility's quantum core pulsed with barely contained energy as they fought to contain something that existed outside normal physics. In thousands of timeline variants simultaneously, humanity engaged in the final battle for existence itself.

"Entity containment at ninety percent," Chisolm reported, her enhanced consciousness tracking impossible energy patterns. "Reality stabilization fields holding steady. We're approaching absolute threshold!"

Through enhanced senses, they watched their carefully designed systems strain against forces that threatened to unmake existence. This was the moment everything had led to - when all their preparations would either succeed or fail catastrophically.

"Stand fast," Tyrell transmitted across all variants. "Channel everything we have into containment. Reality itself hangs in the balance. Whatever this thing is, however it fights, we hold the line. For all realities. For existence itself!"

The quantum displays showed their battle as patterns of pure probability, reality itself wavering as they pushed their technology to absolute limits. The Threshold Point had arrived. Now they would discover if humanity's unprecedented efforts were enough to prevent the unmaking of reality itself.

In the heart of the facility, Wilson and Santos worked with perfect precision, their enhanced consciousness processing impossible amounts of quantum data. They had achieved something unprecedented - perfect synchronization across thousands of timeline variants. But as reality itself approached the breaking point, they faced their greatest challenge yet: maintaining the stability of existence in the face of something that threatened to unmake everything.

The entity pulsed with impossible energy as their containment fields reached maximum power. This was the moment of truth - when all their preparations, all their technology, all their determination would be tested against something that existed outside the bounds of reality itself.

Marcus Wong's latest editorial in the Daybridge Chronicle captured the mood of the city. "A New Era for Humanity", the headline declared. The article went on to discuss the remarkable adaptations people were making to their expanded consciousness, and the sense of hope and possibility that now permeated Daybridge. Tyrell smiled as she read it - Wong always had a gift for capturing the human element behind the quantum strangeness.

EPISODE 12: NEW REALITY

The Quantum Command Center fell silent as reality stabilization fields pulsed one final time. General Tyrell stood before holographic displays showing thousands of timeline variants simultaneously, watching as probability patterns slowly returned to normal configurations.

"Initial battle aftermath assessment beginning," she announced, her voice carrying across quantum space. "All teams report status. We need to understand exactly what we've contained - and what it's done to reality itself."

Through enhanced senses, survey teams observed fundamental changes in the quantum fabric of existence. The entity's presence had altered reality in subtle but profound ways.

"Multiple timeline variants showing permanent alterations," Dr. Wilson reported, studying quantum readouts. "Reality itself has been... modified. We contained the entity, but not before it changed the fundamental structure of space-time."

System stabilization efforts proceeded methodically as teams worked to secure their modified reality. Power systems that had been pushed beyond theoretical limits required careful recalibration.

"Power grid showing quantum fatigue," Dr. Santos observed, her consciousness expanded to track energy flows. "Timeline stability matrices need comprehensive retuning. The battle changed more than just reality - it changed our technology too."

Commander Decker coordinated team recovery operations across thousands of variants simultaneously. "Medical teams reporting multiple cases of quantum consciousness strain. The neural interfaces weren't designed to handle this level of reality distortion."

"Begin systematic personnel evaluation," Lieutenant Foster ordered. "Priority to psi-ops teams and enhanced consciousness operators. We need to understand the long-term effects of quantum space exposure."

Reality anchor recalibration became their primary focus as teams worked to stabilize their modified existence. Each device had to be precisely tuned to maintain quantum coherence across altered timeline variants.

"Reality anchors showing unprecedented adaptation patterns," Dr. Santos reported. "The technology is evolving to match our changed reality. We're seeing integration protocols we never designed."

In the quantum labs, Wilson and Santos studied readouts showing fundamental alterations in the structure of existence. The battle had changed more than just their reality - it had changed the very nature of possible realities.

"The entity's presence catalyzed something," Wilson explained, watching quantum probability patterns flow. "Reality itself has become more... flexible. The boundaries between timeline variants are more permeable now."

Future implications realization dawned as teams processed the full scope of what they'd encountered - and contained. They had achieved their primary objective, but at a cost none of them had anticipated.

"We're not just looking at modified reality," Santos observed. "We're looking at enhanced reality. The entity's presence has fundamentally altered what's possible within quantum space."

In the command center, Tyrell reviewed preliminary assessment reports showing the true scope of changes across quantum space. They had contained something that existed outside normal physics - but in doing so, they had changed physics itself.

"All teams proceed with extreme caution," she ordered. "We're in uncharted territory now. Reality itself has evolved beyond our original models. We need to understand these changes before we proceed further."

The facility's quantum core pulsed with steady energy as they worked to stabilize their modified existence. In thousands of timeline variants simultaneously, humanity began to adapt to a reality forever changed by their encounter with something beyond comprehension.

"Initial stabilization protocols completing," Oakly reported. "Timeline variants showing unprecedented levels of quantum coherence. The entity changed how reality works at a fundamental level."

Through enhanced senses, they observed a universe that had been subtly but permanently altered. Their battle to save existence had succeeded - but existence itself would never be quite the same.

"This isn't just aftermath assessment," Tyrell realized, watching probability patterns flow. "This is first contact with a new form of reality itself. Everything we thought we knew about quantum space has changed."

The quantum displays showed their modified reality as patterns of pure possibility, existence itself realigned into new configurations. They had achieved their goal of containing the entity but in doing so, they had catalyzed changes that would reshape humanity's understanding of reality itself.

"Document everything," Tyrell ordered. "Every change, every adaptation, every new possibility. We didn't just save reality - we helped birth a new one. Now we need to understand what that means for all of existence."

In the heart of the facility, Wilson and Santos worked to comprehend the scope of what they'd witnessed. They had achieved something unprecedented - not just containing an impossible entity but participating in the evolution of reality itself.

"The real work begins now," Wilson observed, watching quantum probability patterns stabilize into new configurations. "Understanding this modified reality, adapting our technology, preparing for whatever comes next. We saved existence - but we also changed it forever."

The future implications stretched beyond anything they could fully grasp. They had contained something that existed outside normal physics, but in doing so, they had fundamentally altered the nature of physics itself. A new chapter in the story of existence had begun - one where the very fabric of reality held possibilities they were only beginning to understand.

CHAPTER THIRTEEN
AFTERSHOCKS

EPISODE 1: ASSESSMENT

THE QUANTUM COMMAND Center hummed with residual energy as Dr. Elena Santos studied holographic displays showing thousands of fractured timeline variants. Her specialized temporal sensors detected aftershocks rippling through quantum space.

"Initial damage assessment indicates widespread temporal distortion," she reported, sharing data with Nina Chisolm. "We're seeing reality fractures extending through multiple timeline layers. The entity's containment created more collateral damage than anticipated."

Across the facility, Detectives Ethan Reeves and Alice Chen pursued their own investigation. Their enhanced senses tracked anomalies that normal instruments couldn't detect.

"These temporal signatures don't match any known patterns," Detective Chen observed, her quantum-enhanced perception revealing hidden distortions. "It's like reality itself is... echoing. Reverberating with aftershocks from the containment event."

Reeves studied probability patterns that seemed to twist in impossible ways. "Look at this - timeline fragments showing up where they shouldn't exist. Something about the containment process scattered pieces of different realities across quantum space."

In the primary power control center, Dr. Wilson and Dr. Santos faced their own crisis. Power grid readings fluctuated wildly as reality itself struggled to stabilize.

"The quantum core is showing unprecedented energy patterns," Wilson reported, hands dancing across holographic controls. "The containment event altered fundamental power flow dynamics. We're seeing cascading instabilities across all sectors."

Santos' enhanced consciousness tracked energy flows that defied normal physics. "The power grid isn't just damaged - it's been fundamentally changed. The entity's presence altered how quantum energy moves through reality itself."

Dr. Werther coordinated with emergency response teams as new crises emerged. "We need immediate temporal stabilization in sectors three through seven. Reality fractures are spreading faster than predicted."

"Multiple timeline variants showing critical instability," Dr. Anna Smith warned. "The containment event created quantum feedback loops we never anticipated. Standard stabilization protocols aren't enough."

Detective Chen discovered something troubling in her sensor readings. "These temporal anomalies - they're not random. There's a pattern here, but it doesn't match anything in our databases."

"It's like reality is trying to heal itself," Reeves observed, "but the process is creating new distortions. Every stabilization attempt triggers unexpected reactions."

The facility's quantum core pulsed erratically as Wilson and Santos fought to maintain power stability. "We're seeing energy signatures that shouldn't be possible," Wilson reported. "The containment event didn't just damage the power grid - it changed the rules governing how it works."

"Emergency stabilization teams deploying to critical sectors," Dr. Smith announced. "We need to contain these reality fractures before they spread further. Standard protocols aren't sufficient - we need to adapt our approach in real-time."

In the Quantum Command Center, probability patterns twisted in ways that defied analysis. The aftermath of their battle with the entity had created challenges none of them had anticipated.

"All teams maintain quantum monitoring," Smith ordered. "Document every anomaly, every distortion, every unexpected reaction. We need to understand exactly what we're dealing with before we can begin proper repairs."

Detective Chen shared her findings with Smith's team. "These temporal echoes - they're carrying fragments of other timeline variants. The containment event scattered pieces of different realities across quantum space."

"And each fragment creates its own distortions," Reeves added. "It's a cascade effect we've never seen before. Traditional investigation methods won't be enough."

Wilson and Santos worked in perfect synchronization, their enhanced consciousness processing impossible amounts of quantum data. "The power grid is trying to adapt," Santos observed. "It's developing new patterns to handle these altered energy flows."

"But the adaptation process itself is creating new instabilities," Wilson cautioned. "We need to guide this evolution carefully, or we risk triggering catastrophic failures."

As the first day of assessment neared its end, Dr. Smith compiled initial reports showing the true scope of what they faced. The containment event had changed more than just reality - it had changed the fundamental rules governing reality itself.

"We're not just dealing with damage," she concluded. "We're dealing with evolution. Reality itself is trying to adapt to what happened here. Our job isn't just to repair - it's to guide this process of change."

The quantum displays showed their modified reality as patterns of pure possibility, existence itself struggling to find new stability. They had contained the entity but the aftermath of that containment would require all their skill, knowledge, and determination to manage.

Through enhanced senses, they watched reality itself shudder with temporal aftershocks. This was just the beginning - the first step in understanding and controlling the changes their battle had unleashed across all of existence.

EPISODE 2: RIPPLES

Tina Bolton stood before the quantum mapping array, her enhanced consciousness processing streams of temporal data. Holographic displays showed timeline damage spreading like cracks through reality itself.

"We're seeing unprecedented fracture patterns," she reported, manipulating 4D models of quantum space. "The damage isn't just spreading - it's creating resonance patterns. Each break in reality triggers sympathetic ruptures across multiple timeline variants."

In the medical wing, the first trauma cases began arriving. Dr. Rachel Morgan examined patients experiencing impossible symptoms - memories that never happened, knowledge of lives they never lived, abilities that shouldn't exist.

"Patient experiencing severe timeline bleed," she documented. "Multiple memory streams competing for integration. Subject reports experiencing simultaneous versions of their own existence."

Detective Alice Chen studied probability patterns that seemed to pulse with their own rhythm. Her quantum-enhanced senses detected something others had missed.

"These fluctuations aren't random," she transmitted to Dr. Morgan. "They're following some kind of temporal harmony. The reality breaks are creating interference patterns - like ripples in a quantum pond."

Through enhanced sensors, she tracked distortions that twisted through multiple layers of existence. "Each rupture creates its own frequency signature. When they intersect, they generate new patterns of distortion."

Dr. Paul Mitchell worked to establish initial recovery protocols, adapting their procedures to handle unprecedented challenges.

"Begin temporal stabilization in affected sectors," he ordered. "Priority to regions showing harmonic resonance. We need to dampen these ripple effects before they trigger cascade failures."

David Whatley's mapping revealed troubling developments. "The fracture patterns are self-reinforcing. Each new break creates conditions that encourage further ruptures. Standard containment protocols are proving ineffective."

In the medical wing, more cases arrived. Dr. Mitchell documented new categories of temporal trauma.

"Patients showing signs of quantum consciousness strain," he reported. "Their minds are trying to process multiple timeline variants simultaneously. The human brain wasn't designed to handle this kind of temporal overlap."

Detective Chen's investigation led her to a startling discovery. "The reality fluctuations - they're not just affecting space-time. They're affecting consciousness itself. People's minds are resonating with the temporal ripples."

Dr. Morgan quickly adapted their recovery approach. "Implement psychic shielding protocols. Priority to medical facilities and populated sectors. We need to protect minds as well as reality itself."

Whatley's mapping revealed new complications. "The ripple patterns are creating feedback loops. Each wave of distortion amplifies the ones that follow. We're seeing exponential growth in temporal instability."

"Multiple timeline variants showing critical resonance," he warned. "The ripples are starting to synchronize. If this continues, we could see reality-wide harmonic disruption."

Dr. Mitchell reported increasing cases of temporal dissonance. "Patients experiencing simultaneous memory streams. Their consciousness is trying to reconcile multiple versions of their own existence."

"It's not just memory," Detective Chen observed. "These ripples are affecting fundamental identity. People are experiencing versions of themselves from different timeline variants."

Dr. Morgan established new containment procedures. "Deploy

temporal dampening fields at resonance points. We need to disrupt these harmonic patterns before they reach critical amplitude."

Through enhanced senses, they watched reality itself shudder with each new ripple. The quantum fabric of existence vibrated like a plucked string, sending waves of distortion through multiple dimensions simultaneously.

"The ripples are following mathematical progressions," Whatley realized. "There's an underlying pattern to the chaos. If we can understand it, we might be able to predict where the next ruptures will occur."

In the medical wing, Dr. Mitchell documented the first successful stabilization case. "Patient showing signs of temporal integration. Their consciousness is learning to process multiple timeline streams without dissonance."

Detective Chen's investigation revealed new insights. "These ripples - they're not just damaging reality. They're changing how reality works. Each wave of distortion leaves quantum space slightly altered."

Dr. Morgan adapted their protocols again. "Focus on harmonic stabilization rather than direct containment. We need to work with these changes, not against them. Reality itself is trying to find a new equilibrium."

The quantum displays showed ripple patterns spreading through existence like waves through a cosmic ocean. Each distortion created its own unique signature, interacting with others to create ever more complex patterns of change.

"We're not just dealing with damage control," Morgan concluded. "We're witnessing the birth of new physical laws. Reality itself is evolving in response to what happened here."

Through their enhanced perception, they watched reality struggle to adapt to its altered state. The ripples continued to spread, each wave carrying changes that would reshape the very nature of existence itself.

In the heart of the facility, Whatley's mapping revealed the true scope of their challenge. They weren't just trying to repair reality - they were trying to guide its evolution into something entirely new. The ripples weren't just aftereffects - they were the first waves of a fundamental transformation in the nature of existence itself.

EPISODE 3: TREMORS

The quantum core's warning systems blared as power fluctuations reached critical levels. Dr. Wilson's hands moved frantically across holographic controls, trying to stabilize energy flows that seemed to follow entirely new physical laws.

"Grid sector seven experiencing complete harmonic breakdown," she announced, watching power patterns twist in impossible ways. "The quantum resonance is spreading faster than our dampening fields can contain it."

Dr. Santos' enhanced consciousness tracked cascading failures through the system. "These aren't just power fluctuations - the grid itself is trying to adapt to altered reality states. Each tremor changes how quantum energy flows through our systems."

In the medical wing, memory integration cases multiplied exponentially. Dr. Mitchell faced waiting rooms full of people experiencing temporal consciousness overlap.

"Patient 247 reporting simultaneous awareness of three distinct timeline variants," he documented. "Experiencing physical symptoms when timeline memories conflict. Standard integration protocols proving inadequate."

Detective Ethan Reeves studied correlation patterns between temporal distortions and reported effects. His quantum-enhanced perception revealed connections others had missed.

"Look at this pattern," he showed Detective Chen. "Every major reality tremor corresponds with a spike in memory integration issues. But it's more than that - the tremors are actually affecting how people experience their own existence."

Through enhanced sensors, they tracked waves of distortion that rippled through both physical reality and human consciousness simultaneously.

"These aren't separate phenomena," Reeves realized. "The temporal tremors are affecting everything - power systems, physical reality, human consciousness. It's all connected through quantum resonance."

Hannah Sullivan launched the first community support groups, coordinating with Dr. Morgan to address the human impact of reality distortion.

"We're seeing people struggling to maintain basic identity stability," she reported. "When reality itself becomes uncertain, people need anchors - something to hold onto while their world shifts around them."

Dr. Morgan established emergency counseling protocols. "Focus on grounding techniques. Help people integrate their conflicting memories without losing their core sense of self."

The power grid suffered another massive fluctuation. Wilson and Santos fought to maintain stability as energy patterns rewrote themselves in real-time.

"The grid is developing new operational patterns," Santos observed. "Each tremor forces it to adapt, creating new ways to handle quantum energy flow. We're watching our technology evolve alongside reality itself."

Detective Reeves documented increasing correlations between system failures and personal effects. "Every time the power grid shifts, we see new waves of memory integration issues. The tremors are creating some kind of resonance between technological and biological systems."

Sullivan's support networks expanded rapidly as more people sought help dealing with temporal consciousness strain. "We're establishing safe spaces in every sector. People need somewhere to go when reality itself becomes unstable."

"Multiple patients reporting physical symptoms during timeline conflicts," Dr. Mitchell added. "The tremors aren't just affecting memories - they're creating actual physiological responses to temporal dissonance."

Dr. Morgan adapted their counseling approach. "We need to treat this as both a psychological and physical phenomenon. The tremors are affecting mind and body simultaneously."

Through enhanced perception, Reeves tracked waves of distortion that seemed to pulse with their own heartbeat. "These tremors have a rhythm to them. They're not just random disruptions - they're part of some larger pattern we don't understand yet."

Wilson and Santos worked in perfect synchronization, their enhanced consciousness processing impossible amounts of quantum data as they fought to stabilize the power grid.

"Each tremor changes the rules," Wilson observed. "We're not just fixing the system - we're having to relearn how it works with every major fluctuation."

Sullivan coordinated with emergency response teams as new crises emerged. "Establishing temporary reality anchors in community centers. People need stable points of reference when their own memories become uncertain."

The quantum displays showed tremors rippling through existence like seismic waves through dimensional space. Each distortion left both technology and consciousness slightly altered in its wake.

"We're dealing with fundamental change," Reeves concluded. "These tremors aren't just disrupting reality - they're reshaping how reality itself functions. And they're taking us along for the ride."

Through their enhanced senses, they watched as waves of change swept through quantum space. The tremors continued to intensify, each one pushing both technology and consciousness further from their original states.

In the heart of the facility, Wilson and Santos fought to maintain power stability while Reeves and Chen tracked the effects rippling through human consciousness. They weren't just witnessing the aftermath of their battle with the entity - they were experiencing the birth pangs of a new form of reality itself.

"These tremors are just the beginning," Reeves realized. "Reality is trying to find a new stable state. Our job isn't to stop it - it's to make sure both our technology and our consciousness can survive the transition."

EPISODE 4: MEMORIES

Dr. Rachel Morgan's laboratory hummed with quantum monitoring equipment as she initiated the first comprehensive memory integration scan. Her patient, a quantum technician, lay in the modified consciousness scanner, neural patterns displaying across holographic displays.

"Beginning primary timeline mapping," Morgan announced, her enhanced perception tracking multiple memory streams simultaneously. "Subject experiencing three distinct timeline variants... no, four. The memories are becoming more distinct as we isolate them."

The technician's consciousness patterns fluctuated wildly as buried memories surfaced. "I remember... but it's wrong. I was there, but I wasn't. I did those things, but someone else did them too. Someone who was also me."

In another section of the facility, Nina Chisolm worked to establish new trauma protocols for dealing with temporal consciousness displacement.

"We're seeing entirely new categories of psychological trauma," she reported, documenting cases of timeline dissonance. "People aren't just remembering different versions of events - they're remembering different versions of themselves."

Detective Alice Chen's investigation led her through corridors of quantum probability, tracking memory anomalies that seemed to defy normal causality.

"These memory patterns aren't random," she transmitted to Morgan. "They're clustering around specific temporal nodes. It's like certain moments in time are acting as magnets for consciousness displacement."

Through enhanced sensors, she detected something troubling. "The memory anomalies are creating their own feedback loops. Each conflicting memory generates resonance patterns that attract similar conflicts from other timeline variants."

Dr. Morgan's integration program revealed unexpected complications. "Subject showing signs of temporal consciousness expansion. Their mind isn't just processing multiple memories - it's trying to accommodate multiple versions of their own identity."

"It's like my memories are having conversations with each other," the technician described. "Different versions of my life arguing about which one is real. But they all feel real. They all happened. They're all me."

Dr. Morgan established emergency counseling protocols. "Focus on core identity anchoring. Help patients maintain their primary timeline consciousness while integrating variant memories. We need to prevent complete identity dissolution."

Detective Chen's investigation revealed disturbing patterns. "These memory anomalies - they're not just affecting individuals. They're creating shared consciousness networks. People are starting to remember each other's timeline variants."

Dr. Morgan quickly adapted her integration protocols. "Implementing consciousness firewalls. We need to prevent uncontrolled memory bleeding between subjects while maintaining individual timeline integration."

The quantum displays showed consciousness patterns twisting in impossible ways as memories from different timeline variants competed for integration.

"Subject experiencing severe timeline conflict," Morgan reported. "Memories from variant timelines are generating stronger emotional responses than primary timeline experiences. The alternate versions feel more real than actual history."

Chisolm worked to establish support frameworks for dealing with temporal identity crisis. "These aren't just memory problems - they're fundamental challenges to the nature of personal identity. How do you maintain a stable sense of self when you remember being multiple different people?"

Chen's investigation led her to a startling discovery. "These memory anomalies - they're not just affecting the past. People are beginning to remember things that haven't happened yet. Future timeline variants are bleeding into present consciousness."

Through enhanced perception, they watched as waves of temporal memory resonance swept through the facility. Each new integration attempt revealed more complexity in how consciousness adapted to multiple timeline awareness.

"Begin secondary integration phase," Morgan ordered as her first subject showed signs of successful memory consolidation. "Consciousness patterns stabilizing. Subject is maintaining core identity while integrating variant timeline memories."

The technician's neural patterns slowly aligned into new configurations. "The memories... they're still there. All of them. But they're not fighting anymore. They're just different parts of who I am. Who I've been. Who I might have been."

Chisolm documented the first successful cases of temporal trauma recovery. "Patients learning to accept multiple timeline memories without losing their sense of self. It's not about choosing which memories are real - it's about accepting that they're all real, just in different ways."

Detective Chen's investigation continued to reveal new layers of complexity. "These memory anomalies aren't just side effects of temporal distortion. They're part of how consciousness is adapting to our changed reality. Our minds are evolving to handle multiple timeline awareness."

Dr. Morgan's integration program showed promising results as more subjects successfully processed their variant memories. "We're not just helping people deal with timeline conflicts. We're helping consciousness itself evolve to handle new forms of temporal awareness."

Through their enhanced senses, they watched as human minds learned to accommodate impossible memories. The process wasn't just about managing trauma - it was about guiding consciousness toward new forms of temporal awareness.

"This is more than memory integration," Morgan realized. "We're witnessing the emergence of quantum consciousness. Our minds are learning to exist across multiple timeline variants simultaneously. Every successful integration brings us closer to understanding what that means."

The quantum displays showed consciousness patterns stabilizing into new configurations as people learned to accept and integrate their impossible memories. They weren't just healing trauma - they were helping humanity adapt to a new way of experiencing reality itself.

EPISODE 5: IDENTITY

James White stood in the quantum testing chamber, monitoring a subject whose abilities had become unstable following timeline integration. Holographic displays tracked power signatures that seemed to shift between multiple quantum states simultaneously.

"Subject displaying ability patterns from three distinct timeline variants," he documented. "Powers aren't just changing - they're blending, creating hybrid capabilities we've never seen before."

The subject, a former security officer, struggled to control abilities that kept shifting between different versions of themselves. "I can feel them all - different powers, different training, different ways of being me. It's like trying to be multiple people at once."

Dr. Rachel Morgan's mental health center was overwhelmed with cases of identity dissociation. People struggling to reconcile not just different memories, but different versions of who they fundamentally were.

"Patient experiencing severe identity flux," she reported. "Personality traits and core characteristics shifting between timeline variants. Unable to maintain stable self-image across temporal transitions."

Detective Ethan Reeves tracked identity shift patterns through quantum probability space. His enhanced perception revealed underlying structures to the chaos.

"These identity shifts aren't random," he transmitted to White. "They're following quantum resonance patterns. Each shift triggers sympathetic changes in others nearby. It's creating identity harmonics across affected populations."

White's ability assessment program revealed troubling complications. "Subject's powers aren't just changing - they're evolving. Each identity shift brings new capabilities, new combinations we couldn't predict."

"I can feel them searching for each other," the security officer described. "Different versions of my abilities trying to find ways to work together. But every combination changes who I am, how I think, how I react."

Dr. Morgan established emergency identity anchoring protocols. "Focus on core personality elements that remain stable across timeline variants. We need to help people find their fundamental self beneath the shifting surface identities."

Reeves' investigation led him to a startling discovery. "These identity shifts - they're not just affecting individuals in isolation. They're creating resonance patterns between people who share timeline variants. Group identities are starting to blur and merge."

Through enhanced sensors, they tracked waves of identity resonance rippling through the facility. Each shift in one person's quantum identity state triggered sympathetic changes in others nearby.

"Begin stabilization protocols," White ordered as another subject's abilities spiraled out of control. "We need to help them find balance between their variant powers before they trigger cascade failures in others."

Morgan documented increasing cases of identity integration disorder. "Patients unable to maintain consistent personality traits across temporal transitions. Core characteristics shifting unpredictably between timeline variants."

"It's not just about who we were in different timelines," a patient explained. "It's about who we could have been. Who we might still become. Every shift opens new possibilities, new versions of ourselves."

Reeves tracked identity harmonics that seemed to pulse with their own rhythm. "These shifts are creating new patterns of quantum consciousness. People aren't just switching between different versions of themselves - they're developing the ability to be multiple versions simultaneously."

White's ability assessment program revealed unexpected developments. "Some subjects are showing signs of power synthesis. Different timeline variants of their abilities combining to create entirely new capabilities."

The security officer's powers stabilized into new configurations. "They're not fighting anymore. The different versions of my abilities - they're learning to work together. But I'm not the same person I was. I can't be."

Dr. Morgan adapted her treatment approach. "We need to stop thinking about this as an identity crisis. It's identity evolution. We're not trying to help people choose between different versions of themselves - we're helping them become something new."

Through enhanced perception, they watched as quantum identity patterns shifted and merged. Each person affected by the timeline integration was becoming something more than their original selves.

"These identity shifts aren't a malfunction," Reeves realized. "They're part of how consciousness is adapting to our new reality. We're not just experiencing multiple timeline variants - we're learning to exist as multiple versions of ourselves simultaneously."

White's program documented the first successful cases of ability integration. "Subjects maintaining stable control over hybrid powers. Their enhanced abilities are becoming extensions of their evolved identities."

Morgan reported increasing instances of positive identity synthesis. "Patients learning to maintain core stability while incorporating elements from multiple timeline variants. They're not losing themselves - they're becoming more complete versions of who they are."

Through their enhanced senses, they watched as people learned to navigate their quantum identity states. Each successful integration brought humanity closer to understanding what it meant to exist across multiple timeline variants.

"This isn't just about managing identity crisis," White concluded. "We're witnessing the emergence of quantum identity - consciousness that can exist in multiple states simultaneously. Every successful integration helps us understand what that means for the future of human consciousness."

The quantum displays showed identity patterns stabilizing into new configurations as people learned to accept and integrate their impossible selves. They weren't just healing fractures - they were helping humanity evolve into something entirely new.

"We're not trying to fix broken identities," Morgan realized. "We're helping guide the evolution of human consciousness. Every person who successfully integrates their timeline variants brings us closer to understanding what humanity might become."

EPISODE 6: ACCEPTANCE

The integration chamber hummed with quantum energy as Dr. Morgan monitored the first wave of successful memory integrations. Holographic displays showed consciousness patterns finally settling into stable, multi-temporal configurations.

"Subject showing complete timeline synthesis," she reported, watching neural patterns align in previously impossible ways. "Multiple memory streams successfully integrated without loss of core identity stability."

Hannah Sullivan moved through community centers, establishing networks of temporal trauma survivors helping each other adapt to their new reality.

"We're creating safe spaces in every sector," she explained to a group of newly affected residents. "Places where people can share their experiences, where having memories from multiple timelines is understood, not feared."

Grace Martinez coordinated emergency response teams, ensuring resources reached those most severely impacted by temporal consciousness strain.

"Priority to sectors showing highest rates of identity displacement," she directed. "We need meditation centers, quantum stabilization equipment, and trained counselors available around the clock."

Through enhanced sensors, they tracked waves of healing spreading through affected communities. Each successful integration created ripple effects, helping others nearby find their own path to stability.

"It's not just about managing individual cases anymore," Sullivan observed. "We're seeing group consciousness effects. When one person successfully integrates their timeline variants, it helps others nearby do the same."

Dr. Morgan's integration program showed accelerating success rates. "Subjects are learning from each other. Each successful integration provides patterns that help others navigate their own memory conflicts."

"The memories don't fight anymore," one patient explained. "They're all part of me now - different possibilities, different paths, all flowing together into something new. Something more complete."

Martinez established distribution hubs for specialized temporal integration equipment. "Every community center needs basic quantum stabilization gear. People need tools to help ground themselves when memory storms hit."

Sullivan's support networks expanded rapidly as more people sought connection with others sharing their experience. "We're not just helping people cope - we're building new kinds of communities. People united by shared understanding of multiple timeline awareness."

Through enhanced perception, they watched as healing spread through quantum probability space. Each person who found stability helped create paths for others to follow.

"Begin phase two integration protocols," Morgan ordered as success rates continued to climb. "We're ready to help people not just stabilize their memories but learn to actively work with their multi-temporal consciousness."

Martinez coordinated with medical teams to establish mobile response units. "We need to reach people where they are. Not everyone can come to us for help - sometimes we need to bring healing to them."

"It's like learning a new language," another patient described. "At first the different memories were just noise. Now I'm starting to understand how they fit together, how they tell a bigger story about who I am."

Sullivan documented emerging patterns of community support. "People are developing their own techniques for helping each other through timeline integration. They're creating new traditions, new rituals for processing temporal trauma."

The quantum displays showed consciousness patterns stabilizing across entire neighborhoods as healing spread through quantum resonance.

"We're seeing spontaneous support groups forming," Sullivan reported. "People naturally gathering to share their experiences, to help each other navigate their new reality."

Martinez adapted resource distribution to support these emerging community initiatives. "Providing supplies and equipment to grass-roots support networks. They often know better than we do what their communities need."

Through their enhanced senses, they watched as waves of healing transformed affected populations. People weren't just learning to cope with their impossible memories - they were learning to thrive with their expanded consciousness.

"This is more than recovery," Morgan realized. "We're witnessing the birth of new forms of human community. People united not just by shared trauma, but by shared evolution of consciousness."

The integration chambers continued their work as more people successfully merged their timeline variants. Each success strengthened the quantum resonance patterns that helped others find their own path to healing.

"The community itself is becoming a healing force," Sullivan observed. "People drawing strength from each other, creating networks of support that exist across multiple timeline variants simultaneously."

Martinez's teams worked tirelessly to support these emerging healing networks. "Providing the resources they need to help each other grow. Sometimes the best thing we can do is empower communities to find their own ways of healing."

Through enhanced perception, they watched as quantum conscious-ness evolved not just in individuals, but in entire communities. People weren't just healing separately - they were learning to heal together, creating new forms of connection that transcended single timeline awareness.

"This is how we adapt," Morgan concluded. "Not alone, but together. Each person who finds their way helps light the path for others. Every successful integration brings us closer to understanding what human consciousness can become."

The quantum displays showed healing spreading like waves through probability space, communities learning to thrive with their expanded awareness. They weren't just recovering from trauma - they were evolving into something entirely new, together.

EPISODE 7: POTENTIAL

The quantum monitoring chamber erupted with unprecedented energy signatures as new abilities manifested across the facility. James White's enhanced consciousness tracked power fluctuations that defied conventional physics.

"We're seeing complete reformulation of quantum interaction patterns," he reported, watching energy flows that seemed to create their own natural laws. "The power grid isn't just adapting to changes - it's evolving to accommodate new forms of human potential."

Dr. Rachel Morgan's laboratory hummed with activity as she documented waves of consciousness evolution. Holographic displays showed neural patterns restructuring themselves into previously impossible configurations.

"Subject displaying quantum consciousness expansion," she noted, tracking brainwave patterns that operated across multiple timeline variants simultaneously. "Their mind isn't just processing multiple realities - it's learning to exist in them all at once."

The Detection Team, led by quantum specialist Maya Patel, investigated reports of increasingly sophisticated ability manifestations.

"These aren't just enhanced versions of existing powers," she transmitted to Morgan. "We're seeing entirely new categories of abilities. People aren't just becoming stronger - they're developing capabilities that shouldn't be possible."

Through enhanced sensors, they tracked waves of potential spreading through the facility's population. Each new manifestation seemed to trigger sympathetic awakenings in others nearby.

"Begin enhanced monitoring protocols," Morgan ordered as power signatures reached unprecedented levels. "The grid is developing new ways to handle quantum energy flow. Each ability manifestation forces it to evolve further."

Patel's research revealed troubling implications. "These consciousness changes aren't stopping. Each evolution in ability seems to trigger corresponding expansions in awareness. Power and perception are growing together."

"It's like my mind knows things it shouldn't," one subject described. "Not just memories from other timelines - but understanding. Knowledge that comes from everywhere and nowhere at once."

The Detection Team documented increasingly complex ability patterns. "Powers aren't just growing stronger - they're becoming more sophisticated, more integrated with expanded consciousness states."

Patel tracked energy signatures that seemed to pulse with their own rhythm. "These power manifestations are creating quantum resonance patterns. Each new ability generates harmonics that influence how others develop."

Through enhanced perception, they watched as waves of potential swept through quantum probability space. Each person who manifested new abilities created pathways for others to follow.

"Subject showing signs of quantum synthesis," Morgan reported as consciousness patterns reached new levels of complexity. "Their mind isn't just processing multiple realities - it's learning to manipulate them."

The Detection Team's investigation revealed unexpected connections. "These new abilities - they're not just random mutations. They're systematic adaptations to our changed reality. People are developing powers they need to exist in multiple timeline variants."

"The energy... it's not just power anymore," another subject explained. "It's like I can feel the quantum fabric itself. Understanding how reality works at levels I never imagined possible."

White adapted power management protocols as the grid evolved to handle increasingly complex energy patterns. "We're not just managing power distribution anymore. We're helping guide the evolution of our technological infrastructure alongside human potential."

Morgan documented accelerating rates of consciousness expansion. "Each successful integration seems to unlock new potential. As people learn to handle multiple timeline awareness, their minds develop new capabilities to manage that expanded consciousness."

The Detection Team tracked ability manifestations that seemed to defy conventional understanding of human potential. "These aren't just powers anymore - they're new ways of interacting with reality itself."

Through their enhanced senses, they watched as human potential evolved beyond what they thought possible. Each new manifestation pushed the boundaries of what consciousness could achieve.

"This isn't just about managing new abilities," Patel realized. "We're witnessing the emergence of quantum-enhanced humanity. Each person who successfully integrates their expanded potential brings us closer to understanding what that means."

Morgan's research revealed patterns of accelerating evolution. "These changes are self-reinforcing. Each expansion of consciousness creates conditions that encourage further growth. We're not just observing evolution - we're experiencing a quantum leap in human potential."

The Detection Team documented increasingly sophisticated ability manifestations as people learned to harness their expanded consciousness.

"Powers aren't just tools anymore," Patel observed. "They're becoming extensions of evolved consciousness. People aren't just using abilities - they're becoming something new."

Through enhanced perception, they tracked waves of potential that seemed to pulse with their own purpose. Each new manifestation brought humanity closer to understanding what they might become.

"We're not just adapting to changed reality," Morgan concluded. "We're evolving to shape it. Each person who successfully integrates their expanded potential helps define what human consciousness can achieve."

The quantum displays showed potential spreading like wildfire through probability space as people learned to harness their impossible abilities. They weren't just developing new powers - they were becoming something entirely new, something that could exist across multiple realities simultaneously.

"This is more than evolution," Patel realized. "We're witnessing the birth of quantum humanity. Every successful integration, every new ability manifestation, brings us closer to understanding what that means for our future."

EPISODE 8: CONTROL

James White stood before banks of quantum monitoring equipment, implementing new protocols as timeline instabilities reached critical levels. His enhanced consciousness processed impossible amounts of data, searching for patterns in the chaos.

"Initiating adaptive control matrix," he announced, holographic displays showing quantum harmonics realigning under his guidance. "We're not trying to suppress the timeline fluctuations anymore - we're teaching the system to flow with them."

Dr. Rachel Morgan's research lab hummed with activity as she documented unprecedented patterns of temporal healing.

"The recovery rates are accelerating exponentially," she reported, watching neural patterns stabilize across multiple timeline variants. "Once we stopped fighting the changes and started working with them, everything shifted."

The breakthrough came during a routine stabilization attempt. White had noticed something unusual in the quantum resonance patterns.

"The system isn't fighting stability," he realized, tracking energy flows that seemed to seek their own balance. "It's trying to establish new forms of equilibrium. We've been fighting against natural healing processes."

Through enhanced sensors, they watched as waves of stability spread through quantum probability space. Each successful integration created ripple effects that helped others find their own balance.

"Begin implementation of harmony protocols," White ordered as the first test subjects showed signs of true stability. "We need to help people work with their timeline variations, not against them."

Morgan's research revealed surprising patterns of natural recovery. "The human consciousness is remarkably adaptive. Once we provide the right conditions, it naturally seeks ways to integrate multiple timeline awareness."

"It's like learning to swim," one subject described. "At first you fight against the current. But once you learn to flow with it, everything becomes easier. The timelines aren't trying to drown you - they're trying to teach you how to float."

White's new protocols showed immediate results. "System stability increasing by 47%. When we work with the natural quantum harmonics instead of trying to suppress them, the whole process becomes self-reinforcing."

Through enhanced perception, they tracked waves of healing that seemed to pulse with their own rhythm. Each person who found stability helped create paths for others to follow.

"Subject showing complete timeline integration," Morgan reported as consciousness patterns aligned in new ways. "They're not just managing multiple memories anymore - they're learning to exist across multiple temporal states simultaneously."

The quantum displays showed stability spreading like ripples through probability space. Each successful integration strengthened the field harmonics that helped others find their way.

"These aren't just control protocols," White realized. "We're developing a new understanding of quantum consciousness stability. Each success teaches us more about how minds can exist across multiple timelines."

Morgan documented accelerating patterns of recovery as more people learned to work with their expanded awareness. "Once they stop fighting the changes and start flowing with them, the healing process becomes almost natural."

"The timelines... they're not trying to break us," another subject explained. "They're trying to teach us how to be more than we were. Once you understand that, everything else falls into place."

White adapted control systems to support these natural healing processes. "We're not trying to force stability anymore. We're creating conditions that allow people to find their own balance across timeline variants."

Through their enhanced senses, they watched as quantum consciousness evolved in ways they never expected. People weren't just learning to control their timeline awareness - they were learning to thrive with it.

"Begin phase three implementation," White ordered as success rates continued to climb. "We need to help people not just stabilize their timeline awareness but learn to actively work with it."

Morgan's research revealed patterns of accelerating evolution. "Each person who successfully integrates their timeline variants helps create quantum resonance patterns that make it easier for others to do the same."

The control systems hummed with new purpose as they shifted from suppression to support. Each successful integration strengthened the field harmonics that helped others find stability.

"This isn't just about control anymore," White concluded. "We're learning how to exist in a new state of consciousness. Every successful integration brings us closer to understanding what that means."

Through enhanced perception, they watched as waves of stability transformed affected populations. People weren't just learning to control their impossible memories - they were learning to exist as something more than their original selves.

"The timelines are teaching us something," Morgan realized. "They're showing us how consciousness can exist across multiple states simultaneously. Each person who finds their balance helps us understand what human awareness can become."

The quantum displays showed harmony spreading through probability space as people learned to work with their expanded consciousness. They weren't just controlling timeline variations - they were evolving into beings who could naturally exist across multiple realities.

"This is how we adapt," White observed. "Not by fighting change, but by learning to flow with it. Each successful integration brings us closer to understanding what human consciousness can achieve when we stop trying to control it and start trying to work with it."

The facility hummed with new purpose as they continued to refine their understanding of quantum consciousness stability. They weren't just managing a crisis anymore - they were helping guide humanity toward a new way of being.

EPISODE 9: UNDERSTANDING

The quantum research chamber buzzed with activity as the first comprehensive ability evolution model took shape in holographic space. Teams of enhanced analysts processed data from thousands of documented cases, watching patterns emerge from seeming chaos.

"The evolution isn't random," Dr. Morgan announced, her consciousness tracking multiple probability streams simultaneously. "There's an underlying structure to how abilities are developing. Each manifestation follows quantum resonance patterns that influence future developments."

Detective Alice Chen's team confirmed the first signs of genuine reality stabilization. Their enhanced perception tracked quantum field harmonics that were finally finding natural equilibrium.

"The timeline variations aren't collapsing into each other anymore," she reported. "They're establishing stable quantum interference patterns. Reality isn't trying to choose between different versions - it's learning to maintain multiple states simultaneously."

Through enhanced sensors, they watched as waves of understanding spread through affected communities. Each new insight into their changed reality helped accelerate the rebuilding process.

"Begin implementation of future integration protocols," Morgan directed as the model revealed new possibilities. "We need to prepare for the next phase of consciousness evolution. This is just the beginning."

The detective team documented increasing instances of natural stability. "People aren't just adapting to multiple timeline awareness anymore - they're starting to understand how to work with it. The fear is being replaced by curiosity."

"It's like learning to read a new language," one community leader explained. "At first it's all confusion and chaos. But eventually patterns emerge, and suddenly you realize there's meaning in what seemed like noise."

Morgan's framework revealed unexpected implications. "These changes aren't just affecting individuals - they're reshaping how human consciousness itself functions. We're witnessing the emergence of quantum-aware society."

Through enhanced perception, they tracked ripples of understanding spreading through quantum probability space. Each person who grasped their new reality helped others find their own path to comprehension.

"Community stability increasing exponentially," Chen reported as more neighborhoods showed signs of successful adaptation. "Once people understand what's happening, they stop fighting it and start working with it."

The quantum displays showed consciousness patterns evolving into new configurations as humanity learned to exist in their changed reality.

"Subject showing advanced quantum awareness," Morgan noted, watching neural patterns that operated across multiple timeline variants simultaneously. "They're not just accepting multiple memories anymore - they're learning to actively work with multiple states of being."

The detective team's investigation revealed accelerating rates of community recovery. "These aren't just coping mechanisms anymore. People are developing new ways of living that embrace their expanded consciousness."

"The changes... they're not something that happened to us," another resident described. "They're something we're becoming. Once you understand that, everything else makes more sense."

Morgan adapted integration protocols as understanding spread through affected populations. "We need to support these natural evolution patterns. People are finding their own ways to exist across multiple timeline variants."

Through their enhanced senses, they watched as quantum consciousness evolved in unexpected ways. People weren't just learning to live with their changed reality - they were learning to thrive in it.

"Begin next phase analysis," Morgan ordered as success patterns became clearer. "We need to understand not just where we are, but where this evolution is taking us."

Chen's team documented emerging patterns of community adaptation. "Neighborhoods aren't just rebuilding - they're reimagining what community means in a quantum-aware society."

The holographic models pulsed with new data as understanding spread through probability space. Each successful integration revealed more about what humanity was becoming.

"This isn't just recovery," Morgan realized. "We're witnessing the birth of quantum civilization. Every person who successfully integrates their expanded awareness brings us closer to understanding what that means."

Through enhanced perception, they watched as waves of comprehension transformed affected populations. People weren't just accepting their impossible reality - they were learning to shape it.

"The evolution patterns are clear," Chen concluded. "We're not just adapting to changed reality - we're becoming something new. Each person who finds understanding helps define what human consciousness can achieve."

The quantum displays showed ripples of insight spreading through probability space as communities learned to embrace their expanded awareness. They weren't just rebuilding what was lost - they were creating something entirely new.

"This is how we grow," Morgan observed. "Not by trying to return to what we were, but by understanding what we can become. Each successful integration brings us closer to grasping our true potential."

The facility hummed with purpose as they continued mapping humanity's evolution. Through their enhanced senses, they watched as understanding spread like wildfire through quantum probability space, transforming not just individuals but the very nature of human society itself.

"We're not just observing change anymore," Morgan concluded. "We're learning to guide it. Every new insight helps us understand not just what we are becoming, but how to help humanity reach its full quantum potential."

The models pulsed with possibility as they tracked the emergence of true quantum civilization. They weren't just managing crisis anymore - they were helping birth a new chapter in human evolution.

EPISODE 10: BALANCE

The power grid control center pulsed with quantum energy as Nina Chisolm watched years of work finally reach fruition. Holographic displays showed energy patterns achieving perfect harmony across multiple probability states.

"Grid stabilization at 99.7%," she announced, tracking power flows that danced between timeline variants with natural grace. "The system isn't just managing quantum energy anymore - it's achieving true temporal resonance."

Detective Alice Chen stood in the quantum observation chamber, her enhanced senses confirming what their instruments had begun to detect. Timeline fractures were healing themselves, probability waves finding natural equilibrium.

"The temporal rifts are self-repairing," she reported, watching reality knit itself back together. "It's like watching a wound heal. The time-lines aren't fighting each other anymore - they're learning to coexist."

Through enhanced sensors, they tracked waves of integration success spreading through affected populations. Each person who found their balance strengthened the field harmonics that helped others achieve stability.

"Personal integration rates exceeding all projections," Dr. Morgan noted, monitoring consciousness patterns that showed unprecedented levels of timeline synthesis. "Once people learn to work with their expanded awareness instead of fighting it, the process becomes almost natural."

The community support networks, carefully built over months of trial and error, hummed with activity. Every neighborhood now had access to quantum stabilization equipment, trained counselors, and groups of peers who understood their experience.

"Network completion achieved," Hannah Sullivan confirmed, watching support patterns spread through quantum probability space.

"No one has to face these changes alone anymore. Everyone has access to the help they need."

Chisolm tracked power signatures that pulsed with newfound stability. "The grid isn't just distributing energy anymore - it's helping maintain quantum field harmony. Each successful integration strengthens the overall system."

"It's like finding your balance on a bicycle," one resident explained. "At first you wobble and fight against it. But once you find that sweet spot, staying upright becomes effortless. Your body just knows what to do."

Chen's investigation revealed accelerating rates of timeline healing. "The probability waves are establishing stable interference patterns. Reality isn't trying to choose between variants anymore - it's learning to maintain multiple states in harmony."

Through enhanced perception, they watched as waves of balance spread through quantum probability space. Each successful integration created ripples that helped others find their own equilibrium.

"Begin final phase protocols," Chisolm ordered as power signatures reached perfect stability. "The grid is ready to support long-term quantum consciousness evolution."

Dr. Morgan documented patterns of natural integration as more people learned to work with their expanded awareness. "Once they stop fighting the changes and start flowing with them, the whole process becomes self-reinforcing."

"The timelines... they're not separate anymore," another resident described. "They're all part of a bigger whole. Once you understand that, finding balance becomes natural."

Sullivan adapted support networks as communities developed their own methods of helping each other achieve stability. "We're not just providing assistance anymore - we're facilitating natural healing processes."

Through their enhanced senses, they watched as quantum conscious-ness evolved into something beautiful. People weren't just learning to manage their impossible reality - they were learning to dance with it.

"System harmony achieved," Chisolm announced as power signatures reached perfect resonance. "The grid isn't just stable - it's evolving alongside human consciousness."

Chen's team documented waves of healing that seemed to pulse with their own rhythm. Each person who found balance helped create path-ways for others to follow.

The support networks hummed with purpose as they shifted from crisis management to long-term stability. Communities weren't just surviving anymore - they were thriving with their expanded awareness.

"This isn't just balance," Morgan realized. "We're witnessing the emer-gence of true quantum harmony. Every successful integration brings us closer to understanding what consciousness can achieve when it finds its natural equilibrium."

Through enhanced perception, they watched as waves of stability transformed affected populations. People weren't just managing their impossible reality - they were becoming something more than their original selves.

"The field harmonics are self-sustaining now," Chen observed. "Reality isn't just stable - it's achieving a new kind of balance. One that can maintain multiple timeline variants in perfect resonance."

The quantum displays showed harmony spreading through proba-bility space as humanity learned to exist in their expanded state of being. They weren't just finding balance - they were becoming beings who naturally existed in quantum harmony.

"This is how we evolve," Chisolm concluded. "Not by forcing stability, but by learning to dance with quantum possibility. Each successful integration brings us closer to understanding what consciousness can become when it finds true balance."

The facility pulsed with achieved purpose as they watched their years of work bear fruit. Through their enhanced senses, they witnessed the birth of quantum harmony - not just in individuals or systems, but in the very fabric of reality itself.

EPISODE 11: CLARITY

The quantum forecasting chamber hummed with crystalline energy as the future path development program came online. Detective Ethan Reeves stood with James White, watching probability streams coalesce into clear patterns for the first time since the temporal event.

"All major timeline variants now mapped and stabilized," White reported, his enhanced consciousness tracking quantum pathways that stretched into possible futures. "We're not just reacting anymore - we're finally able to see where these changes are taking us."

The final ability control protocols pulsed with elegant simplicity, the result of months of refinement and understanding. Each line of code resonated with natural quantum harmonics.

"Control integration at 100%," Dr. Morgan confirmed, watching power signatures that danced in perfect synchronization. "The protocols aren't forcing stability anymore - they're supporting natural consciousness evolution."

Detective Reeves prepared to close the temporal investigation that had consumed years of his life. His enhanced perception traced quantum probability streams that no longer showed signs of instability or collapse.

"Investigation status: resolved," he announced, filing his final report. "The temporal event wasn't an accident or attack - it was a catalyst for human evolution. We weren't victims of change - we were its recipients."

Through enhanced sensors, they watched as waves of clarity spread through the quantum field. Each person who grasped their new reality helped others understand their own path forward.

"Begin future integration sequence," White ordered as the program revealed unprecedented insights. "We need to help people not just exist with their expanded consciousness but actively shape where it takes them."

Morgan documented the final patterns of system integration as quantum technology achieved perfect harmony with evolved human awareness.

"It's like waking up from a dream," one participant explained. "Not because the dream wasn't real, but because now we can see how all the pieces fit together. Everything makes sense in a way it never could before."

Reeves tracked probability streams that pulsed with newfound purpose. "These aren't just random changes anymore. There's a pattern to how consciousness is evolving - a direction that we can finally see clearly."

Through enhanced perception, they watched as understanding rippled through quantum probability space. Each successful integration strengthened the field harmonics that guided humanity forward.

"System completion verified," White announced as the final pieces fell into place. "We're not just managing quantum consciousness anymore - we're ready to help guide its evolution."

Morgan's research revealed accelerating patterns of natural development as people learned to work with their expanded awareness. "Once they understand where these changes are taking them, the evolution becomes almost effortless."

"The paths... they're not separate anymore," another participant described. "All possible futures are connected, parts of a larger pattern. Once you see it, you can't unsee it."

Reeves closed case files that had seemed unsolvable just months before. "We were looking for an enemy, a problem to solve. What we found instead was an opportunity to become something more."

Through their enhanced senses, they watched as quantum consciousness evolved with newfound clarity. People weren't just accepting their changed reality - they were actively shaping it.

"Begin next phase implementation," White directed as future paths became clearer. "We need to help people not just understand their evolution but consciously participate in it."

Morgan documented final integration patterns as systems achieved perfect harmony with evolved human consciousness. "The technology isn't just supporting changes anymore - it's becoming an extension of expanded awareness."

The quantum displays showed clarity spreading through probability space as humanity grasped their true potential. They weren't just adapting to change - they were becoming its architects.

"This isn't just completion," Reeves realized. "It's a beginning. Every successful integration brings us closer to understanding what consciousness can achieve when it sees its path clearly."

Through enhanced perception, they watched as waves of understanding transformed affected populations. People weren't just accepting their quantum reality - they were learning to shape its future.

"The probability streams are stabilizing naturally now," White observed. "Reality isn't just maintaining multiple states - it's evolving along paths we can finally see and understand."

The facility pulsed with achieved purpose as they watched years of work reach fruition. Through their enhanced senses, they witnessed humanity step fully into their expanded potential - not as victims of change, but as conscious guides of their own evolution.

"Case closed," Reeves concluded, sealing the final investigation files. "Not because the story is over, but because we finally understand what it means. Each person who finds clarity helps write the next chapter of human consciousness."

The quantum displays showed understanding spreading like light through probability space as humanity embraced their new reality. They weren't just finding clarity - they were becoming beings who naturally existed in quantum awareness, ready to shape whatever future awaited them.

EPISODE 12: ECHO

The quantum assessment chamber resonated with crystalline harmonics as Dr. Elena Santos presented the legacy impact findings. Holographic displays showed ripples of change extending far beyond their initial predictions, echoing through generations yet to come.

"The temporal event wasn't just a moment of change," she explained, tracking probability streams that pulsed with inherited potential. "It's become part of humanity's evolutionary trajectory. These changes will echo through our species' future."

James White's future preparation framework hummed with elegant complexity, designed to support consciousness evolution across multiple generations.

"Framework integration at optimal levels," he reported, watching quantum signatures that showed how current changes would influence future development. "We're not just preparing for tomorrow - we're laying groundwork for decades of evolutionary echo."

The final recovery phase initiated with quiet certainty, more celebration than crisis management. Through enhanced sensors, they watched as the last pieces of their changed reality fell naturally into place.

"Recovery completion at 99.9%," Dr. Santos confirmed, monitoring consciousness patterns that showed perfect stability. "But 'recovery' isn't quite the right word anymore. We haven't returned to what we were - we've become something new."

Through enhanced perception, they tracked waves of acceptance spreading through quantum probability space. Each person who fully embraced their new reality strengthened the field harmonics that would guide future generations.

"Begin legacy protocol implementation," Dr. Morgan ordered as the assessment revealed unprecedented implications. "We need to ensure these changes are passed on properly, that future generations understand their inherited potential."

White documented patterns of generational evolution as quantum consciousness prepared to echo through time. "These aren't just temporary adaptations. They're becoming part of our species' basic consciousness framework."

"It's like watching ripples in a pond," one observer noted. "Each change creates waves that spread outward, influencing everything they touch. But these ripples don't fade - they become part of the water itself."

Foster tracked consciousness signatures that pulsed with newfound permanence. "We're not just changed beings anymore. We're becoming the ancestors of quantum humanity."

Through enhanced sensors, they watched as understanding rippled through probability space. Each successful integration created patterns that would echo through future generations.

"Legacy stability confirmed," Dr. Morgan announced as impact patterns reached unprecedented clarity. "These changes aren't just surviving - they're becoming fundamental aspects of human consciousness."

Dr. Morgan's research revealed accelerating patterns of generational adaptation. "Future generations won't have to learn these abilities - they'll be born with them. Quantum consciousness is becoming our natural state."

"The echoes... they're not just memories," another participant described. "They're blueprints for what humanity is becoming. Each generation will build on what we've achieved."

White refined preparation protocols as the framework revealed long-term evolutionary patterns. "We're not just planning for immediate future anymore. We're helping guide the echo of quantum consciousness through time."

Through their enhanced senses, they watched as reality settled into its new configuration. People weren't just accepting their changed state - they were becoming conscious architects of humanity's future.

"Begin final phase integration," Dr. Morgan directed as legacy patterns became clearer. "We need to ensure these changes echo properly through time, that each generation builds on the foundation we've created."

White documented waves of acceptance as communities fully embraced their new reality. "This isn't just adaptation anymore - it's evolution. We're watching humanity step into its quantum inheritance."

The quantum displays showed stability echoing through probability space as humanity grasped their role as evolutionary ancestors. They weren't just changed beings - they were becoming the origin point of a new kind of human consciousness.

"This isn't just completion," White realized. "It's genesis. Every successful integration becomes part of the echo that will shape human consciousness for generations to come."

Through enhanced perception, they watched as waves of understanding transformed not just current populations, but the very trajectory of human evolution. People weren't just accepting their quantum reality - they were ensuring it would echo through time.

"The probability streams show generational stability," Dr. Morgan observed. "These changes aren't just maintaining themselves - they're becoming stronger with each new generation."

The facility pulsed with achieved purpose as they watched their work ripple outward through time. Through their enhanced senses, they witnessed humanity not just step into their expanded potential but ensure it would echo through all the generations to come.

"Assessment complete," Dr. Morgan concluded, but with a beginning rather than an ending. "Not because we've finished evolving, but because we finally understand our role. Each person who finds acceptance helps create the echo that will guide humanity's quantum future."

The quantum displays showed understanding spreading like ripples through probability space as humanity embraced their role as evolutionary anchors. They weren't just finding acceptance - they were becoming the source of an echo that would transform human consciousness forever.

"This is our legacy," White observed. "Not just the changes we've experienced, but the future they'll create. Each successful integration strengthens the echo that will guide humanity toward its quantum destiny."

The chamber hummed with crystalline certainty as they watched their transformation echo outward through time, knowing their changed reality would ripple through all the generations yet to come.

EPILOGUE: ECHOES OF TOMORROW

Detective Alice Chen stood at the observation point overlooking Daybridge, the evening air crisp with autumn's first breath. Six months had passed since the final integration protocols were established, and the city pulsed with a new kind of life.

Through her enhanced perception, she watched the quantum field harmonics dance across the cityscape - now as natural as watching clouds drift across the sky. Citizens moved through their daily lives, their expanded consciousness allowing them to navigate multiple timeline variants with practiced ease.

"Beautiful, isn't it?" Dr. Morgan approached, her own quantum-enhanced senses tracking the patterns of stability. "Sometimes I forget how far we've come."

"Almost perfect," Chen agreed, but her brow furrowed slightly. Something about the quantum frequencies had changed in the past few weeks. Subtle distortions that didn't quite fit their established models.

Below, a street musician played saxophone on the corner of 7th and Main, the music seeming to ripple through probability space in ways that shouldn't be possible. Chen had noticed more of these anomalies lately - moments where reality bent in ways that quantum physics couldn't explain.

"Have you been getting the reports?" she asked Dr. Morgan. "About the shadows in Old Town?"

Morgan nodded slowly. "Three cases this week. Enhanced perception shows normal quantum signatures, but..." she trailed off.

"But the shadows move against the probability streams," Chen finished. She'd seen it herself - dark shapes that seemed to exist outside their carefully mapped reality.

A child's laugh drew their attention to the park below. A young girl was chasing what appeared to be floating lights - except Chen's enhanced senses detected no quantum energy signature at all.

"We mapped every variant," Dr. Morgan mused. "Every probability stream. And yet..."

"And yet there's something else out there," Chen said quietly. "Something different."

The sun set over Daybridge, painting the sky in deep purples and blues. The quantum field harmonics pulsed with achieved stability, humanity's new consciousness flowing smooth as silk through probability space.

But in the growing darkness between buildings, in the spaces between timeline variants, something ancient stirred. Something that had been waiting for humanity to evolve enough to see it again.

Chen watched the city lights come alive, each one casting shadows that sometimes moved in ways they shouldn't. Her enhanced perception picked up quantum signatures dancing in perfect harmony - but underneath it all, a different kind of music was beginning to play.

"We've come so far," Dr. Morgan said, turning to leave. "Learned so much about reality."

"Yes," Chen agreed, her eyes tracking a shadow that seemed to move against the quantum flow. "But I think reality has more to teach us."

As night fell over Daybridge, the city hummed with the achievement of quantum evolution. But in the darkness between moments, in the spaces between probabilities, old truths were awakening. And Detective Chen couldn't shake the feeling that humanity's greatest changes were still to come.

The quantum displays in the observation room pulsed with perfect stability, showing a humanity that had mastered its new existence. But as Chen turned to leave, a wind that wasn't wind whispered through the streets below, carrying echoes of mysteries that quantum science couldn't explain.

Tomorrow would come, bringing with it all the promise of humanity's evolved potential. But tonight, in the shadows of Daybridge, something waited. Something watched. Something remembered.

And somewhere in the darkness, a saxophone played impossible notes that danced between realities, calling to things that existed far beyond the realm of quantum probability.

The future was clear. But the past... the past had secrets yet to share.

A SNEAK PEEK AT WHAT'S NEXT!

Thank you for joining me on this journey through *Quantum Detective: The Alice Chen Files.* I hope you enjoyed exploring the mysteries of Daybridge and getting to know its secrets.

The story doesn't end here—there's so much more waiting to be uncovered. I'm excited to give you an exclusive first look at *Synthetic Storm,* the next book in the *Ethan Reeves Werewolf Detective Series.* Dive into the free chapter below and get a taste of what's to come!

Synthetic Storm **Book Seven in the Ethan Reeves Werewolf Detective Series**

PROLOGUE: Echoes of Tomorrow

2:17 AM - Daybridge Corporate Research District

Breach Alert: Lab 7, Quantum Enhancement Division

Sarah Chen's fingers flew across holographic displays as emergency protocols flashed red across the laboratory walls. "They're breaking through the quantum barriers," she warned, watching reality itself fracture around the containment field. "The artifacts are destabilizing."

Fifteen ancient relics, each humming with supernatural resonance, pulsed with increasing power. They had been inert museum pieces until three months ago, when corporate scientists discovered their quantum enhancement potential. Now they threatened to tear reality apart.

"Security teams are eight minutes out," Alice Chen's voice came through the quantum-encrypted channel. Unlike her older sister Sarah, she had chosen government service over corporate research. "Just hold the containment field."

Sarah watched probability waves ripple through supposedly solid matter. The artifacts were reaching out, calling to something buried deep in human genetic code. "This isn't just enhancement anymore, Alice. The artifacts... they're awakening something. Something that's been dormant in us."

Through the observation window, she could see the test subjects changing. Corporate executives who had volunteered for "controlled enhancement" were manifesting abilities that defied traditional physics. One woman phased through quantum states while a man's consciousness expanded across multiple probability streams.

"Ma'am," Lieutenant Foster's tactical team reached the outer security perimeter. "We're detecting massive supernatural energy signatures. Traditional containment protocols aren't designed for this."

"Because it's not just supernatural," Sarah realized, watching ancient symbols materialize in the quantum foam. "The artifacts aren't creating something new - they're remembering something old. A time when reality was more... flexible."

The building's enhancement dampeners whined under increasing strain. In secure labs across the city, other artifacts began resonating in response. Centuries of accumulated supernatural energy sought release through quantum channels that corporate science had inadvertently reopened.

"Sarah, get out of there," Alice's voice carried rare urgency. "The probability models are cascading. This isn't just a containment breach - it's a catalyst event."

But Sarah couldn't move, transfixed by the patterns emerging in the quantum field. Ancient magic merging with modern science. Supernatural potential awakening through enhancement protocols. Reality itself remembering older, deeper patterns.

"It was always going to happen," she whispered, watching probability waves expand beyond containment. "The synthetic formula, the corporate enhancement programs - they just accelerated what was already coming. We're remembering what we used to be."

The artifacts pulsed in perfect resonance as reality's quantum framework began to shift. In that moment, Sarah understood - this wasn't an ending, but a beginning. Humanity's long-dormant supernatural potential was awakening, and nothing would ever be the same.

"Sarah!" Alice's voice crackled through failing quantum channels. "The containment field is..."

The artifacts released their accumulated power in a quantum cascade that rippled through every probability stream. As reality fractured around her, Sarah smiled. The bridge between what was and what could be had finally opened.

The Daybridge Evolution had begun.

ABOUT THE AUTHOR

Rae Stonehouse turned to fiction writing after establishing himself as a prolific author of self-development and professional growth books.

With over 50 published works helping readers navigate personal and professional challenges, he embarked on a new creative path with the Ethan Reeves Werewolf Detective Series.

When not weaving tales of supernatural sleuthing, Stonehouse continues to share his expertise in personal development through workshops and speaking engagements from his home in British Columbia.

The Ethan Reeves series marks his debut in fiction writing, blending his understanding of human nature with a newfound passion for urban fantasy.

~

www.ingramcontent.com/pod-product-compliance
Lightning Source LLC
Chambersburg PA
CBHW061334310726
48974CB00001B/45